Praise for
Once Upon an Effing Time

Compelling and vividly told, with a narrator to break your heart—and, in her brave search for belonging, to bring you hope. I loved this book.
　　—CARRIE SNYDER, author of *Francie's Got a Gun*

Suspenseful circumstances, black humour, catastrophizing characters and an irreverent attitude mark Buffy Cram's *Once Upon an Effing Time*, where the disturbing tension of trying to live up to goodness in a hard world skitters on the surface of every page.
　　— YASUKO THANH, author of *Mysterious Fragrance of the Yellow Mountains*

An unforgettable story about a childhood eked out on the margins and a mother-daughter relationship that swings between tenderness, brutality and betrayal. The style is vivid, hallucinatory and utterly compelling. Buffy Cram has written a remarkable novel about resilience in the face of tragedy.
　　— SUSAN JUBY, author of *Mindful of Murder*

Once Upon an Effing Time may not be a fairytale, but it crackles with a magic-tinged darkness and light of the best of Grimms. Its young hero is a kind of *Girl, Interrupted* meets Dickens's Artful Dodger by way of the tumble-down-the-rabbit-hole Alice. Her tender-tough moxie is both heartbreaking and exhilarating, just like Buffy Cram's debut novel itself.
　　— ZSUZSI GARTNER, author of *Better Living Through Plastic Explosives* and *The Beguiling*

A darkly beautiful, deeply intelligent and deftly crafted tale of heart-rending loss and heart-mending hope that grips, holds and lingers long.
— BOBBI FRENCH, author of *The Good Women of Safe Harbour*

Where does the bitter magic end and the sweet real life begin in *Once Upon an Effing Time*? Margaret and Elizabeth will haunt your dreams as you sit in on the journey of their lives: riding an edgy line of danger, rich with the tenuous bonds of mothers and daughters, wild with the grit of staying alive. Buffy takes a broken world and makes stained glass of it, transforming the poverty of everyday life into a pilgrimage so kaleidoscopic you will want to stay on the Far Out bus, if only to keep plumbing the depths of the haunted adventures Buffy has created.
— CEILIDH MICHELLE, author of *Vagabond*

ONCE UPON AN EFFING TIME

BUFFY CRAM

ONCE UPON an EFFING TIME

a novel

Douglas & McIntyre

DOUGLAS & MCINTYRE
P.O. Box 219, Madeira Park, BC, VON 2H0
douglas-mcintyre.com

EDITED by Peter Norman
COVER DESIGN by Naomi MacDougall
TEXT DESIGN by Libris Simas Ferraz / Onça Publishing
PRINTED AND BOUND in Canada
100% recycled paper

Canada

DOUGLAS & MCINTYRE acknowledges the support of the Canada Council for the Arts, the Government of Canada, and the Province of British Columbia through the BC Arts Council.

LIBRARY AND ARCHIVES CANADA CATALOGUING IN PUBLICATION

Title: Once upon an effing time : a novel / Buffy Cram.
Names: Cram, Buffy, author.
Identifiers: Canadiana (print) 20230440436 | Canadiana (ebook)
    20230440444 | ISBN 9781771623605 (softcover) |
    ISBN 9781771623612 (EPUB)
Classification: LCC PS8605.R347 O53 2023 | DDC C813/.6—dc23

For Alexander, who has supported me every step of the way, and for Mary Mole, whose story I have carried and attempted to reimagine.

CHAPTER 1

AFTER

IT'S MY FIRST-EVER MONDAY MORNING COMMUTE. I'M PACKED IN WITH THE black-raincoat crowd on the #10 bus, headed downtown. We're on East Hastings, four blocks from Main Street. Vancouver's glassy towers loom in the distance but this part, here, is skid row, the worst part of the worst part of the city. The sidewalks are full of people strutting and selling and scavenging, even at this early hour. I scan all the faces, looking for Margaret, my mother. A young woman on the corner teeters on broken high heels, wearing nothing but a bikini and bruises. A man in a kimono grabs his crotch and shouts at traffic, something about Gucci and the end of the world. There's a person in an orange robe, ringing a little brass bell and singing about God. It's like nothing has changed since I've been inside, like no time has passed at all.

It's January 14, 1980.

"It's a big day!" Dr. Mink said this morning, bouncing her eyebrows at me: part thrill, part warning. And she's right, compared to this, the rest of my days have been small.

It's been ten years and five months since I've been out in the world. That's 3,805 days since I've seen or heard from Margaret. If she were looking for me, if she wanted to, say, save me or send me a message, this would be the perfect time, but I'm not supposed to be thinking about that, not today.

I'm supposed to be thinking about how I look: whether I have breakfast seeds in my teeth (I do), if my buttons are buttoned and my shoes are tied (they're not). But instead all I can think about is how tight my collar is and how I got conned into wearing a shirt with a collar anyway. I mean, is a lace collar absolutely necessary for a good first impression? It makes me look pretty, the nurses said. Meaning, probably, more innocent, like one of those good girls who grew up with a mom/dad and piano/dance/swimming lessons, a real Jennifer, the kind of girl who, if she did happen to do very bad things once, a long time ago, must've done so accidentally, the kind of girl who deserves one last chance, even if she will screw it up.

Today is the first day of the rest of your life, Dr. Mink's card said this morning. The cards were waiting for me on a table in the activity room. Dr. Mink, a bunch of inmates and nurses and Jacinda the janitor were all there, watching me.

Dr. Mink's card had a picture of a kitten climbing out of a basket of, for some reason, yarn. *You're just a kitten*, the card seemed to imply. *These are your first steps.* There was a second card with a picture of a man in spandex standing on a mountaintop, taking in the view of a sun that was rising or setting, I couldn't be sure. Inside, it said something about a journey of a thousand steps. It was signed by everyone on the unit. *Follow your dreams!* the nurses had written in bubbly handwriting. *Watch out!* the inmates had scrawled.

They all stood in a circle around me as I read the cards. Then they applauded and walked me down to the main entrance, or in this case, exit. This is what we always did when someone left the Willingdon Youth Detention Centre. Dr. Mink handed me an envelope. Inside was bus fare and a map to Harrow House, where I'd be living for the next seven months. She gave me some final advice about taking my meds, not swearing, not lying and then the door buzzed and I was out in the yard. Another buzz and I was stepping through the chain-link gate, free at last.

Their faces were crowded in the windows. They were waving and pumping their fists in the air. *Good luck out there*, they seemed to be shouting, but their eyes said something else.

The bus creeps across Princess Avenue and sighs up to the curb.

A woman steps on. She has a thin hoodie pulled tight around her head and no shoes, even though it's below freezing, and this is the part of town where you might easily get stuck in the toe with someone else's sad story. She might've got stuck already. Her feet are splotchy and purple and there's a deep gash across the top of one of them that sneers at me like an angry mouth.

She's up there arguing with the driver, explaining that she has no fare, that someone took her wallet and her shoes and she needs to get to her boyfriend's place, that she has no money on her, but he does, lots, if only she can get to him. She looks back at everyone on the bus, all the commuters who will be late for work because of her, and explains that all she needs is a ride, just one ride, and she can get her life together. She can start again.

She removes her hood and looks around at everyone. She's pretty, or was once. Her hair is short, curly, red perhaps, if it were washed. Her eyes are shiny, maybe blue.

She puts two hands together in prayer. All she needs is, like, 75 cents for her fare and maybe enough for a coffee too, she pleads.

But everyone's just looking out the window or at their hands or at their newspapers.

The woman's eyes lock onto my eye patch and brighten with something like recognition. "Got 75 cents?" she says, and that's when I see her broken teeth and what might be a faint blue line running down her forehead. My heart goes *wuh-whump*, an empty box thrown down a flight of stairs. The morning light gathers around her, all pinkish-gold, and then, suddenly, I forget who I am, which version of myself, in which decade, and I think: *It's her!*

She's come to get me, I think. *Just in time!*

"Mom?" I say. "Margaret?"

I step out into the aisle, but I'm too late. The bus driver has already forced her off. We're pulling away from the curb.

I run across the aisle and press my hands to the window.

The woman steps back onto the sidewalk and, as my window passes through her line of vision, she looks up at me. I look into her brown eyes. Definitely brown, not blue.

She raises her middle finger, jabs it up-up-up at me and screams, "Screw you, bitch!"

So, not my mom, probably.

I flop back against the seat.

My heart, that empty box, reaches the bottom of the stairs.

The bus merges into traffic, and I'm definitely feeling the feeling I feel right before a mood swing. It's like someone has put their hand on the dimmer switch. Everything goes grey, and I remember that I'm all alone, living in the afterlands, and everything has already happened.

"*Everything* has already happened, or just a lot of very formative things that you're still untangling with the help of therapy and medicine?" Dr. Mink would say if she were here, in my head, because according to her, words and thoughts matter. According to her, we're all building a story of ourselves in our minds every moment, with every thought, and it's important to be specific. According to her, specificity of thought is the first cornerstone of mental wellness. And mental wellness is the goal, always.

Okay, so not *everything*, but some big things have happened. The best/worst things.

"Really?" she would say. "Best? Worst? How can you be so sure? You're only nineteen, Elizabeth. It seems to me your story isn't finished yet," and then she would wink and smile her doctorly smile at me.

You see how she is.

Another one of the cornerstones of mental wellness, according to her, is honouring my commitments, which is why I absolutely cannot be late on this of all days.

So I straighten my collar and shake it off, this "sighting," as Dr. Mink would call it. I get off just before Main Street and walk through

4

Chinatown, past a grocery store with huge bins of dried fish out front and a restaurant with barbecued ducks hanging in the window. I turn onto Keefer, the long residential street where my new home is supposed to be.

"Try not to think of it as a punishment," Dr. Mink said when she first told me I would be going to Harrow House. "Think of it as having training wheels for a little while. Just until you can ride on your own." Then she remembered that I had probably never ridden a bike and certainly not one with training wheels.

"Think of it as a bridge," she said.

Then, more accurately, "Or a life raft." She pursed her lips and studied me.

We were in her grey office at Willingdon, on opposite sides of her grey, metal desk. A small window was behind her, looking out on a grey sky. My file was open in front of her. My meds were lined up in front of that. She was explaining that it would be my responsibility now to remember which ones to take when: the white one like a little, powdery cupcake, the blue one like an icy planet, the yellow capsule full of tiny beads.

She explained that she thought I might need a little extra help easing into civilian life, that she'd called around and found an opening at a place called Harrow House, an art-based group home. She said the woman who ran it, Bertha, was a little unconventional but was having a lot of success.

She stopped then and, like a daytime talk show host about to say something meaningful, leaned forward in her seat. "Bertha will be able to help you with your writing, Elizabeth," she said. "I think it's important you keep going with that. We all do."

She said some other things too about guilt and letting go of it, about moving on and how every moment was a fresh start.

I wasn't listening to any of that.

I was looking out the window, imagining a grey bird wobbling through the grey sky, flying, but with only one wing, only halfway free.

5

"So it's a halfway house?" I asked.

"Try not to think of it that way."

"But if I make a mistake, I'll be sent back here?"

She swallowed, looked down at her hands.

"Or somewhere else? Somewhere worse?"

Out the window, that imaginary grey bird tipped head-over-ass and plummeted through the sky.

"That won't happen, Elizabeth," she said, "because I believe in you! We all do!"

There's a homeless man limping down Keefer ahead of me. He has a hockey stick balanced over one shoulder with a satchel hanging off the end like some sort of Canadian Huck Finn.

I arrive in front of a brown house with a red picket fence. There's a brick path leading up to some steps. The sides of the steps are crowded with flowerpots that are crowded with dead things. A sign reading "Beware of Artists" hangs from the red door. I look at the address on my sheet. 467. I look at the house. 467. This is it. The place.

When the homeless man gets to the end of the block, he turns to face me, and I see it's him: Michael, my brother. Of course it's him. Because I've just imagined seeing Margaret and the two of us never *could* share a meaningful moment—even an imaginary one—without him. He's much older than I expected—my age, I suppose—but he has the same curly hair, the same eyes that are every colour at once. Underneath his trench coat he's wearing blue jeans, a striped shirt.

I raise my hand.

He raises his hand.

He winks and curls a finger at me. *C'mon.*

And what I want, of course, is to chase after him, to live a life on the run with nothing but my hockey stick and satchel, to feel vivid and alive, scrounging for pizza, dodging police, sleeping in a different bush every night.

But I'm not supposed to follow people down alleys anymore. It's rule number two of my parole agreement.

And if Dr. Mink were here, in my mind, she would remind me that not everything I see is real. She would remind me about the third cornerstone of mental wellness, which is remaining rational and sticking to the actual facts, and the fourth, which is mind control, which is why I have *Is it true? Is it specific? Is it factual? Is it rational?* written on the insides of each of my fingers, so I can sneak peeks throughout the day.

So what do I do? I stop to read my fingers now and ask myself: *Is it? Is it? Is it? Is it?* and by the time I've answered, *no, no, no, no,* I look up and he's gone.

The red door opens. An old woman steps out, looking froggy with her big chest and skinny legs. She has two long, white braids wrapped around her head in a kind of folksy crown, a round, red face, a tray of muffins in her hand. This must be Bertha.

"Hell*ooh*," she says, waving.

She looks nothing like I imagined a halfway-house mom to look. She looks like she might've once danced barefoot at a concert in the rain, like she knows how to use a bong and believes in miracles. She's wearing a homemade dress that is just a bunch of purple things sewn together. She has oatmeal-coloured tights, rubber boots, no bra, which is interesting/challenging.

She comes down the first step. "Yoo-hoo, Elizabeth. Hi Honey."

Two men crowd the doorway behind her. They're slack-faced, round-shouldered. My future roommates, the other halfway people.

My ears are hissing like a radio tuned wrong. *You could still run.*

But mental health is a story I am building every moment, with every positive decision, Dr. Mink always says.

Also: This is it, my last chance. If I screw this up, back in the can I go.

Bertha is coming down the path toward me now. She's waving her muffin tin in the air, and the smell reaches me. Banana muffins, fresh from the oven.

Fuck it, I think.

I reach up and rip the lace collar off my shirt. I stuff it into my pocket and, right away, I feel better. Less like a Jennifer, more like me.

I open the gate and step, not so much toward my new life as toward those muffins.

But I've gotten off track.

This is not a story about muffins. It's a story of rehabilitation: it's about the past and how I am using my tools to overcome it, one moment at a time.

"So what can you tell me about Michael?" Dr. Mink asked once. This was in my early days at Willingdon, not long after I'd been transferred from the Mid-Hudson Forensic Psychiatric Center in New York State.

She must've read the police report. I hadn't said his name, hadn't said a word to anyone since I'd arrived.

A string of drool slipped out the corner of my mouth, landed on my shirt. I was on enough medication to tranquilize a circus animal at the time.

Dr. Mink didn't look at me like the New York doctors had though, like I was a lion asleep at the back of my cage. She looked at me like I might actually have something worth saying.

"Let's try something different," she said, coming around her desk to sit in a chair across from me. She took my hands in hers and got me to take a bunch of deep breaths, in through my nose and out through my mouth. Then she asked me to close my eyes and imagine a long staircase going all the way down to the basement of my mind, and she walked me slowly down the steps, counting them off. When we got to the bottom, she asked me about the beginning of my story, about Ontario. I started to tell her that I grew up in a cheese town, living in a Kraft company trailer parked on company land, but she stopped me.

She wasn't interested in facts, she said. She wanted to know about "sensory details," the smells and sounds and textures of my life back then. It was a doctor trick she knew.

So I told her about the knobby blanket thrown over the back of the couch, the way the kitchen linoleum crackled under my feet when I stood in front of the fridge, the way water screeched through the pipes on cold mornings, and she clapped her hands together, saying, "Good! Great! Fantastic!" Then, when I opened my eyes, she handed me a pen and paper and told me to write a list of everything I could remember, starting with the words "I remember."

I froze.

"Start any way you can then," she said. "Start with 'Once upon a time' if it helps."

So I rolled my eyes and scribbled, "Once upon a fucking time" on the page. I was full of attitude back then.

But then a funny thing happened. When I put pen to paper again, something broke open inside of me. Her doctor trick had worked. In the weeks and months and years that followed, the more I wrote, the more I remembered and the more I remembered, the more I needed to write, until eventually it became this, what you are about to read (or not): a totally true account of how, little by little, one life can go so impossibly wrong.

CHAPTER 2

BEFORE

ONCE UPON A TIME, IT MUST'VE BEEN JUST THE TWO OF US, JUST ME AND Margaret, living in a trailer by the side of the highway, but I don't remember that. I remember it always being her, me and Michael too.

I remember the knobby blanket, the linoleum crackling beneath my feet, the water screeching in the pipes, and Margaret's Ferris wheel moods, how there were long stretches when she couldn't get out of bed. I used to spend hours in the bathroom then, with the window open, because that's where I could hear the neighbour's TV best. I remember sitting in the dry tub with my jacket and shoes on, sipping the "soup" I'd made by swirling yellow powder into warm tap water, or eating beans, cold from the can, and listening to Ed Sullivan and Johnny Carson, all that applause, as if it was coming from a faraway planet.

"You two take care of each other," she'd say whenever she was in one of these moods.

I remember wishing he would, but I couldn't feel him the same way she did.

Sometimes, late at night, I'd hear her talking to him behind the closed door of her bedroom. It sounded like they were arguing about something, but softly, like *swish, swish, swish.* I tried arguing with him too, on my side of the door, but I never heard anything back.

I didn't know much about my brother, Michael, about why I had lived and he hadn't, and I wasn't allowed to ask, but I knew it had something to do with the red scar up Margaret's belly and a matching one up the middle of me from my three heart surgeries—two when I was a baby and one when I was five. I knew it had something to do with my eye patch and her headaches. And I knew she needed him. I knew that without her ever having to say it.

Margaret wasn't always in bed though.

She was a good mother when she could be.

Sometimes she was up, baking cookies and scrubbing the kitchen cupboards with a toothbrush, running her hands through her big orange afro and talking about the size of the universe and how amazing it was that, of all the people in all the world, there was no one quite like me. She'd tap-tap me on my eye patch then and say, "You're gonna do great things, Kiddo. I can feel it." She had so much hope then. I could feel it puffing me up like a balloon that could float away whenever it wanted to, to someplace, anyplace better.

This was in Hell Hole, Ontario, which is not what it was called but what she called it because she had almost gotten away once, had almost been a backup singer for an American rock star, but then something had come up and now we were stuck in a trailer in the middle of nowhere, surrounded by mud flats and broken-down trucks as far as we could see.

It was me and Michael that came up. It was our fault she didn't get away. She never said that, but I knew. Some things you just know.

The rest of the adults called the place Kraft Park because they all worked at the Kraft factory, a large, orange building that sat in the middle of a black field across the road, looking just like a piece of cheese on burnt toast.

That's where Margaret met Rocky, packaging cheese on the factory floor. I was eight years old the night she invited him for dinner. I remember she made a big deal about what kind of car he drove—a Cadillac Coupe DeVille, sky blue with red seats—and she wore lipstick and made her famous Cheddar Broccoli Casserole. I don't remember dinner, but I remember I was sent to bed right after and how, from then on, it was the three of us, like a family, almost.

With Rocky around things were better for a while, not so up and not so down. For the first time ever we had our own TV, and Margaret had a bottle of headache pills that she kept on a shelf above the kitchen sink. She stayed out of bed and stopped talking to Michael. She made breakfast every morning and dinner every night. I remember casseroles, clean sheets and how she started taking me to my eye doctor again. Every night before bed she would even help me with my exercises, removing my eye patch and standing at the far end of the kitchen, holding up different pictures made of red and green dots, asking, "What do you see now?" and, "What about now?" while the lines of the kitchen snapped in and out of focus.

Rocky and her were happy for a while. I remember the way his eyes followed her around the kitchen, how he called her Baby and she called him Babe and how sometimes he looked at her like he was hungry and she was chicken dinner.

I remember always having to go over to stay with Hugo, our neighbour, in his trailer on Thursday nights while they went out dancing at the Legion.

They even talked about getting married. She had a magazine full of white dresses she kept stashed under the couch cushions. I wasn't allowed to touch it in case I streaked the pages, but I was allowed to look over her shoulder and read what it said below each picture because she couldn't. "This one's called Delicate Delilah," I read aloud, "and this one's called Blushing Betty."

I remember Rocky talking about California, where he was from, and how, after the war, he was going to take us back there, so we could all live the rest of our lives in the sun.

I'm not sure how long this went on, the good times. It might've been months. But eventually all that talk of California set her off again.

She stopped taking her headache pills, and I could hear that old Ferris wheel creaking back to life, her mood going up, up, up.

Instead of making dinner, she started sitting at the kitchen table, smoking one cigarette after another and talking about how in San Francisco there were palm trees and beaches and whole neighbourhoods full of famous people, how everyone there walked around without shoes all year round and ate goat cheese and had never even heard of Kraft.

"I'd take any kind of cheese right about now," Rocky said, looking at the empty dinner table.

She started singing at the Legion once a week too. At first it was just for fun, but soon she stopped going to work so she could practise. Then she started keeping me out of school too, so I could help her with the lyrics. While Rocky was at work, we would take his Cadillac and drive it down the highway, all the way to the edge of Lake Huron, where she would sing along to the music coming from America on her short-wave radio, and I would scribble down the song lyrics in a notebook.

"We're destined for better things, Kiddo," she'd say, staring out at the other side of the water, and I believed her, or I believed that *she* was at least. Margaret was one of those people you just had to look at. She had an afro the exact colour of carrots and 1,049 freckles across her nose and cheeks. She had ice-blue eyes that darkened according to her moods and when she sang, her voice was so scratchy it could make a cowboy movie play in your mind.

But Rocky wasn't too impressed with any of that. He wanted a casserole on the table by six every night, not a wife with her head in the clouds.

That's what he said when they fought in the kitchen that last night—that everyone had warned him her head was in the clouds, that he should've listened. She said something about how she was going to be famous, how in California people handed out record deals like candy. Things got quiet after that. I figured they'd made up, but in the morning I found Margaret leaning over the kitchen table, holding her head in both hands, saying he was gone.

"Gone?" I walked toward the window.

"He took the Cadillac," she said before I could get there.

I knew what she was thinking, that now we'd never get to California.

"We'll find our own way," I said. I was picturing us out on the road together, just the two of us, a mother and daughter on a great big adventure. "We'll save up and get our own car!"

But she was making the face she always made right before a headache hit, squinting like something big was being dragged across the floor of her mind. "I'm going to bed," she said. "You two take care of each other."

You two.

So it was back to that again, back to me and Michael.

Then she stood, wobbling slightly, and headed for the bedroom.

I should've known by the way she was moving, delicately, on tippy-toes, like the bottoms of her feet were bruised, that this time things were serious. I should've known by the look she gave me before shutting the bedroom door that it would take a miracle—or several—to get us out of this.

But I didn't know any of that. As far as I knew, the most important thing when Margaret had a headache was to be quiet. Even the sound of a cupboard opening could make her feel worse. So I went outside to play.

Kraft Park was just a handful of trailers arranged in a horseshoe shape around a homemade antenna that Hugo had built so we could all watch American tv. Scattered around the outside of the horseshoe were a bunch of broken-down trucks—Kraft ones and other ones too because Hugo was the company mechanic but also the only mechanic for miles. There were only two places to play at Kraft Park: there was the ditch along the highway that sometimes had interesting garbage in it, and there was the truck cemetery.

I slid onto the seat of an old Ford with no doors, cranked the wheel and imagined I was driving with Margaret down a wide California street with palm trees at the edges. I imagined we were singing along to the radio and the man in the car next to us heard her voice and stopped what he was doing and leaned out his window to listen some more. He was just about to offer me a lollipop and Margaret a record deal when Hugo's tow truck turned into the park, pulling a school bus. I ducked below the dash. Hugo didn't like me playing in the old trucks. I slid out of my seat and ran back home.

I remember I stayed in the living room that night, watching TV with the volume on low.

I found peanut butter way at the back of the cupboard and ate some straight out of the jar, not even using a spoon.

Walter Cronkite came on. He was frowning, talking about all the trouble in the streets.

I watched a show about a dog named Lassie who rescued people and always did what she was told, except when it was better not to.

I watched a show about a woman who could cast spells just by wiggling her nose and another show I'd never seen before, about a family who moved into a house with a ghost, an old sailor, who haunted them by moving things around behind their backs.

At some point during that show, Margaret thumped the wall with her fist, which meant "turn it down," so I did.

I sat cross-legged on the floor in front of the TV, watching with the volume off. I took my eye patch off and my shirt—two things I never did when Margaret was around because she didn't like it, because it reminded her of what she called "our Big Sad Story." I ran my fingers up and down the scar on my chest. It tickled way down inside me.

I was so close to the TV I could see the small squares that made up the picture. I watched the people's mouths, trying to guess what they were saying. It seemed like the ghost wanted something. He stood perfectly still in the corner of the room, watching a woman brush her hair. He even stood over her while she slept. At some point they had an argument and after that they were friends. He did the dishes and helped her around the house.

It had gotten dark. The TV was the only light in the room.

I heard a swish behind me.

I turned to look, but my eyes were funny from being so close to the TV.

"Michael?" I said.

No answer.

"Do the dishes," I ordered.

Still no answer.

I gave up and went to bed. The house was quiet but, lying there in the dark, I thought I could feel him standing over me, watching. He wanted something from me, I was sure of it, I just didn't know what.

In the morning Margaret was still asleep in her bedroom. The TV was still on, the jar of peanut butter sitting there with the lid off. Everything was exactly the same as I'd left it, except—and I know you won't believe this because you are normal and I am a mental patient—the dishes were done. I swear, every single dish was stacked up and drying in the rack.

That was the first miracle.

I waited all morning for Margaret to wake up. I cleaned up her ashtrays and even did some homework. Then, finally, at noon, I made her peanut butter crackers and put them on our fanciest plate. I poured her a glass of milk. I found her headache pills and put one on the plate. I tiptoed down the hall to her room and slowly pushed the door open.

She was still sleeping. The room was hot and dark. It smelled like burnt socks.

I put the plate on the table next to her.

She didn't move.

I called to her.

She didn't answer.

She didn't look like herself. Her hair was plastered to her head like a greasy helmet.

I reached out and rested my hand on her shoulder. "Mom," I said, even though she preferred to be called Margaret.

Her eyes popped open. "What?"

"Michael did the dishes," I said.

"That's good." She rolled away from me. "Atta boy."

I tiptoed out of the room, turning the heat down as I went.

That day I didn't even bother with my eye patch. I ate Rice Krispies with milk until the milk was all gone, then with orange juice until the Rice Krispies were all gone. I finished the orange juice, then the last of the peanut butter. Then there was nothing but a bottle of ketchup.

I watched a show about some cowboys, and another one about a boy and a bear.

I was about to turn the TV off when the second miracle happened. A new show came on, one I'd never seen before. A woman was sitting alone on a stage. She had an eye patch just like me and black gloves and what looked like a shiny towel wrapped around her head. A man with a cane came limping onto the stage. She gestured for him to sit and then stood over him, fluttering her eyelashes and making a face like she was sucking on a sour candy. The lights flashed. She touched the man on the head, right between the eyes. He slid off his chair and lay crumpled on the ground. The woman waved her hands over him, saying what looked like, "Abracadabra." Then, like magic, the man came back to life. He sat up, smiling. When he stood, he was moving differently than before. He was dancing, and he didn't need his cane anymore. The lights in the room came up. There was an audience there. They were all shaking their heads and applauding. The woman with the towel on her head bowed. The audience went wild.

I went and got some of Margaret's gloves from the closet. They were grey, not black, but they would do. I crept into Margaret's room and stood over her. I wiggled my toes for good luck. Then I copied the woman on TV. I pretended I was sucking a sour candy. I waved my hands around and tried to put a spell on her, on us, our whole lives. She kept sleeping.

I went out into the yard and looked back at the trailer to see if anything was different, but from the outside it looked the same as always—too small, once mint green, now freckled with rust. I noticed for the first time that the wheels of our trailer had sunk halfway into the mud. It looked like soon they might be swallowed.

I saw Hugo jump into his tow truck and pull out of the park.

I walked over to the bus he'd towed in the day before. It looked like a regular school bus except it had the words "Far Out" written above the window, where the name of the school would normally be. I pulled the door open and climbed the stairs. It wasn't anything like a regular school bus on the inside. It was like a home. There was a kitchen counter with a sink and, across from that, a padded bench and a kitchen table. There were curtains on all the windows, and a rug on the floor, and a record player, and a bed at the back. It even smelled like a home, like coffee and toast. I wondered who had lived there before—maybe a family with a mom and dad and two living kids. Maybe they were happy and always going places on the weekend. I stayed there, imagining that family's life for as long as I could.

On Sunday, after I looked in the cupboards and found them empty, I closed the doors and went to get the grey gloves. I dragged a chair over, stood up on it and waved my hands in front of the doors, *abracadabra*. I waited for a few seconds and, when I opened the doors again, like magic, I found two handfuls of spaghetti noodles way at the back of the top shelf.

I boiled the noodles, but I must've done something wrong because they all stuck together. Still, I put ketchup on it and brought it to Margaret along with another headache pill.

"Spaghetti!" I said, placing it on her side table, next to the other plate with the crackers and the pill still on it.

She didn't move.

I tiptoed out and ate my own spaghetti. Then I had a stomach ache and had to lie down.

Sometime later I heard Hugo moving around in his yard. I watched him through a slit in the curtains. He kept sticking his head into the open hood of the bus. He'd clang around in there with his wrench, and then climb on board to try and start the engine, but every time it made a sound like *wheee-clunk*.

I liked Hugo. He was nice and interesting. Nice because whenever he babysat me he made me pancakes and let me have a bunch of the little, orange candies he kept for his diabetes. And interesting because he brewed what he called "Kraft Hooch" in big, white buckets in his laundry room and sold it out back of the Legion most nights after closing time. He had a pet lizard called Lizzy that he let walk around his house. He could call her from any room just by clicking his tongue. He also had a tinfoil ball that he'd made by saving the foil from all his cigarette packs. It was nearly the size of my head. He said it would be in *The Guinness Book of World Records* one day.

I always wondered why Margaret didn't date Hugo, someone so nice and interesting whose tinfoil ball would one day be in a book.

But he was too ugly, she said, and it was true. Hugo's face was as round and bumpy as a meatball, with a big scar up one side from a knife fight he'd once been in.

Watching Hugo out there, I couldn't stop thinking about his pancakes. *Paaaaancakes*, I thought. I waved my hands through the air and, just when I did, abracadabra, he looked up and waved back.

I was so hungry I went out to see him.

Hugo invited me inside even though he wasn't babysitting me. His place smelled nice, like soap and cigarettes.

The TV was on, that show I'd seen before with the woman with the eye patch. This time I could hear it. A housewife from the audience came up, bowed and said, "Mademoiselle."

"Sit," the woman—Mademoiselle—said. "Give me your hands and I will read your future."

The housewife sat. Mademoiselle took the woman's hands and ran her fingers over her palms. She made the sour-candy face and fluttered her eyelashes.

Hugo marched over and turned the volume down.

"Wait!" I said. "What is that?"

"Some fortune-teller nonsense." He stood in front of the TV, blocking it.

"What's a fortune teller?"

"Never you mind," he said and then he asked where my eye patch was.

I said I was taking a break from it.

On the TV behind him, Mademoiselle flipped her eye patch up. She had a normal-looking eye under there, just like me. She was saying something important to the housewife, something meaningful. The housewife was crying.

Hugo asked about Margaret.

I said she was fine.

I asked about Lizzy.

He went to the other room to get her.

On TV, the housewife had stopped crying now. She stood and smoothed her dress and reached into her purse to give Mademoiselle a bunch of money.

Hugo came back into the room and put Lizzy on my shoulder. Lizzy froze and looked at me like she always did, sideways out of one huge eye like she knew all my secrets. I'd forgotten how she always did that and how you could see her little heart beating in her throat. I remembered then that I didn't really like Lizzy, that once I'd seen her pull her own skin off and eat it. I scooped her up and gave her back to Hugo.

I asked him to make me pancakes. He said he'd have to go to the store first, but that I could come over later if I wanted. He said I could bring Margaret, that I should.

I said she was probably too tired.

He nodded. Then he stood, went to the kitchen, came back with a bottle of hooch and handed it to me. "For Margaret," he said.

I liked that about Hugo. He knew about Margaret's moods without me ever having to say. He was a real professional that way.

"Well then," he said, which really meant, *It's time to leave.*

He walked me toward the little room where he kept his boots and the pegboard with all the keys to the trucks he was working on. That's when the third miracle happened. He pulled a set of keys from his pocket, dropped them on the top peg, and something about the way they hung there, two keys and a silver feather, I knew they belonged to the bus.

Back home, I went straight to Margaret's room.

She pushed herself up when she saw what I had. She raised the bottle to her lips and gulped. For a second I thought I could see her heart beating in her throat. I looked away.

She patted the bed next to her and asked how I was.

"Fine," I said, sitting. Her two headache pills were still there next to the food on her bedside table. I thought about asking if I could have the crackers, but then she spoke.

"What have you been doing?"

I wanted to tell her about the bus, about how I'd done magic on the cupboard, how there was nothing to eat and Hugo had invited us for pancakes, but it was better not to say too much when she was just getting over a headache.

I shrugged. "Not much. TV and stuff."

"That's good." She took another swig from the bottle.

I waited to see if she wanted to play any of the games we usually played when she wasn't feeling well.

There was TV, where I was the TV and she'd press my nose to change the channels. Every channel had to have a different show on it, a real one or one I'd made up right there on the spot. She'd press my nose faster and faster until I couldn't keep up anymore.

Radio was the same but with songs.

And there was Feel What I Feel, where she'd touch her forehead to mine and half of whatever she was feeling would rush into me. Sometimes I'd report it back to her in a British accent, like, "*Dah*ling, you *aaah* feeling better." That always made her laugh.

But she wasn't in the mood for games just then.

Instead, she asked if I was ready for school the next day.

I hadn't been to school in weeks, not since she'd started singing at the Legion, but I said yes.

"Atta girl." She patted my leg. "Good girl. So smart."

I should've stayed longer. I should've said about the pancakes or reminded her about Michael doing the dishes—anything to keep her talking—but she said she had to sleep some more, so I took the crackers and tiptoed out.

That night I ate the crackers and watched some shows with the volume on low, I don't remember what. At some point I heard Hugo start the engine to the bus. I saw him drive it out one end of the park, down the highway and back in the other side.

On Monday morning I woke at 8:25, right on time.

I washed in the sink and changed my clothes. I stuffed my school books into my backpack and crept into Margaret's room before leaving.

I remember the heat was cranked again, that smell of burnt socks, how I leaned over and did two abracadabras on her but didn't kiss her goodbye because she was too sweaty.

I should've kissed her goodbye.

"Well, well, look who it is," Sister Agnes said, sniffing the air when she saw me come in through the front doors of the school.

That morning she stood at the front of the class and talked about Jesus, about how he could peer into our hearts and tell whether we were good boys and girls. She talked about his sacrifice. "He died so we could live," she said, lowering her book and then her black-brown eyes until she was looking right at me, and my scar turned cold and rigid like a zipper.

All morning she kept glancing at me sideways, like a lizard.

"Sit still," she said, but I couldn't.

"Pay attention," she said, but my eyes kept floating up to Jesus hanging from the cross on the wall above her head. He'd died for me, and he didn't seem very happy about it.

Finally, just before lunch, I was sent for detention in the library. I was told to pick a book and sit at the back of the room.

I found one called *Fun Tricks for Good Christian Children*. It seemed like a good book, but I couldn't concentrate. Another Jesus was hanging above the librarian's desk, watching me. He was really starting to get on my nerves, so when the lunch bell rang, I tucked that book into the back of my pants and walked right past him, and the librarian too, without signing it out.

I was sitting out in the farthest corner of the yard, wishing I had a lunch and minding my own business, when the next miracle happened. Billy Flanders came up to me. I hated Billy. He knew more about me than I wanted because his dad managed the Kraft factory. They lived in a huge brick house on the other edge of town. He always had two sandwiches for lunch—one with ham, one with peanut butter—and perfectly ironed clothes.

"I heard Rocky left," he said.

I looked past him.

"And your mom can't get out of bed again."

I flipped my eye patch up and focused on him just like on the pictures of the red and green dots at home. The lines of his shirt popped forward and back. I thought about Margaret, sweating in her bed back home, and his mom, ironing clothes in her big brick house, and before I knew it, I was up and charging. That's when I felt it: a force at my back, like two hands pushing.

I slammed into him so hard his teeth clacked.

He yelped and the sisters came running.

I had to sit on the hard bench outside Father Perry's office.

The end-of-lunch bell rang. All the other students went back to their classes.

I could hear Sister Ann's class across the hall. They were learning their times tables: *four times two is eight. Four times three is twelve.*

I could hear Father Perry telling his secretary, Gladys, to call Margaret.

I knew how this would go. Father Perry would speak first. He'd say what I'd done and then it would be Margaret's turn. She'd remind him of our Big Sad Story and, at some point, Father Perry's voice would shift to a soft murmur. "Yes, Ms. Squire," he'd say. "We're all praying for you."

I wouldn't get the strap. I wouldn't get any punishment at all except for the way people in that town were forever looking at me and Margaret, always stepping out of our way on the sidewalk and in the grocery aisles, smiling at us in a way that was equal parts kind and cruel.

I'd sit on this hard bench all afternoon writing "I will not push other students" over and over. At some point Gladys would bring me a little glass of milk and some stale ginger cookies, which is what the sisters always ate when they thought God wasn't watching. "Poor dear," she'd say, smiling down at me. At the end of the day, I'd be given a lecture about how we must all try to behave our best, even at the worst of times, and a letter to take home, a letter Margaret would never read because she couldn't. Nothing would change. We'd go on living our Ferris wheel lives, up and down, forever.

Except I could hear Gladys telling Father Perry she couldn't get through. Busy signal, she said.

I remember a strange feeling in the centre of my chest then, like there was a cord attached to my heart and someone was yanking on it. There was a loud static in my ears. Did I hear a voice then too, beneath the static, telling me to go home? I don't know. There is the moment and then there is the story of the moment. Over time, one replaces the other.

I stood and walked down the hall.

Four times nine is thirty-six.

Four times ten is forty.

I slipped out the front doors of the school. Nobody stopped me.

I walked and then ran down the highway, all the way home, and the whole time there was that static in my ears, that cord pulling.

From outside, the trailer looked normal: sad, sinking.

On the inside it was quiet.

I called to her.

No answer.

I tiptoed down the hall and opened the door to her bedroom. The air was thick and hot.

Margaret was there, on her back, in bed, with a blanket pulled over her face. She was making a strange noise, not snoring but gurgling. A glass of water and her empty pill bottle were next to the bed.

I pulled the blanket back and, right away, I knew something was wrong. Her skin was cold instead of hot, grey instead of pink. There was white foam in the corners of her mouth.

So I did what someone on TV would do. I splashed the glass of water onto her face. I shook her and slapped her. That's when her eyes popped open: the fifth miracle. She twisted out of bed, fell to the floor and puked all over my shoes. I remember the pills she'd taken were still spongy and white, like Rice Krispies.

She sent me to get a bottle from the medicine cabinet. I brought it to her. She took some and then lay on the floor, gasping while I went to open the windows. That's when I noticed another blanket had been folded up and jammed into the opening of the heater, the entire length of it. I pulled it out. It was singed brown, the fabric starting to melt in places. I opened the windows, turned off the heat and didn't say a word about it.

"Sorrybabythankyousorry," she kept saying. Then she crawled to the bathroom and everything inside her came out.

That night we lay on the couch together. The TV was on, but the sound was low.

Walter Cronkite came on. He was frowning. Something terrible was happening in the streets somewhere.

Margaret was behind me. She kept kissing my head, calling it a miracle that I had come home in time, that I knew just what to do, that the pills hadn't absorbed. She kept saying, "I couldn't live without you."

I must've told her about the rest of the miracles then: about Michael doing the dishes and Mademoiselle and the keys and the two hands pushing and another one I'd decided to add just then, the voice in my ear telling me to "go home," just in time.

She got quiet then, too quiet for too long, and then, finally, I heard her sniffling.

"I knew it," she said. "I always knew it." She buried her face in the back of my neck, crying softly, and I wondered: *Knew what?*

Another show came on. A cop show.

Her breathing got slow and heavy. I could feel her heart beating into my back. It sounded like a horse galloping through the Ontario mud, trying to get somewhere, anywhere else.

I wriggled out from under her arm.

The TV light flickered across her face, blue and then not.

I lowered down to check if she was breathing. She was. I touched my forehead to hers and felt it then, what she felt: the difference between who she was and who she wanted to be, her bigness against the smallness of Kraft Park, how everyone knowing our Big Sad Story in this stupid, small town was dragging her down, how if we stayed, she would never get a record deal.

Just then, the rabbit ears fell over. The TV turned to static, and in that static I could see Mademoiselle. Her head filled the screen. She flipped her eye patch up and leaned forward to speak. I couldn't quite hear, but I didn't need to. She said just the one word: California.

"How?" I asked.

"You know," she said.

And, like a miracle, I did. I knew exactly.

I peeked out the window and saw that Hugo was still at the Legion, selling his hooch.

I grabbed the flashlight Margaret kept by the door, put on my gumboots and walked over to his trailer. The door was unlocked. I went in. I knew where he kept his money from the hooch. It was the same place he kept his diabetes candies: in a Nabob coffee can on top of the fridge.

I crept into the kitchen. I couldn't reach the top of the fridge, so I dragged a chair over and climbed onto it. I pulled the coffee can down. I put my hand in, and there it was: the biggest pile of money I'd ever seen.

It's possible that I was just pretending up until this point, that I was just going to steal a few dollars and some orange candies and then head back home to live out the rest of my ordinary life. But when I stepped down off the chair with the coffee can in my hand, I felt a soft, wet pop beneath my boot. I pointed the flashlight and there was Lizzy, burst open all over the floor.

I bent over her, crying for a while—I don't know how long—before I realized I'd always known it would end this way for Lizzy and me. Some things you just know. My tears dried up. I found a box on the counter and scooped Lizzy into it. I remember putting all my sadness into the box with her, closing the lid, placing the box on the step outside Hugo's back door. Then I grabbed half the money and put the can back on top of the fridge. I moved the chair back to the table and left out the front, stopping to grab the keys to the bus on the way.

Back home, I shook Margaret awake.

I must've shown her the money and the keys. I must've said they were for a bus called Far Out, that it was like a real home, with a bed and a sink and even a record player, that it ran, that'd I'd seen Hugo drive it. I must've said I'd killed Hugo's pet lizard, that we had to go, that it was now or never.

I remember she sat up and stared into the corner.

"Now we can go to California," I said, "so you can get your record deal."

She was running her hands through her hair, whispering to him, *swish, swish, swish.*

"We're destined for greater things," I reminded her.

Then, the last miracle: I heard the creak of the Ferris wheel, her mood tick-ticking up. Finally, she looked at me. "Yes, we are," she said, and her eyes flashed, bluer than ever.

It was 2 a.m. Hugo would be home in no time. She was trudging in and out of the house, handling the big things: pots and pans, a mop and broom, blankets and records.

I stayed inside, packing what I could: clothes, crayons, the contents of my costume trunk, the grey gloves, the library book I'd stolen.

Before we left, we stood for a moment in the mostly empty kitchen, listening to the whir of the fridge, the rain on the tin roof.

"Say goodbye to this hell hole," Margaret said. Then she took me by the hand and led me out of the trailer, across the yard and onto the bus.

I sat on the bed at the back. Margaret slid into the driver's seat.

She turned the key and the engine roared to life. It was so loud I could feel it in my teeth. We lurched out the long driveway and onto the highway. I watched out the back windows as the cheese factory and the shiny, squat trailers of Kraft Park shrunk to a brown smudge in the distance. It all looked so insignificant, like a place you might drive right by and hardly notice.

"Whooo-eee," she said, smiling at me in the rear-view mirror.

I tried to say "whoo-eee" too, but I couldn't find my voice. I was thinking about Hugo, about how he'd come home soon and search his whole trailer, clicking his tongue, looking for Lizzy. How eventually, maybe tonight, maybe tomorrow, he'd open the back door and find the box. Then he'd find the slimy spot near the fridge. Then he'd look up and see the coffee can and know what I'd done.

At some point I must've slept because next thing I remember, we were parked by a bridge in front of a huge lake, not Lake Huron but another one.

The clock said noon.

Margaret was up on her tippy-toes, fiddling with something at the front of the bus. She cranked a lever and the words "Far Out" disappeared from the display above the window. Now there was a blank spot there, as if to remind us we had no idea where we were going.

"Oh, good," she said when she saw I was awake. "Now listen, we need to get to America—" she pointed across the water, "—but we need to be smart about it."

I noticed she was dressed in disguise, with a bandana tied over her hair and sunglasses that took up most of her face.

She stomped toward me, nudged me off the bed and flung the mattress back. She opened a trap door in the bed frame to reveal a secret compartment—a cool, dark, rectangle of space hidden below the bed. "Get in," she said, handing me a blanket and pillow. "You need to hide."

I must've protested, but I don't remember that.

I remember her putting her hands on my shoulders and pushing me down. Not forcing—she was a good mother—but pushing, saying, "it won't be long" and, "just until we're across."

I was crying, probably, but trying not to.

I remember the last thing she said was, "I need you two to be brave right now."

You two.

Then she closed the hatch, and I was stuck there, in the darkest dark I'd ever seen, with him. I couldn't see a thing, not even my own hand in front of my face.

I heard her flop the mattress down on top of me. She walked to the front of the bus and started the engine. It rattled up my spine and down my legs, jittering every part of me.

I felt the bus turn out of the parking lot and onto the highway, the ridged metal floor against my back, the dark, damp space stretching out on all sides. It smelled like gasoline, rust, blood, like the beginning, before everything.

I thought of me and Michael, tumbling and hiccupping in another darkness so long ago. Brother and sister. A pair. But what had gone wrong?

"You're a fighter, Kiddo, a real survivor," Margaret had said to me one night after the Legion, when her mood was just right.

My scar was heating up now, a white, hot seam of pain right up the centre of me. There was a hissing in my ear. *Who did I fight?* I wondered.

But I knew.

I knew by the way I never got the strap at school, no matter how badly I behaved, by the way Father Perry's eyes changed shape whenever he asked how things were at home, by the way the sisters stood in a huddle, whispering about me in the school yard.

I was a killer. A Lizzy killer, a brother killer, a mother killer, almost.

I could smell singed fabric. I was lying on the same blanket that had been stuffed into the heater at home. Then, like a movie in my mind, I saw what would've happened if Michael hadn't pushed me and I hadn't pushed Billy, if I hadn't left school exactly when I did. I saw the blanket bursting into flames, the trailer burning with Margaret inside.

I felt the bus come to a stop. Margaret was talking to somebody. This was it, the moment when we would or wouldn't cross over.

"I couldn't live without you," she'd said, but I was sure that by "you" she'd meant "you two."

The air was so close it was like a wet hand smothering me. I was gasping. The walls were closing in. I was about to press up on the bottom of the bed when I felt a weight on top of me. It was him. I felt the heat of him, his breath on my face. He was pinning me down, his arms on my arms, his legs on my legs. Then he leaned close, touched his forehead to mine and told me what I'd always known to be true.

You are not enough on your own, he said without saying.

I died so you could live.

You owe me.

I don't remember anything after that.

CHAPTER 3

AFTER

BERTHA INTRODUCES ME TO MY HOUSEMATES, PATRICK AND LEONARD, AND says something about a Heather, who will join us later.

Patrick and Leonard look exactly like mental patients in their matching tracksuits. "Hullo," they mumble to their feet more than to me.

Patrick is so pale he resembles a photo of an old photo. He has blond hair and white-blond eyelashes that he constantly blinks. The whole time we talk, he clenches his jaw and holds his hands in fists at his sides, like he's trying to rein in a runaway stagecoach. His hands are stained with bright splotches of paint. His clothes too.

Leonard looks like Patrick's opposite. He has dark hair and dark eyes that dart around the room as if he's trying to look everywhere at once. He reaches out to shake my hand and leaves it coated with what I hope is flour. He smiles and wink-winks at me.

While Bertha shows me around, they do the pharma-shuffle behind us, dragging their feet and breathing through their noses the way the heavily medicated always do. It's like they're afraid if they lift their feet off the ground, even for a second, the world will rearrange itself.

Bertha shows me the living room, which is almost like a real living room except for bars on all the windows and a fish tank where the TV would normally be. Bertha sees me notice this and says, "We don't do TV here, Hon'. It causes too many problems."

Someone should tell her calling people Hon' can cause problems too.

They show me the art room. It doesn't look anything like the art room at Willingdon, with its vats of sparkles and glue. This looks like a real art room, with easels and tubes of actual paint, not just watercolour pucks. There are the usual motivational posters everywhere, though. A delicate flower pushing up through concrete and something about hope. A cartoon turtle saying, "Slow and steady." A teddy bear climbing up a steep staircase and the phrase, "All things are difficult before they're easy," except someone has crossed out "difficult" and added the word "shit." All things are shit.

Leonard sees me see that and snorts.

The kitchen is almost like a real kitchen, but with locks on most of the cupboards.

"Those are just for safety, Hon'," Bertha says. "Any time you need anything, just ask."

The room smells amazing, like homemade spaghetti sauce.

Somehow Leonard reads my mind. He leans close and whispers, "homemade *lasagna*."

"For lunch," Bertha clarifies. "That's what we'll be having for lunch."

We stop in front of a bulletin board full of charts and lists and chore wheels, and Bertha lays out the house rules: no swearing, no lying, no hurting ourselves or each other. She makes a little speech about routine—how it is an essential part of life here at Harrow House because it makes us feel productive and accountable. She explains that all of us will be expected to pass our high school equivalency tests and apply to college, that I'm expected to apply to college too even though I'm a few months late, but not to worry because I'll have Mr. Twohig and my writing coach to help with that.

Every time she says the word "college," she lowers her chin but raises her eyebrows at me, like we're playing poker and she's just laid a big, fat hand on the table.

Behind her there's a schedule with the days of the week and each of our names. My name is there too and my whole week is mapped out, hour-by-hour, in bright-coloured squares. I see that I will have tutoring with Mr. Twohig, a paper route, sessions with someone named Annie. I can hear Patrick breathing behind me to my left, Leonard to my right. My ears start to hiss. I hear the voice again, *You could still run*, and I start to feel light-headed, but then Bertha opens the lid to a big, green bin, and a pukey smell wafts out, sharpening the air. She explains about compost: something about eggshells, something about coffee grounds.

Then we're out on the back porch. "Greenhouse," she says, gesturing toward a dingy-looking structure at the other end of the yard.

"And boots," she says, pointing to a shelf full of boots by the door, as if I couldn't figure that out for myself.

When we're back inside, she starts leading me toward the second floor to show me my room. We leave Patrick and Leonard at the bottom of the stairs. Patrick tugs on his reins and blinks goodbye. Leonard raises one finger, ever-so-slightly.

At the top of the stairs, a door swings open and a girl is standing there in a cloud of strawberry-smelling steam. She looks tough, even in her towel. Her hair is shaved on one side, and she has a purple scar lifting one corner of her mouth, the flick of a long-ago knife. She has little blue X's tattooed at the top of her cheekbones, and I swear I see a faint, blue line running down her forehead. My skin turns cold. She looks like someone I might've known once. *Does she know me? What I've done?*

"Elizabeth, Heather. Heather, Elizabeth," Bertha says.

Heather looks me all the way down and then all the way up, stopping at my eye patch. There's a kind of static all around her. The air prickles.

"Hi," I say, casually, even though I feel like one of those cartoon characters that has run off a cliff and is hanging in mid-air for a moment, legs pumping, before the fall.

"What're you, a pirate?" she asks.

"No," I say. And then, maybe because I'm nervous or because I want her to know I was somebody once—that I was MeMe Fanta, the Amazing Roadside Wonder—I say, "more of a psychic."

I look at Bertha, who is looking at me. "Or I was once," I correct. "Now I'm nothing."

Heather makes a noise like *hmmph*. Then she turns, stomps down the hall to her room and slams the door.

"Don't worry, she'll warm up," Bertha says as she leads me down the hall toward my own room. It doesn't have a door, just a beaded curtain. She says at Harrow House, a door is a privilege, that I will have the opportunity to earn mine through good behaviour.

She shows me a dresser full of clothes she, or someone, has picked out for me. I see a bunch of tracksuits and turtlenecks, corduroy pants, a vest with little cats embroidered on it. Mental patient clothes. "I hope you like them," she says, "but if not, we can talk about that."

This is a test, I'm sure, so I say I do.

She shows me where the towels are and the soap and the toothpaste, how to turn the heat up or down, where to put my jacket, where I can find extra blankets. She stands in the middle of the room, bouncing up onto her toes. "So, welcome home, my dear. Lunch is at 12:30." Then she twirls away and is gone, and I'm alone in my very own room for the first time in 3,805 days.

The room is too hot. It smells like laundry soap and, faintly, of pee, which is doing a thing to my mind. I walk to the window and try to open it, but there's some kind of safety lock. Bertha isn't taking any chances with me. I look down at the street. Michael is still out there, pacing on the other side of the sidewalk with his hockey stick and satchel, waiting for me. He knows what I know: that it's only a matter of time until I ruin things here, like I ruin everything.

CHAPTER 4
BEFORE

BY THE TIME MARGARET OPENED THE TRAP DOOR, I HAD PEED ALL OVER MYSELF and the blanket and the floor too.

I scrambled out of the hole. "Are we in America yet?"

"We are," she said, but she didn't seem happy about it. She sniffed the air, frowned, went to find a towel to clean up my mess.

Her short-wave radio was on at the front of the bus, tuned to static. It seemed to be morning, but that couldn't be right because I'd gone into the hole just after noon, and she'd promised to come and get me as soon as we were across the border. The sun was slanting in the windows in big dusty sunbeams though, and there was the smell of fresh coffee in the air.

The curtains were drawn all along the sides of the bus, but out the back I could see we were in a parking lot next to the highway. In front of us there was a small brick building and some picnic tables, a man selling hot peanuts from a cart, parked cars and people—Americans— milling around on a little patch of grass.

"Stay away from the windows," she snapped.

I peeled my wet pants off—the only pair I had—and balled them up at the back of my suitcase. I put on a pair of shorts and joined Margaret at the kitchen table. Hugo's money was piled up in front of her.

"How much?" I asked, but she didn't answer.

She stuffed the money into an empty coffee can, stood and started pacing.

I looked into the can and then I knew what she was thinking. The can was half empty. It wasn't nearly enough to get to California. She was thinking what I was thinking: that I should've taken more.

She lit a cigarette and stared out the front window.

I waited until the third puff before speaking.

"You could sing for money!" I said. "And I could do magic!" I started to tell her about the gloves and the abracadabra and the spaghetti at the back of the cupboard, but she shushed me. She wasn't in the mood for any of that.

She sat in the driver's seat and fiddled with the radio. A man's voice rose up out of the static. He was reading a list of names, all the men who had died that day in Vietnam: Bill Cudge, and Joe Hill, and Clayton Thomas and many more.

She pulled out a road atlas and a pen and started writing things down on the pages.

I hovered nearby in case she needed my help, but she didn't, and I knew better than to ask. She had that look she got right before a headache, with her mouth pinched tight and a deep wrinkle between her eyebrows.

I sat on the bed and flipped through the pages of my book, *Fun Tricks for Good Christian Children*.

Chapter 1 was all about being a good boy or girl, and using tricks to bring joy to the people around you, not fool them. I skipped that chapter.

Chapter 2 was about throwing a quarter really quickly from one hand to the other without anyone noticing, but I didn't have a quarter.

Chapter 3 was something to do with a penny and three cups. I skipped that one too.

After a while, the man's voice disappeared into static. The radio got quiet. Margaret was hunched forward in her seat with her head in her hands, muttering to herself, or to Michael, I couldn't tell.

I shut the book loudly.

She didn't move.

I sighed.

Still nothing.

"I have to pee," I said.

She opened her eyes and shook her head at me. "Again?"

I stood, blinking, in the bright American sun. My ears were full of static. The edges of everything were vibrating and blue because Margaret had decided at the last minute to take my eye patch off, in case anyone was looking for us.

"Keep your head down," she'd instructed. "And be quick. And don't talk to anybody or look anyone in the eyes." Then she'd pulled the big lever to open the bus doors.

There was an American family at the picnic table in front of me. They looked like they were straight off a TV show. The mom had pink lipstick that matched her shoes. She was unpacking a picnic basket and yelling at her kids: *Jeffrey, watch for cars*, and *Gracie you get back here this minute*. Jeffrey had crisp pants and a collared shirt. Gracie had a lemon-yellow dress and a bow in her hair. Their dad was frowning down at a map he'd unfolded over the hood of his car, just like a TV dad would. They even had a dog who looked like Lassie. She ran up to me and stood on her back legs, whimpering and pawing.

Jeffrey came running after her, saying, "Down, girl." He had a ball in one hand and a little paper cup of peanuts in the other. "Wanna throw?" he said, offering the ball. I wished he'd offered the peanuts.

I looked back at the bus. Its brown curtains were pulled tight all around. I couldn't see Margaret, but I could feel she was in there, watching.

I shook my head no and ran for the bathroom.

I counted to a hundred four times before coming back out, but when I did, Jeffrey and his dog were still there, waiting.

"She wants you to throw it," he said, tossing me the ball. Lassie barked in agreement.

I threw the ball and was about to walk away when he offered me some peanuts.

I looked at the bus. Margaret hadn't said anything about not eating peanuts. He poured some into my hand. I ate them all in one handful. They were delicious, coated in some kind of salty, sweet candy and still warm from being roasted.

"What's your name?" he asked, giving me another handful.

Before I could think to stop myself, I answered. Then I looked up and saw Margaret standing in the bus window, drawing an imaginary line across her neck.

I was barely in the door when Margaret got me by the collar and yanked me up the stairs. "What did you say to that boy?"

"Only my name," I choked.

"And what did I tell you about that?" she shouted. "What did I *just* say?" My collar was twisted up in her fist, tighter than she probably knew, the buttons digging into my skin.

"This isn't a game. You have to listen when I tell you things." She was holding me up, just slightly off the ground, and shaking me harder than she probably meant to. The bus walls were starting to pulse, the edges of things going bright, then dark, then bright again.

The radio squealed. A woman's voice came on. *Give your children a hearty breakfast*, she said. *And be sure to start the day right!*

Margaret looked at me as if she was surprised to find me there, gasping in front of her. She set me down, smoothed my shirt, then turned and went back to the driver's seat. She put her bandana on and her dark glasses. She started the engine, and we pulled out onto the highway again.

I crawled to the bed. I took my shirt off and got under the covers, but I could still feel her hands around my neck, and I wondered, *Is that how I had done it to Michael? Had I strangled him without meaning to?* I didn't move or say a word for miles. I counted telephone poles out the back windows and tried not to think about how many to Ontario, how many more to California.

Much later, when it was dark and I could tell she had calmed down, I crept up to the front of the bus. I slid into the seat across from her, quietly.

The radio was on, making her hair glow green. She had a bottle of hooch pinched between her thighs. Her eyes kept sweeping left-right across the road. I counted out the seconds under my breath, waiting for her to forgive me.

"I know you didn't mean to do that," she said, finally. "But we have to be careful. We can't talk to anyone or tell people our names. They're probably looking for us by now."

"Who?" I asked. "Hugo?"

"Hugo, the cops, highway patrol, the FBI, you name it." She pulled a cigarette from behind her ear, put it in her mouth and tried to light a match while still holding the wheel.

I jumped up. "Let me."

"Okay, but don't inhale," she said, handing it off.

I'd seen her do it enough times to know what to do. I lit the match and sheltered it. I brought it to the end of the cigarette. I puffed and spat the smoke out and only coughed a little.

I handed the cigarette back to her. My mouth tasted like a house on fire.

"Atta girl," she said, looking at me, then the road, then me again, like she was seeing something new in me, something to be proud of.

The highway buzzed beneath us. We passed one neon sign after another. They were advertising for all kinds of things, but mostly bowling alleys and buffets.

"We have to change our names," she said, looking at me in the mirror. "We can't be Margaret and Elizabeth anymore. Those people are gone, understand?"

I nodded.

"And we can't say the word Ontario anymore. Or Canada. Or Kraft Park. We can't say any of that stuff to anyone. We're nobodies now, from nowhere."

I nodded. "So what are our names if people ask?"

"Don't know." She blew a smoke ring and, for a moment, it clung to her hair like a fancy hat.

"Clarice?" I tried. "And Eleanor?" They were names that fit her hat.

But she shook her head no. Too fancy.

I suggested Crimson and Clover, but those were too silly.

And Sally and Jane were too boring.

I watched the wrinkle appear between her eyes and, even though I knew I was risking being sent to bed, I tried again. "What about Fran and Sisco?"

A huge smile spread across her face, the first since Ontario. "Yeah," she said. "Yeah, I like that."

I didn't bother asking who was Fran and who was Sisco that night. It didn't matter, as long as I was back in her favour again.

In the morning she was curled up behind me in bed, her arm draped over my waist, all my earlier mistakes forgotten. We were at the far end of a big parking lot with a bowling alley in the distance.

I slipped out from under her arm. I looked around for my magic gloves but couldn't find them.

I counted the money in the can: thirty-nine dollars.

The bus was hot and stuffy and was starting to smell like a mouth, so I tiptoed around and opened some windows. She slept right through.

I flipped through the pages of the atlas. There were fifteen pages between Ontario and California, and each one looked like a tangled spiderweb. I saw Margaret's writing all around the edge of the pages, not letters but strange symbols, like little stick people and houses. It embarrassed me somehow to see that. I closed the book and opened my magic book instead.

The next trick in the book was a card trick where you ask someone to pick a card, any card. You pretend to memorize it and put it back in the deck, but with a little nick in the side. You sort through the deck and make small talk about Jesus and the weather until you find the right card. Then you wave your hands, *abracadabra*, and show it to them.

When Margaret finally woke up, I wiggled in next to her with the cards. I went through the trick, asking her to take one, putting it back, nicking it, shuffling. I did everything like the book said except I skipped the small talk because she hadn't had any coffee yet.

"Pretty good," she said when I finally showed her the right card, but in a voice that sounded like "whoop-de-doo." Then she stood and moved to the front of the bus. She sat, turned on the radio and said to pipe down, that she needed time to think.

She spent the whole day up there, thinking, smoking, tuning and retuning the dial, scribbling in her atlas. She gave me a box of saltines in case I got hungry and a bucket to pee in. She didn't say what to do if I had to do the other thing but, luckily, I didn't have to. I tried to be quiet, but everything I did seemed to annoy her and, as the day went on, the list of things I wasn't allowed to do kept growing. I wasn't allowed to squirm or tap my fingers against the wall. I wasn't allowed to ask questions. I wasn't allowed to hum under my breath, or step off the bus, or look out the windows, or even go near them. It wasn't safe, she said. They could be out there.

"They-who?" I asked.

"The Man," she said.

I snorted—*how could they be a man?*—but then I noticed she was looking all around as if, whoever he was, he might be out there in the parking lot.

Every once in a while, a snippet of music would emerge from the static. Then she'd find me in the rear-view mirror and ask, "What was that?"

If I knew the song, she was pleased. If not, that wrinkle between her eyes would deepen, so I started making up song names. That's "Moonlight on a Field," I said, or, "Pam, I Love You," or, "Baby, I'm Leaving."

Sometimes the static would disappear and there'd be long periods of silence, but I wasn't allowed to talk then either. She sat perfectly still, with her head tilted, as if she was listening to faraway instructions and the slightest noise from me would interrupt them.

Eventually it started to rain. The drops sounded like lizards scurrying over the roof. The windows fogged up so much they started to drip on the inside, but she didn't seem to mind. She turned the radio off and leaned back in her seat with her eyes closed and, for the first time all day, the wrinkle between her eyes smoothed out.

I stayed busy.

I practised the quarter trick with an eraser, the penny trick using some stray bolts I'd found on the floor.

I drew faces in the condensation on the cold metal walls: scary ones, ugly ones, pretty ones.

I tried to read my book, but the next trick was one involving a ball and a stick. I closed it and tried to play the TV game by myself. I closed my eyes, pressed my own nose and imagined changing the channels, but every show was about a mother and daughter living in a small box. Every day the daughter annoyed the mother even though she tried not to. Every day the box got a little bit smaller.

Finally, when it was dark, she got up, put her boots on and grabbed a soup pot. She stood at the front of the bus with one finger held to her lips—*shhhh*—tipping her head back and bouncing her eyebrows at me like we were finally about to do something fun.

We crept off the bus and made our way toward the tree line at the back of the parking lot. She got me to climb down into the ditch to fill the pot with mud, then pulled me up and led me back toward the bus. It was only once we were crouched behind the rear bumper that she explained what we were doing.

While I painted over the licence plate with mud, she stood back, whispering instructions. When I added too much mud, she said, "Don't *cake* it, fling it. It's got to look natural." When I added too little, she said, "You've got to cover the *letters*. I can still see the *letters*." Then, once I had got it right, when both plates and my hands and clothes were covered in mud, we climbed back onto the bus and finally drove away from that parking lot.

Margaret said we needed a gas station but every time we saw one, there was something wrong with it. She'd slow down in front and crane her neck around, then shake her head and speed away again, saying it was too bright or too busy, pressing down on the gas pedal so hard the engine clanked like Hugo was down there with his wrench.

When she finally did find a suitable one, what she called a "Mom and Pop" place away from the highway, she told me to lie on the floor while she gassed up and went in to pay.

She came back with a loaf of bread, a box of raisins, a newspaper and a frazzled look in her eyes.

"Stay low," she kept saying until we were back on the highway again.

Then, when I finally did get up, she made me flip through the whole newspaper, even the funnies, looking for any mention of us.

"Nothing!" I said once I'd finished.

"You sure? Nothing about a mom and daughter on the run? Nothing about a school bus?" She seemed disappointed, but I couldn't tell if it was in the newspaper or in me.

She made me check again and a third time, too. Then she told me to keep watch out the back window.

"For what?"

"Anything suspicious," she said. Then she clarified: I was to watch for lone men in black cars, men with serious-looking hats and moustaches. She said if I saw one, to write down his licence plate and what kind of car he was driving. She said to do a quick sketch of him, especially his moustache. I thought I saw the flicker of a smile when she said that, so I leaned against the back doors, eating raisins and watching half-heartedly out the windows, thinking it was just a game she'd made up to keep me busy, like how sometimes on Sunday mornings she used to ask me to organize Rocky's records alphabetically, so the two of them could sleep until noon. Every week those records were all mixed up. Every week I put them back in order.

In the morning, she was in bed behind me again, her arm wrapped around me, everything forgiven. She'd left the radio on at the front of the bus. I put on my shorts and crept up there to turn it off. Out the window, I saw we were parked at the far end of a parking lot, another bowling alley in the distance. When I reached for the dial, there was a squeal and a woman's voice saying, "Give me your hands and I will read your future."

"Mademoiselle?" I whispered.

"Shhhht," Margaret warned.

So I found my magic book and tiptoed back to bed to read quietly beside her. There were only two tricks left.

The first was another useless trick involving more things I didn't have, this time a bunch of string and a top hat.

There was only one trick left now.

I closed my eyes, made the sign of the cross and prayed like the sisters had taught me at school: *Please God, Jesus, Mary and Joseph, let this be a good trick that makes us money.* All we needed was one good trick. It could change everything.

I opened my eyes and turned the page.

But the final trick wasn't a trick at all. It was all about how if you let Jesus into your heart, you could find your own special tricks. It said to make a list of what my talents are and use those to impress people. Our own special tricks are God-given and always best, it said. I thought about that and made a list in my mind.

I could play the TV game pretty fast.

I knew most of the lyrics to most of the songs on the radio and, when I didn't, I was pretty good at making them up.

I could bend my thumb really far back toward my wrist in a creepy way.

I could hum and whistle at the same time.

But I couldn't imagine how any of those things could make us money.

I read the instructions again. Maybe the problem was I'd never let Jesus into my heart.

I lay back, rubbing my scar, trying to open my heart and, for a moment, I did feel something like a door creaking open. I imagined Jesus, crawling through on all fours in his weird diaper, grumpy-faced in his crown of thorns, and then the thought made me laugh and the laugh

44

made me cough and the cough made me poo my shorts. It went squirt and, right away, there was the smell, and I knew I was in trouble.

I tried to keep it between me and Jesus. I managed to pull the sheet out from under Margaret without waking her. I wrapped it around me and made it to the front of the bus and out the front door.

In the parking lot, I stripped everything off. I balled up my shorts and hid them above the wheel well. I used the sheet and some puddle water to wipe myself off.

But when I turned to come back onto the bus, she was standing at the top of the steps, holding her nose and shaking her head at me.

"What happened?" she said, even though she knew.

I tried to speak, but I couldn't find my voice.

"It's okay," she said, looking at me funny, "we'll clean it up." But I knew, even then, she would never sleep in the same bed as me again. I had ruined everything. And I knew I would have to do whatever I could, and become whatever she wanted me to be, to try and undo the damage.

We had to throw out most of the blankets and drive with all the windows open.

Since I didn't have any other clothes, I had to wear the red velvet Rapunzel dress from my costume trunk.

"Need to stop?" she kept asking without taking her eyes off the road, like I was a big baby who might do it again.

It was like that all afternoon. She wouldn't look directly at me. I knew what she was thinking though. She was thinking she'd have been better off with Michael. I heard her muttering to him up there while she drove. *Your stupid sister*, I thought I heard her say.

Lying at the back of the bus, my ears were hissing loudly and my chest ached from when the door of my heart had slammed back shut. I wanted to pray, but to who? Not Jesus. So I rubbed my scar and prayed to Michael for the first time. I asked him to help me use my life, ours. To help me help her, to give me just one good trick that could erase this mistake and get us to California.

I waited. Nothing happened.

The road hummed and thwapped beneath me. The sun was going down now. Strange shadows swooped and dove across the ceiling, chasing strange bars of light. Margaret was up there, her hair glowing red like an angry planet, one that was getting farther and farther away from me by the minute.

I slept then, must've, because I dreamed I was in a dark room, sitting across the table from someone I couldn't quite see. The room was full of shadows, but I could make out the eye patch, the shiny towel, a crystal ball sitting on a bed of feathers. It was Mademoiselle.

"Give me your hands and I will read your future," she said. She reached across the table, took my hands in hers and traced the lines with icy-cold fingertips.

Behind her there was a TV. It was staticky at first, but then it started changing channels quicker and quicker, one image after another flicking past. She leaned forward and, when the shadows shifted away from her face, I saw that it wasn't Mademoiselle after all but a boy, my age. He looked just like me—grey eyes like mine, curly hair like me— except, where his mouth should've been, there was a straight slope all the way to his chin. His cold hands clenched mine. He reached out to put a hand on my chest and, as soon as he touched me, the words arrived in my brain just as if he'd spoken them. *Be like Mademoiselle*, he said without saying. *Let me speak through you.*

I woke in a sweat. We were in another parking lot in front of another bowling alley. The sky was just getting light around the edges. Margaret was asleep in the driver's seat, as far away from me as she could get. The radio was on, hissing instructions.

I went to my suitcase. In with the clothes from my costume trunk I found a long, gold scarf and another one made of purple velvet. I twisted them up and tied them around my head. In the boxes of kitchen stuff Margaret had packed, I found a small glass bowl. I placed it upside down on the kitchen table like a crystal ball. I found a shiny, pink headband with white feathers all over it. I pulled the feathers out one-by-one and placed them all around the bowl. Then I sat before it, at the kitchen table, and coughed loudly.

Margaret sat up. "What the—?"

"I am Mademoiselle," I said in a mysterious voice. "Give me your hands and I will read your future."

She stood and stepped toward me, scratching her head.

"Sit," I said.

She sat and, sighing, extended her hands across the table. "Okay, go."

This was it, my chance.

I took her hands in mine. I closed both eyes, sucked an imaginary sour candy and waited for it, to feel what she felt. I felt her irritation, that in another few seconds she would get tired of this and say she needed a coffee. Then she would turn on the radio, and it would be another endless day trapped on the bus.

I had to get her attention. I opened my eyes and looked at her hands. I pointed at one of the lines there and, in a very serious voice, said what I knew she'd always wanted to hear: "Says here you will be famous."

She looked at me for the first time since the accident in my shorts.

I tapped another line. "Rich too." I heard that hissing in my ears again, like I was a radio tuned wrong, and then my mind turned on like the TV set in the dream. On the TV was an image of Margaret spinning in the middle of a crowd of people.

"You'll be the centre of attention, surrounded by people," I said, or must've. I don't remember exactly because it was like what Michael had said in the dream, like someone else was speaking through me.

On the TV, Margaret was spinning and smiling, chanting something over and over. Her eyes were closed, her mouth open. The people all around her were clapping and singing. They were cheering her on, answering her over and over.

I must've said that, about her singing, about the crowd, about everyone cheering her on. I must've made it sound pretty good because when I opened my eyes, she was staring at me with a look of wonder. "Amazing!" she said.

"Amazing?"

She was trembling a little. "How did you learn to do that? It's like you were in a trance or something."

I knew exactly what she wanted to hear.

"Michael," I said.

She hung her head and made a strange sound, like the air being let slowly out of a birthday balloon. I wasn't sure what was happening until I saw her tears hit the tabletop.

I came around and sat next to her. She put her arms around me and said the same thing she'd said before, that she always knew it.

"Knew what?" I asked this time.

"That you two were destined for something special," she said. She squeezed me then, a little too tight for a little too long, until I couldn't quite breathe.

For the rest of the morning, Margaret was buzzing. She wanted to work on what she called "our act."

She said I would need a new name, that I couldn't just be Mademoiselle, I had to be Mademoiselle *Something*.

I can't remember who came up with Mademoiselle Fantastico, only that once it was said, the name stuck.

She said we'd need a sign. She took apart an old cereal box, turned it inside out and got me to write my new name on it. I didn't know how to spell Mademoiselle, but I thought I remembered the abbreviation. My letters were so big I had to split Fantastico over two lines, but Margaret didn't notice. She said it was perfect. After I was done she even took the sign and drew some of her strange symbols on it.

She took the scarves off my head and braided them into a proper crown, then she went through my costume trunk and found a patchwork hat and a fancy scarf for herself.

When she was done dressing us, we stood at the back of the bus, bobbing our heads around to try and see ourselves in the rear-view mirror. She seemed pleased. She said we looked mysterious, that that was good, that people would pay more for that.

"People?"

"Customers," she said.

"*Customers?*" I had thought we were just playing dress up.

She led me by the hand toward the front window of the bus and pointed at the building in the distance. "See that diner? We're going to go in there and work the lunch crowd." She tousled my hair. "You're going to read their palms and make us a ton of money."

It was a diner, not a bowling alley. I could see that suddenly. I saw the signs advertising coffee and pie, the menu taped to the window, and I wondered why I hadn't noticed them before.

"But I can't," I said. "I don't know how."

"Nonsense! You just did it for me."

"But I *know* you. I don't know them."

"Listen," she said, spinning me around. "I saw what you did just now. You've got a gift, Kiddo. And I'll be right there with you. I'll be right by your side, okay?"

I nodded okay. I didn't have the heart to tell her I was a liar.

For the next hour she kept giving me all kinds of instructions: that I should stare at people's hands like I was reading a book, that I should trace the lines of their hands instead of just pointing, that just before I spoke, I should tilt my head to one side, like I was listening to something in the next room. She reminded me not to use our real names, that she was Fran Sisco and I was Mademoiselle Fantastico.

I tried to listen, but the hissing sound was back in my ears, like somewhere at the back of my mind, a tea kettle was about to boil over.

When it was time, she took me by the hand and we walked across the parking lot. I could barely feel my knees. We entered the diner and took a booth at the back, near the kitchen. She ordered a coffee for herself, a 7 Up for me. She winked at me as she slid our homemade sign toward the edge of the table.

"I don't think I can," I whispered.

"Nonsense," she said. "You were born for this." And I understood then that playing this game was the only way I could make up for what I'd done to Michael and the whole Big Sad Story of our lives.

I faced her. She faced the door. Every time someone came in, she reached up and pretended to stretch, which, because she wasn't wearing a bra, either made them look or made them look away.

The first person to come to our booth, about a half hour later, was a man. I saw Margaret's eyes narrow and move up-down while he approached, just like when she was trying to read the atlas.

"Trucker," she whispered, "unmarried, Texas plates." She flashed a smile and stuck her chest out a little. Then he was upon us.

He stood in front of our table, legs wide, arms folded across his chest, looking at our sign. He wasn't a big man, but he was pretending to be. "MeMe Fanta," he read aloud.

"Mademoiselle Fantastico," Margaret corrected. "My daughter here is a fortune teller. She'll read your fortune for a buck." She wasn't herself. She was waving her hands around and talking in a strange accent. She was Fran Sisco, confident and American.

"That right?" the man chuckled. He looked at her nipples, at me. Then he dug in his pocket and laid four quarters on the edge of the table.

She slid over, patting the bench next to her.

He looked at her and licked his lips. Then he sat.

"Give her your hands," she instructed.

He extended them across the table.

I took his hands even though I hated the way this man was looking at Margaret. I closed my eyes and waited for the TV to come on in my mind, but nothing happened. My mind was blank. My mouth was dry, my throat cinched tight like a knot.

"It'll just take a minute," Margaret—Fran—said. "She's just speaking to her brother now. He's on the other side."

My eyes shot open.

"Other side of what?" the man asked.

"The divide," she said. Then she leaned forward and came out with it, the whole Big Sad Story, all the parts I'd never heard before. She said we'd been twins, but there hadn't been enough for the two of us, so I had

50

lived and he had died. But we were still connected, she said. He could talk to me and send messages from the other side.

All the colour drained from the man's face. "So they're, like, what? Siamese?"

"Yes!" Fran said, perking up. "Just like that."

She kicked me under the table. They both turned to look at me.

I closed my eyes and tried to think of something to say, but I kept hearing that word, *Siamese*, hissing in my ears like a snake.

The man sighed. In a moment he would give up. He'd take his money back and tell the waitress about us. She'd call the cops and we'd be arrested.

I grabbed his hands tighter.

"Here we go," Fran said.

Margaret believed in me, I could feel that. She believed that I was born for this, that this moment right here could make our whole lives worthwhile.

I could hear a clock ticking on the wall, the chatter of the room, a fryer spitting in the kitchen, the radio on in there.

In the kitchen, the cook was whistling along to the music, Bob Dylan's "Like A Rolling Stone." I remembered that knowing all the words to songs and being able to make them up was my number two God-given talent, and I suppose that's how the idea came to me.

I must've said something about a man alone on the road, about having nothing and nothing to lose, maybe even something about not knowing the way home, about rolling like a stone and never arriving.

I might've flipped my eye patch up and asked, "How does it feel?" I must've because when I was done, he looked right at me and answered, "Feels pretty crummy alright."

"Is there someone you should call?" Fran asked. I don't know what made her say that, but it was the exact right thing, at the exact right moment.

His eyes welled up, and his breath turned ragged. He hung his head, for just a moment, then stood, rapped his knuckles on the table, said "thankya," and left.

As soon as he was out of earshot, Margaret looked at me with eyes brighter than I'd ever seen. She reached over and squeezed my elbows. "See?" she said. "I knew you could do it!"

We made three dollars off three truckers that day. I stuck to Bob Dylan. She always ended with the same question—*Is there someone you should call?*—and every time there was.

At the end of the day, Margaret said I could order whatever I wanted off the menu. I had a root beer and a grilled cheese. She had a turkey sandwich.

She decided we didn't have to drive that night. Instead, she flicked the lock on the door, and we spent the night in the parking lot.

She was in a great mood. She lit a few candles and kept the radio off for once. She whistled a tune while she swept and did dishes and unpacked her suitcase. I watched her fold her clothes neatly and place them in a cupboard above the bed, like maybe it was finally worth unpacking because this was all going to work out after all.

"You're good, MeMe. Really good," she said. "And your eye patch is perfect. I bet we can do this all the way across the country. People are going to love you. They're going to line up for miles."

I was at the kitchen table, flipping through my notebook of song lyrics, trying to find other ones I could use on truckers, but I kept thinking about what she'd said, about Michael and me, that there hadn't been enough for the two of us. *Not enough what?* I wanted to ask, and, *Who had decided who lived and who died? The doctors? Her? Me?*

I was waiting for her to slow down so I could ask, but she was in one of her way-up moods, chattering about all the places we'd go on the way to California: the Grand Canyon, the Mississippi, a certain buffet she'd heard about in Las Vegas that had forty-nine kinds of Jell-O.

"Maybe even grapefruit Jell-O!" she said. "Or chocolate! Do you think there's such a thing as chocolate Jell-O?"

She twirled around to look at me and what I saw in her eyes then, for the first time in such a long time, was hope.

So I nodded yes—my first lie—even though everyone knows there's no such thing as chocolate Jell-O, only pudding.

I didn't ask about Michael that night and, by the time I woke up the next morning, it was too late. We were already driving to the next diner. She was dressed as Fran, in her hat and scarf, and had found a new name for me: MeMe Fanta, the Siamese Wonder. She wanted me to make a new sign. And she'd thought of a way to do my eyes, so I looked more Siamesey. And she had an idea for my hair too.

"You're amazing!" she said, looking at me in the rear-view mirror. "You're MeMe the Amazing Wonder!"

And the truth is, it felt great to be amazing. The only problem with being amazing is, you can't ever go back.

CHAPTER 5

AFTER

BERTHA WASN'T KIDDING ABOUT ROUTINE.

Every morning, Monday to Friday, from nine to eleven, I have tutoring with Mr. Twohig, a retired high-school teacher who is kind and sad and wears all different shades of brown, as if he has been trampled. I don't mind Mr. Twohig so much, even though I'm pretty sure that's not his actual name. He's a realist. He agrees that I may not need to know the Pythagorean theorem or the exact year the czar of Russia abdicated the throne way back whenever in order to live the rest of my life. But I do need to memorize it for now, he insists, in order to get my high school diploma, which is something I very much will need for the rest of my life.

Mr. Twohig is big on "the rest of my life." Every time he says it, he gazes out the window and his eyes flicker with his high hopes for me. Then he clears his throat and returns to the present, where he must teach me $A^2 + B^2 = C^2$, the difference between affect and effect, and how one thing after another led to World War I.

Mr. Twohig is a master of hoping high but aiming low like that. While I practise multiple-choice questions, he slips in the odd comment about how I might like to go to university one day, how I might like Europe, how I might decide to have a family or start a business. He is one of the few people who sees me not for what I've done, but for who I could be.

On Mondays and Fridays, from one to three, I have writing with Annie, my "writing coach."

Annie was a real poet once, before she gave up on all that. So now she's just a regular twenty-seven-year-old who cares a lot about metaphors and similes and finding all the specific but surprising ways one thing is like another.

Annie is a yoga teacher too, which is why she wears pants without zippers and starts every one of our sessions by getting me to stand and swing my hips around like I have an imaginary hula hoop, saying, "Let's just move and get a little bit loose." She's big on getting a little bit loose. Getting a little bit loose is necessary for art, she says. It's the first step.

Annie's a real professional though, so right after stretching, we get down to it. She reads the pages I've written for homework, circling misspelled words and scribbling little notes in the margins, like: *Be specific!* and, *Is that how it really really felt though?*

Sometimes she gives me a serious talking to about my punctuation. Then she usually ends each session by ranting about how important this work is: how writing is alchemy and I'm writing my story in order to unwrite and on and on.

I don't always listen to Annie when she rants. Mostly I stare at the walls.

Slow and steady, says the turtle.

All things are shit, says the teddy bear.

One good thing about Annie is she never stops me staring at the walls. The poet in her knows it's necessary. Staring at the walls is your jam, she always tells me. This is how she tries to relate to me, by saying things like, "your jam," instead of, "coping mechanism" or "self-soothing technique."

I still like Annie though, even though my jam is totally different from her jam.

The first time I showed her my writing, I handed her the messy file folder I'd been shoving little scraps of paper into since Willingdon. She sifted through, reading a few pages. Then she sighed, threw her head back and sat with her eyes closed for a long time as though she was either very impressed or very tired. When she finally opened them again, she closed the folder and ran her fingers over the title: *Once Upon a Fucking Time*. She knew it was against the rules to swear. She knew I knew. I watched her weigh that for a moment. Then she leaned in to whisper, "You've got real talent, Elizabeth, but we've got to get this effing folder organized!" She laughed then in such a way that I could see all the way to the back of her mouth. I could see her grey/pink tongue, and I got a feeling about her, that she still was a poet, deep down, and always would be. I sensed that she believed in art more than medicine, love more than reason, and that it was probably safe to tell her my story because she might actually believe it.

That day she handed me an empty red binder. She said she wanted me to transcribe all the messy pieces of paper from my folder into the binder in chronological order, rewriting along the way, because, she said, I owed it to myself.

On Tuesdays and Thursdays all of us have group therapy with Bertha, which is where I learn that we all have problems with voices. It's our jam, why we're all here.

I learn that Patrick once heard the voice of Bob Barker speaking to him through his toaster. For a long time the voice told him to do good things, like mow people's lawns for them while they were at work, but then, once, it told him to burn down his elementary school, which he did, with two people in it. It was an accident of course. It was spring break and the people weren't supposed to be there, but still, damage done.

I learn that Leonard once held up a famous newscaster at knifepoint for six hours because of certain messages he was receiving from an army of houseflies that he had trained with his mind to do something or other—that part is unclear, even to him. The newscaster wasn't hurt and, actually, his news career got a real boost, but that didn't help Leonard's case any.

I learn that Heather doesn't have a blue line down her forehead after all, or not a permanent one at least. She just likes to draw things on her face and body with a ballpoint pen. I never do learn what she did to end up here or what her issue is with voices, but I know there is cruelty in her past. I know because of the cigarette-sized scars on her back, between her shoulder blades, right where she couldn't possibly have done it herself. She doesn't talk about any of that though. Mostly she talks about California, which is where she says she's going as soon as she gets out of this shithole.

"S-hole," Bertha corrects, and Heather rolls her eyes.

Together we're learning that it's okay to have made mistakes, even very bad ones, as long as we're trying to make better choices now. We're working on acknowledging and negotiating with the voices in our heads, on knowing when to be at peace with the voices and when to tell someone about them. The voices are not the problem per se, Bertha says, it's what they're telling us that sometimes needs to be run by a trusted friend.

I wish she wouldn't say that. Per se. It makes my skin feel one size too small.

On Wednesday afternoons I have therapy with Bertha, alone.

On Saturdays I'm scheduled to go out and deliver newspapers around the neighbourhood with everyone else from the house, but I've been given a free pass on that for now because Bertha says it's probably too upsetting for me. So instead I stay home and clean the fish tank and "try to stay where my hands are," which is a skill I'm working on.

Sundays are my favourite though. Sundays are for tomatoes.

Bertha is as big on tomatoes as she is on routine, which is why we have, like, five hundred seedlings growing on heat mats out in the greenhouse. She says caring for tomato seedlings is a lot like caring for ourselves. We're probably supposed to learn something about giving ourselves exactly what we need in exactly the right amounts, something about rooting down while also reaching up.

When the tomatoes are "mature," she says we'll sell them at the farmer's market to help pay for our college educations, and she makes that face again, the poker face that says, "ante up."

Everything is going fine at Harrow House. Fine*ish*. I get through ten sessions with Mr. Twohig, four with Annie. I eat thirteen of Leonard's gourmet dinners—cauliflower gratin, and chicken catchya-something, and polenta something-something, and I listen politely while he explains in great detail how he made it all. I sit through four group therapy sessions and two with Bertha. I even meet with my parole officer, Rhonda, who is also Heather's parole officer. Rhonda is a fierce-looking woman with tight pants and a tighter bun, whose life has not worked out quite how she'd hoped, but she says I'm "settling in just fine," which is a high compliment coming from her.

Then, one day after Group, Heather corners me in the hallway.

"You know there was a girl, Krissy, who lived in your room before you," she says. She's standing so close I can feel the warmth of her breath on my face.

"But then she offed herself." She holds a fist above her head like a fake noose, cricks her neck and sticks her tongue out sideways.

"So?" I know better than to show a reaction.

"So, don't you have a thing about ghosts?" she says. "Can't you feel her haunting you?"

She's referring to Michael of course, which is something confidential from Group, which is against the rules, which is why I push her against the wall, which is how I end up being pulled into Bertha's office to discuss why Michael is such a "trigger point" for me. Then, next thing I know, Bertha wants to know all about him—when I saw him first and when I saw him last and what he said and how it made me feel—and she starts writing everything down in her notes.

At the end of it all, she says she thinks we need to start meeting more regularly.

She says she wants to see me "engaging more in Group too," meaning she wants me to talk about my crimes.

I nod. These doctors are all the same. They get off on confession.

"So you agree to dig a little deeper?" she says.

I nod some more.

Before I leave, she clarifies that Krissy didn't kill herself, she simply decided group living wasn't for her. I feel like simply deciding the same thing, but I can't because Margaret might be looking for me and everyone knows if you're lost in the woods, you're supposed to stay in one spot until rescue. Plus I'm in the middle of weening.

Every day, I sneak into the bathroom, unfurl the paperclip I've stashed behind the toilet tank and use one pointy end of it to shave just the smallest powdery sliver off my white and blue pills. I crack open the gel cap of my yellow pill and remove a few glistening beads before closing it back up again. It rattles like a tiny tambourine when I bring it to my mouth, like the opening to "Yellow Submarine" and then I remember that I was somebody once, that I was MeMe Fanta, healer of hearts and minds and bum trips, and could be again, if only I can get off this submarine.

CHAPTER 6

BEFORE

SOON ENOUGH, MARGARET AND I HAD A ROUTINE.

Every morning we woke early and muddied our plates before driving to a new diner. Margaret would turn into the parking lot and roll past slowly, waiting to get a yes/no feeling about the place. She said there was nothing more important in life than the yes/no feeling, that she'd never understood why they didn't teach *that* in schools.

If the diner was a yes, we'd park and do a bunch of "warm ups," which meant she'd think of a colour or a word and hold it in her mind until I guessed it. Then, when I did, she'd squeeze me and say, "See how incredible you are?"

While we waited for the diner to fill up she'd remind me to pay attention to the cues, to a person's clothes, their hair, their hands and what they did with them. She said to notice if they were tired, if they were clean, where their eyes went when they talked, if they had a wedding ring or not. She said people were giving themselves away all the time, that it wasn't unusual to notice this stuff, it was unusual *not* to.

When we finally entered the diner just before noon, she'd have a few words with the head waitress and give her a dollar for her trouble. We always sat at the back, near the bathrooms, where people had no choice but to walk past.

"Hey you," Margaret would say, leaning out of the booth. "Ever met a Siamese psychic before?" That made most people run but, every so often, someone would sit and stay awhile.

It was mostly truckers. Sometimes a housewife or a lonely man eating lunch alone. Margaret always did a quick read of them as they approached. She always knew when someone was in trouble. "Heavy drinker," she'd say or, "This one likes to gamble." If anything, she was the real psychic. But I was the one with the eye patch and the story, and that was pretty much the whole hog right there, she always said.

As the days went by, our story grew. Soon she was saying Michael and I had been joined at the heart, that we were joined still. She said the doctors had told her to choose between us, but we had worked it out ourselves—his heart for my eye. That's why I could see the future, she said. I had one eye in this world, one in the next.

Sometimes, for the doubters, she'd pull down the collar of my dress to show off my scar. "See?" she'd say, "What'd I say? Joined, right there!"

She was full-on Fran in those moments, waving her hands in front of my chest, her eyes big and spooky.

And I was playing the part too. I traced people's palms. I pretended to hear a voice speaking to me from far away. I flipped my eye patch up and quoted Bob Dylan: songs about heartache and being far from home, songs about soldiers, songs about hobos.

Everyone we saw seemed to be sad or lost, so in a way it was easy. I even learned to do a thing where I made a little small talk first and then, whatever clues I learned about their life I echoed back to them later.

When I'd said enough, Margaret kicked me under the table and swooped in to collect the money.

I don't know how long this went on. Weeks? A month? Two?

I don't remember, and it didn't matter. She was happier than I'd ever seen her. We were meeting new people every day, hearing their stories, making seven, eight, nine dollars a day and eating three square meals. We were living her American Dream.

Most nights we'd climb back onto the bus together and sit at the kitchen table, talking about the events of the day. She'd give me tips on how to improve my act—that I should roll my eyes and flutter my hands and flatten out my vowels so I sounded less Canadian.

Once, she asked me to teach her to read. At the Kraft factory she'd been able to get away without being able to, she said, but on the road, things were different. So we spent that night and many after sounding out words and learning how to write them.

"How come you never learned in school?" I asked, even though I already knew the story: how the sisters had beat her so bad for using her left hand—"the Devil's hand" they'd called it—the words had started to float around on the page.

"Because I was never taught right," she said. Then she raised the crayon she'd been writing with and pointed it at me. "And don't you ever tell anyone."

"Our secret," I promised.

In return, she taught me the few things she'd memorized in Morse code: "S-O-S," and "I love you," and, "Enemy near."

I asked how she knew all that. She said her dad had taught her, that he'd learned it in France, during the war.

I stayed perfectly still then, hoping she'd say more about the grandpa I'd never met, but she didn't. For Margaret, the past had always been strictly off limits. Anytime I tried to ask about it, she said she'd grown up in the middle of nowhere and that's all there was to say about that.

My favourite days were the ones when we drove away from the diner parking lots, out along winding country roads, stopping wherever we felt like it.

Once, we stopped at a farm stand to buy some apples and, in behind the stand, we saw a group of women seated in a circle playing music together. One had an instrument made out of a bucket and mop and one had a washboard. If it weren't for the one playing the banjo, and their sad, sad song, I might've thought they were doing laundry.

Another time we came across a man trotting down the side of the road on horseback. Behind the horse was a goat and behind the goat, a dog and behind the dog, a donkey and behind that, a pig. They were walking all together, all in a line, and the man at the front kept turning around on his horse to see if they were all still there.

We saw people selling pies, selling jam, selling homemade doilies. They waved, we waved back.

"That, right there, is the real America," Margaret always said when we drove away from these people, and I wondered why we couldn't live here all the time, in the real America, instead of along the highway.

Whenever we crossed a bridge with a nice-looking river beneath it, we'd park and scramble down the banks to clean ourselves. I loved those days, sitting in the sun by the side of a rushing river, daring each other to go into the cold water. It felt like we were finally free then, like we'd put Ontario and our big sad past behind us.

If we could've gone on this way forever, until she could read and write and I could tap out anything I wanted in Morse code, I would have.

But one afternoon, after working the lunch shift at a place called The Blue Fox, we came back to the bus and, when Margaret turned the key in the ignition, it made that old sound: a *wheee* followed by a *clunk*.

Margaret talked to one of the waitresses who phoned a guy, Ray, who knew how to fix school busses. He came out that evening to take a look. Margaret told me to lie on the floor at the back, but I crept into the driver's seat and spied on them. Ray had a big belly and greasy hair that hung in his eyes. He stuck his head under the hood and tapped around down there. Then he stood up, closed the hood and wiped his hands on his overalls. "Starter's shot," he said, "have to order a new one."

"How much?" Margaret asked.

His eyes travelled her body. "Seventy-five, give or take."

She said we only had thirty.

He took a step toward her and said he'd be open to arrangements.

"Absolutely-fucking-not," I heard her say. She turned away, came stomping back onto the bus and started making coffee, noisily, at the stove.

Ray stood out there for a while, whistling and packing up his tools as slowly as possible. Then, before he left, he wrote his phone number on a piece of paper and tucked it under the windshield wiper, shouting, "In case you change your mind."

We stayed on the bus that night with the door locked and the curtains drawn all around. I didn't say anything about Ray. Neither did she.

Together we were trying to remember the words to "Boots of Spanish Leather" because, she said, as long as the bus was broken, we should stick to Dylan's more obscure songs. We had to be more careful about everything and keep an eye out for anything peculiar.

"Peculiar how?" I asked.

But she didn't answer. She said I'd better get to bed, that I had a big day ahead of me. She walked me to the back of the bus and started making the bed for me—something she never did. When she tucked me in, I hung on to her neck and tried to pull her down with me. She pushed me away though, saying she was busy. Then she went to sit up front. I watched her blow out the candle. I heard her turn on the radio and tune it to static. She was flipping through the atlas even though it was too dark to read, scribbling on the margins of the pages again.

The next day I did five truckers and a housewife. I made nine dollars by the end of the lunch rush, my best day yet, but Margaret hardly noticed. All day it was like she was on the other side of a glass wall, like she could see me but not quite hear me. Her eyes were dark and darting all around the room.

We didn't eat in the diner that night, even though they had a special of roast beef with mashed potatoes and gravy. She said we had to save our money, so we had stale bread and butter on the bus, stale raisins for dessert. I wanted to take my eye patch and crown off when I ate, but she wouldn't let me. She said if someone saw, it wouldn't be good for business. All the curtains were drawn, but she still paced back and forth, peering out of one window and then another. She said something about all the men in brown hats. "Didn't you notice them?" she asked. "We were surrounded by them all day."

I tried to get her to sit with me and practise reading.

I tried to get her to work on the words to "Ballad of Hollis Brown" but she was unreachable.

She sent me to bed even though I wasn't tired. Then she sat up front, smoking one cigarette after another until the smoke had gathered around her head like a storm. Ray's phone number was still out there, flapping in the wind. She sat perfectly still, more still than I'd ever seen her, staring at it.

The next day, my third at The Blue Fox, was my worst. All day long I kept checking the faces of the men who walked into the diner. I checked their hats, their clothes, what they ordered, if they wore wedding rings. I never did see a man in a brown hat, but I did notice a woman with a tall, black one, like a magician's hat. She was sitting in a booth in the far corner of the restaurant, right in my line of vision. She had a cup of coffee and was pretending to read a book but was really watching me. I studied her around the edges of the menu. She had blond hair in two long braids and a strange blue dress with pieces of string hanging off of it. There was a stack of cards sitting in front of her on the table like she was about to play Solitaire, but she never did play. I noticed the waitresses ignored her, even when she tried to wave them over. I thought about telling Margaret about her, but she was on the other side of the glass wall again, and I didn't want to make her feel any worse.

It was dead all day, but in the late afternoon, as soon as Margaret stepped away to use the bathroom, the blond woman rose from her seat and went to the jukebox. She pressed some buttons. An old familiar song came on, one Margaret and I used to sing along to back in Ontario.

A moment later, a farmer slid onto the bench across from me. He was a huge man, practically bursting out of his overalls. He had a red bandana tied around his neck and he was chewing on a long piece of hay. I remember thinking something wasn't quite right about him, that he looked more like the idea of a farmer than an actual farmer.

"Howdy," he said. "What's all this?"

I explained that I could read his future for a buck. I left out the part about being Siamese.

"All righty then," he said, pushing a dollar across the table at me. He started rambling then, something about a business deal, about not wanting to be foolish, not wanting to rush in. Then he gave me his hands before I had a chance to ask.

I took them. I should've noticed they were too smooth for a farmer's hands. I closed my eyes and waited. Nothing was coming.

"Is there a problem?" he asked.

"No problem," I said, but my head was spinning. I was searching my brain for the right song.

Bob Dylan would have been fine probably, or Joni Mitchell or Joan Baez. But instead, all I could hear was that song in the background. I remembered it now. It was Etta James, the one about being a fool and rushing into love. I quoted it to him, the line about fools rushing where wise men don't.

The man snatched his hands away. "You talking some Etta at me?" he shouted. His voice was so loud it carried across the whole restaurant. People put their forks down and looked.

Margaret, who had just stepped out of the bathroom, came rushing over. She apologized and offered to give the man his money back, but he was already calling the waitress.

"C'mere, Betsy," he said. He repeated what I'd said about fools rushing in. "Ain't that Etta she's talking?"

It was Etta, Betsy confirmed. It was, in fact, the song that was playing on the jukebox right that moment, word-for-word.

The man was up out of his chair now, still shouting. "What kind of scam is this?" he shouted. "If I wanted Etta, I'd turn on the radio for free." He said maybe he should call the cops and see what they had to say about all this.

"Now, now," Betsy said, stepping in front of him. She managed to calm him down a little, but then she turned to us and said we should leave and probably not come back.

"Yeah, or you'll go to jail," the man shouted over her shoulder.

Back on the bus, Margaret stomped around, smoking one cigarette after another. She was pacing and looking out the windows again. Then she sat behind the wheel and flicked on the radio. She was rocking back and forth to the static, whispering to Michael. They were arguing. I heard her say, *No, uh-uh, no way.*

I stayed quiet. Of all the songs in all the world, I'd had to choose Etta. Nothing could've been more stupid. She was probably trying to decide whether she should just ditch me there and go to California by herself. She probably would've been better off.

She tried the ignition again. There was no sound this time, not even the *whee-clunk.* She tried again and again before she gave up and crumpled over the steering wheel, her head resting against it.

I stayed at the back of the bus, doing silent abracadabras on her, on the bus, but it wasn't working. I wasn't magic, never had been. I was a liar and a fake.

Eventually, she got up from her seat. She stooped to look at herself in the mirror, fluffed her hair a little, then spun around and pointed a finger at me. "Stay here," she said. "And don't move a muscle."

I nodded, using as few muscles as possible.

I sat, frozen, as she stepped off the bus, closing the front door behind her. Then I watched her reach up and pluck Ray's number from beneath the windshield wiper and walk away from me, to the far end of the parking lot and beyond, out along the highway where I lost sight of her completely.

When she came back a few hours later, she stumbled up the steps and flopped down on the bench.

I came to her side.

She reached out to touch my face but changed her mind halfway. "Don't worry," she said, with her hand hanging there in the air between us. "We gotta plan now."

She tried to smile, but her mouth wasn't working right. And her eyes kept circling and circling my face, never landing.

Ray was going to order the part, she explained. She'd have to visit him in the evenings and Michael and I would have to take care of each other.

"Is he your boyfriend?" I asked.

"*God* no," she laughed, and I noticed her hooch breath. It sharpened the air around us. She closed her eyes. Her face kept changing: happy then sad then scared then, eventually, mad. "Go to bed," she ordered. "I hafta think."

She stayed up, smoking and thinking, for some time. She lit a candle and hunched over it, running her finger back and forth through the flame until I could smell singed skin.

In the distance, the lights of the diner turned off.

I heard the last waitress get in her car and leave. Then, a few minutes later, there was a soft knock at the door.

I sat up.

Margaret picked up the heavy black frying pan from the stove and moved toward the door.

"It's just me," a woman called. "I just wanted to see if y'all are okay."

I shook my head, *no*, but Margaret didn't see.

She put the pan down, flicked the lock, and a woman stepped on.

It was the blond woman from the diner.

"Hiya," she said. "I'm Lucky." She was carrying a big backpack with a tin cup and a pot hanging from the frame. Her long, shaggy dress had bells sewn to the hem, so every step made noise. She stood at the front of the bus, jingling and clanging, looking all around with her mouth hanging open. Her hat was nowhere in sight.

"Come in," Margaret said, waving her toward the table like she was an old friend.

I scrambled out of bed. I had to warn Margaret about the woman, how she'd been watching us all day, how she was one of them, the men with brown hats.

The woman sat. "I saw what happened at the diner earlier."

Margaret sat across from her, with her back to me.

I was knocking out Morse code on the edge of the bed—S-O-S and Enemy near—but Margaret didn't notice.

Lucky leaned to the side to peer around Margaret. "Would you like to come and join us, MeMe?"

How did she know my name? The candle flared like a warning.

I came to the table. I tried to give Margaret a look, but she was busy staring at the woman. I knew what she was thinking: this was her first real-life American hobo, straight out of a Bob Dylan song.

"Where's your hat?" I asked.

Lucky pulled a leather pouch out of her pocket and started to roll a cigarette. She licked the paper, spat a piece of tobacco. "Hat?" she asked. She looked at me, smiling, and that's when I noticed how strange her eyes were. Her pupils were huge and black with just the thinnest ring of blue around the edges. And her smile was strange too. It was relentless and phony like the sisters at school when they were mad but pretending not to be.

Then she changed the subject. "So you two are in some kind of trouble?" She looked from Margaret's face to mine.

Margaret started to mumble something about how we were fine, that we had a plan, but Lucky interrupted.

"Let's see," she said, counting our troubles off on her fingers. "You're on the run from something. You're far from home. You've been banned from the diner. Your bus is broken. And—" using her thumb now— "you're counting on Ray to bail you out of this mess?"

Margaret froze. "You know Ray?"

Lucky lit the cigarette she'd rolled. She took a drag and held it in so long it made a clicking sound at the back of her throat. Then she exhaled, still smiling, and passed it to Margaret. "Any woman around here who's in any kind of trouble knows Ray. Consider it his specialty."

The bus filled with her green-smelling smoke.

Margaret tried to copy what Lucky had done, but she ended up coughing. Lucky rummaged around in her bag and came up with a thin, metal bottle. She passed it to Margaret.

"I have a proposition for you, and I want you to think about it very carefully. Because here's the thing," she held one bossy-looking finger up in the air, "I'm a psychic too. A real one. And this here used to be *my* restaurant. Well not my *restaurant*, but my territory. I make my living here. Or I did, until you two came along."

She reached across and plucked the cigarette out of Margaret's fingers. Then she continued, her voice firmer now, louder.

"You two have become a real pain in my ass, see? So rather than call the cops and have them send you back to wherever it is you're from, I suggest you come with me to where I'm staying." She stopped to inhale, long and slow, held it in, then exhaled. "It's a special place, full of people just like you—" she looked at Margaret and winked, "—people who just want to step off the wheel for a little while and get free."

The wheel: how did she know?

She handed the cigarette back to Margaret, said to take it slow, then continued.

"In the next few days I'll get my friend, Mick, to come out and fix your bus and, in the meantime, I'll teach MeMe here how to do *real* readings"—she looked at me—"not that Etta James crap you've been doing." She turned back to Margaret. "What do you think?"

Margaret inhaled slowly through her teeth. She looked out the window toward the highway. I tapped out S-O-S again on the tabletop, and I thought I saw her nod. I thought I knew what she was thinking, that in a second she'd say, "absolutely-fucking-not," lunge for the frying pan and kick this woman off our bus, but when she finally spoke, she turned to Lucky and said, simply, "Okay."

I must've made a real scene because, next thing I knew, I'd been sent to bed, and they'd stepped off the bus to talk without me.

If I pressed my head to the wall, I could hear them out there. They were talking fast about everything all at once: about growing up in stupid, small towns, about Vietnam, Nixon, marriage, divorce, the race to the moon.

I noticed Lucky did a thing like what I'd learned to do in the diner. She let Margaret speak first, then just echoed whatever she'd said.

When Margaret said, "I don't actually *like* Baez all that much," Lucky agreed, saying, "*Waaay* too warbly!"

And when Margaret said, "I don't know if we should even be going to the moon," Lucky added, "Yeah, how about making things better here on Earth?"

I heard Lucky ask Margaret where we were headed.

"San Francisco," Margaret said.

"No *way*," Lucky said. "I was *just* there!"

Lucky's voice got low then, and she told a story about getting robbed in broad daylight in the middle of Golden Gate Park. They took everything, she said, even her shoes. Then she said something else I couldn't quite hear, something about bad drugs and the whole place cracking up and how the '60s were over.

I kept waiting for Margaret to say we weren't going there for any of that, that we were going there to eat goat cheese and get a record deal, but she didn't.

Lucky's voice ticked up and she started talking about where she lived now, that they were working on something new, a way to wake people up. She started talking about someone named O and someone else named Samuel and how they had a plan, a way forward. They were really going to shake things up, she said, and get things back on the right track again.

They got quiet then. I stood up on my knees in bed and peered out around the side of the curtain. They were sitting side by side on the curb out there. They stared at each other for a moment. Then they leaned forward. Margaret's arms went up, around Lucky's shoulders. Lucky's went down, around Margaret's waist. Their faces came together and didn't come apart again, not for a long time.

CHAPTER 7

AFTER

THE RAIN LETS UP FOR ONCE AND THE VANCOUVER SKY TURNS A SLIGHTLY lighter shade of grey.

Every day, I shave a little more off my blue and white pills. I crack open the yellow submarine and remove another few beads. I'm feeling it now, big time. One minute everything's fine and the next, my brain is a startled bird flapping around in its cage, wanting out. I have to keep reminding myself that Margaret wanted me to be here, in Vancouver; that someone started the process that got me sent back to Canada and, specifically, to Willingdon. It must've been her.

Plus, there have been signs.

Once, last week, while walking, unsupervised, through Chinatown, I found a packet of red Kool-Aid where it shouldn't be, sitting right in the middle of a shelf full of noodles in Yuen Fong Supermarket.

And a few days later I saw a puff of orange hair bobbing above the crowd ahead of me. I chased after. I couldn't catch up, but I came to a brick wall with the words *I am* freshly painted on it. Then, a few blocks later the word *here*, written in chalk on the pavement.

So she's near. She'll come and get me soon. She's just waiting for the right moment.

I've started leaving my own signs: *Margaret Squire, your daughter is at 467 Keefer*, written on little folded-up notes buried in the bins of dried fish in front of Yuen Fong; *I'm here too*, scrawled on the steamy windows of the dumpling restaurant.

Mr. Twohig and I blow through the eleventh grade at what he calls "lightning speed." I learn the complicated relationship between X and Y, how to conjugate verbs in Spanish, that Romeo and Juliet were doomed from the start. I learn the phrase "star-crossed." I write, *Estoy star-crossed* on the palm of my hand just to see how that feels. It feels true.

Annie reads the new pages I've written for the red binder and doesn't say anything about the new title page I've made: *Once Upon A Fucking Time* with lightning bolts all around the F-word. She makes little smiley faces and check marks in the margins and, every time, something leaps inside me. I live for those smiley faces. I live for those check marks. She usually gives me a new assignment, something to "fill in the gaps in my story." Then she gives me a pep talk about writing into the darkest places and how every story needs a hero at its centre. That's the work we're doing here, she says. I'm moving to the centre of my own story, the centre of my hula hoop. I'm getting loose and finding out how I *really* really feel about things. I notice she doesn't talk as much about how every story needs conflict though—a protagonist, yes, but also an antagonist. This, she assumes, I already know.

In the greenhouse, more and more tomato seeds crack open. The seedlings peek out, then unfurl like little green question marks, like: *Am I? Am I really?*

Whenever I'm alone with Bertha, she always wants to talk about Michael now. And she's always writing it all down, everything I say.

She says she's trying to identify what she calls my "trigger points" because these will be the biggest hurdles to my healing. She says each one is like a snake in the game Snakes and Ladders. "You'll be going about your day," she says, "and something from the past will come up, say a smell or sound. You'll go shooting down the snake and, sometimes, you'll have to work really hard to find the ladder."

"You don't know Snakes and Ladders?" she asks when she sees I have no idea what she's talking about.

I shake my head no.

So she changes tack and says each of my trigger points is like a trap door to the past, which is finally something I can relate to.

Bertha is big on trigger points. She's writing a chapter on it for her next book, so in Group she's always encouraging us to say when we're being triggered by each other.

This is how I find out Patrick gets triggered when I sit too close to him.

Leonard gets triggered if I make direct eye contact.

Heather says she is triggered by my face.

"Can you be more specific than that please?" Bertha interjects.

With some work we figure it out: Heather is triggered by a certain way I scowl. It reminds her of her mother.

"And is there anything about Heather that triggers you, Elizabeth?" Bertha asks.

I shake my head no. I don't know how to explain that every time Heather talks about California, it makes me feel like this whole thing is a setup, that I keep expecting Margaret to come bursting through the wall like the Kool-Aid Man and say "just kidding" and take me back to my real life. I don't know how to describe the sudden loss of hope whenever this doesn't happen.

I keep shaving my pills. Every day I crack open the yellow submarine and let a little more of the music out. My mind plunges, an elevator cut free of its cable. The ground yawns at my feet and I wonder, which is worse: going on drugs or coming off them?

Still, I proceed.

We all live in a yellow—

We all live—

We all—

"Are you okay?" Annie asks. She stops swirling her hips. "Do you need to sit?"

Mr. Twohig rests his pencil. "Shall we take a little break?"

"I'm fine," I say. "Everything's fine." But I know how I look. I look exactly like a mental patient. I am clenching my fists at my side, trying to rein in my own runaway horses like Patrick. My eyes are darting around the room like Leonard's.

I think I'm getting away with it and then, one Saturday, I reach for the paperclip behind the toilet and it's not there. Later that afternoon, after I've cleaned the fish tank, Bertha pokes her head out her office door and invites me in "for a chat."

I step in. She's barefoot, wearing a dress that looks like old bandages wrapped around and around her body. I find myself wishing, not for the first time, she would dress a little more normal. What's so wrong with jeans and a sweater? What's so wrong with a bra? Incense is burning. Joe Cocker is playing on the record player. She's been getting loose in here, definitely.

She points at the record, "Is Joe going to be a problem?"

I shake my head, even though his voice has opened one of those trap doors to the past, and I'm suddenly remembering what it's like to fall asleep alone, in a barn, with only a chicken to keep me company.

"Sorry, Hon'," she says, turning it off. "Have a seat."

She gestures for me to sit on the floor, so I do. I kneel and, as soon as I'm down, I see it: my paperclip, right there on the coffee table in front of me.

She flops down, cross-legged, on the other side of the table in such a way that I catch a glimpse of her underwear, which, thank God, she does wear.

"Listen, I'd like to discuss whether you feel you're on too much medicine," she says.

She cranks her eyebrows up and smiles at me, a little too kindly. It's a trick, I'm sure. Trick kindness to make me admit that I've broken rule number one of my parole agreement. She probably has a hidden recorder somewhere.

"Don't worry," she says. "You're not in trouble or anything. I'd just really like to know, honestly, if that's how you feel."

I want to tell the truth, of course. I want to say that, for the past ten years I've felt like a fat, pharmaceutical zombie with lead feet and a hollow head, moving through a sterile world without magic or music or any meaning at all. I want to say how often I've found myself staring into the middles of rooms with my mind wiped clean of any and all thought, that once, the week before I started shaving my pills, I fell through time and went away for who-knows-how-long, to who-knows-where and, when I came back, I had drooled down the front of my own shirt. I want to say that people like her have got it all wrong about people like me, that I can't possibly move to the centre of my own story if I'm not actually living, which I'm not because I'm a fat fucking zombie trapped on a yellow submarine.

But I don't say any of that because I'm not allowed to swear or come off my meds. It's written into my parole agreement.

So instead I say what all mental patients say when they've been caught shaving their pills. I say, "I felt dizzy."

It usually works. Usually there is a flash of pity, a slight adjustment.

But Bertha just fixes her eyes on me.

"Because I feel you are," she says. "On too much. Maybe even far too much. And if you're interested, I feel that is something we could work on together."

Michael is hissing in my ear. *Never ever trust a doctor.* I'm looking around for the hidden camera, a hidden doctor perhaps, crouched behind her filing cabinet, and then I'm remembering those first days in the hospital, so long ago. How I woke to a bright, white whirring, my arms covered in small, pinch-sized bruises and strapped to the bedframe. Dr. Singh standing over me, his flashlight in my eyes, asking: "Can you tell me your name? Where is your family? Do you know which drugs you took?"

Michael was in my ear, advising me not to talk. I couldn't answer anyway. I was so sedated, my mouth wasn't working right. Everything came out as a kind of meow.

"Righty-oh," Dr. Singh said, making a note and twirling away.

Days smudged by. Nurses came on squeaky shoes to deliver my meals: always some sort of soup followed by some sort of Jell-O, as if I had no teeth. They must've lessened my medication. I remember it felt like swimming up from the deep.

Dr. Singh returned, always with the same questions and a few more too, about whether I'd recently been in New York City, whether I knew anything about a Cosmic Garage.

I kept up with the meows for a long time. *Never ever trust a doctor.* Then, one day, I realized that nobody was coming for me and that, if I ever wanted out of there, I'd have to do something about it. So I told the truth, or what I believe to be the truth at the time. I said I *had* been in New York, at the Cosmic Garage, that my brother and I had hurt someone in order to save Walter Cronkite. I must've said some other things too, about the moon landing and spraying the city blue and the end of capitalism.

"*Oooh*key-doke," he said, scribbling something on his clipboard.

The diagnosis came a day later: paranoid schizophrenia. Nothing I said after that could convince anyone otherwise. I was committed to the Mid-Hudson Forensic Psychiatric Center for a period of one-day-to-life. The police and the lawyers came later. I was made an example of and charged as an adult, but I don't remember much about that. By then I was medicated. Back down I had gone—glub, glub, glub—seven leagues down, and there I stayed for the next three thousand and something days of my life, until one year ago, when Margaret hired the lawyer who filed the papers that brought me to Vancouver, to Willingdon, where I met Dr. Mink.

"Hell-*oh*," Bertha says, snapping her fingers to bring my attention back to the room. Out the window, the sky does a thing. A ray of light—not quite sun but almost—slides through the curtains. It brightens the edges of everything, making the moment seem more real.

I look into her eyes for maybe the first time, and there I see what I've been sensing since I got to Harrow House, that she is a doctor, yes, but she's nothing like Dr. Singh. I mean, her clothes for one. And her hair. And Joe Cocker. But I see something else too: that she actually, truly cares for me. Also that I am drowning and she is probably my last, best chance of rescue.

So I sit up tall and say yes.

Bertha sits up tall too. "Yes?"

"Yes, okay, please."

"Wonderful!" She jumps up, comes around the table and pulls me into a squishy, braless hug.

"This won't be easy," she says, patting me on the back. "It's going to take some work, but it will *absolutely* be worth it, trust me."

And with those two little words—*trust me*—the trap door swings open, and I am riding that snake or ladder or whatever all the way back to the past again.

CHAPTER 8
BEFORE

IN THE MORNING, MARGARET SHOOK ME AWAKE. SHE HANDED ME A BLACK garbage bag and said to pack some things because we were going with Lucky.

"Going where?" I asked, and, "For how long?" and, "What about the bus?"

But she wasn't in the mood for questions. She was busy packing her own bag.

It was Lucky who bent down to comfort me. "Don't worry, MeMe," she said, "Everything's going to be just fine. Trust me."

I didn't trust her, though. Somehow, overnight, she'd lost her creepy smile. And her eyes had changed colour, from shiny black to blue. And where was her hat?

We walked out along the highway, sweating in the heat, garbage bags slung over our shoulders. They were ahead of me. Lucky was talking about all the different concerts she'd been to, how she'd once stood close enough to Bob Dylan to almost touch his foot, how she knew a guy who knew a girl who knew Janis Joplin. She talked about all the different protests she'd been to and how they were just a useless distraction, that The Man would never change, that O and Samuel were working on a way to *really* change people's minds and Margaret kept nodding her head—*yes, yes*—like she was buying it all.

Each time a car passed, I got hit with a whoosh of air so big I thought it might lift me off my feet. I thought it might send me cartwheeling down the highway, all the way back to Canada, and the two of them wouldn't even notice.

About a mile down the road, we turned into a gas station. We put our bags down by the corner of the building. Lucky undid her braids and shook her hair out. Then she said, "watch this," and walked up to the different pumps, talking to people while they got their gas, flicking her long blond hair and smiling her now-beautiful smile.

When she finally found someone who could give us a ride, she waved us over. It was an older man with a brown station wagon and a white moustache. Margaret and I climbed into the back seat, pushing aside stacks of newspapers and magazines. Lucky got in front.

"Where to then?" the man said, and Lucky explained how to get to the farm.

"I know the place," he said. He looked at Margaret, then me in the rear-view mirror. His moustache twitched. "You sure?"

"We're sure, Man," Lucky said. "We're all sure." She flashed her best smile, reached over to turn on his radio and said, "Let's blow this popsicle stand."

We drove out along a country road, past barns in fields, cows in fields, kids fishing off bridges. Lucky kept flipping stations and singing along to all the songs but always just slightly before the singer. The man kept looking at her chest.

At some point he pulled over. "I won't take you in."

"No problemo," Lucky said, and we all got out and stood in a line, waving at him like he was our good, old friend.

"Creep," Lucky said when he was gone, and then, "Follow me." We walked over a little hill and then down a long driveway that cut through a sea of tall, golden grass. It rippled in the breeze, shiny and then not.

In the distance there was a house that had probably been beautiful once. It was tall, with a pointed roof and a wrap-around porch. Now it was painted all different colours though—pink and yellow and brown and blue—with garbage bags where windows should've been and holes in the walls and little lean-tos and teepees scattered all around it.

On the other side of the driveway there was an old barn and a concrete building that looked a bit like the cheese factory, with all kinds of chimneys coming off of it.

"Welcome to the compound," Lucky said as we came down the hill toward the house. Just when she said that, a black dog came barrelling across the field toward us.

"Hands in your pockets," Lucky ordered.

I didn't have pockets in my Rapunzel dress, so I put my arms up over my head, which only made the dog more excited. It was barking and leaping at my hands.

Margaret and Lucky drifted off toward the house together. They went up the steps and in the front door. I couldn't follow. The dog was snarling, winding tighter and tighter circles around me.

Finally, there was a high whistle from across the field. A bald man with two tufts of red hair above his ears shouted, "Stella, down." The dog whimpered and sank back as if she'd been kicked.

I followed after Margaret.

When I stepped onto the porch, I noticed a man standing in the corner. He was facing me with his arms stuck out straight at his sides. I waved, but he didn't seem to see me. He kept squeezing his hands, and he had a look on his face like when you've lost something and are trying to remember where you put it. There was a cigarette pinched between his lips, all-smoked. Now it was just a long tube of ash drooping past his chin. If he sneezed, it would scatter.

There was no door to the house, so I walked right in, into a kind of kitchen area. The only light was daylight seeping in through the cracks in the walls and up through the floorboards too, but in the half-dark I could make out a long table with a huge pot on top—the biggest I'd ever seen—and piles of dirty dishes all around it. The middle of the room was swirling with flies. There was a man curled up under the table, sleeping.

I heard Lucky laughing somewhere near the back of the house.

I moved down the hall.

There was a room on my left with people sleeping all over the floor, like they'd been playing Ring Around the Rosie and they'd all fallen down, all at once, and then just decided to sleep there.

On my right was another big room with bed sheets hung from the ceiling to make walls. Behind the sheets, people were snoring and murmuring, and one woman was moaning *oh-oh-oh* like she had a toothache.

A chicken burst out from behind one of the sheets and ran for the door at the end of the hallway, not a door really, but a hole that led outside. I thought I could hear Margaret and Lucky out there, giggling at one of their private jokes, but when I got outside, they were gone.

Instead, there was a girl washing clothes in an old kitchen sink that was sitting on a stump. She had long, brown hair in braids, and she kept smiling down at the water. She looked old enough to be a babysitter but not old enough to be anyone's mom.

"Hi, you," she said when she saw me. "Are you MeMe?" Then she giggled, adding, "You-you, me-me," while she plunged her hands into the blue-grey water. It was sloshing and spilling over the edges.

I couldn't speak. I felt like the man on the front porch.

She stepped toward me. She was wearing a scruffy, blue dress with threads hanging off it, just like the one Lucky wore, but hers had colourful patches sewn all over it and she had a red bandana tied around her neck. When she got close, I saw she had a thin, blue line right down the middle of her face, like she'd drawn it there with a pen. It started at her hairline and stopped in an *X* at the tip of her nose.

"I'm Sammy," she said. "Your mom said I should show you around."

"Where is she?" I walked past her, to the corner of the house, and looked back up the driveway. There was endless grass stretching out in all directions. My stomach swooped. They could be anywhere.

"Don't worry, they'll be back," Sammy said. "You like chickens?"

She didn't wait for my answer. She strode off toward the other corner of the house, reached into a bag hanging from a hook and threw a handful of seed at my feet. A bunch of chickens came darting out from under the house and rushed at me, pecking at my heels and between my toes. It tickled so bad it made me giggle and hop around, which must've looked pretty ridiculous. Sammy bent in half, holding her stomach and laughing through her teeth like *tssst-tssst-tssst.*

"Want to see the chicks?" she asked next and, before I could answer, she was leading me down the side of the house, past the front porch, where the man was still standing in the exact same position.

"What's wrong with him?" I whispered.

"Who, Larry?" She waved a hand in the air like she was swatting a fly. "He just does too much sometimes."

"Too much what?"

But she didn't hear. She was already across the driveway and halfway to the barn.

The inside of the barn smelled like hot wax. A group of people were standing in a cluster, turning a big wagon wheel that hung from the ceiling by a rope. The wheel had strings tied to every spoke. They were pouring the wax over each of the strings, one-by-one, and arguing among themselves.

"Get it *straight*, Bonnie," someone said.

"Go slower," said someone else.

Another group was standing over a bench, hammering something.

Over in the corner, a few women were using a paddle to stir what looked like pudding inside an old bathtub.

Nobody noticed us. They were all so busy with what they were doing.

Sammy led me toward the far corner of the room where there was a cardboard box with a lamp in it. She grabbed my hand and pulled me to the edge. There, inside the box, were a bunch of fluffy, yellow chicks. She named them as they ran from their bed to the water dish and back: Stew and Dumpling and Drumstick and Gravy and Meatball.

"Oh, and I almost forgot," she said, stopping to untie the bandana around her neck. She cradled it in her hand, opening it very carefully, and what stepped out was a tiny chicken, about half the size of the others. He was pink instead of yellow, with a translucent beak and feet. He blinked up at us with huge, black eyes.

"This is Runt," she said. Then, when she saw I didn't understand, "It means smallest."

She reached into one of the colourful patches on her dress, which I could now see was actually a pocket, and pulled out a little brown bottle. She unscrewed the top and held a dropper above Runt's head. He tilted back and opened his little clear beak to drink. After a few drops, he blinked and shuddered and toppled over, and we both laughed. I tried laughing like her, like *tssst-tssst-tssst*, and I liked it.

We stayed there, feeding Runt while the others bustled and argued around us.

I asked what was in the dropper.

She said sugar water.

I asked where Runt's mom was.

She said with the other chickens, under the house.

What if she was looking for him? I asked.

She said chickens weren't sentimental like that. Then, before I could ask, she said sentimental meant emotional.

I asked why she didn't put Runt in with his sisters and brothers.

She said they'd peck his eyes out. Then she looked at my eye patch and brought her hand to her mouth. "Oh, sorry Honey." She came to my side and put her arm around me. That's just how it was with chickens, she said. The strong picked on the weak. It was survival of the fittest, which was a law of nature, but only among animals, not people. She was rubbing my back and smiling down at me, so close I could smell her sour breath.

Thankfully we heard a bell ringing in the distance.

"Dinner!" she said. While everyone else drifted out of the barn and toward the house, she folded Runt back into her bandana. She lifted him carefully, tied him around her neck and we followed after.

A bunch of people were gathered around a fire pit in front of the house. I scanned the crowd, looking for Margaret or Lucky.

"Don't be scared, we're all a big family here," Sammy whispered as she led me to the edge of the circle. But looking around at all these strange, sleepy people, I was scared.

There was a woman sitting on a cushion at the top of the circle. She had long, black hair and a headband with what looked like chicken feathers stuck to it. Her eyes were closed, but everyone was watching her, waiting for her to do something. She was wearing one of those long, shaggy blue dresses. All the women were. And the men all had the same-coloured overalls. All of them, the men and the women, had tangled hair and strange, dull eyes and drifty smiles.

I looked around the circle. Lots of people had those blue lines down their faces, like Sammy. On some, the line went all the way to their chins. When my eyes landed on the farmer from the diner, I jumped.

He winked and waved at me. He was wearing Lucky's tall, black hat.

For a moment the world tilted beneath my feet, and then I understood: we'd been tricked. It was all a big setup. Lucky and him had lured us here together. We had fallen right into their trap.

I looked away.

Sammy crawled into the middle of the circle. The giant pot was there. She scooped some food into two bowls with her bare hand, then crawled back and handed me one.

The woman on the cushion started talking, something about all the people in the city and how they were all one but had forgotten. She said they were trapped on a big wheel, running and running and they didn't even know why or to what. She said Samuel was going to give us the medicine we needed to show them the truth. She said something about blue ink and awakening people through their skin, something about stepping to the very edge of what was known, and how it took great bravery to do that.

When she talked, she kept her eyes closed and stayed perfectly still, like she was balancing a teacup on her head.

The food was yellow mush and I had no spoon, but I was so hungry I slurped it off my fingers.

The woman said capitalism had run its course, that it was up to us to usher in the next thing. We were soldiers, fighting a war, she said, a spiritual one. We had to have the courage of soldiers and the discipline of soldiers. Her eyes popped open suddenly and travelled around the circle until they landed on me.

"Who's this?"

Everyone turned to look at me.

I put my bowl down and that's when I noticed I was the only one eating, that everyone else's bowls were still resting at their feet.

Sammy sat up tall and did a strange bow. "O, this is MeMe."

So this was O, the woman Lucky had spoken about, the one who had a plan.

"MeMe just got in today with her mom," Sammy continued. "I guess she's very hungry."

A few people around the circle laughed at that—*tssst-tssst-tssst*—but O didn't. She was looking at me the way the sisters used to look at me at school, right before I was sent to detention. "We don't allow children here," she said.

"Um, okay, but Lucky brought her?" Sammy said. "I believe she's a travelling psychic? And her mom has a school bus?"

O was staring at me so intently it made my body fill with heat. I thought about what Sammy had said about the strong picking on the weak, and how Runt's mother had left him just because he was weak—how she was living under the house now with all the other chickens and had probably forgotten all about him. I sat up taller. I tried to look older than I was, and Siamese and psychic. I flipped my eye patch up and fluttered my eyes the way Margaret liked me to.

O turned away from me. She closed her eyes again and talked about how we were here to fight the system, but we also had to follow our own systems. She said that, by now, everyone should know there was no such thing as an individual need. There was only the Family and the Cause.

When she was done talking, everyone closed their eyes and stayed like that for a long time until, finally, there was a crash, and two chickens came high-stepping into the middle of the circle. They were flapping and chasing one another. Some people laughed. Some leapt up to shoo them away. O didn't move a muscle. She stayed just as she was, balancing that imaginary teacup on her head.

Once things had settled back down again, she nodded her chin ever-so-slightly and everyone started reaching for each other's hands. Sammy's hand was still goopy from scooping out our dinner, and the woman on my other side was squeezing way too hard. When everyone was holding hands all around the circle, they bowed their heads and chanted, "One heart, one tribe, one cause," pumping their hands while they said it. Then they let go and a chatter rose around the circle. Everyone reached for their bowls and stood and mingled. O stood too and walked away, and with her long, blue dress reaching all the way to the ground, it looked like she was floating.

I slipped away from Sammy and went into the house to look for Margaret.

There was a man standing in the middle of the room where everyone had been sleeping before.

"Have you seen my mom?" I asked.

"Hello?" he shouted. He waved his hands through the air like a blind man.

"Have you seen a woman with a big red afro?"

"Hello, are you there?" He was looking all around like I was a ghost, like he could sense me but not see me. I backed away.

I searched behind all the sheet walls and even under the house. I walked along the driveway, calling her name into the long grass. Then I went over to the building with all the chimneys and walked around it.

There were lots of windows, but they were all painted black. There was a whirring coming from inside and a smell like vinegar. When I came around the last corner, toward the door, the black dog leapt up from where she'd been sleeping and lunged at the end of her chain. She was snarling and showing her teeth.

The barn was empty now. I visited the chicks, but they were sleeping. At the back of the barn, I found a ladder leading up to a hayloft. There was a big, square doorway cut into the wall up there, a door that led nowhere, only down. I took a step toward it and stood right at the edge. O had said something about going up to the edge. She'd said it was brave. From up there I could see the house with everyone milling around it. I could see we were in a kind of valley with a river snaking down its centre. There was only one other house, far in the distance. The lights were on. Someone lived there.

I scanned the whole place for a flash of red hair. I tried to feel her, but I couldn't.

What if she'd left? I thought. What if she and Lucky were halfway to California without me? I kept imagining her on the back of a motorbike, heading west with the wind in her hair. The thought made me feel sick.

I lay on a hay bale and watched the sky turn orange and then pink and then purple. When it was finally dark, I started to smell smoke. I crawled to the edge of the doorway. Someone had lit a bonfire in front of the house. I heard music. A crowd was starting to gather. I felt a yank in my chest. She was there, at the fire, I could feel it. I climbed down the ladder and walked toward the house.

In the middle of the driveway, I passed two women playing a strange game. They were face-to-face, gazing into each other's eyes. One moved her hand up and then down like she was polishing an invisible window between them. The other one copied. They went up-down and side-to-side, faster and faster until eventually they were like perfect mirror images of each other.

I passed a man on all fours, digging for something in the dirt with his bare hands.

Closer to the house, there was a woman leaning out of the branches of a tree screaming, "Land ho." A few people were gathered beneath her saying, "Come on now, Lacey. Come back down here. This isn't funny."

When I got to the fire, I saw Larry, the man from the porch, sitting on a rock. He looked better now, like he'd found whatever he was looking for and maybe showered too. I waved, but he didn't wave back.

There was a record playing somewhere inside the house, something I'd never heard before, strange music full of gongs and loose piano notes.

I saw Lucky standing near the house. She was deep in conversation with someone, probably trying to trick them.

I saw Sammy. She had just told a joke. She was bent in half, laughing.

And then, through the flames, I saw Margaret.

I walked straight over to her. I hooked my finger into the pocket of her pants, so she couldn't get away again, and asked where she'd been.

She smacked my hand away and scowled as if I was a pickpocket. For a second I wondered if I had the wrong person. She didn't look quite like herself.

"I've been looking for you," I said.

She stared at me.

"Were you in the field with Lucky?"

A smile flickered across her face.

"I was looking for you all day," I said.

She kept smiling, not at me exactly, but through me. It was like the sides of her mouth had been hitched up by a string, like she couldn't stop smiling even if she'd wanted to. An awkward silence stretched out between us. I couldn't think of what else to say.

I took a step toward her. "I saw the farmer from the diner," I whispered. "He lives here too. He's one of them."

"Elizabeth!" she gasped as if she'd only just recognized me. She bent down. Her eyes locked onto mine. They were strange-looking—shiny, black and swirling inwards. She put her hand on my chest, right over my scar. "I'm going on a kind of vacation. Actually, I'm already gone. So be good and take care of each other, okay?"

I nodded even though it felt like someone was tugging on that cord between us.

Just then, O started talking from the top step of the porch, something about taking Samuel's medicine and emptying out and letting go of our own individual stories, something about being wiped clean. Margaret dropped her hand from my chest and stepped toward her, listening, with her eyes closed and her mouth hanging open. She was swaying and doing that thing Larry had done earlier, squeezing her hands at her sides. Everyone was doing it.

I backed up to the edge of the firelight.

O came down from the porch and started weaving between everyone. They all stood perfectly still, like it was a game of Frozen Tag and she was It. She was circling the fire, talking about how we're all one, all connected, and about the evils of capitalism, how it keeps us living a lie, locked inside our own individual struggles. Every once in a while she would stop in front of someone and look at them and whisper a few words. Then she'd take them by their shoulders and get them spinning, slowly, on the spot. She did that over and over until, eventually, everyone was spinning.

"This is how we deprogram ourselves," she said. "This is how we unwind the lie."

When it was Margaret's turn, O said something I couldn't hear and then got her spinning too, like everyone else.

The music sped up. On the record a man started singing, but it sounded like he was at the bottom of a well. It sounded like moaning. The people sped up and started moaning too. They had their hands out at their sides now, their heads thrown back.

O was clapping, saying, "Faster, faster," and they all obeyed. They weren't just spinning on the spot anymore. They were starting to circle around the fire too. I wondered how they were able to do that without crashing into each other.

The first person to fall was a woman a little older than Sammy. She went spinning out of orbit and skidded to the ground. O went and stood over her. The woman was shaking and crying. O said something encouraging and put her hands on the woman's head until she quieted down. Then, when she was better, O helped her up, and she started spinning again.

Another person fell and another, and O did the same for each of them. Eventually they were all back up, spinning even faster than before.

"This is the medicine," O called out to the group. "First we awaken ourselves and then we awaken the world."

When Margaret fell, she let out a terrible howl. I stepped into the firelight to run to her, but Sammy got to me first.

I thought she was going to warn me, *kids aren't allowed here*, but instead she clutched my dress and asked, "Do I have teeth?"

I looked at Margaret. O was straddling her now. She had Margaret's head in her hands.

Sammy was running a finger back and forth over her teeth. "Are they still there? I can't feel them." She was desperate, almost crying.

"Yes," I said. "You have all your teeth." I tried to squirm out of her grip.

Margaret was crying now, and O was crouched over her, whispering something into her ear.

"Thankyouthankyouthankyou," Sammy said. She pulled my face close to hers. "Please," she pointed at Runt, "take him."

She couldn't untie the bandana herself, so I helped. She handed me the brown bottle from her pocket and then went off to join the rest of the spinning people. I stood at the edge of the firelight with the bandana in my hand. I could feel Runt in there, his little feet, delicate as twigs.

O bent down and touched Margaret on her stomach, right above her scar, and Margaret really lost it then. She was weeping great big harmonica sobs and saying his name, saying Michael, over and over. O was hugging Margaret and rocking her in her arms. "Good, let it all out," she kept saying. Then she touched Margaret between her eyes and said, "You are forgiven," and that seemed to help. Margaret quieted down, and O moved on to the next person.

I wanted to go to Margaret, but I was scared. Her sadness was too big, and besides, it was Michael's name she'd said, not mine. Runt was wriggling around inside the bandana. I lifted him carefully and tied him around my neck. I took one step back, away from the fire, and then another and another and, the whole time, I felt that cord between me and Margaret stretching.

That night I lay on a bale of hay in the loft. I could hear everyone moaning and whooping in the distance, going up to the edge or breaking through or whatever. I unwrapped the bandana. Runt stood on my chest, right on top of my scar, and stared at me with his big, black eyes.

"What?" I said.

He was looking at me out of one eye and then the other, trying to figure out if he could trust me. He was so small and delicate, I could squish him between my hands and nobody would even notice. Then, finally, he made up his mind. He took a step forward.

"I wouldn't," I said.

He took another.

"I'm a killer," I warned.

But he took another few steps and tucked in right under my chin anyway. I felt his breath, warm against my neck. I heard the tick-tock of his little heart and, before I knew it, I was feeling what he felt. I felt his loneliness, how he had lost everything, his mom and brothers and sisters. His sadness went all through me.

CHAPTER 9

AFTER

"HOW DID IT FEEL TO BE ABANDONED SO OFTEN, AT SUCH A YOUNG AGE?"
Bertha asks in one of our sessions. I'm pretty sure Annie has been
showing her my writing. They've been having secret meetings about me.

"I wasn't abandoned," I say. "Margaret was always with me."

She tilts her head, says, "Oh?" and waits.

The silence stretches out between us. Oldest doctor trick in
the book.

"Okay, not always *with me*," I say, finally. "But always nearby, and
with me when she could be."

"Okay then," she says, writing something in her notes.

"Okay then," I say.

She says she wants us to do a "thought experiment" and then she
pulls out a big piece of paper and a bunch of coloured pens. She draws
a line down the middle of the page—her side, mine—and says she
wants each of us to write a list of what we think are the characteristics
of "a good mother." She says there are no wrong answers, to just write
whatever comes to mind. Then, when we're done, she folds the paper
in four, tucks it inside the file she's keeping on me and says we can add
to it as we see fit. So now every time I meet with her, I will have to see
that stupid piece of paper. My list: *tries to take care of you, makes you soup,
remembers your birthday, nice hair.* Hers: *reliable, responsible, always puts the
child first, unconditional love.*

When we're done, we sit back down and she starts talking about "different kinds of love," like, for example, love that is freely given versus love that has to be earned through certain types of behaviour. She talks about love that is transactional, love that is reinforced through punishment, love that is driven by fear.

"How would you describe you and Margaret's love?" she asks casually, as if the thought has just occurred to her.

I know what she's getting at. It's what she's been driving at all along. She would like nothing more than for me to blame everything on Margaret.

I think of my mom how I remember her best: sitting in the car, staring out at Lake Huron, dreaming of a better life for us. I picture her fiddling with the radio, looking for just the right song, something we could both sing along to. And I think of the look on her face whenever she found a good one, something with harmony that we both knew all the words to, how she'd turn to me then, saying, "This is it!" making two guns with her hands and pointing them at me like *stick 'em up*, except we both knew those weren't ordinary guns, they were show business guns and this was my big moment. Then, with spotlights in her eyes she'd say, "you go high, I'll go low," even though we both knew she was better with the high notes. That's the thing I can't explain and Bertha will never understand: that Margaret always wanted me to hit the high notes. She was more than just a good mother, she was a good friend and because of that the rules are different.

I look at Bertha, her head tilted, her pen raised like a sword. She is waiting for me to say that Margaret was a bad mother. But I won't. She was a good mother when she could be, and once in a while, occasionally, the best mother of all. For me that is enough.

"Our love was like this," I say and I raise both hands to make the motion of paper-covers-rock, except the paper is more aggressive, it swoops down on the rock like a hungry mouth, it wraps around the rock and swallows it whole. I even make a swooping-mouth sound.

"I understand," she says, even though she doesn't really, never could, any more than a rabbit can "understand" it is caught in the mouth of a lion.

94

CHAPTER 10

BEFORE

THE NEXT MORNING I FED RUNT AND TIED HIM AROUND MY NECK. THEN I WENT to look for Margaret. I found her standing on top of a rock in the field behind the house, staring at the sky with her mouth open. She was naked, her clothes crumpled on the ground beneath her.

I wanted to tell her that I'd seen a house in the distance, that we could go there and ask for a ride back to the bus, but she spoke first.

"Do you see that?" She pointed up.

The sky was empty, not a cloud.

"All the shapes?"

I flipped my eye patch up and looked again. I did see something then.

"Like bubbles?" I tried. "Going up?"

"And do you hear that? That beautiful humming?"

I listened. I heard wind in the trees, what I thought might be a highway in the distance, and it did sound beautiful in a way, like waves.

"Isn't it wonderful?" she said, stepping down from the rock and crouching in front of me.

The sun was coming up over the hills behind her, filling her hair with a pinkish-gold light. "Doesn't it feel like we've arrived, MeMe? Like we're finally home?"

My heart dropped, a yo-yo plummeting toward the end of its string. It's not what I'd expected to hear or what I wanted. I wanted her to say she'd had enough of this place, that we were going back to the bus and, after that, to California.

But she was staring at me and smiling, and I had to admit, she looked better than she had in a long time. Her eyes were bluer and her freckles darker, like she'd been coloured in with brand-new felt markers overnight.

"But you were crying," I said.

"I was just letting go of some stuff."

"But the farmer from the diner is here," I insisted. "He's friends with Lucky. He's wearing her hat! The hat *she* was wearing in the diner!"

She sighed, closed her eyes and brought her forehead to mine—Feel What I Feel. She breathed slowly through her nose a few times and then said, "Do you feel that? The beautiful feeling?" For a second I did feel something like a strange calm washing over me. "Those are all just details, MeMe," she said. "What matters is we're home now." We took a few more breaths together and I tried to feel good about that, like she did, but it didn't last.

When she pulled away from me, all my worries came rushing back. Runt was wriggling against my neck. My heart was still plummeting. In the distance someone had started banging a pot with a spoon.

"All better?" she asked, standing.

I wanted to say no. I wanted to explain again—just in case she'd missed it—how exactly we'd been tricked and that the hat was proof, but she was so happy, happier than I'd seen her in such a long time.

I tried not to look at her naked body, the small red puff between her legs, her pink-brown nipples, the puckered scar up the centre of her stomach, like a zipper sewn in wrong.

"Yes," I said, even though it wasn't true. My second lie.

I picked up her clothes and pushed them at her.

I wanted her to cover up before anyone else saw what I'd done to her.

Everyone was gathered in a circle again. The farmer was there, wearing Lucky's hat. He watched Margaret and me approach. He smiled at her. She smiled back. My ears grew hot.

Once everyone was settled, O swept a hand through the air and said, "Judy."

Judy stepped into the centre of the circle. She didn't look like the others. She was older and was wearing regular clothes: a shirt and pants, socks and shoes. She had a clipboard in her hands. "Okay folks," she said loudly, "we've got a big push coming up, so we need all hands."

She called out different jobs—going to town, hitching to the gas station, watering the garden, folding pamphlets, peeling potatoes. People raised their hands and she took down their names: women named Star and Vesper and Raven, a man named Eight, another named Jelly Roll.

She said she needed someone for printing.

Margaret's hand shot up, and Judy wrote her name down.

I raised mine too, but Judy had already moved on to the next job.

"Can't I work with you?" I asked Margaret.

She was busy talking to the person next to her.

I tugged on her sleeve. "Can I go with you? Please? Shouldn't I?"

I couldn't get her attention. She and her neighbour were laughing about something and then the farmer chimed in and they were all laughing together even though he was a liar and I'd told her that.

I'm not sure what made me do it. Maybe I was just tired, or sick of not being listened to. Or maybe I sensed that this was my last chance to pull her back to me.

"But how *can* you print," I shouted, louder than I meant to, "when you don't even know how to write?"

People turned to look. Some laughed: *tssst-tssst-tssst.*

Margaret blushed a deep red.

The farmer looked at his hands.

There was a long silence, then O started speaking again about the forces that were against us. She said we all had to remain vigilant and remember that every job was important.

Everyone nodded and *mm-hmmed.*

I reached for Margaret's hand but she swatted me away.

My whole face was hot now.

I had broken my promise. I had told her secret to everyone.

"Let's tune in," O said, and she started humming. Everyone joined in, humming the same note, a long, low Oh. The sound circled and swelled, and the air started to buzz. After a while O went up to a new note and, one-by-one, everyone joined. They were all looking around and smiling at each other. Finally, O made a hand signal and everyone stopped, all at the same time. They closed their eyes and sat there, in total silence, smiling and swaying for what felt like forever, and I wondered if they were all feeling it, the beautiful feeling. I closed my eyes and tried to feel it too, but I only felt sick.

As soon as everyone did the chant—oneheartonetribeonecause—Margaret stood and walked away from me. I tried to follow, but Lucky cut across my path. She had my crown with her. She put it on my head and said, "You ready to go to work, MeMe?" It sounded like a question, but I knew it wasn't. It was an order.

Margaret was way over by the building with the chimneys now. The door opened. She stepped inside without even looking back.

By the time I had climbed into the back of a blue pickup with Lucky, my ears were ringing. The truck bed was full of people sitting on top of boxes. Lucky introduced them all. There was someone named Mick, who Lucky said was going to fix our bus, and then a bunch of other people—Grace and Donna and Trixie and Tex and Effie, who were all dressed like clowns, with white faces, red noses, creepy smiles and thick, cartoonish eyebrows.

"And you've already met Roland," Lucky said, gesturing toward the farmer from the diner, who was in the process of painting his face like everyone else's.

Roland lowered the mirror he'd been using, did a strange bow and held his hand out to me. "Sorry about the other day."

But I didn't want to take his hand. I'd already made that mistake once. I folded my arms across my chest and turned my back on him.

The clowns gasped.

"Ouch!" said one.

"Sizzle!" said another.

"I understand you're mad," Roland said to my back. "But I do hope we can be friends one day."

"I *do* hope too," said one clown.

"I do-do too-too," said another and then the rest of them laughed.

Lucky banged the side of the truck, and we pulled away from the house.

We drove down one long winding road after another. At one point I had to lean over the edge of the truck and puke. One of the clowns gave me water, and Lucky said not to worry, that it was just car sickness, but I knew that wasn't it. I was sick about telling Margaret's secret.

Eventually we arrived in a small, dusty town. It was only about a block long. There was a pharmacy, a grocery store, a butcher shop, a bank, a diner. That was all. It looked like we could be in Ontario, except for the American flags hanging everywhere.

The truck pulled up in front of the diner. Lucky and I got out. Roland and the rest of them blew big, exaggerated clown kisses as the truck drove away.

We went in and got a booth near the back.

There was only one waitress. She seemed to know Lucky and didn't seem to like her much. Lucky had to flag her down to get her to come over. She ordered a coffee and a ginger ale for me.

When the waitress—Dell was her name—came back with the drinks she said, "Pay up," and then stood there with her arms folded over her chest while Lucky dug around in her purse.

She looked me up and down. "You need anything, Hon'?"

Runt wriggled against my neck. I thought about saying, *Help, my mom and I have been kidnapped.* I even started to say it, but Lucky ground her heel into my toes under the table.

"We're fine, thanks," she said, handing over the money.

Once Dell was gone, Lucky leaned across the table, raised a bossy finger at me and said she didn't want to see any more shenanigans like that. She pulled a big deck of cards out of her purse and unwrapped it as though it were the most precious thing in the world. "Tarot," she said when she saw me staring. "You'll learn about that later." Then she said I'd better sit up straight and pay attention because she was about to teach me the only three questions I'd ever need to know.

I was really starting to hate her.

The first question was, "Have you lost something?" because, she said, anyone who sat down in front of a roadside psychic had probably lost someone or something and not too long ago. She said to point that out to them right off the bat created trust and, in this business, trust meant money.

The second question was, "Does your heart hurt?" because, she said, that's who we'd be making our money off of, the broken-hearted. "And what is it the broken-hearted want more than anything else?" she asked.

"Their moms?" I tried.

"No," she said. "Hope! They need hope, and we're in the business of giving it to them."

"How do I do that?" I asked.

She said to tell them whatever they most wanted to hear and, when I asked what that was, she said the key was to get people talking and then to listen very carefully. She said people always revealed what it is they most wanted to hear.

The third question, my real money-maker, she said, seeing as how I was Siamese, was to ask if they wanted a message delivered to anyone on the other side. She said that'd make them crack like an egg. She said after that, the rest was easy.

"But I'm not Siamese," I said.

She stopped and looked at me with a very serious expression. "I don't ever want to hear you say that, MeMe." She raised her bossy finger in the air between us again and explained that what I'd said was very unprofessional.

Then she softened a little. To tell the truth, she said, it really didn't matter too much what I said. People would pay me either way because I was a kid and I had an eye patch and a good story.

She made me practise the questions with her a few times, with her playing different customers, easy ones and difficult ones. Then, finally, she said I was ready. She put a sign out on the edge of the table: "MeMe Fanta, Siamese Medium."

Then we sat and waited, and I tried my hardest not to think about Margaret because, every time I did, I thought I might puke again.

Lucky rolled one cigarette after another. People came in, glanced at her, at me in my Rapunzel dress, and then went to sit in a different part of the restaurant. It reminded me of the way people used to treat me and Margaret back in Ontario, like our Big Sad Story might be contagious.

I asked if I could feed Runt.

"Okay," she said, "but be quick."

I untied him and stood him on the table while I fed him. That's when our first customer of the day came over, a trucker. I tried to ask Lucky's questions in the right order, but I was tired and hungry and I kept screwing it up. Fortunately, he was much more interested in Runt than in either of us.

Then came a housewife who knew a little bit about chickens. She watched me feed Runt and then said he was ready for solid food. She got Dell to bring over a little bowl of oats. I quoted "Girl from the North Country" to her. "Yeah thanks," she said, handing over a dollar, but I could tell she wasn't really impressed and neither was Lucky.

"What's the matter with you?" Lucky said once the woman had left. "I thought you were supposed to be good at this."

"I don't feel good." I clutched my stomach even though it wasn't my stomach exactly that hurt.

She lit another cigarette and squinted at me through the smoke. "You homesick or something?"

I nodded. That sounded about right, although I didn't know where home was anymore.

"Well you'd better figure yourself out," she said. "I can't cover for you forever."

"Cover?"

"You heard O. Kids aren't allowed at the farm. She even sent her own daughter away."

My stomach did a somersault. "Away where?"

"New York City."

"Alone?"

She nodded.

"How old is she? What's her name?" I managed to ask before my voice gave out.

"Rainbow," she said, exhaling two columns of smoke through her nose. "And I think she's younger than you, but never mind that." She leaned forward with her finger held up between us again. "The only thing you should be thinking about right now is money. As long as we make enough money, you won't be sent anywhere, got it?"

"Got it," I said.

We did two more readings that day, or Lucky did, and Runt and I watched. All the while I kept thinking about the girl named Rainbow. Who took care of her? Where did she sleep? The idea of her wandering all alone in the big city lodged in me, a sick flutter in the pit of my stomach.

At the end of the day Lucky wrapped up her fancy deck of cards. I put Runt on my shoulder and we walked to the far end of town to wait for our ride. People passed in their cars, one happy American family after another. Their heads swivelled to take us in: two real-life hobos and a chicken stranded by the side of the road.

Lucky was sitting on a rock, drawing shapes in the dust with a stick. She didn't feel like talking and neither did I.

The sky turned the colour of a bruise. Runt burrowed in under my hair to stay warm. I wondered if we'd have to spend the night there, curled up in a ditch. I wondered if Margaret would notice or even care.

Eventually there was a familiar roar in the distance and then two headlights. When the lights slowed to a stop in front of us and I realized what I was seeing, I jumped up and hugged Lucky without meaning to.

All the same people from that morning were on the bus, except Mick who was following behind in the blue truck. Tex was driving.

There was one new person, Rebecca. She looked nothing like the others, more like a teacher or a store clerk with her ordinary jeans and button-up blouse. She kept looking around at the clowns with wide, frightened eyes, and I wondered if she'd been kidnapped too on her way home from work. I tapped out S-O-S on my knee and tried to catch her eye, but she wouldn't look at me.

The clowns were seated all over the floor of the bus. They had bags of gas-station food, and they were passing a jug of wine back and forth. The radio was on. They were laughing and chatting and singing along. It felt good to be back on the bus, a little like being home again, only with all the wrong people.

"How'd it go at the diner?" Roland asked.

"Runt stole the show!" Lucky said.

"That good, huh?" He offered me a stick of pepperoni.

I shook my head no.

"Peanuts?" Effie offered.

I said no to those too.

"Better eat while you can," said Trixie.

"Yeah, unless you like yellow mush," Tex shouted from up front and everyone laughed.

We drove on. When all the food was eaten, Roland gathered all the wrappers. He raised his fingers to his lips—*shhhh*—and dropped them out the window.

Lucky rolled a cigarette and passed it around.

The Stones came on. Tex turned it up and everyone sang along at the top of their lungs: *I can't get no. Satis-fac-tion.* They hammed it up, singing into their fists, pounding their chests and pretend-fainting into each other's arms.

It was funny but I couldn't laugh. Something still had ahold of my stomach.

It was the new girl, Rebecca, who, a mile or so down the road, stood up on her knees and said, "Can we now?" She was talking to Lucky.

"Not yet," Lucky said, sticking her chin in the air.

But then the rest of them crowded around her too, with their hands in prayer, chanting, "Please, Miss. Can we now? Can we, please?" until, eventually, she gave in.

She dug around in her purse and came up with a sheet of paper filled with little blue dots with smiley faces in them. Everyone lined up. She ripped a dot off for each of them and placed it on their tongues, except for Rebecca, who only got half.

"Trust me," Lucky said when she complained.

"Trust her," the clowns echoed.

Then they all flopped back in their seats and got really quiet. They lay there, smiling up at the ceiling all the way back to the farm.

I waited for Margaret by the fire for what felt like hours. When she didn't appear, I went looking.

I made a wide loop around each of the buildings, calling her name.

In the field by the barn, I saw the clowns playing a game. Roland was up on a ladder, calling out different words, and the rest of them were acting out the words without making a sound, using only their bodies.

I crouched in the grass and watched.

"Rage," he said, and everyone screamed, but silently. They thumped their chests and pretend-pulled their hair.

"Sorrow," he said, and they all crumpled up, small and sad.

"Glee," he said, and they leapt like ballerinas.

They did Mischief and Greed and Love, but Awe was my favourite. They fell to their knees, mouths open, hands praying to the sky as if begging forgiveness for all the bad things they'd ever done.

After a while Roland clapped his hands and climbed down from his ladder. He told everyone to shake it off and gather around. He saw me then even though I tried to duck out of sight.

"Come and join us, MeMe," he said, but I had already turned and run.

I made my way back to where Tex had parked the bus by the house. On board, I found a small box and lined it with a kitchen towel. I put in a little cup of water and the handful of oats I'd pocketed at the restaurant and then put Runt inside.

I lit a candle and sat at the kitchen table, waving my hands in front of it, spelling out S-O-S, praying for Margaret to see it and come to me.

I noticed for the first time how the bus windows were streaked with greasy finger marks, probably from when this was an actual school bus. I imagined all the kids pressing their faces to these windows, waving goodbye to their parents every morning. A thousand kids, a thousand goodbyes, nobody knowing if it was for the last time, and maybe sometimes it was. That world seemed so far away now, the world of school busses and moms and dads. This was a new world now, with new rules. I just wished I knew what they were.

I heard a swish behind me.

The candle flickered out.

"Michael?" I said.

I thought I could feel him then, a presence on the bus with me.

I closed my eyes. "What do I do?" I asked. "How do I bring her back to me?"

There was a soft static rising inside me, and below the static, a voice. *Put yourself at the centre*, it said.

"The centre of what?" I asked. "How?"

There was no answer.

I opened my eyes and looked all around for him, but he was gone.

It was just me and Runt.

I brought the box to bed with me and pulled the covers over our heads. I could hear everyone whooping out by the fire again.

I slept and dreamed I was a small boat drifting out to sea in a storm. The shore was far away, getting farther.

The next morning I woke up early to look for Margaret, but I couldn't find her anywhere. She wasn't in the house or the barn or in the fields around them. She wasn't at the breakfast meeting. And none of the clowns who climbed onto the bus to head into town had seen her either.

When I asked Lucky where she was, she said, "initiating." I was sitting across from her at the diner. Runt was tucked up against my neck, under my hair.

"What's initiating?"

"Never mind," she said. "You'll probably see her tonight."

"*Probably?*" All the energy drained from my body. My head dipped on my neck, too heavy to hold up.

She gave me a look: *poor thing.* Then she pushed her coffee toward me, said to drink up, that it would make me feel better.

She said if I did a really good job, she'd make sure Margaret came to see me that night.

"Promise?"

"Cross my heart and hope to die." She held a finger up between us, "*if* you do a good job today."

She spent the morning teaching me how to read auras. She had a formula: name a colour, name a feeling, end with a song lyric, easy-peasy.

She said to stick to the five main feelings. She counted them off on one hand: anger, sadness, fear, guilt and grief. But grief was our main money-maker, she said. Most people who came to see a medium would be dealing with grief. That was a no-brainer.

"What colour is grief?" I asked.

She thought about that for a moment, then decided: purple.

She added some more milk and sugar to my coffee and laid out the rest of the rules for the day: that I shouldn't be so afraid to speak, that I should relax and let my mind wander a little, that I could use Bob Dylan lyrics if I wanted but no Etta James, that Runt could stay on my shoulder, but off the table because we weren't a circus act.

"Got it?" she asked.

"Got it," I said. I could feel the coffee working in me now. It felt like an engine had been turned on at the base of my spine, like my brain was a rocket about to take off. I was having a hard time sitting still. I wanted to get up and run but also to sit still and get organized. I asked Lucky for a pen and paper so I could write down her rules.

"That's the spirit!" she said, handing them over.

With her own pen she added the word "auras" to my sign. She pushed it to the edge of the table and we waited.

Nobody came all morning.

There were two waitresses: Dell and a younger one, Pam. I watched them making small talk with everyone who sat down. I noticed the difference between them: how Pam bounced up on the balls of her feet when she walked, but Dell moved like she had heavy stones in her pocket, how Pam's smile was real, but Dell's disappeared from her face as soon as she turned away from her customers. I thought maybe I could see something like an aura around each of them. If Pam's was yellow, then Dell's was dark purple, like she had the Biggest Saddest Story in town.

"You okay?" Lucky asked. Her aura was grey, definitely, like a storm cloud.

I nodded.

"You sure? Because your mouth's hanging open."

I closed it.

Every once in a while, Lucky would sit up tall and say, "here comes one," but everyone was always just headed for the bathrooms.

The lunch rush came and went.

Lucky tipped our sign over, grabbed her purse and said she was going to take a short break. "Be good," she said, pointing at me and Runt, "both of you." Then she was gone.

If I leaned back in my seat, I could still see her. She was out in the parking lot, smoking and talking to a man with long hair, probably about O and this amazing place she knew where he could get off the wheel for a little while. She stood with one hip higher than the other and kept twisting her hair up between her fingers.

She smiled.

He smiled.

She flicked her hair.

He flicked his.

Poor guy. Soon he'd be eating yellow mush and listening to O's lectures like the rest of us.

The record on the jukebox changed, then changed again. It was the lull between lunch and dinner. The restaurant was nearly empty. There was a commotion behind the counter, over near the coffee machines. Pam had burned herself and Dell was rubbing an ice cube on it. "This'll help," she said, and somehow I could feel that ice cube sliding over my own wrist. Pam was about to cry, and Dell was saying, "Now, now."

I felt woozy. I put Runt on the table and lay my head down next to him. I closed my eyes and remembered my dream from the night before, that I was a small boat lost at sea. It seemed some part of me was still out there, drifting, even now. I could hear the creaking of ropes, water sloshing against my sides. There were waves of bubbles rising up through me and a small voice, far away, asking me something.

I opened my eyes.

Dell was standing there with a bowl of oats for Runt, a soda for me. She slid my drink across the table at me. Ginger ale. I could taste it already, just looking at it. The bubbles rising up through it were the same bubbles rising up through me.

I flipped my eye patch up. I saw that dark purple haze all around her now.

"You're so sad," I said.

She flinched, like I'd slapped her, then shook her head and walked away.

I leaned back to look for Lucky. She wasn't in the parking lot anymore.

I looked at Runt. He had a pinky-gold aura all around him, like an afro at sunrise. Everything had an aura now, even the cash register, even the coffee machine, and I could hear every little noise, the buzz-click when the jukebox switched records, a fly bumping up against a window at the front of the restaurant, wanting out, the crinkle of a man's newspaper. Every sound seemed unbearably close. My mind was being tossed at sea. My ropes were creaking. I felt suddenly seasick. I took a sip of my drink. I could feel the bubbles of soda tickling over my tongue. It made me laugh. I closed my eyes and felt the bubbles rising up through me.

"Are you okay?" someone asked. It was Dell again. She was sitting across from me now.

I wanted to answer, to tell her that my mind was a boat lost in a storm, but then I remembered Rainbow, and that if I didn't do a good job today, I'd end up like her, sleeping all alone in a dumpster in New York City.

Runt stepped across the table and tapped her watch. It was way too big for her, a man's watch. He tapped it again. He was trying to tell me something. I reached out for the watch and as soon as I touched it, I knew it was her husband's, that he was dead now. I can't say how I knew. Some things you just know.

I tried to remember Lucky's questions. "Is it grief?" I asked.

A single tear slid down her cheek and, when it hit the tabletop, a strange thing happened. My mind went up and emptied out all at once, *pffft*, like a helium balloon let go in a room. My head filled with static. The TV set came on. On it, I saw a picture of a small brown and white trailer next to a creek. I saw a big yard with a fence all around it, a red truck in the driveway, tall purple flowers growing all along the fence. Then the channel changed. Another picture, of a small room, a kind of workshop out behind the trailer. I could see its low beams and cluttered shelves. The channel changed again and, like watching a movie in my mind, I saw a man's hand sliding a letter between two jars of screws. The man was wearing the watch, the same one Dell was wearing. It was her husband's watch, her husband's hands. Then the TV turned off.

I opened my eyes. Dell was staring at me. Her mouth had fallen open.

Lucky was standing there too, behind Dell. I hadn't heard her come back. Her mouth was the opposite of Dell's—pinched shut.

"He left me a letter?" Dell asked.

I must've spoken without realizing it. I must've said what I'd seen on the TV.

Lucky was shaking her head no, but I could see the letter being slid between the jars. I could smell the room—engine oil, sawdust, paint—so I said yes.

Dell put her elbows on the table and her face in her hands. Was she angry? Was she crying? I couldn't tell.

"That's enough of that," Lucky said, stepping forward. I had just enough time to put Runt back on my shoulder before she grabbed me by the hand and hauled me out of the diner, down the sidewalk, past the butcher and the pharmacy and the grocery store and clear out of town.

While we walked, she talked. This was worse than Etta James, she said. Much worse. I had broken every rule she'd taught me. I'd gone way off script. And I'd messed with that poor woman's feelings, that poor woman who had been through so much.

"So much what?" I asked, but I already knew. The TV set in my mind had turned on again. I saw her husband swinging from the rafters of his workshop. I heard the creaking of the rope, the same creaking I had been hearing all along—his rope, not mine. It felt like a punch to the stomach. It knocked the air right out of me.

"Did you ever think that we have to come back here?" Lucky said. She was trudging down the road ahead of me. "Did you think about what happens when she doesn't find any letter?" She twirled around to wag a finger at me, but when she found me curled up into a ball on the ground, she came back and helped me up.

"I just don't like you making promises you can't keep," she said, dusting me off.

But the promise would keep, I knew it. She would find the letter. I knew because there was a voice—Michael's—saying so in my mind.

That evening, on the bus on the way back to the farm, Roland asked how it had gone at the diner again.

"Fantastic!" Lucky said, shooting me a look.

"Do me," Effie said, crawling across the aisle, pushing her hand into mine.

Lucky was shaking her head at me—*don't even*—but I could still feel the coffee working in me. I took Effie's hand and closed my eyes. I felt that strange feeling again, the *pffft*, the going up. There was static and then the TV came on. I saw a big, old tree with twisted limbs running parallel to the ground.

"That's the oak tree in my front yard!" Effie said. "Oldest tree in the county."

The clowns sat up.

"What else?" she asked.

Another image, of a small yellow house on a hill.

"That's my house!" she said. "The one I grew up in!"

Tex turned down the radio.

The clowns crowded around.

Something strange was happening. One picture after another was flashing through my mind now, like a TV on the fritz. I saw an empty kitchen, the oven door flopped open, a dropped pie all over the floor, cherry pie. I saw the front door standing wide open, firetrucks in the snow, that big, old tree split open and in flames. My ears were full of static and words were rising up from the static, coming through me, even faster than the pictures.

Lucky marched down the aisle, clapping her hands and saying, "Okay, that's enough. MeMe needs to rest now."

"Is there someone you need to call?" I managed to spit out before Lucky pulled me away, to the back of the bus. She made me put Runt in his box and get into bed and lie down next to him even though I wasn't tired.

The clowns nodded and backed off, but the whole rest of the ride I could feel their eyes on me and my ears were still hissing and the TV was still flickering in my mind—one image after another, things I'd never seen before, not from my own life but from someone else's.

Back at the farm, Lucky made me stay on the bus while everyone else left.

She reached into her purse, found a bottle and shook out a little handful of powdery pills. They were orange-flavoured, like Hugo's diabetes candies.

While I sucked on one after another, she looked around in the cupboards and found a can of soup. She heated it up on the stove and brought me a bowl—Cream of Mushroom—but I couldn't eat it. It looked like Elmer's glue and my stomach was still at sea.

"You've had a big day," she said, sitting across the table from me while I stirred and stirred my soup. "I want you to stay here on the bus tonight and rest."

"Am I still in trouble?" I asked. "Will I be sent away?"

"No," she said, but then she got quiet and looked at her hands for a while as if she might be considering it.

"What's capitalism?" I asked. I didn't plan on asking, it just came out.

"It's a system," she said, looking suddenly very serious, "something that keeps us under pressure, so we all have to behave ourselves. But don't you worry about that just now." She reached across the table to brush my hair away from my face and smiled at me. I saw that her grey aura had little flashes of pink in it, that she could be kind, when she wanted to.

She made me eat four spoonfuls of the glue soup. Then she held Runt while I wiggled out of my Rapunzel dress. She tucked us both in— him in his box, me in my bed—and made me promise we would stay there, on the bus, for the rest of the night.

I reminded her of her own promise: that she would find Margaret and make sure she came to visit me.

She said she'd arrange it.

"Cross your heart?" I asked.

"And hope to die," she said.

Then she stepped off the bus, taking the broom with her. Before she left, I heard her wedge it into the handle next to the door and then tuck it behind the side-view mirrors, locking me in from the outside.

It was early in the morning when I felt Margaret climb into bed behind me. She curled around me—big spoon, little spoon—and kissed me on the back of my head twelve times. She smelled like campfire, vinegar, onions.

"I missed you," I said.

"I missed *you*," she said.

"I'm sorry," I said. I meant for telling everyone she couldn't read, but also for all of it, for stealing the bus keys and not enough money and getting us into this whole awful mess.

"No, *I'm* sorry," she said, and I stayed quiet, hoping she would say for what.

Instead she squeezed me. "I hear you're doing great."

"Great?"

"At the diner. Lucky says you're doing a great job."

It was a lie. Lucky was covering for me, for now. But I knew if I didn't do a better job soon, I'd be sent away like Rainbow.

I was crying. I didn't want to, but the tears were coming fast.

"What's wrong?" She sat up on one elbow.

I was tired of this new life, tired of playing MeMe and working in diners, tired of Lucky and the clowns and all these weird people. I wanted it to be just the two of us, to go back to Canada and live an ordinary Ontario life together.

I buried my face in my pillow. "I don't want to be MeMe anymore," I said. "I want to go home."

I felt her body jolt.

She yanked me back, so she could face me. "What did you just say?"

That's when I saw it: a thin, blue line running down her forehead. It stopped between her eyes in a small *X*, and it wasn't just drawn with a pen. It was red and inflamed, like a bee sting.

I reached out to touch it. When she lifted her arm to block me, I saw she was wearing one of those blue dresses too, with the threads hanging off of it.

"Listen, MeMe," she said. "This *is* our home now. We're finally part of something here, something big. Please don't take this away from me."

She looked at me for a long moment. Her eyes were searing, doing that thing, swirling in and in. I remembered all the things I had already taken from her and thought I heard a silent "too" on the end of her sentence: *Don't take this away from me too.*

CHAPTER 11

AFTER

BERTHA WANTS ME TO MEET WITH HER THREE TIMES A WEEK NOW, TO "TOUCH base."

She wants to talk about "clairvoyance" a lot, about whether there really is such a thing as "clairvoyance," or whether it might be reframed as my own special form of anxiety.

I can tell by how she makes air quotes with her fingers every time she says the word that she doesn't actually believe in clairvoyance, that in her mind it's right up there with talking houseflies. And maybe it's because I want to prove her wrong or because my whole past depends upon it, but we're in her office one day when, suddenly, a MeMe feeling comes over me. I feel the *pffffl*, the going up. The TV comes on in my mind.

I can see her as a younger woman, living in a big house somewhere far from here, eating breakfast alone. She's terribly lonely, trapped in a bad marriage.

"Were you trapped in a bad marriage once?" I ask.

She looks at me like, *Please.*

The channel changes. I see an old woman in a wheelchair. "Were you caring for an older parent?"

"Eliza*beth*," she says, peering at me over the top of her glasses.

"Okay but *were* you?"

She doesn't answer, but it doesn't matter. I'm sensing money troubles. "And you were broke?" I try. "Scraping together every last dollar?"

She tries to wrestle back control of the conversation. "Do you think it might be possible that rather than '*reading people's minds*'"—here she flutters her hands in the air—"you were just trying, desperately, to please your mother?"

I'm sensing despair, loneliness. "And you were lonely?" I try. "Very lonely?"

She persists. "Do you think it's possible that at least some of those times when you could see and hear Michael, you were drugged?" She leans forward in her seat. "Do you think you might have just *imagined* it was his voice speaking through you?"

My head feels like a barrel full of rocks kicked down a hill. She has found it: my number one trigger point.

"I wouldn't know," I say. "I've never *not* been drugged." Then, just to make a point, I say "fuck" and stomp out of her office, slamming the door on the way.

It doesn't stop there though.

Mr. Twohig and I start reading Hamlet together. We talk a lot about the ghost in the story and what purpose he serves and was he *really* real or just real to Hamlet. We talk about the end of World War I, all those reparations and how they eventually led to Hitler getting power. "So you see," he says, "there is such a thing as paying too much for the past," and he looks at me like he's not just talking about Germany anymore.

Annie's in on it too. She draws a lopsided triangle on the blackboard. One side is a steep slow climb. "Rising action" she writes above this. The other side is a short, sharp drop-off. "Denouement," she writes here. Right at the peak of the triangle, she writes "Climax." Then she comes back to the table and explains that a climax is a turning point and every story is barrelling toward one. "For example," she says, "in many stories the character starts out believing a lie about themselves, like that they are trapped, or too weak, or not good enough on their own. But often, by the end of the story, that lie falls away. They find their courage. They break free."

"What if it there is no climax though?" I ask. "What if the person wants to just stay comfortable in the lie forever?"

"They can't," she says. And then she explains how every story throughout the history of time has followed this formula, that stories are about change and change always boils down to one pivotal moment, a breaking point, after which nothing can ever be the same.

The tomatoes grow taller every day: two inches tall and then three. When I step into the greenhouse now, I can smell their spicy, peppery breath. Bertha shows us how to pinch off the new baby branches, so the plants don't spread themselves too thin. She shows us how to make tea out of the kitchen compost and feed it to the tomatoes. We're supposed to learn from this, I'm sure: something about yesterday's garbage and the dangers of overreaching.

Every day I check the bulk bins in front of the Yuen Fong Supermarket, but there's nothing for me. I stand on corners, waiting for Michael to pass by, but he's vanished. I leave notes at the pharmacy and the liquor store and the neighbourhood pub: *Margaret Squire, come and find me, please hurry.* At night, just before bed, I tape two signs up in my bedroom window: "HE" and "LP." Every morning I remove them again and hide them in my desk.

In Group, Bertha talks a lot about Love, Care and Attention™, which she always says all at once like, "lovecareandattention," because she is an expert on it and has written a book about it. Before she started Harrow House, she used to travel all around the country teaching corporate types how to provide themselves with lovecareandattention in the workplace, which as far as I can tell means stopping every two seconds to ask yourself, "And what am I feeling now? And what about now? And what about now?"

Another part of providing oneself with lovecareandattention, she says, is knowing how to say "no," so in Group we do role plays to practise. We stand with our feet firmly planted on the ground and puff our chests out like Superman and say, "NO, you *cannot* sit so close to me," or, "NO, you *may not* borrow my favourite pencil," while Bertha gives us pointers on how to remain assertive but calm.

Whenever someone asks us for something, we're encouraged to stop, take a deep breath and "check in with our boundaries." We're encouraged to wiggle our toes and identify our feelings using a chart on the wall.

Heather smirks at me.

I accidentally smirk back, a big mistake because, after that, she thinks we're friends.

She comes up to me after Group, grabs my hand and looks at my palm. "Estoy star-crossed," she reads. "Rad!" She flashes her own palm at me, and there in the centre is a heart with the word Tad written inside. "My boyfriend," she says. Then she wink-winks at me and, just like Lucky all those years ago, says, "We're gonna blow this popsicle stand." My knees do a thing like they're no longer part of my body.

I have to find a way to warn her about me.

CHAPTER 12

BEFORE

BECAUSE OF WHAT I'D SAID TO DELL, LUCKY WOULDN'T TAKE ME BACK TO THE same diner any more. Instead we had to work at a seedy place near the highway where the truckers were mean and the coffee was sour. Then one day Effie finally called home and found out I was right about everything—the lightning strike and the fire and even the cherry pie. After that Lucky changed her mind.

One morning, she showed up at the bus door at the usual time, with the usual cup of coffee for me, and this time she had a gift too. She slid a brown paper bag across the kitchen table at me and said, "go on." Inside was a black, satin eye patch. It had jewels glued to the front and the word MeMe stitched on it in red. She told me about Effie, about the tree, the cherry pie. "You're the real deal, MeMe," she said, "I'm sorry I ever doubted you."

"Oh, and this!" she said, reaching into her pocket. She pulled out a small, tinfoil crown with matching jewels glued to it and put it on Runt's head. He sat up tall and strutted around the table like a little prince.

"Does this mean we can go back to see Dell?" I asked.

"Just because you were right about Effie doesn't mean you were right about Dell," she said with one finger in the air. "But, yes, we can try."

As soon as Dell saw us sitting in our usual spot, she made a beeline for our table. She laid out two menus and said, "Anything you want."

Lucky peered up at her. "What do you mean?"

"I mean whatever you want, it's on me," Dell said. Then she spun and walked away, and I thought I saw the slightest bounce in her step.

Lucky had a cheeseburger with fries and ordered apple pie with ice cream for me. She made me eat at least half of it, too, even though I wasn't hungry. She was always watching me now, always counting my bites and reminding me I had to eat.

Dell never did say that she'd found the letter or what exactly was in it, but she didn't have to. Some things don't need to be said.

That day I met Dell's friend Flo, a round ball of a woman in a floral dress who had also lost her husband. She came to the table, clutching his tie in her hand and asking if we had any messages from her Robert.

Lucky gestured for her to sit.

I took the tie in my hand. It was brown and white striped, with a red stain on the front. I closed my eyes and waited for the TV in my mind to come on, but it was unplugged. I opened my eyes to look for Flo's aura, but she didn't have one. I couldn't even think of a good song lyric.

Dell and the other waitress were watching from the other end of the diner. Everyone was. I had to do something.

Michael was hissing in my ear, saying just one word, over and over: *listen.*

So I decided to get her talking. "What was Robert like?" I asked.

Lucky kicked me under the table. This wasn't one of her money-making questions. But Flo perked right up and told me all about him, that he'd been a math teacher and a softball coach, that he was great with kids, although never a father. She said he was good and cheerful and patient, that he had a special way with animals, that he was a kind soul, taken far too soon. It had been a genetic thing with his heart, she said. Nobody saw it coming.

I ran my hands over the tie while she talked, waiting for a feeling.

"Is there something you'd like me to tell him?" I asked.

Lucky shook her head at me. I was way off script.

"Oh, yes, please," Flo said. She reached into her purse and pushed a folded-up note toward me.

The note was three pages long and full of all the things she wanted to say to Robert: that she was sorry she'd never taken an interest in his softball, his model airplanes, his big-band music, that she wished she could have given him a son, she wished they'd taken that trip to Australia, she wished she'd tried harder with his mother, that she'd been more patient, more loving and, more than anything, she wished for just a little more time.

After I read the note, I closed my eyes and sat still for a long time, probably too long. I was imagining a cord running from me up to Robert, wherever he was, and I was trying to send all that love up the cord.

When Lucky had had enough, she coughed and said, "Thank you, Flo, that'll be a dollar."

I opened my eyes.

Flo was digging around in her purse, but she looked a little disappointed. The coffee had finally kicked in. I could see something like an aura around her now. It was green as guilt.

I wanted to do more for Flo, to take her guilt away, so I did the only thing I could think of. I copied what I'd seen O do to Margaret that first night at the farm. I reached out, touched Flo between the eyes and said, "You are forgiven."

She looked at me. "Is that—? Does he—? Is that what he says?"

Lucky nodded, almost imperceptibly.

I nodded too.

Flo put her face in her hands and fell apart. She was crying and thanking me and blowing her nose in great big honks. "Oh boy, did I ever need to hear that," she kept saying. Then, when she was all done, she stood and gave me three dollars before shuffling away.

I expected to be in trouble for what I'd said. I expected Lucky to know I'd used O's trick, to say it wasn't for kids and I'd better not do it again, but instead, as soon as Flo was gone, she turned to me and said, "Wow!" She folded up one of the dollars into a little compact square, placed it in my hands and said I'd earned it, that I was developing a really good instinct about people. She said to hide the money well though and not to tell anyone, not even Margaret. I agreed and, later that evening, I stashed my money in the empty Cream of Mushroom can on the bus and hid it under the sink.

After Flo, I hit my stride.

Every morning Lucky came to find me on the bus with a cup of coffee in her hands and watched while I drank it. I would feed Runt then we'd head to the breakfast circle.

When we approached, all heads turned our way, even if O was already talking. They'd all heard about me by then. They knew Effie's story and that I was making money at the diner every day.

If Margaret was there, I always tried to squeeze in next to her. Sometimes, while O talked about the war on the other side of the world and the war here at home and that they were both a symptom of capitalism and it was up to us to wake everyone up, Margaret would put her hand down by her side and let her pinky rest against mine. It felt like there was electricity travelling between us then, like the cord between us wasn't broken and never could be.

By the time we arrived at the restaurant, someone would always be waiting for me with their object—a tie, a hat, a piece of jewelry—and would want to speak about whoever they'd lost. I would take their hands in mine and listen to their stories. The TV would turn on. Scenes from their life would flash across my mind. Michael would speak to me from the static, telling me just what to say. The words came through me. Sometimes I'd quote a song or give some advice. Sometimes I would just ask questions and listen. In the end that's what most people wanted—to be heard. I would always finish by saying they were loved and forgiven, and that always seemed to be enough. Everyone wanted to be forgiven for something. They would say thank you and pay their money, often even more than what was asked. At the end of every day, when Lucky counted the money up, she'd always take a few dollars off the top of the pile, fold them into a tiny square and pass them to me with a wink: *our little secret.*

When we got back to the farm in the evenings, sometimes Margaret would come and sit with me at the fire. She always knew exactly how much money I'd made. "Fifteen dollars!" she'd say, putting her arm around me and asking me about my day. I would tuck in against her and tell her about the different people I'd met and the messages Michael and I had delivered. She would listen carefully, with a crooked, silly smile on her face, like I was absolutely fascinating. "I always knew you were amazing," she'd say, full of pride, and I couldn't tell if she meant me or him or both of us, but it didn't matter because I had her full attention for once. On a good day, she'd pat the ground in front of her, inviting me to lean against her knees so she could run her fingers through my hair.

"You're doing *so* great, Elizabeth," she'd say, working out a knot. "You're really helping the Cause."

I'd nod, hoping she couldn't feel what I felt: that I didn't care about the Cause or even understand it, that all I cared about was this time with her, her fingers in my hair, her calling me by my old name.

Still, no matter how much money I'd earned, as soon as O came toward the fire, our time was over. Margaret would pat me on the shoulders and move away to stand before her, listening with her hands squeezing at her sides.

Sometimes I'd hang around and stand at the edge of the firelight to watch everyone spin. Margaret was one of the fastest now. She'd tilt her face up to the sky and stomp and flap her arms, saying, "hup, hup, hup" while the strings on her dress took flight, blurring her edges.

I could never stay for long though. If I did, one of the new people would find me and push their palms into my hands, saying, "Please, MeMe. Can you do me?" To avoid them I had to disappear into the tall grass, or hide in the hole at the back of the bus.

There were always new people arriving at the farm in those days. They'd be sitting on the bus with the clowns at the end of the day, or they'd come walking down the long driveway with their backpacks and bedrolls. Usually they'd heard about O and the Cause. But sometimes they had heard about me, about the girl who could talk to the dead.

Everyone always gave the new people special attention, showing them around, assigning them a job, saying that this was a family, that everyone took care of each other here. Around the fire, O would do to them what she had done to Margaret. She would spin them until they broke and then she'd kneel over them saying, "Let it all out," and, "You are forgiven." The next day they'd look different, scrubbed clean and with a strange inner light beaming up through them. Then, a few days later, they'd have a blue, shaggy dress or overalls and a line down their face and they'd be talking about capitalism and the Cause, just like everyone else.

Not everyone stayed though. Some people couldn't handle the spinning, the letting it all out. These people might spend the whole night curled up in a ball, crying, and nothing anyone did could console them. Or they'd stand, frozen in one spot, staring straight ahead and squeezing their hands all night, totally unreachable. There was one man, Dave, who climbed up onto the pointiest part of the roof and wouldn't come down for days. He was ranting the whole time, rhyming and spouting an endless stream of words about how he was the *real* son of God. The Human Radio, everyone called him. He might've never stopped if Roland and Tex hadn't climbed up there to pull him down.

It seemed like there was always someone freaking out around the bonfire, but these people never lasted. In the morning, I'd see them walking back up the long driveway with their belongings, and it was never clear to me whether they were asked to leave or whether they left on their own.

"We're not all cut out for the Cause," O announced at the breakfast circle one day. "It takes true inner strength to change the world. The Cause doesn't choose everyone"—here she looked all around the circle until her eyes landed on Margaret, "—but it has chosen you."

Work around the farm was increasing. A weekly Renaissance Fair had started a few towns over, so all week long people were busy making soap and candles and tie-dyed shirts to sell there. I liked to help with the work when I could. I stood around the wagon wheel, pouring wax over the candle wicks with a big ladle. I helped the ladies stir the ingredients for the homemade soap in the big old bathtub. I helped untie the tie-dyed shirts and spread them out over the tops of the tall grass to dry.

Then, on Saturdays, we'd pack all our goods onto the bus and travel to the fair grounds. I was never allowed to help selling soap or candles though. I had to stay on the bus, waiting for customers with Lucky, even though MeMe Fanta wasn't such a big hit with the Renaissance crowd. But sometimes, at the end of the day, I was allowed to wander in between the tables and tents for a while, watching the people pack up their crates of vegetables and homemade goods. Sometimes a kind farmer would give me a box of strawberries that hadn't sold or a handful of lettuce for Runt. Sometimes his wife would give me a leftover piece of pie and, when she saw the state of my Rapunzel dress, a look like, "Oh dear."

I loved the Renaissance Fair more than anything. I loved seeing so many people going about their ordinary lives, wearing normal clothes and talking about the weather or what they'd seen on TV the night before. It was the real America. If only Margaret could have seen it.

But Margaret was always in the printing shed. Sometimes a week would pass and I wouldn't see her. I started hanging around outside the building, hoping to catch a glimpse of her. Every few days a big truck would arrive with pallets of boxes and barrels. Men with leather vests and tattooed arms tipped the barrels onto their sides and rolled them into the building. Lucky said to stay away from those men, but that was easy. They went into the building and didn't come out again.

I never did see Margaret, but once I saw the bald man with the two tufts of red hair come out to feed Stella. He left the door wide open behind him and, through it, I saw a bunch of big machines that looked like tractors, with wheels and cranks. The machines were whirring and spitting out paper. In the background I saw a bunch of those papers drying on a line—a thousand blue dots, fluttering in the breeze.

The nights were long and boring without Margaret. I put Runt on my shoulder and wandered the property, looking for something to do.

One night I came across the clowns playing that same game again, where Roland stood on the ladder and shouted out commands to everyone. This time they were acting out animals.

"Penguin," he shouted, and everyone shuffled around with their arms stuck to their sides.

"Lion," he said, and they strutted and roared, but without making a sound.

He saw me watching and invited me to join. This time I did.

I was a giraffe. I was a ladybug. I was a butterfly. It felt good to be something else for a while: to be tall, to be small, to be light.

"Good. Now Catharsis," Roland said, clapping his hands together and stepping down from his perch.

For Catharsis everyone had to lie on their backs in a circle with their heads on each other's stomachs. At the top of the circle, Roland started laughing, a big, deep belly laugh. The person with their head on his stomach started laughing too, and the next, and the next until it had gone all around the circle and we were all laughing.

Then, at some point, Roland switched to crying. His crying was just as contagious. It travelled all around the circle, belly-to-head-to-belly. When it got to me, I felt a hot lump in my throat. I thought of the last time I'd cried—the night I'd asked Margaret if we could go home— and of the time I'd cried before that—over Lizzy the lizard, lying in her box outside Hugo's back door. I remembered how I'd shut the lid tight, sealing all my sadness in with her, and I shut it again now. I wouldn't let myself cry in front of everyone. I was MeMe Fanta. It would have been very unprofessional.

After the crying, Roland said, "now Peace," and he got quiet and tried to send peace around the circle, belly-to-head, but it never came to me, or it passed me right by.

After Peace he asked us all to sit up and gather around for a talk. I expected him to talk about the Cause and how we all had to be good soldiers, but instead he looked around the circle and asked, "How was that?"

One-by-one, people talked.

"I'd like to talk about love," Effie said, "because I noticed that we were all expressing it pretty different, like some were holding their hearts, but some were holding their stomachs."

"Good point," Roland said. "Let's explore that."

People talked about love and where they felt it most. They talked about sex-love and friendship-love and the kind of love you have for an animal. Roland stood to demonstrate how he might clown these different kinds of love—with the first one he looked like he was being dragged across the circle, crotch-first and with the last he swooned, holding something small and precious to his heart. When he was done, everyone applauded. He lifted a pretend hat off his head and bowed and sat back down again.

Someone brought up pity and they talked about that for a while.

Then someone else said, "Can we talk about these bikers? How they're, like, polluting everyone with their hard drugs and their bad attitudes?"

Roland glanced at me and then away. "Catharsis isn't the place for this," he said. "But we can certainly talk about fear."

At the end of it all, Roland said sitting in a circle like this and exposing our biases was an important part of clowning because, when it came time to clown, we needed to set those biases aside. He said we needed to be able to empty ourselves out and let something else take over for a while, just like in Catharsis. Catharsis wasn't easy, he said, but it was necessary for the clown to get to know their own inner landscape.

"For example," he said, "if you aren't able to feel sadness, why is that? And if you aren't able to feel peace, why?" He smiled all around the circle, stopping to wink at me. Then he clapped his hands, and everyone stood and hugged one another, saying, "love you, love you, love you too."

I tried to get away but got caught in one of those hugs. "Love you," a woman said to me, and I felt the lid on Lizzy's box wiggling loose again.

I had ten dollars in the mushroom soup can, then twelve, then fifteen.

Word kept spreading about me. More and more people came to see me at the diner, from farther and farther away. Sometimes there was even a lineup. "The pirate girl," some started calling me, probably because of Runt and my eye patch.

Lucky wasn't happy about this. She wanted me to work on my delivery of "you are forgiven" because she said it was my money-maker. She wanted me to get quiet before I said it, to tilt my head and scrunch my face like I was listening to a far away voice. She wanted me to stay like that until I'd counted to ten. Then, when I spoke, she wanted me to act like the forgiveness was coming from the dead person, whoever the customer was trying to reach, not from me. She wanted me to say it with conviction, like I was acting the words, not just saying them.

"You want me to clown?" I asked.

She thought about that for a moment. "Yeah," she agreed, "I guess I do."

Lucky wasn't happy with my outfit either. My Rapunzel dress was worn thin by then. So one day we hitchhiked to another town to visit a thrift store. There, she found me a black velvet dress with secret pockets and a matching cape. She got me a shiny gold headband too.

When I was all dressed, she took me by the hand and led me toward a mirror. "Look how elegant you are," she said, pointing. I jumped when I saw my reflection. I didn't look anything like my old self anymore. I looked like I'd been walking for days through bad weather without a hairbrush.

"But you know what isn't so elegant?" Lucky said. She pulled my hair back to reveal Runt, standing on my shoulder. She plucked his tinfoil crown off and said maybe it was time to let him live with the rest of the chickens.

"No," I wailed. "They'll peck his eyes out!"

She laughed. "Who told you that?" Then she reassured me that's not what would happen, that he'd have a long and wonderful life with both eyes in his head.

I looked at him. He was older now, almost the same size as his brothers and sisters. He had all his feathers, and his beak and feet had darkened. Still, I felt the lump rising in my throat, the lid to Lizzy's box coming loose. I clutched her arm. "Please don't take him from me," I begged. "I need him."

Lucky gave me a strange look, but she agreed. I could keep Runt with me for just a little while longer. "But be careful," she warned, one finger in the air between us. "Don't let anyone else see how attached you are, especially not O."

The truth is, Runt was the only thing keeping me going at that time.

Every day was the same. I drank my coffee. I waved my hands and fluttered my eyes. I said, "Your aura is green/red/blue/purple." The TV came on, the channels changed. The static rose in my ears. I said, "You're grieving / you're angry / you're sad / you're forgiven." I don't know what I said. The words came through me.

Back at the farm at night, people were always following me around, falling on their knees before me, pushing their hands into mine, saying, "What do you see?"

I had to keep moving. If I stopped, even for a moment, they were upon me.

I hardly saw Margaret at all anymore and, when I did, she wasn't herself. She didn't come to sit with me at the fire anymore. She didn't ask about my day. She waved at me from a distance with a quick flick of the hand, like she didn't have the strength for anything more. I noticed her fingers were stained blue up to the knuckles. She had blue smudges on her skin and in her hair. She looked tired, more tired than I'd ever seen her, but startled too, like she was being pulled in two directions at once.

I wanted to sit next to her, to put my forehead to hers and take away half of what she was feeling. I wanted to tell her I had thirty-two dollars saved in the can, almost enough for us to get out of there and catch a bus to wherever we wanted to go. But I couldn't get near her. O was always by her side, telling her what to do. Neither one of us could stand still anymore it seemed.

At night I lay awake in the hayloft in the barn, or in the tall grass, or in the hole at the back of the bus with Runt at my side and my mind, that small boat, sloshing out at sea. I couldn't feel my feet or hands. I couldn't feel my face. The TV was on in my mind, tuned to static. I couldn't turn it off. Michael's voice was hissing in my ears all the time now, saying something I couldn't quite make out, something that sounded like a warning.

CHAPTER 13

AFTER

BERTHA AND I DECIDE TO LEAVE THE MICHAEL THING ALONE FOR A WHILE. Instead she wants to talk about drugs, about what it felt to be on them all those years in the hospital—my "lost decade" she calls it—and what it feels like to come off them now.

"It feels like a lobotomy reversal," I say.

But what I'm really thinking is it feels like coming back to myself, like the two torn threads of my life are connecting. If only Margaret would come for me, I could mend them. I could build a bridge between then and now.

Bertha puckers her mouth like she wishes I would be more eloquent, so I decide to give her something good for her book.

"It feels like the opposite of compression," I say. "Like swimming up from deep water."

"Lovely," she says, making a note. "And how does *that* feel?"

That's, like, her number one doctor trick: to dive into the feeling, then the feeling behind the feeling. She never tires of it.

But if I'm honest, it's not all swimming up. There are hard parts too.

For example, I'll be out in the world, waiting at the bus stop, say, when a woman a little younger than me walks by and, whether she's all put together and going to her office job or pushing a shopping cart and begging for money, pretty soon I'm doing the math in my head, thinking she would have been about five in 1969 and then, next thing I know, *pfffft*, I'm up and out of myself, seeing her whole life flash past, all the years since then, all the ups and downs, the beautiful and bad and wonderful moments, and I'm thinking she might have kids one day, and those kids might have kids and then I'm thinking of the importance of a life, the size and measure of it, and then one of those trap doors opens up beneath my feet and, suddenly, I'm on my knees, right in the middle of the sidewalk, weeping and thinking about the before and after of my life and all the things—but especially the one thing—I can never take back.

I keep finding myself crying on street corners, in department stores, in front of the barbecued chickens twirling on their skewers at the grocery store.

"That's to be expected, Hon'," Bertha says when I tell her. "It's what I call 'the thaw.' It's a perfectly normal part of coming off your meds. All those emotions that were suppressed for so long are welling up now."

Bertha is a relentless cheerleader. With her, everything is perfectly normal as long as it can be contained by quotation marks.

She teaches me to write down every one of these "episodes" in a journal that I carry with me. So when I see that woman on her way to work or whatever, what I'm supposed to do is stop right there in the middle of the sidewalk and measure my feelings. I'm supposed to think to myself, *I feel 80% guilty and 20% sad.* I'm supposed to say to myself, *I'm having an episode and that's okay*, and, right there, in the middle of the sidewalk, I'm supposed to place my hand over my heart and wiggle my toes and take three deep breaths. Then I'm supposed to measure my feelings again and see if they have gone down at all and, you know what? Usually they have.

She calls this "tuning in," which is part of Radical Self-Compassion™, which is the topic of the new book she's writing. Patrick and Leonard and Heather are in the book as case studies, and she's asked if she can put me in there too, as a Radical Self-Compassion success story.

"But I'm not a success," I say.

"Oh yes, Hon'," she says. "I think you are."

In fact, she says, I'm doing so well, it's time I get a job like everyone else in the house. She says it will help with my parole review, and that, actually, she's called in a favour with a friend and it's all arranged. I'm expected to check in for my first shift tomorrow at a video store nearby.

"No, uh-uh, no way," I say. "I can't. Can-fucking-*not*."

She smiles, letting the swear go. "Sure you can."

"But I'm not ready!" I am 80% terrified, 10% angry, 10% about to run away.

"I'll let you in on a little secret, Hon'," she says with a wink. "Nobody is. We're all just pretending. And it's perfectly okay for you to do the same until you get the hang of things."

But it's not the beginning I'm worried about, not the getting-the-hang-of-it part. It's the end I'm worried about because I know I will ruin this like I ruin everything.

CHAPTER 14

BEFORE

I WAS A SUCCESS AS MEME FANTA. I HAD A GOOD RUN. AND I WOULD'VE KEPT on running that way all summer. I would have run myself right off a cliff if not for my mistakes.

My first mistake happened late one night when I decided to follow Margaret. I had been trying to sleep up in the hayloft. I had been thinking of some of the kids I'd known in Ontario, imagining them in their big, comfy beds with fluffy pillows and perfect sheets when I saw Margaret walk past, below. I scrambled down the ladder and ran after her, catching up just in time to see her duck into a teepee. I circled it. It was all lit up, an orange triangle against the night sky. I heard soft murmuring inside, the sound of two women talking. I saw their huge shadows moving around. Then they sat down, side by side. The other woman lit a candle. There was the clang of metal, as if they were sorting cutlery, then a hiss, then a long silence. I saw Margaret fall back. I saw the other woman climb on top of her. She lowered her face to Margaret's face as if she might kiss her or eat her alive. I pressed my head to the wall. "Pssst," I said, and then—I couldn't help myself— "stop that."

The shadows came apart. There was a commotion inside the teepee, then I was yanked back by my ear and thrown to the ground.

It was O standing over me. It had been her in the teepee, her who'd been kissing Margaret.

"What are you doing here?" She barely lowered her chin when she spoke to me, as if she was still balancing that imaginary teacup on her head.

"I wanted Margaret," I said, but Margaret was behind her, shaking her head no.

"We don't *do* neediness here," O said.

"But I was just—"

"Neediness is for children," she boomed, loud enough for anyone nearby to hear. "And children aren't allowed here." Then she turned and ducked back into the teepee, leaving me and Margaret alone.

Margaret came to my side to help me up. I tried to hug her, but she put her hand on my chest to hold me back.

"Do you love her?" I asked, but I already knew the answer. I could see it in her eyes. And I could see something else too: that that love wouldn't work out, that it was already taking too much from her, giving too little back.

She was trembling. Her lips were thin and blue and she was so tired she could barely keep her eyes open. "Go back to the bus," she said, blinking slowly. "And dial it down a little."

"Dial what down? How?" I asked, but she had already turned away from me.

The next morning at the breakfast meeting, O sat at the top of the circle, talking about attachment and how dangerous that was for a soldier of the Cause.

Margaret was sitting next to her, looking down at the ground.

"Attachment means we are less willing to make the necessary sacrifices when we're called upon," O said. "It makes us weak and inefficient."

Then she opened her eyes and clapped her hands loudly. "Wake up, people," she shouted. "This is war. We must be efficient. We must root out and sever our attachments." Her eyes travelled all around the circle, one face at a time, until they landed on me. "And anyone who is not up to the task will be asked to leave."

I witnessed my first critique a few days later.

When Lucky and the clowns and I came home on the bus one evening, we saw a bunch of people gathered in a circle down by the house. They were all standing except for Sammy, who was seated on a chair in the middle. O was talking and waving a wooden spoon around. Sammy was curled up into a little ball on the chair.

As soon as we were parked, Roland barged off the bus and down the hill toward them. The rest of us followed.

Up close, I couldn't see what was happening inside the circle, but I could hear it. "I've noticed there is a laziness in you," O said. "And an imprecision to your actions, almost as if you don't want to do things well because that would mean you're fully engaged, and my sense, Sammy, is that you don't want to be fully engaged in anything. My sense is you are playing the role of the small, helpless girl, the unwanted child, poor little Sammy, out of laziness and habit. But that's not what we're about here. We're a family, but not *that* kind of family. We are soldiers with important work to do. My own sister is rotting in a prison cell. There's no room for laziness here, no room for little girls."

"What is this?" Roland said. He was strutting around the outside of the circle, looking for an opening, but people had linked their arms together and wouldn't let him pass.

"This is a critique," O said. "A necessary part of things."

I ducked down to peer between people's legs. I saw Sammy bury her face in her knees and start crying. Nobody went to her.

O passed the wooden spoon to Margaret.

"I've noticed that too," she said. "Your laziness. And your helplessness. It's like you're always waiting for Daddy to come along and do the thinking for you."

Everyone nodded and that word—Daddy—went around the circle. Margaret passed the spoon.

The next person started and then the next.

"I've noticed your breath stinks," someone said.

"And you never clean up after yourself," said someone else.

One-by-one, they attacked her. They talked about the way she looked, the way she did her work, how she talked, her posture. And she sat through it, curled up on the chair, crying and nodding, taking it all in.

"That's enough," Roland said at one point. He forced his way into the middle of the circle, scooped Sammy up and carried her away in his arms.

"Here comes Daddy," I heard someone say, but by then I was already on my way back to the bus. I climbed on, locked the door, got into the hole at the back and shut the lid.

I was crying and shaking all over. I wanted to be alone, but Michael was there, hissing in my ear, *How long before it's our turn?* he said, and, *What will they say about us?*

By morning, Sammy had left. And soon other people started to follow.

First was Larry. One day he was on the porch, squeezing his hands and staring off into space, and the next, he was gone. Someone said they'd seen him walking up the driveway. Someone else said they'd seen him get into a cab and drive away.

Then it was the man named Jelly Roll.

Then it was Judy.

One day we were all at the breakfast circle. O was talking. She closed her eyes and seemed to be finished, so Judy stepped into the middle of the circle and started calling out jobs. But O wasn't finished.

"Excuse me," she said.

Judy stopped and lowered her clipboard.

"Ex*cuse* me," O said again.

Judy stepped back to the edge of the circle.

"I think your time here is done, *Judy*," O said, turning to look at her finally.

"Sorry, I just—" Judy started to say.

"I'm not interested in sorry," O said in a voice so loud it hurt my ears. "I think it's time for you to pack your bags and leave." Then she closed her eyes, end of discussion.

Judy bowed and left the circle. A few moments later we all watched her drag a plaid suitcase up the driveway.

But my biggest mistake was a few days later.

Lucky and I had had a good day at the diner. We'd made fifteen dollars before noon, so we hitched back to the farm early, rather than wait for the bus. But when we came over the rise in the driveway, we saw the bus was already back, parked in front of the house. And when we got to the end of the driveway, O was standing there, waiting for us. She stepped forward and took Lucky by the hand. "I'd like to invite you to step into the circle," she said. She nodded toward the house. There was a single chair standing there with a circle of people gathered around it.

Margaret came up next to me and slid her hand in mine. "You too, MeMe," she said. I looked up at her to try and figure out what was going on, but she wouldn't look back at me.

"Sure!" Lucky said, and we all walked down toward the house. Lucky sat on the chair and it began.

O picked up the wooden spoon and talked about ego and the dangers of not belonging. She said there was nothing worse than pretending to be a part of something while having one foot out the door. She said it had been discovered that Lucky was keeping secrets and putting her own needs above the interests of the group. She bent down and picked up a soup can from her feet, my can, the one with my thirty-two dollars in it.

I tried to step forward, but Margaret's hand was clamped over my own. She was holding me firmly in place.

"It's true," Lucky said. "I was skimming off the top of MeMe's earnings."

O spun around to look at me. "Is that true, MeMe?"

Behind her back, Lucky was nodding at me, ever-so-slightly. *Say yes.* I nodded.

"You've been spending a lot of time with Lucky," O said, stepping forward to hand me the wooden spoon. "You must have something to say about her."

I looked at Lucky. I thought of all the things she'd taught me, all her rules, how bossy she could be, but also how she'd taken care of me. She looked so small sitting there on the chair.

"I like her," I said.

O sighed. "Whether you like her or not is irrelevant, MeMe. We *all* like her. What I'm asking is if you've noticed any behaviour that goes against the Cause."

I wanted to say that I didn't even know what the Cause was, or care, but Margaret was squeezing and squeezing my hand—S-O-S—and Lucky was giving me a look that said, *speak*.

"She's bossy," I said. "And she's always making up rules."

Some people laughed: *tssst-tssst-tssst*.

"Great," O said. "What else?"

I remembered then how we'd first met, how her and Roland had tricked us into coming to the farm.

"She lies," I said.

"She lies!" O repeated. "About what, MeMe?"

I shrugged. "Lots of stuff."

O crouched down to look at me. It was my first time being so close to her. I noticed her eyes were hard and glinting, like hammered-down nails. "Like what?" she asked.

"She says you have a daughter in New York City that you don't even care about," I said. Her face twitched. She stood and addressed the crowd. "*Niece*, folks," she said. "Rainbow is my *niece*, and I *do* care about her, and she's doing just fine." Then she plucked the wooden spoon from my hand. "Thank you for revealing the truth to us, MeMe," she said before passing the spoon to the next person.

Lucky looked down at her hands.

The critique continued, but I didn't stay. I walked away, straight out into the tall grass where nobody could find me.

In the morning I waited for Lucky on the bus, but she didn't come. The clowns didn't come either. I found Roland in the barn. He wasn't dressed for the day. He looked sad and ordinary without his clown paint.

I asked if we were going to town.

He said no.

I asked where Lucky was.

He said gone.

Gone where? I asked.

He said nobody knew. Then he reached into his overall pocket and pulled out a note, folded up into a perfect square. "She said to give this to you."

I quickly stuffed it into my dress pocket in case anybody was watching and snuck back out into the tall grass to read it. "Thank you for everything, Elizabeth," it said. "I'm not mad at you. You did the right thing. Don't forget, you are still a child. Love, Lorelai." There was a ten-dollar bill folded up with the note. I stuffed the note and the money back into my pocket. Then I lay back in the grass and wept.

My final mistake happened later that night. I was walking toward the fire, looking for Margaret, when a man, a newcomer, spotted me. He came over and knelt in front of me. "Please," he said, showing me his palms, "tell me what you see."

I looked into the man's face, his greasy, knotted beard, his strange eyes and broken, yellow teeth. I remembered seeing him at Lucky's critique the day before and I didn't want anything to do with him. I didn't want to take his hand, but a crowd was forming around us.

I pretended to look at his palm. I ran my finger over the lines and fluttered my eyelashes. "You shouldn't be here," I said. "You should go home."

He snatched his palm back and looked at it. Then he came at me again. "I don't think so." He pushed his hand into my chest. "Try again."

I tried to step around him, but he was blocking my way. He was thrusting his hand at me, so I decided to cut right to it and give him what I knew he wanted, what everyone always wanted, whether they knew it or not. I put my hand between his eyes and pushed him back, hard enough that he fell in the dirt. "You are forgiven," I said.

He lay on his back, thinking about that.

I stepped around him and was about to walk away when I saw Margaret. She was standing outside the circle of people, watching, with her head at an odd angle, her hands shoved deep into her dress pockets.

Her eyes were black and dull, like the windows of the printing shed. I couldn't read those eyes, couldn't tell if she was proud or angry.

I wanted her to finally see me in action, to see what I had become without her, how important I was.

When the next person knelt before me, I pushed her palms aside. I said something about being Siamese, about having a brother on the other side. I said he had a message for her, that he wanted us to put our foreheads together so I could feel what she felt.

I thought I saw a little smile flicker across Margaret's face.

I brought my forehead to the woman's forehead and then it happened, the whole MeMe routine: the *pffft*, the going up, my ears hissing, Michael's voice whispering to me. The TV came on. Images flashed past. I saw glimpses of the woman's life on the road, thumb out, catching rides with strangers, good rides, bad ones, one that ended with a knife to her throat.

I don't know what I said exactly, only that I was full-on MeMe. The words came pouring through me. I said something about her mother, something about the daughter she'd left in her care, something about a friend she'd lost touch with. I was like the Human Radio, shouting from the rooftop. Then, at the end of it all, when the woman was crying and confessing her sins to me, I put my hand between her eyes, pushed her back and told her she was forgiven too.

When I looked up, Margaret was shaking her head at me. Her eyes swung up and past me. I turned to see what she was looking at, and that's when I saw O. She was standing behind me, watching. Her face was twisted into a scowl. Then she tipped her chin down to look directly at me, and that teacup I'd imagined her carrying on top of her head for so long tumbled. I watched it fall. I felt it break.

The next morning Margaret came to find me on the bus.

I seem to recall she sat across from me at the kitchen table and said that this MeMe thing had to end, that I had pushed it too far. Or did she say this Michael thing had to end? That I had pushed *that* too far? I can't remember.

I do remember her taking my chin in her hand and telling me something important and serious. Did she decide to finally tell the truth about Michael and me? Did she even know the truth herself? I wish I could remember. I've tried and tried, but there is a blank spot here, a black hole of memory. Some truths are just too hard to face.

I remember her saying she had to get healthy, that it was something she had to do on her own and I'd have to fend for myself for a little while. Then she broke the real news: I would be going with the clowns to stay in the city.

I remember I could barely hear her over the hissing in my ears. It was as if she was talking to me from the end of a long tunnel that was full of wind.

"But I don't want to go to the city without you," I pleaded. I came around the table and grabbed her arm. I was thinking of Rainbow, sleeping in her dumpster. I started crying, tears and snot dripping down my face and—I don't know what made me do it—I wiped my face on her sleeve.

"It's the centre of the world, MeMe," she said. "You're going to love it there. And I'll be *right* behind you."

"But how will you find me?"

"I'm sure I'll find you at the centre of things," she said, smiling down at me, loosening my fingers from her arm, one at a time.

I was confused. "At the centre of the centre?" I asked.

"Yes," she said, "and I'll be able to join you there because I'll be doing much better."

She was trying to sound upbeat, but she was lying. I knew it, even then. One liar always recognizes another.

"Okay then," she said, leaning over to give me one last hug. "You be good. Do what is asked of you." I remember that hug, how her arms felt light as air. I remember how the world was spinning in tatters, coming apart all around me, and how it felt like my yo-yo heart had finally reached the end of its string.

CHAPTER 15

AFTER

MY NEW JOB IS AT A PLACE CALLED THE VIDEO STATION.

I'm allowed to walk there and back on my own. I earn $4.25 an hour, and I can keep all the money as long as I put half of it in a bank account for later, when I'm in college. While I work, I can drink as much lemonade as I want and eat as much popcorn and buy candy at half price.

I don't even have to talk to customers. I'm not supposed to. I'm supposed to stay in the back, rewinding and cleaning the returns. Then, when the store is quiet, I tiptoe out and restock the shelves.

It's a good job. I could ride it out until the end of my time at Harrow House, easy. I could save up money and have a little stash for when I'm free. But of course, I screw things up.

I start slipping notes in with the rentals: *Margaret Squire, please contact your daughter at 467 Keefer.*

I start making long-distance calls whenever Mike, my boss, steps out. I call the places I can remember, like The Blue Fox Diner in upstate New York. But I also call every garage in New York City asking, "Are you cosmic? Do you know a woman named O? Do you know any clowns? Have you seen a woman with a big, red afro?"

I start stealing licorice too even though I get it cheap; it's an old habit, hard to break.

Then, one Tuesday afternoon, Mike leaves me alone while he goes to get a pizza next door, and I see a woman wandering through the aisles, looking lost. I get that old feeling again: the *pffft*, the going up and, next thing I know, I'm sensing things about her: how she lives in a big house with a husband who loves her but desires someone else, how he hardly comes home for dinners anymore, has even started staying away on weekends. I see that she is in a delicate place, teetering right on the pointy edge of her climax, the moment when she finally understands what's really going on.

So even though I'm not supposed to talk to her because I am a junior convict and new to The Video Station, I feel like I have to warn her. I come up beside her where she's browsing rom-coms and say, "Hey, *pssst*, show me your palm."

I don't mean for it to become a thing, but it does. The woman comes back a few days later, thanking me. She tells a friend who tells a friend and soon word spreads. People start showing up, asking my boss Mike if the palm reader is in and then, before long, the gig is up.

"Way to blow your first job, genius," Heather says, smirking at me over breakfast.

"Don't admit to anything," Patrick says.

"There are much more important things going on," Leonard says, holding one finger up and swirling it to take in the room or, perhaps, the flies in the room.

Eventually, Bertha pokes her head out of her office and asks me to come have a chat, which is how I know I'm in big trouble. Also because, once inside, she gestures for me to sit on the couch instead of the floor.

"I'd like to talk about what happened at the video store," she says.

I look at my hands. It's a junior-convict trick I know: don't speak until you know what, exactly, you're in trouble for.

"Did you feel you had to perform in that way?" she asks. "Did you feel it wasn't enough for you to just stock the videos?"

I'm still not sure which of my transgressions she's referring to, so I shrug.

Outside, the sky is a cliché: clouds are gathering, darkening.

She's looking and looking at me, so much there is a kind of heat building in the air between us.

"Listen, Elizabeth. I've been trying to steer you toward something delicately, but I suppose it might be better to just take the plunge and rip the Band-Aid off." She must be nervous. She's mixing metaphors, flapping her hands about.

"I've consulted with Dr. Mink and some others and we're all in agreement that you were most likely misdiagnosed," she says. "We don't believe you were ever suffering from schizophrenia, like was previously thought. We believe you were suffering from something called folie à deux."

"Folie a *what*?"

"Deux," she says. "It means a madness shared by two. You and your mother in this case."

I look at her finally. Her hair is different today. It's gathered into a bun that's pierced through with chopsticks.

She moves closer to me on the couch.

"It happens when the parent is unwell and suffering from delusions. The child loves the parent so much, and wants to see what the parent sees so badly, they take on the delusions. They sort of catch them in a way, like a virus. They may have visions or hear voices or believe they have special powers. Like, for example, clairvoyance."

So it *is* the palm reading I'm in trouble for.

The first drops of rain hit her office window.

"The point is," Bertha says, "eventually a separation must occur. The delusions must come to an end. The parent must go their own way, and the child must return to reality. Which can be quite painful, as you know."

Climax, she's saying, denouement.

There are so many things I want to say just then. Such as: where exactly is the line between illness and imagination, between helping someone with a story and harming them? And what exactly is the difference between hope and delusion, between thinking you are something and actually being it? And besides, isn't all love a form of delusion?

I suppose she will add that to her "good mother" list later: *no delusions, not ever.*

I want to tell her that, for me, there had only ever been two outcomes: to be disabled or to be extraordinary, that Margaret was a good mom who gave me the best story she could. What's so wrong with a love like that? I want to ask, or do, because she answers.

"There's nothing *wrong* with it, Hon'," she says. "But I think you deserve to know the truth." She stands and goes to her desk. She picks up a piece of paper, brings it over and lays it on the table in front of me, carefully, like it might burst into flames.

It's a photocopy of a newspaper article. "Miracle baby born with heart outside body," the headline reads. There's a photo of Margaret in the hospital. She's leaning on the edge of the bed, holding a baby: me. "Margaret Squire and baby Elizabeth," the caption says. I'm swaddled and she's smiling for the camera. The article talks about how I was born with a rare heart condition, about how my mother had to have an emergency c-section, how, in my first weeks of life, I underwent two separate surgeries to repair my heart and almost didn't make it. There's no mention of Michael. No mention of Margaret having to choose between us. No mention of us being Siamese or joined.

The ground is breathing beneath me, like I'm perched atop a sleeping giant who is about to wake up.

She hands me another piece of paper, a hospital birth record. My name is listed there, next to Margaret's. Only my name.

She hands over a third and final piece of paper, a different kind of record, dated three years earlier. She tap-taps her finger on the date. Then she points to some other words directly across the page, the words *Michael Squire* and, *Stillborn.*

"I'm sorry but it seems you never had a twin brother, Elizabeth," Bertha says.

She slides closer to me on the couch. "I believe that was a story your mother told you because she was unwell. She was grieving the loss of her first child and maybe she felt guilty, maybe the guilt was unbearable, and she wanted you to carry some of that burden."

Feel What I Feel, I'm thinking.

Outside, the rain is coming down the way it does in this part of the world—in sheets, actual sheets.

"I believe that Michael was your first shared delusion," she continues. "She believed in him, so you did too, and everything went from there."

I've never sat in this particular spot on Bertha's couch before. From here I can see a framed needlepoint on the wall next to her bookshelf. It's old and unremarkable, something bought at a garage sale maybe. "Is it possible to overcome the past?" it asks.

It's strange that it's a question. Wouldn't it be more cheerful to say, "It is possible"? Wouldn't that be more appropriate for an office where such conversations take place?

"What do you think about all this, Hon'?" Bertha asks, coming closer. "I know it's a lot. Do you have any questions?"

That needlepoint is one of Bertha's doctor tricks, I'm sure of it. She probably made it herself and then rubbed coffee grounds into it to make it look old. I imagine her placing it here, at eye level, right before I came into the room just to provoke me.

"Stay with me, Hon'," Bertha instructs. She reaches for my hands and takes them in her own. "Stay where your hands are."

And then, to my surprise, I do have a question. "Did Margaret bring me here?" I ask. "Was it her who hired the lawyer who brought me to Willingdon? To Vancouver?"

She swallows hard. It makes a sound like *galump* at the base of her throat. She squeezes my hands harder than she probably means to. "No, Hon'. You were repatriated. Margaret had nothing to do with that."

So she *wasn't* behind it. She *isn't* coming for me.

I feel that old feeling again, that my heart is a yo-yo that has reached the bottom of its string.

Annie is right. Every story has a climax, a breaking point. Every life is hurtling toward it. Eventually every life goes shooting off that cliff edge.

My eyes are crying even though the rest of my body hasn't given permission.

Bertha comes around to my end of the couch and catches me, just as I fall sideways. She holds me as I fall and fall and fall apart.

It's not possible, I decide. It's not possible to heal from the past, not when your life, your whole life, is based on a lie.

CHAPTER 16

BEFORE

MY LAST MORNING AT THE FARM, THE CLOWNS LOADED THE BUS UP WITH BOXES and suitcases while I hung around in front of the house, waiting for Margaret. She never appeared.

When it was time to leave, I stuffed my feelings into an imaginary box and closed the lid tight. I set Runt down on the ground and walked away from him. He tried to follow, but I shooed him until he disappeared under the house with the rest of the chickens. I made sure I had Lucky's ten dollars tucked into my dress pocket. Then I climbed onto the bus and we drove away from the farm for good.

While we drove, the clowns talked about New York City. "Wait'll you see the place!" they said, and, "You won't believe the hotdogs!" They were trying to cheer me up. They kept saying that New York City was the centre of everything, that it was the belly of the beast, that when you were there, nothing else mattered.

But I didn't care about any of that. I lay on the bed at the back, picking the jewels and stitching off my eye patch. I didn't want to be MeMe the Amazing Wonder anymore. I didn't want to be anybody. I wanted to disappear.

We drove for hours. I could feel the thread between Margaret and me stretching out like an elastic band, pulled so tight it could break. The bus was roaring loud enough to cancel out all thoughts, all feelings. Eventually, I slept.

It was Roland who poked me awake. "Look," he said, pointing out the window. We were halfway across a long bridge. I sat up and saw a city shimmering and floating above the water in the distance, and for a second I wondered if it had been built that way, like a ship in the sky.

But the rest of the clowns were gathered at the windows with their mouths hanging open.

"It's like some sort of mirage," someone said.

"Like an optical illusion," said someone else.

We kept driving and, by the time we got to the end of the bridge, the mirage was over. The buildings were back on the ground again, wavering in the heat.

We were moving down a never-ending street. All the stores had bars over the windows. Every street corner was crowded with people. They were spilling off the curbs, wheeling in circles, selling bracelets, watches, uppers, downers, tickets, suitcases, balloons, hotel rooms. I'd never seen so many people selling so many things. People of every age and colour. They were shouting from the corners, shouting at traffic, at friends passing by, at the cops who pulled up in their cruisers.

It was like watching a parade except we were the ones moving. I pressed my face to the window, wondering where the centre of everything was and how Margaret would ever find me in this sea of people.

Eventually, we turned off that street and drove through a leafy neighbourhood with brick houses painted yellows and reds and browns. Each house had a staircase that spilled onto the sidewalk like a lazy tongue. Each staircase was crowded with people sipping drinks and eating dinner and playing dice.

Near the end of a long, dead-end street, we pulled over and parked in an alley.

"Welcome to Queens," Roland said and then we all piled off the bus and stood there, sticky with heat, next to a house the colour of earthworms.

The house had a large, paved yard with a chain-link fence around it and a sign that said "Garage" in thick black letters. Someone had added the word "Cosmic" above it in blue paint.

Roland rang the bell next to the sign. Standing there, waiting for someone to come, it did feel like we were in the belly of something. The air smelled like every kind of food all mixed together—spaghetti and curry and onions and bacon—and it was full of sounds—music, babies crying, laughing, pots clanging and, somewhere in the distance, a violin. I could sense all the people living all around us, next to each other and stacked on top of each other.

Finally, a man appeared. He waved, wearing rubber gloves that were stained blue to the wrists, and then opened the gate. We followed him into a garage with concrete floors. Two machines like the ones I'd seen at the farm were standing in the middle of the room. People with gloves and plastic gowns were hovering around them, putting paper in and pulling paper out the other side, wet with ink. These papers were passed carefully, person-to-person, until, finally, they were clipped to a line to dry. One whole side of the room was full of these drying papers, and each paper had a big blue sun on it.

"I'll show you to your room," Roland said, steering me past.

We went up some wooden stairs and into a grimy kitchen. I saw a leaning tower of pizza boxes, a sink overflowing with dishes. We stepped through a beaded curtain into a hallway. There was a staircase going down to my right. The floor and walls and ceiling were covered in gold shag carpet. It looked so inviting, like a fluffy tunnel. I turned to go down, but Roland got me by the shoulder and steered me straight, into a room with tall windows that faced the street. He spun me around to face him. "I don't want you going down those stairs, okay?"

When I asked why, he said the people who went downstairs didn't always come back.

I nodded and promised I wouldn't.

We were in a big room with an old fireplace and mantle. In a normal house this would have been the living room. There would've been a couch and a TV. But here there were only a few cushions lying around on the floor. There was a record player tucked in where the fire would've once burned. The walls were painted deep red and were crumbling in places, with bare patches where the bones of the house showed through. The windows were wide open to the street. A warm breeze blew through. Crumpled paper scuttled across the floor.

I missed Ontario suddenly. The nights curled up with Margaret on our couch, listening to our short-wave radio, dreaming about America. I missed *that* America, the one we had dreamed of.

"This way," Roland said, leading me up a flight of stairs.

The second floor was a long hallway of closed doors. Roland swung the first door open and said, "bathroom." We walked past four more closed doors and then he opened the last one at the end of the hall, saying, "your room."

It was a small, square room with writing all over the walls. There was a mattress in the corner that looked like a piece of toast—brown in the middle, white at the edges—and a sheet tacked to the window as a curtain. A candle stuffed into a wine bottle stood in the middle of the floor. The candle was burning. Someone's clothes were scattered across the floor. A pair of sneakers were parked by the bed.

Clearly it wasn't just my room. I would be sharing it with someone. Someone who'd just stepped away and would be right back.

Roland twirled a full circle in the middle of the room, looking pleased. "I have to go talk to some people, but I'll see you at dinner, okay?"

I nodded and he left.

I spun, reading what was written all over the walls: *Fuck the pigs, Love is all you need, Turn on.* And right there, on the wall above the mattress, the words *Rainbow wuz here.*

I heard her then, a high metallic voice floating in through the open window. It was getting louder, closer, and then the curtain was shoved aside and she came climbing into the room, feet first.

"Thought we heard you," she said with a smile. She was younger than me, but tougher than I'd imagined. She was missing both front teeth and her hair was clumped together in thick, tangled ropes. She was dressed ordinarily enough, in a striped tube top and jeans, but she looked like the kind of person who'd steal your lunch if you weren't careful.

A tall, Black boy climbed through the window after her. "King," he said. He reached out to shake my hand and gave me a weird smile, with his lips all scrunched up like he was about to kiss a strange aunt. He was older, and he looked as if he came from a real home where someone washed his clothes. He was wearing brown bell-bottoms with crisp creases on the legs and a shirt with the collar buttoned all the way up, the cuffs buttoned all the way down. He had a tidy afro and a thin line of peach fuzz above his top lip.

"You wanna help us find Spots?" he asked.

"He escaped this morning," she said. She sprayed her *s*'s when she talked—*ethcaped*—and her tongue poked out between her teeth. It was stained dark purple.

"*She*, stupid," King said. "Ever seen a *he* lay an egg?"

Rainbow didn't seem to mind being called stupid. She laughed and pulled a packet of Kool-Aid from her back pocket. She licked her fingers and dipped them in, then brought them to her mouth and sucked. I noticed her fingers were also stained purple from doing that.

"Want thome?" She held it out to me.

I shook my head no.

She shrugged, tucking the Kool-Aid into her pocket again.

King led us back out the window, onto a wide stretch of roof. There were some plants growing in buckets out there and a lean-to made out of apple crates with the words "Chicken Koop" painted on the side. We went around a corner and up a ladder that led to a higher roof. The surface was covered with broken glass, but we kicked it aside and sat, looking out at the city that stretched as far as I could see in all directions.

King pulled a flat, metal bottle from his back pocket. He took a few sips and squinted out at the view. "She'll be someone's dinner if we don't find her."

"Yup, fried chicken," Rainbow said, squinting just like him and swirling her finger in her belly button, which was also stained purple.

I thought of Runt and then Margaret, and it felt like someone was squeezing my heart in their fist. I checked to see if Lucky's ten-dollar bill was still in my dress pocket. I tried to guess how far it was to the farm, and I wondered if ten dollars would get me there.

Just then, Rainbow leaned in, wrapped her sticky purple fingers around my arm and said, "What'd you do?"

I pulled my arm away. "What?"

"To get sent here," she said. "You musta done something."

"Or *didn't* do something," King said, handing her the bottle.

"Yeah, like I didn't do what I was told," Rainbow explained, "and he got stung by a poison bee. That's why we're here."

"Not a *poison* bee," King corrected. He turned to me as if only I could understand what he was about to say next. "I'm *allergic*. My tongue swells up."

"You both used to live at the farm?" I asked.

"Years ago," Rainbow said, taking a sip from the bottle and scrunching her face up like a walnut.

"*One* year ago," King corrected, but the way he said it, it sounded like, "one year ago, *stupid*."

"So what'd you do?" Rainbow asked again.

They were both looking at me, waiting for an answer.

I thought of telling them about my mistakes: how I'd said too much and been too needy, how at first I wasn't good enough at my job and then I was too good. But instead I said, "I don't really know."

They both nodded like that made perfect sense to them.

King nudged Rainbow to pass me the bottle. I was so thirsty I took a big sip and immediately had to spit it out. It tasted like a burnt eraser.

They both started laughing. It was the exact same laugh, high pitched and out of control, except he covered his mouth when he laughed and she did the opposite. She threw her head back, and I could see all the way down her purple throat like she was a baby bird.

"C'mon," King said when they'd both recovered. He climbed down the ladder and reached back to help me. Rainbow came last.

We walked to the fire escape at the edge of the lower roof. We stood on its platform and looked down at all the things going on below us. A man rattling a shopping cart full of bottles down the alley. A couple of dogs bickering over a bag of open garbage. Kids playing jump rope. Mothers leaning out of windows, shouting their names, calling them home for dinner.

I raised my hand to my eyes and peered out at the city. I tried to find the street we'd come in on, but I couldn't. There were too many buildings.

"Where's the centre of everything?" I asked.

"There," Rainbow said, pointing to the tallest buildings, way off in the distance. "That's Manhattan, but we're not allowed."

She was standing so close to me, I could smell her. She smelled like garbage and something else I couldn't quite place: *flowers? pee?* I stepped away, but she followed, tripping over her own feet.

"Guess she's gone," King said, sighing down at the neighbourhood with his hands on his hips.

My stomach dropped. He meant Spots of course, but all I could think about was Margaret.

"Did your moms say they'd come and get you?" I asked.

They looked at me blankly.

"When you were sent away, did your moms say they'd come right after you?"

King stood tall and lifted his chin. "I don't have a mom."

"And I only got Thamuel," Rainbow added.

I wanted to argue with them, to say that everyone has a mom, even if she's not around much. And I was about to remind Rainbow that she had her aunt, O, but King was staring at me like I'd better shut up.

"Who's Thamuel?" I asked instead and that made them both break into that high-pitched laugh again.

Before they could answer, a cowbell started clanging somewhere below us.

They straightened up and King handed me the bottle again.

This time I was ready. I took a small sip. I felt it burn all the way down and, to my surprise, this time I liked it. It melted the lump that had been in my throat all day.

Everyone was gathered in the living room for a meeting. There was a clown standing in front of the fireplace, waiting to start. He had black diamonds painted around his eyes and a big red frown painted over his mouth. He kept sighing and checking his watch. "Somebody want to go downstairs?"

The woman with the cowbell jumped up and went over to the gold shag staircase. She hit the bell a few more times and, pretty soon, people started coming up the stairs. I remembered what Roland had said, about how the people down there didn't always come back and they did look strange, like they hadn't seen daylight in a while. They found places at the edges of the room and the meeting began.

It was like a regular dinner meeting only it was all about clowning and there was pizza. They passed boxes of it around so everyone got to eat while they talked about how many posters and pamphlets they had, and who would deliver them and where. I noticed the boxes we'd brought with us on the bus were stacked in a corner of the room.

Rainbow knelt next to me, carefully picking the pepperoni off her pizza and stuffing it into her pants pockets. That's what that smell was, I realized: old pepperoni.

On the other side of her, King was doing something strange too. He was rolling the pizza up into a tube and stuffing it carefully into the side of his mouth. "What?" he said when he saw me watching.

The clown talked about how there were a few big concerts coming up, how people would be coming from all over the country, and this was a good opportunity to reach a new audience. He said if we did things right, each person would take the message back home with them and spread the word wherever they were from. "Remember, we aren't just delivering the message, we *are* the message," he said. "Our words, our deeds, our acts, all of these are the message. We need to *be* the love. *Be* the courage. *Be* the message."

A few people clapped and he sat. Then another man stood. It was the man I'd seen outside the factory, back on the farm. He looked a little like a clown himself. He was bald except for two tufts of red hair that stood out from his head in perfect triangles. He was wearing a rumpled corduroy suit and he had thick, round glasses that made his eyes look faraway and raisiny. He kept scratching his head, looking around nervously. "No offence, but I do believe the time for that type of activity has passed. A war is raging on the other side of the world, folks! We need to be working on something a little bigger now." He talked about something called "an intervention," and something else called "Cosmic Blue." He said he had perfected the formula, that we could wake people up through their skin now, even those who didn't want to be woken up, but he needed help. Then he acted like Judy, naming jobs and spinning in a circle while people raised their hands, calling him "Professor" and "Samuel."

"That's Samuel?" I asked Rainbow.

"My thtep dad," she said without looking up. She had moved on to picking the onions off her pizza now. These, she flicked onto the floor in a small circle all around her.

"Watch it," a woman said when one landed on her foot. She flicked it back at Rainbow, and it landed on her arm with a wet smack.

The sad clown stood again. He said that maybe we should be focused on reaching the people who *wanted* to be reached. There were all kinds of people out there who were searching for something, he said. Nobody should be forced.

Samuel tilted his head back, closed his eyes halfway and spoke in a sleepy voice about how every civilization throughout the history of the world went through this: a time of expansion followed by a time of decline. He sounded just like O when he talked, half-bored and half-awake. He said the signs were always the same: war, oppression, one man up, another man down. He said that the pinnacle of our system had been reached, and now it had to be dismantled, that there was no more time for clowning or volunteerism anymore. He said it was time to make a pow.

"Excuse me," a man sitting at the back of the room said, "but violence only leads to more violence." The crowd parted so he could push his wheelchair forward. He only had one leg and looked like he might know a thing or two about violence. "If you ask me, what you're proposing is violent," he said. "It may not involve guns or bullets, but it *is* violent."

The clowns clapped.

Some of the downstairs people chimed in, and then the room erupted into a bunch of different arguments. People were up, shouting at one another.

"Let's go," King said. He turned and walked toward the front door of the house, grabbing a backpack off the hook on his way out. Rainbow scrambled after him, a limp piece of pizza still in her hand. "You too," she called back to me, so I followed.

The sun had just gone down, but it was still sticky-warm outside. Neighbours were still sitting out on their front steps, drinking lemonade and fanning themselves. They watched as King pulled a long beige jacket out of his backpack and put it on. I thought he looked very professional with that jacket, like a businessman about to make a deal, but the neighbours were shaking their heads at him. He had a jacket for Rainbow too, a short, puffy red one. I was glad he didn't have one for me.

"Boogie time," he said once they were both dressed. Then he led us down the block, right down one alley, left down another and straight into a gang of skinny dogs. They circled around us, snarling and showing their teeth.

King extended his arm in front of me. "Don't move."

"They're furled," Rainbow said, bumping into me from behind.

"Not *furled*," King corrected. "*Feral*," and once again I thought I heard that word, *stupid*, haunting the end of his sentence.

I could see it then, how dirty the dogs were, with bald patches and mangled fur. I wondered if they'd belonged to families once and what had gone wrong—if they'd got lost, or if they'd made a mistake and been locked out on purpose.

"Watch this," Rainbow said, reaching into her pants pocket to pull out her wad of pepperoni. She threw it to the dogs and then we were able to pass.

"Rule number one," King said as we ran past. "Always have pepperoni."

We ran down one alley and then another. While we moved, King pointed things out and listed more rules. Rule number two was always take the alleys. Rule number three was always walk down the middle of the alleys, especially in our neighbourhood, and *extra-specially* after dark.

"How do I know what's our neighbourhood?" I asked.

He pointed up at an empty pole. "By the street signs."

"But there is no sign."

"*Exactly*," he said. Then he kept on with his rules. I didn't mind though because he talked in poems. He called feet *dogs* and dogs *mutts* and men *cats*. He called faces *mugs* and hands *mitts*. He talked about the police a lot, but he called them the Fuzz. "The Fuzz is everywhere," he said, circling his finger in the air, "and don't ever forget it."

Rule number four was don't trust anyone, not even the hennies, which is what he called the women who hung around on corners in short skirts and tall boots, calling out to us whenever we passed. He said they wanted what we had and, therefore, couldn't be trusted.

"What do we have?" I asked, but just then a door swung open and a flaming pan came flying out. It soared through the air like a UFO before skidding to the ground. A man in a white hat came after it, swearing and batting at it with a towel. We hid behind a dumpster until the man went back inside again. Then we ran.

"Rule five," Rainbow said, once we'd stopped to catch our breath a few blocks later. "Watch out for flying frying pans."

"Or frying flying pans," King added and then they both broke into that high-pitched giggle again.

"No, but seriously," King said, once he'd regained control. "Rule number six is don't be seen by anyone when we're working."

"Are we working?" I asked and then they both looked at each other and rolled their eyes.

We were crouched against a wall in the mouth of an alley. There was a bright, busy street in front of us. People were shopping, busses were roaring past, taxis were pulling up, people getting out, other people getting in. I had that feeling again, that I was watching a parade. It seemed like this city was full of every kind of person, wearing every kind of clothing, with every kind of haircut. I wondered how many of them had mothers at home, how many had lost one along the way. But I didn't have time to dwell on this because Rainbow had pulled a new packet of Kool-Aid out of her back pocket, red this time. She ripped the top open and spat into it. Then, while she squished it all around, she said, "He'll go first, then me, then you."

"Yeah, so act like you don't know us," King added. "And count to twenty after Rainbow leaves."

He glanced out at the street before adding one last thought: "And whatever you do, please, *please* try to play it cool."

I nodded, even though I had no idea what either of them were talking about.

King was watching the foot traffic. He seemed to be waiting for something.

"Rule theven," Rainbow whispered, so close I could smell her pizza breath, "don't ever feel bad about it."

"About what?"

"Watch," she said.

Then they both pushed off the wall and stepped out into the human parade.

I followed.

We walked half a block and stopped in front of a small grocery store. We were wandering in among the bins of apples and potatoes outside the door, pretending not to know each other, playing it cool.

King went into the store first. The door chimes rang. Rainbow was looking at some potatoes but counting under her breath. I could see her mouth moving—*five, thix, theven.* When she got to twenty, she went in after him. I ran my hand over a pile of shiny red apples, counted to twenty and followed.

It was a small store with low shelves. Rainbow was over by the fridges. King was near the door, looking at the bubble gum. I pretended I didn't know them. I went over to the cereal section. I was looking at the boxes, making up a story in my mind: that I lived around the corner, that my mom had sent me to get breakfast for tomorrow.

The shopkeeper was behind the counter. The TV news was blaring back there. Walter Cronkite was on the screen, talking about all the trouble in the streets. I was so happy to see him I almost waved at the TV. It was like seeing a long-lost uncle.

I was trying to play it cool, but my head kept darting around. I was trying to watch Cronkite and Rainbow and King and the shopkeeper all at once.

The shopkeeper wasn't looking at me though. His eyes were on King, following his every move. "May I help you?" he asked.

"No, *Sir*, I'm doing *just* fine!" King said.

Then there was a smash and a squeal. Rainbow had dropped something. The shopkeeper ran out from behind his counter. I came running too, even though King was shaking his head at me.

Rainbow was standing in a puddle of spilt milk, crying. She was bent down, collecting the pieces of broken glass. There were bright drops of blood in the milk. Blood was running down her hand.

"Stop. Please, allow me," the man said. Then, when he bent down to clean up the mess, she nodded to King, who began filling the pockets of his jacket.

"You missed one," Rainbow said to the shopkeeper. She was pointing to a piece of glass in the milk behind her. The man circled behind her to get it.

That's when King made a run for it. The bell rang as he went. The man stood. "Hey you. Get back here you little—" He tried to step around Rainbow, but she was blocking his way.

"Wait," she said, grabbing his arm. "I should pay you for the milk."

The man pushed her aside and went after King. He opened the door and looked up and down the sidewalk, but he was gone. He came back inside. "Did you know that boy?" he asked her.

She blinked up at him. "What boy?" She was a good actress. She could be in movies someday if not for her hair, I thought.

The man gave her a new bottle of milk and threw in a box of Band-Aids. She tried to pay him, but he refused to take her money. She shoved the Band-Aids in per pocket, and said sorry for the mess. Then she left and he went back to the fridge to finish cleaning up.

I stood in front of a wall of soup cans—mushroom, tomato, chicken noodle—counting to twenty, remembering how Margaret used to make me chicken noodle soup whenever I was sick back at Kraft Park. I wanted that chicken noodle soup now, more than anything. I reached for it and tucked it up inside the sleeve of my dress. Cronkite frowned down at me. With the soup in my sleeve, I walked to the end of the aisle and turned to leave.

"Do you know those two?" the man said, coming up beside me. "Were you all in on this together?"

My mouth flapped open-closed. I couldn't lie to the man, not with Uncle Cronkite watching. But I didn't have to.

He looked at my eye patch and something softened in him. He took a pack of gum off the rack and handed it to me. "Never mind," he said. "Come again."

I found them behind a dumpster, halfway down the alley. Rainbow wasn't crying anymore. She was gulping milk from the bottle.

"Did you really cut yourself?" I asked.

"Course not." She smiled and wiggled her Kool-Aid-stained hand at me.

"Give me that," King said. He poured some of the milk out on the ground and dumped two tubes of Whoppers into the bottle. He tipped his silver bottle over the top too and shook it all up. "Eggnog," he said. Then we leaned against the dumpster, passing it back and forth and that's exactly how it tasted, like Christmas in a big, fancy house somewhere far away.

King showed us what he'd got: gum, licorice, a handful of matchbooks, two bags of peanuts, some pepperoni, three chocolate bars. It all came tumbling out of his pockets and he dumped it into his backpack.

I showed what I'd got: the soup and the gum and a shiny, red apple I'd grabbed on my way out.

King snatched it all up and put it in the backpack too. Then he changed his mind and gave the apple back. He held it out to me, scrunching his lips into the kiss-face, which I now understood was his version of a smile. "Pretty good for your first time," he said.

"Totally feral," Rainbow said, giving me a high-five.

We stayed there, eating and drinking, and King explained that that's how it worked every time: one of us was the klutz, one was the helpful stranger and he got the goods.

He pulled a list out of his pocket of all the different things we were supposed to get that night and checked things off. I saw matches on the list and tape and nails.

"Next time you'll be the klutz," he said. "You ready for that?"

"Do I have to cry?"

"Yes and you have to bleed," Rainbow said, handing me the packet of red Kool-Aid.

"Can you?" King asked.

I thought of Margaret, so far away, doing who-knew-what without me.

"Yes," I said, "definitely."

We did two more corner stores and then a hardware store, although I was only allowed to watch there because it was harder. In that store there were no milk bottles to break, so Rainbow had to knock over a display of boxes and then fake some sort of attack, twitching and shaking where she lay, while King filled his pockets with nails. We would've stopped after that, but Rainbow claimed there was a new, blue Kool-Aid that had just come out, so we went to a few more stores looking for it.

While we walked between stores, King explained that we should never feel bad for what we were doing because we were just evening the score. We were sticking it to the Man, and the Man deserved it because he was always sticking it to us.

I stopped in the middle of the alley, climbed up on an overturned milk crate and asked: "Okay, but who is the Man? Like who *actually* is he?"

I must've said it in a funny way because they broke into that high-pitched laugh again, snorting and falling into each other, and the whole rest of the night, wherever we went, they climbed up onto things saying, "Okay but who *actually* am I?" and, "What *actually* are we doing?"

Rainbow and King knew their way around the neighbourhood. They knew which stores were best to steal from and exactly where to hide after. They knew the best fire escapes to climb up on and one place where, at 11 p.m. on the dot, a fat man in an apron came slamming out a metal door and dumped a whole crate of perfectly good donuts into the garbage can behind his building. As soon as he was gone, we opened the lid and took the best ones off the top of the pile.

They knew another place where, every night at the same time, we could stand in the bushes behind an apartment building and watch Johnny Carson through someone's open window.

And they knew a place where we could sneak in through the back door of an Italian restaurant, down some stairs and into a room full of booze. I stood watch while they took what they could, stuffing it into the backpack. King got a bottle of rum and a couple boxes of straws. Rainbow stole a jar of cherries and a box of little paper umbrellas.

Back out on the street again, we stood on a corner shouting about our straws and umbrellas, trying to sell them, and it occurred to me how quickly I had become one of those people I'd seen on my way into the city, that I was part of the human parade now too.

Nobody wanted what we were selling so we started home. "Pay attention," King said, pointing at me. "Because next time you lead the way."

"Rule one hundred fifty forty," Rainbow said, pointing a bright red finger at me too and scrunching her mouth in an impression of King, "Know your own way home," and then we all burst into the same high-pitched giggle.

Back at the house, King handed the backpack over to some people in the living room and we went upstairs.

In the bedroom, he stepped into the closet to get undressed. I saw him fold his pants over a hanger and then lick his fingers and very carefully pinch the creases all the way down each leg. He placed his shirt on the same hanger and buttoned all the buttons. Then he disappeared into the back of the closet. When he reappeared, he had two fuzzy blankets with him. He lay one on top of the mattress, straightening and smoothing it until it was just right.

"Get in," he said.

Rainbow took her shoes and jacket off and flopped down next to the wall. I lay next to her. He spread the second blanket over us and tucked it in neatly all around the edges of our bodies. Then he blew out the candle and wiggled in between us, with his head at the opposite end of the bed.

When we were all settled and Rainbow had finally stopped squirming, he said, "Remember the time we had to show Elizabeth around Queens?" He was chuckling to himself.

"Yeah, 'member she almost got hit by a flying frying pan?" Rainbow added, laughing too.

"And remember she kept asking about the Man?" he said.

"And she didn't even know how to get home?" she said.

They went back and forth this way for a while, "remembering" all the funny things I'd done that night and giggling about them until, eventually, they both fell asleep.

I lay awake, listening to them breathe, wondering why they wasted their time remembering things that had just happened. Then I thought of Margaret and Michael. I tried to imagine what Margaret was doing back at the farm at that very minute. Spinning around the fire probably.

I closed my eyes and tried to feel what she felt, and then I did. I was spinning too, spinning so fast I thought I might be sick.

I got up and climbed out the window just in time to puke Christmas-tasting milk all over the roof.

I wiped my mouth, walked to the edge of the roof and stood, looking down. So many people were moving through the streets, even at that hour. I took a step closer to the edge. There were so many lights on in so many windows. The flashing of a hundred TVs. I could hear the same show playing at the same time from a few different windows. How strange, I thought, to have so many people doing the same things at the same time and not even knowing it. Is this what O meant when she said people in the city were all one but had forgotten?

I tried to feel Margaret again, to feel what she felt across the miles, but I couldn't. Every part of me ached from missing her, even my ankles, even my elbows.

I rubbed my scar and said, "Michael, where are you?" but I couldn't feel him either.

There was a breeze coming up from the alley. I curled my toes over the edge of the roof and put my arms up. The wind caught the sleeves of my dress and, for a moment, it felt like I was flying.

I thought about tipping off. Would she feel it as a yank on her end of the cord like I had that last day at Kraft Park? Would she come to me then and sit by my bed, nursing me back to health just like at the beginning of our story?

I tipped my head back and closed my eyes. The wind filled my sleeves. It would be so easy to fall, I thought.

Then I heard a, "Hey you." I opened my eyes, expecting to see Michael, but it was a shirtless man leaning out the window across the alley. "You crazy?" he shouted. "Get offa there." He threw something at me, a chicken bone.

I picked up the chicken bone, waved and walked back to the window. I climbed back into the room and lay down. Rainbow rolled toward me, snoring softly. I imagined it was Margaret sleeping beside me and finally drifted off.

CHAPTER 17

AFTER

IT'S SUPPOSED TO BE SPRING NOW. VANCOUVER PUTS ON HER OTHER FACE, THE one that doesn't know anything about endless rain or low, grey skies. She's a liar, this Vancouver. She lures you in with her false weather.

I'm completely off my meds. I've whittled my pills down to their last sliver of dust. I've removed every last bead from the yellow submarine. There is nothing left now, no more extra padding between me and my mind, my mind and the world.

I collect my notes from the fish bins of Chinatown, from the pharmacy and liquor store and pub too, wondering why I ever thought Margaret would be in Vancouver anyway, feeling stupid for thinking she cared enough to bring me here.

I've given up on all that now, on her, wherever she is. I've given up on rescue. Whenever I think of Margaret, I can only think of the lie she let me believe: that I had a twin brother, that he'd died so I could live, that I owed him for that, that I owed her too. I think of how she planted the lie and tended it and watched it grow, and of how, over time, that lie devoured my whole life.

Everything is a trigger these days: Pepsi, pineapples, sunlight, the Sunlight soap in the kitchen, certain shades of blue, people standing on corners, businessmen in their suits, the smell of gasoline, garbage, coffee.

I find myself approaching people, wink-winking at them because they look like somebody I knew once, or who that someone might've become. "King?" I'll say to the mailman who has pulled up to the curb beside me to deliver a package; "Roland?" to the bus driver who doesn't look quite like a real bus driver, but like he might be clowning; "Lucky?" to the woman working behind the deli counter and then, when she doesn't respond to that, "Lorelai?" But it's never King, never Roland, never Lucky or Lorelai.

"It's perfectly normal to be reminded of the past," Bertha says. "It's what you do with those reminders that counts. And from what I can see here, you're really engaging with the process!" She's flipping through my weekly journal, my record of "episodes" and how I got through them. But my journal is mostly lies. I haven't said about the wink-winking at people. Never trust a writer to tell the truth.

I haven't said how, at certain times of day, everybody I pass on the street looks familiar, like somebody I've known and let down before.

Or how sometimes, walking home, I'll get a whiff of old pepperoni and I'll turn around, and then around again, thinking it's Rainbow sneaking up on me after all these years.

I haven't said how, when this happens, I have to come straight home, straight up to my room and climb into the cool dark of my closet for a time. Or how, when I'm sitting there, sometimes I run my fingers up and down my scar and talk to him, Michael, because even though I've given up on Margaret, I'm having a harder time giving up on him.

"You're doing great, Hon'," Bertha says. "Just great."

She's a liar too. It's the "just" in "just great" that gives her away.

Mr. Twohig and I are reading *The Metamorphosis*. We talk a lot about what it must feel like to wake up, suddenly transformed, in a world that doesn't make sense anymore. "Or is it the world that's transformed?" he asks. "Is it ourselves that don't make sense anymore?" We don't always find the answers, me and Mr. Twohig, but that doesn't seem to be the point. The point seems to be to ask the questions.

Annie has heard about my "lost decade" and, knowing I'm reluctant to talk about it, she decides to teach me how to write haikus because, she says, 5-7-5 is a great way to sneak up on what is most painful or fleeting. She decides this is the perfect opportunity to teach me how to type too. So I spend an entire session sitting at Bertha's typewriter, pecking out what it's like to live in a dorm full of other criminally insane people, "growing fatter-er" and "more mushroomy-y" by the day before she finally grows weary of syllables and asks me to just write free-form, by hand.

So then I write about the grey blur, about being so medicated I couldn't tell the days apart, couldn't remember who I was or how I'd got there. I write about the noises at night: people howling, the squeak of the nurse's shoes rushing down the long hallways toward one emergency or another. I write about my roommate, Daisy, who only ever talked about her mother's apple-raisin pie, sometimes chanting the words so fast they became a prayer—*appa raise up high*—until the day she got tired of all that and bit her own tongue in half. Or my other roommate, Wynona, who kept stealing things from me—my hairbrush, my best pen, a Slinky toy one of the janitors had given me— and distributing them to the other inmates on our floor. I write about how, once, we entered the art room to find a girl named Rhiannon—a girl I had liked, who sometimes gave me her unwanted toast—hanging from a window latch with that Slinky, which had been painstakingly uncoiled and smoothed flat, wrapped around and around her neck. I write about how a life on the inside is like that: one thing piles on top of another until, eventually, you are buried.

I never do go back to the video store. Bertha assigns me and Leonard to look after the sick tomato plants in the greenhouse, the ones that look like they might not make it. There is a metaphor in this that I don't want to know about. Leonard teaches me how to repot the plants, crushing up eggshells and adding them to the new soil, propping the plants up with popsicle sticks if they need it. I even catch him talking to one. "You can do it," he says, stroking its leaves. "You're stronger than you feel." And the crazy thing is, I start to notice that plant doing better than the rest, little yellow flower buds appearing at the ends of its branches. Leonard says each of these flowers will become a tomato one day, but I don't believe him. I don't believe anyone anymore.

In Group, we're working on making amends. We make lists of all the people we need to apologize to. Then we practise by saying sorry to each other.

Heather keeps winking at me. She thinks we're friends, which is why, one day, I decide to confess. I stand before everyone in Group and tell them about my crime—the whole, ugly truth. I admit to my mistakes, and then that my mistakes weren't actually mistakes but poor choices I made, one after another. I wear the blame squarely on my shoulders. I even cry a little. And it feels good in a way.

But it doesn't work. Once I'm done, they all look at me like I'm a good person who did a bad thing, like there is still hope for me and I am, in the end, forgivable.

Bertha applauds.

Patrick hugs me too tight, for too long, saying, "I know, I know."

Leonard shakes my hand.

And after Group, Heather comes up to me all the same. "Pssst, Killer," she whispers with something like admiration in her eyes. Then she tells me Tad just bought a van, that they're leaving soon and I should definitely come with.

That weekend, perhaps as a reward for my confession, Bertha rents a car and takes Patrick, Leonard, Heather and me to a place called, appropriately, Wreck Beach. She brings a basket full of egg-salad sandwiches and we all sit, huddled on a blanket in the middle of a crowded beach, blinking into the wind, looking exactly like mental patients. But then, later, the wind dies down and we roll up our pant legs and walk to the water's edge. Once we're in up to our knees, *ooohing* and *aaahing* at the different shells we see, we blend right in with the rest of the people. Or they blend in with us. We all look equally mental, and I wonder for a moment if we aren't all the same, if all of us don't have lost years and stolen Slinkys and huge mistakes we have to live around the edges of.

CHAPTER 18

BEFORE

IN THE MORNING KING KNELT OVER ME, SHAKING ME AWAKE, SAYING, "THESE are your good-girl clothes. Put 'em on." He handed me a stack of clothes: a blue plaid dress with a belt, socks and shoes, a ribbon for my hair. Then he shoved me aside so he could fold our blankets and tuck them away at the back of the closet again.

In the middle of the room, Rainbow was already wiggling into a dress that was more ridiculous than mine. It was pink and poufy, with a huge bow in the back. She tied her hair with her own pink ribbon and then helped me do mine.

When I was dressed, she stood back to look at me. "Lady!" she said, but like *laaay-dee*, as if it was a huge compliment. She rummaged through a bag in the closet and came up with a bottle of perfume. She sprayed it on her wrists and dabbed it behind her ears. Then she sprayed some on me and we went downstairs, smelling fancy.

The morning meeting was already underway. The clowns and the downstairs people were arguing again. Some people were ripping open boxes, pulling out stacks of paper and stuffing them into canvas bags. Others were trying to stop them.

I moved around the edges of the room, looking up at every face, tugging on sleeves and asking, "Have you seen Margaret? Or Fran? Or Sisco?"

"Who're they?" people asked.

I explained that she was only one person but with many names. I described exactly how she looked—her eyes and her freckles and her red hair that could sometimes change colour if she was standing in front of a bright light, but nobody knew anyone like that.

Then, finally, a man told me the bus was making another trip later that night, that she'd probably be on it. I felt a yank in the centre of my chest and decided to take that as proof she was on her way.

Just then, Rainbow and King came up behind me, saying, "Let's go." When they turned to leave, I noticed they each had a heavy-looking canvas bag slung over their shoulder.

I remembered Margaret's last instructions to me: to behave myself and do what was asked. I followed after them.

Out on the sidewalk, we walked past a bunch of kids who were lined up, waiting for their school bus. They had backpacks, bright scrubbed faces, perfect clothes, probably moms and dads.

We weaved in between them saying, "excuse me, sorry, excuse me."

"Look, it's the stinkies," a boy said, holding his nose as we passed.

Rainbow took a step toward him with her fists up but, luckily, King was right behind her. He pulled her back by the bow of her dress and led her away.

We walked in silence for a while. Rainbow's hands were still clenched into fists and King was muttering to himself, so I tried their trick. "Remember the time Rainbow almost beat up a schoolboy for calling her stinky?" I said.

They both laughed and, after that, their moods improved a little. I understood then why they were always remembering everything. It made the bad things seem farther away.

Eventually we entered a nicer part of town with cafés and proper street signs. King led us to an intersection. There, near the mailboxes on the corner, he pulled a wad of rubber gloves out of his pocket and threw them in the garbage behind him. Then they each reached into their canvas bags and grabbed a stack of pamphlets.

I took one off the top of Rainbow's pile. It was folded into three and on the front there was a blue sun. The rays went all the way to the edges of the page and were crowded with writing. The centre of the sun was a blue dot with a smiley face in the middle, the same blue dot I'd seen drying in the printing shed back at the farm. I reached down to touch it, but Rainbow snatched it back.

"Don't touch any more than you have to," she said.

"Why?" I asked.

"You're not ready," she said, and before I could ask what that meant, King started explaining the day's rules.

Rule one was we weren't allowed to go back home until our bags were empty.

Rule two was to always watch for the Fuzz. "And remember," he said, "the Fuzz can be undercover. They can look like anything, even a housewife or a hobo."

"So how do we recognize them?" I asked.

"Watch for the giveaways," Rainbow said.

Before I could ask, King listed the giveaways. One was if the person was too clean—if they smelled like laundry soap, or their fingernails were too nice. Another was if they were too friendly, asking where I lived and where my mom and dad were. "If anyone's asking questions like that," he said, "cut and run."

Cut and run, Rainbow explained, meant walking up to the nearest mailbox, dumping our pamphlets in and running.

It was a busy intersection. We stood there watching for a minute. Every time the light changed, people would form a big crowd on the corner, waiting to cross. King waited until the crowd had reached its peak and then he pushed off into the middle of it, snaking between people, asking,

"Tired of the grind?" and, "Want to know what real freedom feels like?" He had pamphlets spread out in his hand, like *pick a card, any card*, and he kept jabbing them at people, saying, "Take one. It'll change your life." Then, when the light changed and the crowd stepped into the street, he went with them, stuffing pamphlets into people's hands and pockets and purses all the way across the intersection until he was on the other side.

That's when Rainbow made her move. "Stay here," she said, stepping into the crowd on our side of the intersection.

She had a different approach. She didn't talk nearly as much. Instead, she came up next to people and leaned against them the way she did with me. When they looked down and saw her, and then smelled her, a look came over their faces. I knew that look. It was the same one the shopkeeper had given me the night before, the one people always gave me back in Ontario too. It was pity. People felt sorry for Rainbow and, for the first time, I could see how there was power in that. She held a pamphlet out and smiled up at them. They smiled back and took it. She didn't even have to say anything. Then she moved on to the next person.

When Rainbow and King crossed paths in the middle of the intersection, they pretended not to know each other. Then they waited on opposite corners and did it all again.

After they'd crossed back and forth a few times, they both returned to me.

"How many?" King asked.

"Forty-five," she said.

"Liar," he said. Then he looked all around, said, "Let's go," and we were on the move again.

We had to walk six blocks until we found another suitable corner. That was another one of his rules: never work corners too close together.

"Why?" I asked. But I knew the answer as soon as the question was out my mouth.

"The *Fuzz*, Eliza*beth*," they both said at the same time.

We worked for hours, moving from one corner to another. I wasn't allowed to hand out any pamphlets for a long time. Instead, I had to stand behind the mailbox and keep an eye out for clean men who asked too many questions. I had to hold each of their bags and make sure I didn't mix them up because it was a competition to see who had handed out more.

Once, while they worked, I pulled a pamphlet out of the bag and looked at it. The rays of the sun were crowded with questions: *Would you like freedom from working for the Man? From meaninglessness and loneliness? From playing the role society has given you?* Every ray had an arrow pointing toward that smiley face in the centre of the sun. The second page was all about returning to oneness, how it was the ultimate truth but somehow we had all forgotten. The page was crowded with those strange symbols Margaret used to draw on the atlas back on the bus—a village of little stick people and their houses. I ran my fingers over them, trying to feel her, until my fingertips were coated in blue ink. The last page was about the evils of capitalism and how its time was nearly up. I tried to read as much as I could, as quickly as I could, but King was watching me from the other side of the intersection.

After working corners, we moved on to subway stops. Rainbow and King stood at the tops of staircases, sticking their hands out into the stream of people coming up. They didn't bother with the people going down because they all seemed to be late and grumpy about the day ahead. I thought of what O was always saying back at the farm, about how everyone in the city was trapped on a big wheel, running and running, and standing there, watching them all pass with scowls on their faces, it seemed true.

I wasn't allowed to help until later, after we'd taken a bus to a busier part of town. There, Rainbow and I stood in front of a Macy's that looked like a big, round spaceship, holding the doors open for people, offering them pamphlets and wishing them a nice day.

King stood off to the side, watching us work. He couldn't hand things out here, he'd explained. And he was right, the shoppers got a pinched look on their faces when they saw him. They drew their purses in close to their bodies and rushed past.

Eventually, a man in a grey uniform came along and told us to beat it. After that, we walked across the highway, down a treeless street and then around a corner, into a rougher part of town. Here the sidewalks were full of people with bad teeth, who all seemed to be wearing either too little clothing or too much. None of them seemed to be going anywhere at all. They just strutted the same block all day long, bouncing their eyebrows up-down at people, saying, "*Pssst, whachyouwant?*"

In this neighbourhood it was easy to hand out pamphlets. All we had to do was stand on the corner and the people came to us with their hands out. I gave them two, three, four pamphlets each. I would've given more, but King had a rule about that.

I liked this neighbourhood. Everyone knew each other's names. People yelled to one another from across the street. They yelled up to the windows above, too, and their friends threw things down to them. There was a blind lady standing on the corner selling little pies she'd baked. A woman in a bikini smashed a watermelon open on the edge of a fire hydrant and was giving away the jagged pieces. There was a man sitting on an empty bucket, playing it like a drum and, all up and down the sidewalk, people were dancing to his music, even if they didn't know it. Margaret would have loved it there, I remember thinking. It was the real America.

The corners were full of the women King called hennies. When they saw us coming, they called out to us, "Hey babies, got some for us?"

Rainbow and King kept walking, but I stopped and one of them came over. She bent down to look at me. Her boobs were squeezing out the top of her shirt. Her eyelids sparkled purple.

"Lulu's a big believer in what you're doing," she said, reaching out to take my hand in hers. She smelled like peaches and cigarettes.

"Who's Lulu?" I asked. "And what am I doing?"

She threw her head back and laughed. "Sometimes I sure do wonder that myself." She was squeezing my hand so tight and her peach smell was so strong it was making me dizzy.

I was starting to get a MeMe feeling about her, a feeling about what was behind the big laugh and the peaches. I sensed her sadness and how tired she was of pretending to be happy all day long. I sensed that her name wasn't even Lulu, that she had left her body and her name a long time ago, that part of her was way up in the air right this minute—*pffft*—looking down on everything. And I sensed that we were the same, me and Lulu, always having to perform, always leaving ourselves behind.

I handed her a whole stack of pamphlets even though it was against the rules. She smiled and folded them into her purse.

"You keep doing what you're doing, Hon'," she said, patting my hair.

It felt so good to be patted and called that, I leaned in for a hug.

"Okay, Sweetie," she said, "we can do that." She sat down, right there in the middle of the sidewalk and pressed my head to her chest and rocked me back and forth, making little cooing sounds at the back of her throat. We must've stayed like that for a long time, too long, because a tall man in a leather jacket came hissing around the corner. He hit me with his cane on the back of my legs and told me to keep it moving.

I stood and that's when I noticed his aura. It was reaching up around him like flames. Then I saw that everyone on the sidewalk was trailing a different colour behind them, everyone was in flames.

"Git," the man said. He raised his cane again and I saw a long, thin lizard tongue flash out his mouth.

I ran down the block. I saw Rainbow up ahead of me. She was dancing in the middle of the sidewalk, grooving to some music I couldn't hear.

I ran over to her. "Do you feel funny?"

"Very!" she shouted over the music in her mind.

That's when King came marching up to us. His eyes were huge. "Cut and run!" he said. "Cut. And. Run."

We made a beeline for the nearest mailbox and dropped our remaining pamphlets in the slot. "Come *on*, man," the people on the sidewalk groaned behind us.

We ran into the park. King made us do a few laps around the path. Then, when we'd convinced him nobody was following us, we sat down on a bench near a fountain.

"Act like a norm," he said out the side of his mouth.

What's a norm? I was thinking to myself.

But Rainbow had already read my mind. "A *normal*," she whispered.

The park was full of norms: business people on their coffee breaks, moms pushing strollers, kids just out from school. Some teenagers were blowing bubbles on the other side of the fountain. A man was playing a guitar. Someone was selling hotdogs.

We sat there for a while, acting like one of them. Nobody could tell we weren't. We were watching the fountain, the bubbles, the people. We were smiling but not too much. The air filled with hotdog smells and mist from the fountain. The sun danced through the trees and little patches of rainbow hung, impossibly, in the air.

Something strange was happening. I could hear my heart beating in my ears, but it seemed a long time between each beat. And in between each beat there was a rush of thought, each thought like a domino falling into the next, and then I felt how many thoughts in a second, all falling together every hour of the day. I felt how many were worries and how many were fears and then, all at once, all those dominoes in my mind, all those thoughts, lay down, all at once, and my mind was empty. Very empty. And still. Very still.

Hello, I thought, *here I am*, which made me wonder where I had been before.

I breathed.

I was very empty, very still.

I could see the air, what it was made of—tiny little pieces of dust, like a beautiful, twinkling soup—and I wondered why I had never seen that before, or if I had, why I had chosen to ignore it every moment of my life until now. Each piece of dust was spinning, sparkling, and all for me it seemed.

I turned to Rainbow and King. They were staring at the air too, with their mouths hanging open.

"It's all—"

"Squiggles," she said.

"Shapes," he said. He smiled at me—his first real smile—and I could see what he'd been hiding all this time. His mouth was crowded with teeth, teeth upon teeth, like he'd never lost a single one, and one of them—top, front—was grey and rotten. It let out a long, low *whooomp* like a foghorn and I had to look away.

I looked at the air again. Now it was full of shapes, and those shapes seemed to be moving, or sort of breathing, coming together and then drifting apart again.

"Everything's all—"

"Bigs," Rainbow said, grinning at me, "and smalls." She moved her hands like *abracadabra*. Hand open: bigs. Hand closed: smalls.

That's exactly what it was. Bigness followed by smallness.

I thought about that. We all did. We stared ahead, squeezing our hands open and closed over and over, feeling the bigs and the smalls, watching the beautiful dust making beautiful shapes in the air.

The rest of the afternoon passed like a strange dream. We played a game called Every Little Thing, where we all took off our shoes and crawled very slowly through the grass, looking at every little thing very carefully. "Look," one of us would say and then we'd all crowd around to look at whatever we'd found. Once, it was an ant travelling on a hidden highway beneath the grass, carrying a piece of cracker bigger than himself. Once, a bee rolling around inside a flower until he was coated in yellow dust. Everything seemed to be humming and buzzing, even the leaves, even the stones. And then I knew, this was it, the beautiful feeling Margaret had talked about that first morning on the farm. I was finally feeling it too. I couldn't wait to tell her.

When we approached the house that evening, I saw the bus standing empty in the alley. I ran up the front steps of the house and opened the door, shouting her name. A bunch of people were crowded in the entryway. They turned to me with fingers over their lips, saying, "shhhht."

The living room was crowded too. People were even lined up along the stairs. All these people were here to listen to someone. A woman's voice was coming from the living room, talking about the Cause and how we were all part of something big and important.

It was Margaret, I could feel it. She was finally here.

"Margaret?" I shouted again. I was shoving past people, saying, "That's my mom. I need to get to my mom."

Margaret kept talking about how there were two Americas. How we were awake to the truth but they were not and everyone was *mmm-hmmming* and nodding.

I pushed my way into the living room.

Most people weren't brave enough to act, but *we* were, Margaret said. We were the last hope. Only our pamphlets could turn things around.

I was stepping on toes, hooking my fingers into people's back pockets and launching myself forward. I was getting closer to her. I could see her blue dress through the crowd. I was just about to reach out and tug on it when I heard a "not so fast." I felt two big hands around my waist. It was Roland. He lifted me up, threw me over his shoulder and carried me out of the room. It wasn't until we reached the top of the stairs that I was able to look down and see my mistake. It wasn't Margaret sitting in the middle of the room, but O. And next to her was Samuel, one whole side of his body touching one whole side of hers. Then while everyone in the room broke into applause, I saw Samuel lean over. He put a finger under O's chin, tipped her face up to his and kissed her right on the mouth.

"Where is she?" I screeched as soon as Roland set me down on the mattress. I scrambled up and charged at him. I couldn't control myself anymore. The lid on my feelings had flown right off. Tears and snot were running down my face.

"Not here," Roland said, holding me back with one arm.

"Then where?" I was kicking and throwing punches at him. It was him that had got us into this mess, I remembered, him who had tricked us that day at the diner.

He let me flail for a while, but after I'd got him in the shins a few times, he swooped down and caught me up in a bear hug. "You need to get yourself together," he said, squeezing all the air out of me. Then, when even that didn't work, he put his mouth to my ear and said that she was nearby, that she was sick and trying to get better for me.

With that, the fight went out of me. My body went limp. "Sick how?"

"She's trying to quit a bad habit," he said, loosening his grip and setting me back on my own feet.

"But is she up or is she down?" I asked.

He looked at me, puzzled.

"Does she have a headache or is she talking about the size of the universe?"

He still didn't know what I was talking about.

I kept seeing the same image, of her that day I had found her in bed at Kraft Park, her grey skin, the foam in her mouth. I was having trouble breathing. The edges of the room were closing in, darkening. Then my knees gave out.

"Elizabeth?" Roland said, stepping forward just in time to catch me.

"Go get some water and a cool cloth," he said to Rainbow and King, who must've been watching from the doorway the whole time. I could only imagine what they were thinking: *Remember the time Elizabeth lost her cool completely.*

He lay me down on the bed. He placed the back of his hand on my forehead, then my cheeks. "Jesus, what did you guys get into today?"

"Pamphlets," I heard Rainbow say.

"In the park," added King.

He asked if we were wearing our gloves.

They lied and said yes.

He asked what we'd eaten, whether we'd had anything to drink.

They answered, but I wasn't paying attention anymore. I was thinking about Margaret, thinking if O was kissing Margaret, then why was she kissing Samuel too? Had O and Margaret broken up? Had they fallen out of love?

Roland placed a cool cloth on my head. "Don't worry," he said, "it's probably just a bit of heat stroke."

But it wasn't me I was worried about. It was her. Only I knew how sick Margaret could get when she had lost the person she loved, how she would do anything to erase the pain.

That evening Rainbow and King had to go out to get supplies, but Roland stayed with me. He gave me a little lecture about always wearing gloves when I was working. He made me drink two full glasses of orange juice and eat a piece of pizza, crust too. Then he tucked me into bed and told me to close my eyes and try to think about something nice. He said he'd be right outside the window, to just holler if I needed him.

I was alone then, for the first time in days.

I could hear the city buzzing all around me, the clowns rehearsing outside the window, a group of pigeons out there asking *Who? Who?* over and over.

I closed my eyes and tried to think of something nice. I tried to feel Margaret, wherever she was—nearby, Roland had said—but I felt nothing, a dropped line. Maybe she'd already done it, I thought and then I kept seeing all the ways she could have. It was playing like a movie in my mind. She was jumping off a bridge, taking a fistful of pills, getting into a car with the wrong man. The thoughts were so unbearable they knocked the wind right out of me, so unbearable I had to reach out for something, anything, to make them stop.

There was a shard of broken glass on the floor next to the candle. I picked it up and ran it over the skin of my upper arm. The first time I did it lightly, just to see how it felt and, to my surprise, it felt good. I ran it over my skin again, harder, and this time the skin opened easily, like a zipper. There was blood, but it didn't hurt, or not in the same way as the thoughts. It was an easier pain, neat and tidy and concentrated in one spot. A straight line, less than an inch long, with a beginning and an end. Could she feel that, wherever she was? Could she feel what I felt?

I lay back in bed and had a memory then of waking up in the hospital after my third and final heart surgery, when I was five. I remembered how, as soon as I opened my eyes, Margaret was there, standing over me.

"Eliza*beth*!" she said, bending to kiss me all over my face and forehead—big, wet, sloppy kisses. I laughed and, when I lifted my arm to wipe my face, winced. She saw that and rang the bell to call for the nurse.

A minute later, when no nurse had appeared and there was nothing else she could do, she said, "Here, give half to me." She lowered her face to mine and, miraculously, when our foreheads touched, half the pain did leave my body and go into hers—I know because she told me and because I saw it flicker across her face.

I heard the clowns laughing outside the window. There was a faint *shhhh* in my ears and then, for the first time since arriving in the city, Michael was there, leaning over me, his breath warm against my skin, his voice in my ear, saying: *Get yourself together* and *Look for her at the centre of things.*

CHAPTER 19
AFTER

WINTER IS STILL HANGING ON. I CAN FEEL IT LURKING DESPITE THE CHERRY blossoms, the big show of daffodils and tulips.

Bertha wants to meet all the time now to talk about the hardest parts of my story. She calls this "stirring the pot." She says it's necessary for healing.

She wants to talk about the different stages of grief: the anger part, the denial part, but mostly the part that makes me feel like I can't possibly go on living.

She wants to talk about cults and how sometimes a person can end up in one without even realizing it.

She wants to talk about guilt.

Then, when she sees me shutting down, she asks whether I'm still getting "feelings" about people.

But there'll be no more of that, I insist. I tell her I'm all done with magic.

"Oh, there's still plenty of magic in the world, Hon'," she says. "You just have to know where to look."

I am doing everything asked of me. I'm eating three meals a day and typing haikus and confronting the hardest parts of my story and doing my homework and making amends and going to Group and doing my chores and even passing my twelfth-grade exams, one after another, with what Mr. Twohig calls "flying colours." I'm doing all the things and yet I keep finding myself standing in the middle of the grocery store, resisting, but just barely, the urge to climb the shelves of the drink aisle and flip the lids off of Pepsi bottles. And not because I'm thirsty. Because of something else, call it an itch.

Then, one day last week I was in the produce section, admiring all the exotic, expensive fruit, when the itch returned. I couldn't resist it this time. I picked up a pineapple and sniffed it, the way I have seen people do. I cradled it in my arms and walked toward the front door. I hesitated there for a moment, bouncing it on my hip like a strange baby. I even smiled at the cashier. She smiled back and said, "Have a nice day." So what choice did I have but to walk right out the front doors with it? I was a block away before I realized I wasn't even hungry for pineapple.

Bertha continues to stir the pot.

Let's talk about how it felt to be all alone in New York City, she says.

Let's talk about how vulnerable you were.

And then, finally, she says it: "Let's talk about Rainbow and King and how you feel you let them both down." It's so strange to hear their names come out of her mouth, in this city, all these years later, so strange to hear her put it that way, that I let them down—such a neat, tidy box for such a big, sprawling feeling—that my stomach does a somersault and I have to nosedive for the garbage can in her office. I get there just in time for everything inside me to come out.

These setbacks are normal, Bertha reassures me.

Puking is normal.

Temptation is normal.

Even itches are normal, as long as they're well managed.

But then, one ordinary Monday morning, when I'm standing in the kitchen, feeling reasonably sane and even somewhat optimistic about the day ahead, having just poured the milk over my Cheerios and snapped the lid back on, instead of putting the milk bottle back in the fridge and getting on with my day, I drop it. Understand, it doesn't slip from my hand. I'm not startled or distracted. I simply open my hand and the bottle falls to the floor and shatters—an explosion of milk and glass from one end of the kitchen to the other, with me at its centre. And in the few seconds I have alone, before Bertha comes running, when I'm stranded there in the middle of my puddle of spilt milk, I think of Rainbow and King. Then I kneel down and grab the shards of glass. I hold them in my hand and squeeze until I see the blood mixing with the milk, and I will admit, something about that pleases me.

When Bertha does arrive, she's concerned, of course. But she's also furious.

I say it was an accident.

She hands me a towel and reminds me self-harm isn't tolerated at Harrow House.

I say I slipped in the milk, that it won't happen again.

But she isn't buying it.

She lowers herself down to the floor, looks me in the eyes and says, "Are you done paying for the past yet, Elizabeth? Are you ready to talk about this guilt of yours?" and something about seeing her there, crunching around on all fours in the middle of a puddle of milk, makes me finally give in.

In the weeks that follow, Bertha and I talk a lot about self-harm, about inside pain and outside pain and the difference between them. We talk about guilt, finally, and its antidote, self-compassion. She makes me have long conversations with an empty chair, imagining Rainbow or King are sitting in it. Then, after I've talked to the chair enough and I've usually cried, she lets me put on a record and we sit on the couch in her office, not talking, just looking out the window while eating crackers with cheese and pickles, because, she says, this is part of healing too, knowing when to just take a break and have a snack.

CHAPTER 20

BEFORE

I WOKE TO THE SOUND OF RAINBOW AND KING SNORING LOUDLY AT THE OTHER end of the bed, and Michael still in my ear saying, *Look for her.* I slid my legs out from between them and got up. I rummaged through Rainbow's jacket until I found the Band-Aids the shopkeeper had given her the night before. I put two over the cut on my arm and pulled my sleeve down over it. I checked to make sure I still had Lucky's ten dollars tucked into my dress pocket. Then I shook Rainbow and King awake, saying, "Let's go."

That morning I was finally given my own bag of pamphlets. While we walked to our first corner, Rainbow and King didn't crack any jokes about how I'd behaved the night before. They didn't say a word about it. They did laugh at the rubber gloves I was wearing though. "Do you *want* to get arrested?" King asked. So I took them off and threw them in the garbage. Then we got to work.

I had a plan. I was going to target moms. I could always spot one. It was a look in their eyes: a mix of tiredness and kindness.

Whenever I saw one, I walked right up and stood beside them, like Rainbow. I tugged on their clothes until they bent down to look at me.

"What's wrong, Honey?" they asked, pity all over their faces. "Are you lost? Where's your mother?"

When I handed them a pamphlet, they gladly took it. Then, once they'd looked at it and their faces had changed—a crinkle to their brows, mouths clamped tight—that's when I held my hand out in the air between us. I pointed at my empty palm. *Help*, I said without saying. I was doing what Roland had taught me. I was clowning. And it worked.

They got an *Oh dear* look in their eyes. They pulled out their wallets and gave me fifty cents, sometimes a dollar, and I didn't even have to say a word. It was the easiest money I'd ever made. Then, as soon as they gave me the money, I turned and disappeared into the crowd without looking back.

King wasn't pleased when he found out I was getting money from strangers.

"I don't know," he said, glancing over each shoulder. "If Samuel ever found out." King turned a full circle, as if he expected Samuel to be watching from the crowd somehow. But by the time he'd come back around to me, he'd changed his mind.

"Okay, but you give us half," he said with his hands on his hips.

I put my hands on mine. "Only if you take me to Manhattan."

Rainbow reminded us we weren't allowed, but King shot her a look. "*Where* in Manhattan?"

"The centre of things," I said.

He looked at Rainbow, who shrugged.

Then he added a few more terms: I had to buy each of them a juice, plus we had to get a pineapple for him and some Kool-Aid for her.

I agreed to all of it and we shook on it right there in the middle of the sidewalk, sealing the deal—his fate and, in a way, mine too.

We worked a few more corners and another department store. While Rainbow and I held the door open for strangers, asking about their day, King was over by the mailbox, doing the strangest thing. He was tearing pamphlets up into little pieces and holding each piece up to the sun. Then, depending on what he saw, he either threw the piece away or scrunched it up into a little ball that he put in his pocket for later, except for one time when I saw him throw one of those balls into his mouth and swallow it whole.

When it was finally time to head to Manhattan, we walked to the nearest subway station. King knew a trick. He made a big scene at the kiosk while Rainbow and I ducked under the turnstile. Then we descended into the cool, engine-tasting air.

While we waited on the platform, they pointed out the rats darting across the tracks below us. They showed me the map on the wall and tried to explain how to read it—the different trains marked by different colours, the black dots that were stations, the white dots where you could switch trains—but I could hardly understand it. The funny feeling was starting again. My thoughts were turning to dominoes and the ground seemed to be breathing beneath my feet.

Once we were on the train full of swaying, sweating people, Rainbow leaned close and shouted a few of her own rules over the screeching wheels. She said the first rule of Manhattan was not to look anyone in the eye, to look straight ahead and act like I was late to meet my aunt who was just up ahead. And the second, she said, was not to show any fear.

"Or what?" I asked.

"Or they'll eat you alive," she said, smiling, and I noticed that her eyes were like two shiny, black marbles.

We came out at Forty-Second Street and walked toward a strange glow in the distance.

"What is that?" I asked.

"Times Square," King said. "The centre of the world."

But it wasn't until we were in the middle of it all, standing under a huge billboard the size of the bus, that I could feel he was right. The street was crowded with tour busses and honking cabs. The edges of the sidewalk were full of performers and people selling things. The middle was filled with tourists—you could tell by their sandals and the way they were looking all around with their mouths hanging open.

King looked at me with glassy, neon eyes and ordered me to buy them each an orange juice. So we stood in front of a place called Elpine Drinks, sipping our juices and watching the people drift past. Rainbow and King were both strangely quiet, taking it all in.

There was a man on the corner singing a sad song about a pirate. He had a guitar and a harmonica strapped around his neck. Most people walked right past, but some threw money into his guitar case.

A little farther down the block, a magician was performing. A crowd had gathered around him, *ooohing* and *aaahing* while he did something with a top hat and a rose.

"This is where people come to be discovered," King said, and as soon as he said it, I knew she was near.

When they were done their juices, King looked at Rainbow. "Ready?"

"Ready!" she said, tap-dancing and flapping her arms like a chicken.

He shoved his empty cup at me and said, "You collect."

Then they moved to an empty spot on the corner, right next to the guy with the guitar, and started performing. They had a routine figured out. He pulled three balls out of his bag and started juggling. While he did that, she marched around him in a circle, pumping her hands in the air like she was playing an imaginary trombone. She was babbling, saying, "This one's for the ones who forgot they were one with all the others and got too small in their bigs and too big in their smalls." She said something about how everyone was living in a small, grey cage with all the other small greys. She ended with a rhyme, saying, "That's why it don't feel right, people, why it all feels so tighty-tight."

Then they switched. King dropped his juggling balls. She flipped upside down and walked around on her hands, scissoring her legs while he spouted his own strange poem. "That's right," he said, "eat your chicken noodle duty, boys and girls, and do your spelling and always shake the hand of the Man! Bright and shiny now! Whipper snapper now!" He accused everyone of being crispy square crackers, then of being hamsters, then sheep.

They went back and forth like this a few times. They were grinning and juggling and flipping upside down and the whole time the words were pouring out of them in an endless flow.

A crowd had started to form around them, their faces blank with alarm as if they couldn't quite figure out what they were seeing. I walked through the crowd, nudging people to put money into the cup and some did, out of confusion more than anything.

When they were both done and the crowd had drifted away, Rainbow and King stood before me panting.

"What *was* that?" I asked. But I already knew. They were like the man, Dave, on the roof back at the farm. They were Human Radios.

"What *actually* was that?" Rainbow said.

"What was that *actually*?" King echoed and then they both started laughing and didn't stop until the man with the harmonica told us to move it along.

They had made $1.15 with their performance. King knew a place that sold cotton candy at the other end of the block so, once they'd caught their breath, we started heading in that direction. That's when I saw her. She was wearing a strange frilly dress, but I knew it was her by her hair. I saw it bobbing above the crowd like a carrot-coloured dandelion puff. I ran forward, pushing past tourists and calling her name until finally, at the end of the block, she stopped. She was turning in a slow circle, searching for me. I snuck up beside her. "Here I am," I said, slipping my hand into hers.

She yanked her hand back.

"Mom, it's me," I said, stepping forward to clutch her dress.

But it wasn't her. Her eyes were brown, for one, and so was her hair.

The woman retreated from me, and I stood on the corner, rubbing my eye, wondering what was wrong with it. Then I tried to make my way back to where I'd lost Rainbow and King.

I must've paced up and down the block, all the way to Elpine Drinks and all the way back fifty times looking for Rainbow and King, but instead, I kept seeing Margaret. I saw little bits of her in the faces of every passing woman. Some had her eyes. Some had her freckles. Some had her mouth. Nobody had her hair, but she could've cut that, I told myself. She could've been wearing a wig. I approached one woman after another—redheads and blonds and even brunettes—saying, "Mom?" and "Margaret?" truly believing each time that it was her because I could feel it. I could feel the cord stretched between us. And I could hear Michael in my ear saying, *You found her!*

But I was wrong every time. Every woman stepped back from me. One even threatened to call the police.

Eventually I stopped. I closed my eyes and stood, swaying in the middle of the sidewalk, trying to picture her actual face, but it kept skidding off to the edges of my mind. I couldn't hold it in the centre. That's when I heard a soft tinkling sound in front of me.

I opened my eyes. There was a man standing before me, wearing an orange bedsheet draped across one shoulder. He had the most impossible hair—bald but with a little ponytail at the back—and he was holding a brass bell.

He tilted his head and looked at me with eyes that were too kind. "Did you lose your mother?"

"No," I said, remembering Rainbow's rules and looking past him for my imaginary aunt, who would be here any moment.

"Would you like a healthy, warm meal?" he asked.

My stomach rumbled. I did want that, more than anything.

He stepped forward. "Would you like to feel the love of the universe?"

I accidentally looked at him again.

He reached out a hand and when he did, I saw that, beneath his bedsheet, he was wearing what looked like a cloth diaper. It probably wasn't a good idea to trust a man in a diaper with such strange hair, I remember thinking. But I really wanted the healthy, warm meal, so I put my hand in his. I probably would have gone with him, too, wherever he was leading me, and who knows, my life might've even turned out better. Instead, King found me.

"She's with me," King said, grabbing me by the arm and pulling me away, all the way up the sidewalk toward Rainbow, who was standing on the corner, shaking her head at me.

He said it was time to make good on my promise, that I owed him a pineapple and her some Kool-Aid, and while we walked away from Times Square, toward the nearest grocery store, they explained how that man was a hairy Krishna, that if I'd gone with him, he would've eaten my brain and next thing I knew I'd be wearing a diaper too.

The grocery store was much bigger and brighter than the ones we were used to. It was busier, too, which was good for us, King said.

"Count to a hundred and meet me at the pineapples," he instructed. Then we went inside, one after another, and each went our separate ways.

I wandered over to where the drinks were. I meant to just take a look, but at the beginning of the aisle there was a big display, a cardboard sign with the words "Pepsi Sweepstakes" and a picture of a waterfall on it. A woman was standing under the sign, next to a pyramid of Pepsi cartons. She explained that I could collect the little rubber caps inside the lid of each Pepsi bottle and, when I could spell the word Vacation, I would win an all-expenses-paid trip to Niagara Falls.

"Ontario?" I asked.

"Ontario!" she said.

I looked at the picture of Niagara Falls. I remembered Margaret saying she had taken a trip there once, long ago, with the rock star, before everything went wrong with Michael and me. *This is it*, I remember thinking, *a way for us to go back to the beginning.*

"How would I get there?" I asked.

"By airplane," she said.

I pictured me and Margaret sitting on a plane, looking out the window, sipping our Pepsis, high in the sky, saying, "Remember New York City?"

The woman was talking to another shopper now, telling them about the hotel they would stay in if they won, that it had a view of the falls and an all-you-can-eat buffet.

I pictured us at that buffet, filling our plates with macaroni salad and all the different kinds of Jell-O: grapefruit and watermelon and even chocolate. She would eat and eat until the empty part of herself, the part that always needed to fall in love, always with the wrong person, was full.

I opened my eyes. VACATION: it was so easy, just eight letters—seven really—that could change everything.

I took the woman's bottle opener and one of the cartons of Pepsi. I started walking down the aisle, flipping the cap off one bottle: an A. I flipped one off the next: another A. Then an I, two more A's, another I.

I set my carton down and was about to go back to grab another when I heard a commotion up near the front of the store.

I got to the end of the aisle just in time to see two policemen carrying King out the door.

I had forgotten all about him.

They had him by the arms and legs like they were about to give him the birthday bumps. He was twisting and squirming, but he was no match for them. A pineapple fell out of his jacket and rolled across the sidewalk—the pineapple I was supposed to help him get. I thought of the ten dollars in my dress pocket. I could give it to the men and probably sort this all out, I thought. But I didn't move. I just stood there, stupid and frozen, while they swung him into the back of their car like a sack of flour and shut the door on him.

Rainbow appeared next to me. She slipped her sticky fingers around my arm. "C'mon," she said, "cut and run."

Back at the house, we told one person who told another who told another. Eventually, someone rang the bell, and everyone gathered for an emergency meeting.

O and Samuel came up the basement stairs and took their places at the front of the room.

"Another one of our soldiers has fallen," she said, stifling a yawn. "Let us have a moment of silence." She hung her head, and it looked like she might have fallen asleep.

Some people hung their heads with her, but others were looking at each other in disbelief.

After a moment, O jerked her head back up and asked something routine, a question about posters or pamphlets.

"Hold on," Roland said, rising. "Is that all you're going to say about that? King has been arrested and you're just going to carry on as usual?"

A few other people stood too.

"*Many* of us are in jail for the Cause," Samuel said. "He's not the first, and he won't be the last."

"But he's a child," someone said.

"We're all children when seen from the perspective of what it is we're trying to accomplish here," Samuel said. "We're all just beginning."

"No, but he's an *actual* child. Like *actually*," Roland said in a voice so big it rattled the windows.

Samuel stood and shouted back at Roland, something about how the Cause is advanced one person at a time, that it takes many soldiers, many sacrifices, that if Roland didn't agree with that, he and his clowns were free to leave.

Everyone was up on their feet then, shouting. We didn't stay to listen. I took Rainbow's hand and led her outside, into the alleyway and onto the bus. I locked the door and we sat down, side by side, on the bed at the back.

She was crying softly. "I wasn't watching," she said. "I turned away for one minute and he got got."

"It's not your fault," I said.

She turned to me then and I confessed it all: that I hadn't even made it to the fruit section, that I'd been distracted by the Pepsi and lost track of time, that it was my fault we were even in that store, my fault we were in Manhattan.

We sat in silence for a long time. They were still arguing in the house. Their voices were floating across the alley, but I couldn't make out what they were saying, my ears were ringing too loud.

I thought of the ten dollars in my pocket and how it probably could have saved him but decided not to say anything about it.

She lay down and curled up into a little ball. I tried to put my arm around her. She shrugged me off. I told her about the Pepsi Sweepstakes, that if I won, I'd take her on an all-expenses-paid trip to Niagara Falls, where the buffet never closed. We could drink every kind of Kool-Aid and eat every kind of Jell-O, I said, even bubble-gum Jell-O, even chocolate.

"No such thing," she said, but the way she said it, it sounded like "No such thing, *stupid.*"

My heart swung heavy.

She was right. The day was a total failure. I *was* stupid to think I could find Margaret in a city so big, with so many people in it. And in the process of looking, I had let everyone else down. It was all my fault King was gone. She knew it and so did I.

CHAPTER 21

AFTER

SUMMER IS NEAR. THE CHERRY BLOSSOMS ARE LONG GONE. EVEN THE DAFFODILS have shrivelled on their stems, like used-up suns.

Every day I talk to the empty chair and unearth a little more of my guilt.

Everyone thinks I'm doing better after my episode in the kitchen. I'm more open, Bertha says. More focused, says Mr. Twohig. More calm, says Annie.

And maybe because of all that, I've arrived at the makeover part of my rehabilitation.

Bertha brings me to an optometrist, Dr. Bowman, who, after taking my history and peering into my eyes with bright lights, decides I don't need my eye patch anymore.

"And I never did?" I ask.

"Well, I don't know about *that*," he says.

He's being polite, but I'll chalk it up as another one of Margaret's lies.

He says I should remove the eye patch for a little longer each day. He prescribes me a special pair of glasses and teaches me a bunch of different exercises to help strengthen my weak eye. So now every night I have to stand in the kitchen with Bertha while she holds up different red and green pictures, saying, "What do you see now? And what about now?"

Everything shifts into tighter focus around me.

The past curls in on itself.

Bertha takes me clothes shopping at a thrift store.

While we wander through the aisles, placing items into a shopping cart, she very casually asks, "Have you ever thought about what you'd like to do as a job when you're older?"

I know what she's getting at. All of us at Harrow House have our parole reviews soon, one right after another. In order to earn our freedom, it's necessary for each of us to be enrolled in college or a trade school.

She keeps placing different coloured turtlenecks into the cart. "What kind of life do you want to have, Hon'?"

But I don't have an answer for her, or not one that makes sense anyway. If I told her what I really want is to be a Jennifer, she wouldn't know what I'm talking about.

I recall a piece of advice a henny gave me once, a long time ago. "I think I'll marry rich," I say, placing a long, velvet dress into the cart.

She frowns, takes the dress out, puts a pair of brown slacks in instead. "What about being an English major?"

Mr. Twohig says I've basically passed the twelfth grade, that the rest of our time will be spent learning how to write my resumé and cover letter, which is a skill he says will carry me through the rest of my life. So I learn how to parse my life into organized paragraphs, how to talk about my strengths in a way that doesn't seem like bragging, how to hint at personal ruin without delving into it.

Annie says in addition to my other work, I have to start working on my letter to the parole board.

She says it has to be typed because they won't read anything written by hand and arranges for a typewriter to be put into my room. Then she teaches me the format for the letter, which is: taking responsibility for my crime, showing remorse, talking about the present and all the things I'm learning, ending, finally, with my dreams for the future.

"But I don't have any dreams," I say.

That does something to the poet in her. For a second her eyes get wet, but then she digs around in her bag and comes up with a pamphlet for a teen memoir contest run by one of the local papers. It's called Write What You Know. She says I should enter, that she'll help me.

"No," I say. "Nope, no way."

She screws her face up. "Why not?"

"Because—" I look up at the ceiling. Some sentences don't need to be finished.

Bertha brings someone in to teach us meditation. So now, on Sunday afternoons, we all sit on cushions in the art room while a woman named Francine coaches us on how to be still and not think, which, it turns out, is a very difficult thing to do. She teaches us how to follow the air as it travels through our nostrils, down to our bellies and then back out our mouths. It turns out we're very bad at this. Heather hums under her breath the whole time. Leonard twitches. Patrick keeps scratching. But still, we sit. Francine says my mind is like a puppy on a leash, that it will wander and get distracted, but I can always tug it back, gently, to the present.

I like how it feels, the coming back part. I like how sometimes I can get the puppy to sit and stay, just for a minute. My mind empties out. Time slows. For the first time in a decade I can feel every second and every second is sweet.

"Should I put that in my parole letter?" I ask Annie. "That I'm working on meditation?" We're still stuck on the part about what my dreams are.

"*Maaay*be," she says, meaning absolutely not. The Honourable Members of the Parole Board are all about diplomas and vocational programs. They want me to become something tangible—a dental hygienist or a client services representative at the bank. They know nothing about the sweet stillness of the mind, nothing about nothingness.

Everyone thinks I'm doing better. I'm more open and focused and calm. I have new glasses and clothes. But still, every once in a while, I'll find myself circling the big, old houses of my neighbourhood, knowing which ones are empty and wanting to step inside, just for an afternoon, just to take a nap on some Jennifer's bed and imagine a different kind of life. Sometimes I'll even open the front gate and walk up the steps to look for a key. Sometimes I'll catch a whiff of perfume, there, by the front door, and I'll look up and see Rainbow darting away through the darkened rooms—not her as she would be now, but her as she was, and then I know the past isn't done with me. It's a hungry animal nipping at my heels.

CHAPTER 22

BEFORE

AFTER KING'S ARREST, THE HOUSE SPLIT INTO TWO. THE CLOWNS STAYED
upstairs, rehearsing and holding meetings on the roof. Samuel and
O and their people stayed downstairs. They only met in the middle
once a day for the dinner meeting, and even that always turned into
an argument.

Samuel and O kept talking about how important it was to step up
the intervention and spread our message to as many people as possible.

Roland said we should be taking care of our own people first. He
demanded O hire a lawyer to find out where King was, and she kept
promising she would.

In the meantime, the one thing they could agree on was that there
was work to do. Everyone was busy now. The clowns were always
rushing off to do performances throughout the city. There were people
printing pamphlets and posters at all hours, and every day a whole army
of us went out onto the corners to distribute them. At night, groups of
us were sent to different stores to fill our pockets with the supplies on
our lists.

Rainbow and I were still on pamphlets. Without King and his rules, we
could leave the house whenever we wanted, and we didn't even have to

wear our good-girl clothes. As soon as we were out of sight, we dumped our pamphlets into a mailbox, saving just a few for the hennies.

"They'll still get *somewhere* right?" we said to one another. "Nobody said we had to actually put them in people's hands."

After that we were free, or Rainbow was at least.

I'd made a bunch of posters telling Margaret I was looking for her and where to find me. There was a sketch of her and a bunch of those symbols she used to draw on the road atlas.

I wanted to walk around the neighbourhood, putting my posters up, but ever since my confession of guilt on the bus, Rainbow had had the upper hand. We always had to do what she wanted, which meant going to one store after another looking for Pepsi and blue Kool-Aid. She made me run distraction while she flipped the lids off of bottles. She even kept all the rubber caps—hers and mine too—in her own pocket. Once in a while though, when she wasn't looking, I was able to convince a shopkeeper to put one of my posters up near the cash register.

When it got too hot on the streets, Rainbow always wanted to take the bus to Macy's. She liked to wander in among the glass counters on the first floor, talking to the perfume ladies and begging them to squirt things onto her wrists. It was a waste of time for me—I knew Margaret would never show her face in a place like that. But Rainbow was boss, and sometimes she agreed to go with me up to the second floor where there was a model train set that ran in circles all day long. It had a glass wall around it but, when nobody was looking, we could reach over and drop something onto the tracks to make the train derail. We usually got told to leave after that.

In the afternoons we visited the hennies. We gave them the pamphlets we'd saved, and they let us hang around on the corner with them for a while. When I asked them to help keep an eye out for my mom, they crowded around, asking what she was like. I described her afro, her 1,049 freckles, her moods that went up and down like a Ferris wheel.

After that they all started calling me Baby Girl. They were always offering to braid my hair and asking me what I wanted to be when I grew up. And they were always giving me advice. Stay in school, they said. And marry rich. And don't give your whole life away to the first man who calls you pretty.

Sometimes Rainbow wanted to play The Dad Game, where she would pick a man walking through the streets and pretend he was her dad. I didn't mind this game, even though it had nothing to do with finding Margaret. We'd follow the man, making up stories about him: that his name was Bruce and he had a swimming pool and played drums in a famous band. She liked to imagine that as soon as he laid eyes on her, he'd know she belonged to him and would invite both of us over for spaghetti with meatballs. The game ended when she gathered the nerve to walk up alongside him at a crosswalk, slip her hand into his and say, "Dad?" Then she'd hold on for as long as she could, without saying another word, that was the rule. We never did get invited to anyone's house for spaghetti, but she did hold a man's hand for fifteen seconds once.

Sometimes in the afternoons we'd sneak onto a city bus through the back doors while everyone else was stepping off. We'd ride around for a while until we were in a neighbourhood we didn't recognize. Then we'd get off and go to a few stores. She'd look for Pepsi and blue Kool-Aid and I'd try to put up posters.

Once in a while we'd pick a nice street and walk down it and I'd imagine out loud that this is where King lived now. "That one," I'd say, pointing at a big house with a yard and a swing set. "And he has three sisters and a pet bunny." Then I'd point at another. "Or that one. And he has four moms, so if one gets lost, he always has a spare."

Rainbow was always quiet when I played this game, until one day when she stopped in the middle of the sidewalk, turned to me and said, "You know he's not coming back, right?"

I stopped too. "What do you mean?"

"I mean he's *Black*."

"Yeah, so?"

She sighed, like she was tired of explaining everything to me all the time. "So the rules are different for him, Elizabeth." Then she turned and walked away from me, and it felt as if I'd swallowed a cold stone because I knew she was right. I'd known it all along, every time we entered a store together.

It was later that day, on the long bus ride home, that I finally asked Rainbow who her real mom and dad were. She looked out the window and explained that she didn't know her real dad, but her mom, April, was in jail for the Cause.

I wanted to ask whether she'd ever get out, but I was too scared.

Luckily Rainbow changed the subject. She said April and Samuel had been married once.

"But now Samuel's kissing O!" I said.

"Yeah, so?" she snorted, like it was no big deal who kissed who, but I noticed her hands were curled into two tight fists in her lap.

Once, we fell asleep on one of our long bus trips and didn't wake up until the driver turned off the engine and announced, "Hempstead. End of the line."

We stepped off the bus and looked around. Hempstead was a little village full of one-storey shops with flower boxes on all the windows. There were people eating and drinking at tables set right out on the sidewalk. They were all smiling and saying hello to one another.

It didn't seem like the kind of place Margaret would be. "We should head back," I said. A group of schoolgirls had just walked past though, wearing matching plaid uniforms, and Rainbow couldn't take her eyes off them.

She bounced her eyebrows up-down at me.

I shook my head no.

But if my guilt was a lock, Rainbow had the key.

"King would want us to," she said.

So we followed after them.

The girls turned onto a side street. They had matching plaid backpacks with little metal hearts and bells hanging off of them. They were talking about their teachers, about homework, about a boy named Billy and a girl named Suzie, and what had happened at recess: Billy had said something, then Suzie had said something, then Billy had said something else. I tried to imagine their school, a place where everyone wore plaid and took turns speaking.

Soon we were in an area where each house was huge and totally separate from the ones around it. There were no alleys here, no dumpsters or stray dogs. Every house had a yard with a swing set. These girls probably lived in one of these big houses with their own bedrooms, I was thinking. They probably had art/music/dance lessons and knew how to ice skate and had their own bicycles.

Their ponytails swung left-right when they walked, almost as if they were doing it on purpose. Their hair smelled like apples.

We followed as closely as we could, leaning in, trying to hear every last word they were saying. But at one point, when we were all stopped on the same corner waiting for a car to pass, we got too close. They spun around all at once, like a gang of angry ballerinas, and asked, "Who *aaare* you?" Their eyes travelled up and down our bodies.

"Lulu," I said without thinking.

"Lulu-*who?*" they asked.

"Lulu the henny," I said, and then they burst into giggles.

Rainbow stepped forward then and growled like a feral dog. They screeched and ran away.

I thought it was funny, but Rainbow was shaking mad. "We'll show them," she said. Then she ordered me to follow her.

We circled back a few blocks, to head home I thought, but instead she went into the post office. I saw her talking to the lady in there and when she came out a few minutes later, she had a white box hanging from a piece of string with the word UNICEF handwritten on it in red letters. She ordered me to hang it around my neck, explaining that from this moment on I would have to act blind and deaf.

"No way," I said. "This is stupid. Let's go home."

I had already started walking away when she finally said it out loud for the first time, the thing she'd been holding over me. "I'll tell everyone it's your fault King got arrested," she said with her chest puffed out and her chin in the air.

I put the UNICEF box around my neck and we walked back to where the girls had run off. She was looking carefully at every house we passed, sniffing the air, as if she might be able to pick up their apple scent.

We must've walked past forty houses before she found one she liked. It was a big, white house with wide steps leading up to a red door. There were newspapers piled up in front of the door. The curtains were drawn. The driveway was empty.

"I don't think they live here," I said, but she opened the gate and marched up the front steps anyway.

She kept sniffing the air. She rang the bell once and then a second time before she started looking around—under the mat, under the planter, all around the door frame. When she found a key taped to the bottom of the mailbox, she held it up, grinning.

"What are you doing?" I whispered.

She pointed at her ears, reminding me I was supposed to be deaf, and jiggled the key in the lock. Eventually it clicked. Then she swung the door open. We stepped over the newspapers and stood in the entranceway. It smelled like a real home, like soap, coffee, bananas.

"Hello, UNICEF," Rainbow called.

No answer. The tick-tock of a clock somewhere in the distance.

"Yoo-hoo, we're collecting for UNICEF," she called again.

Still no answer.

"All clear," she said. She closed the door behind us, went over to the stairs and started walking up them without any fear at all, just like it was her own house.

I stood frozen in the entranceway. The house was ticking and creaking all around me. I could hear Rainbow walking from room to room upstairs, opening drawers. I would stay right there by the door until this was all over, I told myself. I didn't want any part of this. But I could see the kitchen in the distance. I could smell its banana smells.

I tiptoed forward. I found the bananas in a bowl on the counter. There was a chocolate cake sitting right next to it, under a glass lid, half-eaten. I wondered what kind of a person would leave a perfectly good chocolate cake sitting on the counter like that. A person who wouldn't notice if some was missing, I decided. So I found a knife and cut myself a piece and ate it. Then I closed the lid and went to the sink to clean the knife. The sink was empty. Not a dirty dish in sight. There was a bottle of Sunlight soap sitting next to the tap. I squirted some onto the knife and, as soon as I smelled the bright lemony smell, I pictured Margaret dancing around the kitchen back at Kraft Park, singing along to the radio, soap up to her wrists, talking about how we were destined for better things. I wondered what she'd have to say about who I'd actually become. I squeezed some Sunlight out onto my wrists and rubbed them together. I dabbed it behind my ears the way Rainbow did with her perfume. I wanted to keep that smell with me, always.

I could hear Rainbow crashing around upstairs. I went up to tell her I'd had enough and was heading home, that this was too dangerous, that we could go to jail just like King.

I found myself in a carpeted hallway with a bunch of closed doors. One door had the word "Jennifer" written on it in sparkly letters. I thought I would just take a look and *then* tell Rainbow it was time to go. Sometimes life is like that: the biggest moments, the ones that really change you, hang from the smallest hooks.

Jennifer had a desk and a pink, frilly bed with about a hundred teddy bears on it. She had a bulletin board crowded with pictures of her perfect life: her riding horses, playing volleyball, blowing out candles on cakes. There was one of her on vacation. She was standing under a palm tree on a white-sand beach with her mom and dad. I lay down on Jennifer's bubble-gum-smelling bed. I imagined myself walking home from school with my friends, eating cake and bananas whenever I wanted, going on vacations with my mom and dad, and then, suddenly, I had a memory of Margaret leaning over me in my own bed back at Kraft Park, saying, "What do you want to do today, Kiddo?" This was not long after my third heart surgery. And even though we were broke and it was the middle of winter, I said, "I need a vacation." I don't know what made me say that. I don't think I even knew what it meant. It must've been something I'd overheard at the hospital.

But she knew what it meant and, without a pause, she said, "Okey-doke" and jumped up to make it happen. Within an hour she had borrowed a car and we were driving toward Ottawa with stupid straw hats on our heads, singing along to "Good Vibrations" on the radio. We pulled up in front of the biggest hotel we could find. She walked inside, right through the front doors, and somehow worked her magic because within a few minutes a bunch of men in funny hats and red jackets were rolling a wheelchair out the front door to get me. They picked me up and put me in the chair, calling me "Little Miss Squire." Then they wheeled me all the way to the hotel pool where we spent the day "on vacation," listening to muzak and sipping fruity drinks with umbrellas.

I felt a strange, floaty feeling in the very centre of me when I thought about that, like my heart was a balloon going up. I had been loved once too, just like Jennifer, I thought. It might not have looked the same or smelled as good, but it was still love. I was able to float on that feeling for maybe a full minute before Rainbow came slamming into the room, swinging a woman's purse and ordering me around.

"Get up," she said, heading for Jennifer's closet.

She was rummaging through the shelves, throwing stuff onto the floor, making a huge mess. I followed after her, trying to tidy things back up.

When she finally found something she liked, she slipped out of her old clothes right there on the spot. She put on a pair of denim overalls and a T-shirt with a pony on it.

"Now you," she said, handing me a blouse with long, billowy sleeves and a pair of pink velvet bell-bottoms.

I tried to get Lucky's ten dollars out of the pocket before slipping out of my old velvet dress, but she was watching me.

I let my dress fall to the floor and wriggled into Jennifer's clothes.

"Holy Mama!" Rainbow said, once I was dressed.

I bent down to pick up our old clothes, but she brought her foot down on top of them.

"Leave them." Her face was suddenly stern.

An oniony, animal smell was wafting up from them. "But they stink," I said.

"Exactly," she said, laughing, the same high-pitched laugh her and King used to share. Then she said, "Come on. We gotta go."

We stepped out of the closet. I had no choice but to leave my ten dollars on the floor. There was nothing I could've done. If I'd dug it out, Rainbow would have known that I'd had it all along and could've saved King with it. And who knows how she would've used that information against me.

She kicked the closet door shut behind us. When I saw my reflection swing past in the full-length mirror, I jumped. Even with Jennifer's clothes on, I looked like the kind of person you wouldn't want to sit next to on the subway. I looked like someone who'd lost nearly everything.

We boarded the same bus back to the city. We begged the driver to let us on, explaining that we'd lost our fare, that we were going to visit our aunt in the city, that we had to get there in time for dinner. He looked at us and nodded. It must've been our new clothes.

Once we were seated at the back of the bus, Rainbow opened the purse she was carrying. She took out a tube of lipstick, uncapped it and traced her lips carefully, stopping to draw two sharp peaks on her top lip.

"Where'd you get that?" I asked.

She didn't answer. Instead, she pulled out a bottle of perfume and squirted it at me. It smelled like roses. Then she showed me a handful of rings with coloured stones in them: red, dark blue, green. She put them all on at once and twinkled her fingers at me.

"You *stole* those?" I whispered.

She rolled her eyes. "Why, what'd you get?"

I shook my head.

"*Nothing*?" she said and there was that word, *stupid*, tacked onto the end of her sentence again.

It was a long drive back to Queens. The whole way, Rainbow was acting fancy, sitting with her legs crossed and flapping her hands around to show off her rings. She was talking about all the other houses we'd break into and enunciating her words extra carefully because of her lipstick. I noticed she was wearing a gold necklace with a heart-shaped locket. It was probably Jennifer's mom's necklace, I was thinking, probably given to her by *her* mom. And it probably would've been given to Jennifer someday, to give to her own daughter, if not for us.

By the time we could see the Manhattan skyline I had made up my mind. I was sick of Rainbow bossing me around, always telling me what to do and calling me stupid. She was nothing like me, I decided. I was a Jennifer with a mom who loved me, and she was not.

I rang the bus bell, then turned to her and said, "I'm not going back to the house."

"Oh yes you are," she said.

I stood up from my seat.

"I'll tell them everything," she said, rising too.

"And if you do *that*," I said, grabbing her bejewelled hand, "I'll tell them about this." Then, just for effect, I added the word "stupid" before stepping off the bus.

I shouldn't have said that.

I snuck onto a bus to Manhattan, getting off somewhere near the middle of things.

I wasn't sure what to do. I had no money and nowhere to go. I only knew that I needed to find Margaret.

It was six o'clock. The sidewalks were full of people in business clothes, going places. I went against Rainbow's advice. I looked into each and every face and every time someone looked back at me, I stopped them and asked, "Where is the centre of everything?"

Their answers were different. Some said Times Square. Some said Wall Street or MOMA. One person said Lorna's Pie Shop and drew me a map on the back of a receipt. But many, most of them, said Central Park. So I asked where it was and then that's where I headed. "You'll know it when you see it," people said, and when I saw it, I did.

I went down some stairs into the park. I was on a cool, shady path that curved around a pond. There were people sitting on benches along the side of the path, fanning themselves in the shade. I'd never seen so many benches in one place. It was like a big living room where everyone sat next to each other but minded their own business, like there were imaginary walls between them. People were eating ice cream, reading books, playing cards, knitting, walking their dogs, feeding the pigeons, riding bikes, pushing baby carriages. One man was giving another man a haircut. I saw someone walk by with a parrot on his shoulder. I saw a woman in a winter coat digging in the garbage and telling everyone around her about "the jackals" who were hounding her. I felt sorry for her until I saw her dig a perfectly good sandwich out of the garbage and stuff it into her pocket for later.

This was it, I remember thinking, the real America, exactly the kind of place Margaret would be. All I had to do was wait for her, I told myself, and in the meantime earn some money.

I sat on a bench next to a woman and her dog.

"Give me your palm and I'll read your future," I said.

She was pretending there was that imaginary wall between us.

"*Pssst*," I said a little louder. "Have you lost someone recently? Or something?"

She turned to me then. "Go away," she said, pulling her dog close.

"But I can see your aura," I said. "I'm getting a special feeling about you."

After that she took her dog and left.

I waited a moment before trying the person on the other side of me. It was a man reading the newspaper.

"Hey you," I said. "I got a message for you from the other side."

He didn't flinch.

"Hey *pssst*, I'm the real deal," I said. "Wanna see my scar?" I was lowering my shirt to show him, but he didn't care. So I decided to stick to Bob Dylan.

"Want to know how many roads you'll have to walk down before you're considered a man?" I asked.

He cleared his throat, turned the page.

"Hey, something's happening here and you don't even know what it is," I said.

The benches around us started to clear.

"The times are a-changing," I shouted after everyone. "But I can help you sort it all out for a buck!"

When everyone was gone, the man finally lowered his newspaper and looked at me.

"You need a better act, kid," he said.

"But I'm MeMe Fanta," I said, sitting up taller, flipping my eye patch up and fluttering my eyes at him. "And if you just give me seventy-five cents, I'll tell you everything you need to know."

He raised an eyebrow at me. "That might've worked wherever you're from, but it ain't gonna work here." Then he lifted his newspaper again and continued reading.

But I was determined.

I kept moving down the path.

I approached people, telling them about their auras—that they were green or red or purple. I grabbed at their palms, asking, "Don't you want a message from the other side?"

"Get lost," they said, one after another.

One man gave me a dime just to leave him alone.

It wasn't until an older woman tried to hit me with her purse that I stopped.

I sat on a bench, holding my head in my hands and trying not to cry. The man was right, I was thinking: I did need a new act.

I don't know how long I sat there feeling bad, but by the time I came to my senses, the sun had disappeared behind the buildings. All along the edges of the path, men were packing up their food carts, dumping hotdog-smelling water into the grass behind them while the crows yelled at them. I stood before one of these men with my stomach growling, trying to work up the courage to ask for a hotdog or at least some hotdog water, but without even lifting his head he said, "Gedouddahere."

I kept walking. The lights came on in the buildings beyond the park—a wall of windows reaching into the sky. Margaret was near, I could feel it. This was the centre of things, everyone had said. I just had to find the centre of the centre, I thought, and she would be there, waiting for me.

The lanterns came on alongside the paths. Nearly everyone had gone home, except for the men in long coats who hissed at me when I passed, asking if I needed a place to lay my head.

I ran from them, past some rocks and another pond and through a small forest. In the dim light I saw dark shapes hunched together. They were rolling around, whimpering and exploring their feelings, like clowns practising Catharsis.

I ran over a bridge and under a bridge and over another. The moon was out. Bats were swooping above my head.

I was walking down a wide path, trying to catch my breath, when a bunch of people came hurrying past me in the dark.

"Here they come," a man said as he went by. I saw him duck into a bush, so I did the same on the opposite side of the path. The bush I chose was wide and hollow. It had cardboard boxes laid down as a floor and was almost like a little room. I crawled over the cardboard and peered out at the path. Two men were coming toward me, sweeping their flashlights left-to-right, shouting at everyone to go home.

The men passed without seeing me. Once their lights had retreated in the distance, I crawled out of the bush and continued down the path.

I could sense people in the bushes all around me now. I heard them muttering. I saw the flick of their lighters. I smelled their smells.

She was close, I could feel it.

So I went around to the "back door" of each bush.

"Knock, knock," I said. "Is Margaret here? Or Fran? Or Sisco?"

"Excuse me, have you seen a woman with a red afro?" I asked.

"Well if you do see her," I said, "can you please tell her Elizabeth is looking for her?"

But people weren't in the mood for a visitor.

They told me to scram.

They spit at me.

They threw rocks and whatever else they could find.

One man grabbed me by the arm and twisted, demanding I give him my shoes.

Then, once I'd handed those over, he wanted my socks too.

I kept moving, barefoot now.

Eventually, I came to a grand staircase that led down to a big, open circle and there, in the middle of that circle, in the middle of a fountain, I found a statue of a woman who looked just like Margaret. She was wearing a long dress. She had a tidy afro and a familiar look on her face—the one Margaret always got when she was about to have a mood.

She had huge, concrete wings, too, but that didn't bother me. This had to be it, I thought to myself, the centre of everything. I had arrived. So I sat on the ground with my back against the fountain, listening to the trickling water, and it was just like being with her. I could hear her scratchy voice singing to me. I felt her hands in my hair and the wind of her big wings flapping.

I must've slept because next thing I knew a man was standing over me, offering to take me home and treat me right.

I ran away from him, toward the edge of the park. The sky was getting lighter. The regular world was starting to wake up just beyond the trees. For the first time I started to doubt myself. Would Margaret even be here, I thought? Central Park wasn't the kind of place you'd go to get a record deal or be discovered. It was more like the end of the road.

Just then, I smelled something delicious coming from the garbage can next to me. I put my hand into the opening and pulled out a perfectly good hotdog. It had no ketchup on it, so I reached back into the garbage can and—you wouldn't believe it—I found a mostly empty bottle of ketchup. I sat on a nearby bench, laughing at my good luck, saying, "Thank you, New York," while I applied the last drizzle of ketchup to the hotdog.

An ordinary man in a hat, a norm out for an early-morning stroll, walked past just as I did that. I saw him quicken his pace and then I realized how I must look: like the jackals were after me too.

While I ate my hotdog, I spoke to Margaret. "Are you even here?" I asked. "Do you even want a record deal anymore?"

I closed my eyes and tried to feel what she felt, but I felt nothing.

And it was while I was doing that, while I was sitting with my eyes closed, listening desperately to the air, that the woman with the knife snuck up on me. Before I knew it, she was in front of me, saying, "Give me your hotdog or else."

She had short reddish hair with twigs in it and what might've been freckles beneath the grime.

"Mom?" I said, stepping forward.

But the woman wasn't in the mood. She jabbed the air with her knife and asked if I wanted to die.

So I handed over my hotdog and my last dime and left the park for good.

Margaret wasn't there. There was no centre of the centre. I had failed again.

I started the long walk home, and the whole way I felt a strange wind at my back, as though Margaret's big wings were flapping behind me.

CHAPTER 23

AFTER

THERE'S A PLUMBING LEAK AT HARROW HOUSE. THEY HAVE TO RIP UP THE floor of my room to find the leak, so I have to move in with Heather. We're given bunk beds, which isn't protocol, obviously, because bunk beds have never been good for anyone's mental health. But it's only temporary, Bertha reminds us, just until they patch the leak.

So now I have to listen to Heather's wild talk all night long. At first she's just talking about California and her dreams of becoming a tattoo artist but then, pretty quickly, she starts going on about Jerry Garcia and the Family. She says Jerry owes her money, lots of it, and that after her hearing in a few months, she's going to collect and join the Family and lose herself in the music.

Down on my bunk, I'm having a hard time breathing.

She says her boyfriend, Tad, has agreed to drive us for a hand job each. But before we hit the road, she says I'll have to promise to work on my fashion choices.

Her head hangs down from the top bunk. "You *do* know how to give a hand job, don't you?"

"Sure," I say. *How hard can it be?*

"It's not that it's hard really," she says, reading my mind. "Just gross."

She flops back onto her own bunk and, in her best Mr. Twohig voice says, "Good. I think you'll find the hand job is a very fine skill for the rest of your life."

She talks some more about Jerry and how there's this thing where you can show up at a Dead show with, like, nothing, not even a ticket or a place to stay, how you can just walk down the road, holding a finger in the air, and the Family will see it, and they'll all pitch in to provide you with whatever you need.

But I'm not listening. My ears are full of static and my throat has gone dry. It's all this talk about Jerry and the Family. It's sending me on a snake ride all the way back to the part of my story I haven't told anyone, the part I'd most like to forget.

In the days that follow, Heather gets to work on me. She shows me how to rip the sleeves off my T-shirt and then fasten them back on with safety pins. She shows me how to tight-roll the cuffs of my jeans, how to line my eyes with black eyeliner and then spit on my fingers and smudge it around so I look like I've been up all night, which is a good thing, she says, because it makes me look slutty and dangerous. She shaves a little patch of hair above my right ear and lends me a feather earring to wear on that side. Every day before we leave her room, she covers my face with so much foundation and powder, it feels like I'm wearing a mask, like if I smile it will crack.

Bertha notices the changes right away and wants to start meeting at least once a day to "keep in touch."

"How's it going with Heather, Hon'?" she always asks. "Is she pressing your buttons?"

She talks a lot about "coming under the influence of others" and "knowing the difference between my stuff and someone else's stuff."

She says it's good this plumbing situation has come up now, that it's a great opportunity to work through some of my issues around friendship, which only makes me suspect the whole "situation" is a set up.

Then, at the end of each of our talks, she asks about my future, about what I want to do with my life and, when I say I don't know, she always hands me a different pamphlet: one for the journalism program at the community college, one for horticultural school, one for a women's carpentry course.

But it all feels so forced. I don't want to just *decide* I'm a journalist or a gardener or a carpenter. I want to be like the tomato plants and grow into myself, miraculously.

At night, in our bunks, Heather goes on and on about California: how everything is better there, how it's always sunny and you can swim in the ocean even in January.

Meanwhile, down on my bottom bunk, I'm having a hard time telling the difference between the before and after of my life. I'm having a hard time feeling my limbs, blinking, swallowing.

She talks about the Dead, too, about how they're the best jam band in the history of the universe, how they've never played the same song the same way twice, how they're all on one wavelength, so they can just read each other's minds or whatever.

"Like us," she says, hanging her head over the bunk.

And it's true, she has been reading my mind a lot lately.

Like how the other day she said, "Want a tattoo?" and then, without any hesitation at all, she lifted up my sleeve and found all the scars on my upper arm, as if she'd known they were there all along. She didn't say anything, just ran her fingers over them gently, inhaling through her teeth. Then she pulled out a ballpoint pen and drew a yin-yang symbol on top of them with the words "best" and "worst" written inside each half of the circle. While she drew, she talked about how sometimes the worst things that happen to us are actually the best things in disguise, and I had that feeling again, that I wanted to warn her about me. But I couldn't. Maybe because she was stroking my scars, or because I was in her room, wearing her clothes. Or maybe because it was already happening, that thing that always happens whenever I get too close to anyone. I could feel her mind swooping down on my own, like paper-covers-rock. I knew that soon I would be swallowed and that there would be consequences for that, because there always are.

CHAPTER 24

BEFORE

I GOT BACK TO THE HOUSE JUST IN TIME FOR THE MORNING MEETING AND, AS soon as I entered the room, I knew I was in trouble. Rainbow was sitting up near the front, right next to Samuel, looking proud of herself.

She had told him, of course. She had told them all.

Samuel was saying something about how things were heating up, how the cops were on to us and we all needed to be more vigilant.

People nodded. I scanned the room for Roland, but there were no clowns in sight.

Samuel was saying something about a new mode of delivery, something about hiding in plain sight, and then he turned to Rainbow and announced it was her who had given him the idea.

There was some applause and then he said to stay tuned, that there would be big changes coming.

I turned around and tried to tiptoe out the front door, but he saw me.

"Elizabeth," he boomed. "I need a word with you."

So while the meeting broke up and people got to work all around me, I stood by the door, waiting for my punishment. Eventually Samuel came over, took me by the hand and led me toward the carpeted staircase. He took a step down into that fuzzy golden tunnel, but I kept my feet firmly on the top step.

He reached into his pocket and pulled out one of my posters. He shook it in the air and asked if it was true I'd been putting them up all over the place.

I hung my head and nodded yes.

He asked if I knew I was putting everyone, the whole Cause and especially Margaret, at risk.

I shook my head no.

He asked if I would please stop with the posters and recommit to our common goal.

I nodded, even though I didn't know what that meant exactly.

"Excellent," he said, placing a hand on my shoulder and smiling down at me. "Because I have a very special assignment for you and Rainbow. It is absolutely essential to what we are trying to do here."

I looked up at him then. "But where is she?"

He blinked his raisiny eyes at me. "Who?"

"Margaret."

"Oh," he stiffened. "She's doing something for me, back at the farm. She'll be here very soon. Don't you worry."

But I knew he was lying. It was the "very" in "very soon" that gave him away. That and the way he kept nodding his head, like he was trying to convince himself as much as me.

I was introduced to Dee, who Samuel said would be helping me and Rainbow with our special assignment. Dee had just arrived from Detroit, he said, so we'd have to show her the ropes.

Dee had short hair like a boy. She was wearing a black turtleneck, black pants and a black leather jacket, even in the heat.

She stepped forward to shake my hand. "I've heard so much about you," she said, smiling like an old friend, but I knew what she really was—our new minder. And she proved it right away by ordering us to go upstairs and get changed into our good-girl clothes.

"Did you tell them about King?" I asked Rainbow once we were finally alone in our room together.

"No," she said. "Only the posters," and for a moment she seemed almost apologetic.

Then she remembered herself. "And I got rid of the rings, so don't even think about telling." But I noticed she hadn't gotten rid of Jennifer's mom's locket. It was still hanging around her neck.

When Dee stepped into the room to join us, she looked like a completely different person. She was wearing a knee-length red dress with buttons up the front and lipstick and pantyhose and brown pumps. And she was talking like a different person too.

"Shall we go shopping, girls?" she said, shoving a purse into each of our hands. Then she looked down at my bare feet and asked where my shoes were.

I said a man had taken them.

"For fuck's sake," she said, sounding like her old self again.

She stomped down the hall and came back with someone else's strappy sandals for me to wear. They were far too big, but she cinched the straps tight around my ankles. Then she herded us down the stairs and out the front door.

That day we caught the train to Manhattan, where we went to one department store after another. While Dee chatted with the perfume-counter ladies, trying different fragrances and telling them about her imaginary husband, Carl, Rainbow and I circled the counters, tipping the fancy bottles into our purses.

Then, when our purses were full, one or the other of us would come back around to her and tug on her hand, saying we had to go to the bathroom. "Excuse me," Dee would say. "Where's the powder room?"

Once we were out of sight of the perfume ladies, we headed out the exit and then toward the nearest park, where we'd stashed our backpacks. There, Dee opened each bottle and dumped the perfume into the bushes while Rainbow whined behind her, saying, "Can't we at *least* save that one?"

But Dee didn't care much for perfume. While we worked she talked about how it was a symbol of everything wrong with our society, that it was created by the rich and was meant to separate us from our own true natures.

She talked about the importance of our work too. She said something big was coming, that Samuel and O were counting on us, that time was running out.

"Time for what?" I asked.

She looked at me with eyes like dull pennies and said, "Time to break the machine."

"What machine?" I asked.

"This one." She waved her hands through the air to include everything all around us—the buildings, the block, the whole city. And even though there was no expression on her face, I could sense her rage. I sensed that she was the kind of person who could be very angry at you, and who could save that anger up secretly, bit-by-bit, without you ever even knowing.

At the end of the day, when our backpacks were full, Dee bought us each a piece of pizza and a lemonade. She smoked two cigarettes in a row while we ate. Then, finally, we took the subway home.

As soon as we got to the house, I said bye and turned to walk toward the bus. I wanted to climb into the hole under the bed and go to sleep for a week, but Dee hooked her finger inside the belt loop of my dress and pulled me back to her. "Not so fast, little lady," she said. "You've still got work to do."

She led Rainbow and me into the living room, where she handed us an empty backpack and a list. She told us not to come back until we had everything on it and the way she said it, I could sense her rage again. Then she steered us out the front door and shut it behind us.

Out on the stoop, I unfolded the list. It said masking tape, rubbing alcohol, matches, screws, Bazooka bubble gum.

"Good," Rainbow said, snatching it from my hands and marching away, down the sidewalk.

"Good?" I followed after her. "It'll take all night."

"It's important, *Elizabeth*," she said.

"Why?" I stopped and folded my arms over my chest.

She stopped too and looked at me like I was an idiot. "For the *Cause*."

"Yeah, but *why*?" I stood tall to remind her I was older. "And what is the Cause, exactly? Do you even know?"

"The end of things," she said.

"The end of *what*?"

"All this," she said, windmilling her arms.

"And that's a good thing?" I asked.

"Yeah," she said.

"Why?"

She thought about that for a moment. "Because it isn't working anymore," she said, finally. "Can't you feel that?"

She had me there. Things weren't working. I *could* feel it. And I could feel that she really believed what she was saying. She was practically trembling with belief.

So that night we moved through the streets, getting all the things on our list because even though I had no idea what I was doing anymore or why, it was a relief to know she did. And while we worked, something strange happened. I felt her belief wash over me. It felt like it was washing me clean.

With Dee in the picture, every day was the same for a while. We woke early and got dressed and went out to different department stores, acting innocent while we gathered perfume bottles. In between stores, Dee droned on about the importance of our work, and about the machine, and how trouble was coming, and Rainbow lapped it up like a hungry dog.

"What kind of trouble?" I asked, but she never did say.

As soon as we got home at the end of the day, we were sent right back out again with an empty backpack and another list.

It was impossible to look for Margaret. I could hardly find a moment alone. Sometimes, late at night, after Rainbow had fallen asleep, I would crawl out onto the roof by myself. I tried to feel Margaret then. I tried to remember her smell, the sound of her voice, but it was like all our memories were stored in glass jars on a high shelf I couldn't reach anymore.

Sometimes the movies would start in my mind, and I'd have to run a piece of glass over my skin again, always in the same spot, up by my armpit, where nobody would see. Michael would come to me then, a warm presence all along the length of my body, and then I'd know she was still out there somewhere, alive. He'd wrap his hand around my arm, over the place I had cut, squeezing and squeezing like he was trying to tell me something in Morse code, something I couldn't quite understand.

At the morning meetings we were always told who had been arrested the day before. There was usually some argument about getting a lawyer. Once in a while someone would mention King, but there was never any news about him. The meeting always ended with us being told which corners were hot and what parts of town to avoid.

There should have been less of us at the house except that new people were always arriving. They weren't clowns though, and they weren't from the farm either. They were from Detroit and Chicago and California and they looked like Dee, with leather jackets, dark glasses and big boots that clomped when they walked.

I stopped some of them and asked if they knew Margaret. I described her hair, her freckles, her singing voice that made you think of cowboy movies.

Nobody knew her. One man smiled and said he wished he did.

But most of them just said, "Outta my way."

Eventually, once we'd collected enough perfume bottles, Dee was reassigned. It was just me and Rainbow then for a while. We were put back on pamphlets, which should've been a relief except that Rainbow was bossier than ever. We weren't allowed to dump our pamphlets in the mailbox anymore, she said. We had to hand them out one-by-one. And we weren't allowed to sit in the park or look for Kool-Aid or Pepsi bottlecaps either. I couldn't even talk her into visiting with the hennies or playing The Dad Game. Instead, we spent long, hot days working one intersection after another, jabbing our pamphlets at people until the air went funny.

"Let's play Every Little Thing," I tried then.

Or, "Let's play Bigs and Smalls."

Or, "You do poems, I'll collect the money."

But we couldn't, she said. She always gave the same reason: because time was running out. And when she said it, I sensed that the two of us were rushing toward some future I couldn't quite see. I could feel it though, rumbling in the distance.

The clowns were busier than ever in those days too. Sometimes they went away to do a show and didn't come back for days. Whenever I saw him, I ran up to Roland and asked about Margaret. His answer was always the same: that she was sick and trying to get better, that she loved me and would be with me as soon as she could.

"But are those *her* words or yours?" I asked, and "How long will it take?" and "Where *is* she exactly?" and "When's the last time you *actually* saw her?"

He never had time to answer me straight, except for once when he bent down and admitted he didn't know *exactly* where she was, but that if a person is lost in the woods, it's always best to stay calm and wait in one place.

"Is she lost in the woods?" I asked. "Which woods? Where?"

"No, Elizabeth," he said, taking me by both shoulders. "You are."
Then he widened his brown eyes and gave me a warning. He said

I should keep my head down and stay out of trouble. He made me promise. We even shook pinkies on it.

But in the end it was a promise I couldn't keep.

One morning Rainbow and I woke early and came downstairs to find the clowns standing in the living room, getting ready to go out. The women were wearing white coveralls. Their faces were painted white and they had dark circles drawn around their eyes. The men were dressed normally but had heavy backpacks. They were divvying up change, arguing about whether they should take the subway or a cab.

"Definitely the subway," someone said.

"But a cab is more discreet," said someone else.

Rainbow and I stood in the corner of the room, listening while we filled our canvas bags with pamphlets. I could feel a strange energy coming off the clowns. They were buzzing with excitement.

In the end, they decided to go by train. They left the house, arguing about which route and who was carrying what.

I bounced my eyebrows up-down at Rainbow.

She scrunched her lips like King and was about to say no.

But I had learned from the best.

"I'll tell Samuel about this," I said, reaching over to tug on the heart-shaped locket hanging around her neck.

We slung our bags over our shoulders and followed after the clowns, trailing by half a block so they wouldn't see us. We followed them all the way to the subway station, then down onto the platform and even onto the same subway car. They were headed to Manhattan. We were close enough that they could've seen us if they'd tried, but they were too busy bickering among themselves. They didn't notice when we got off at the same stop, or when we all came out into the same small park.

They seemed to be in a hurry. They strode across the park. Then the men and women split off in different directions. The women went and stood behind some dumpsters alongside a huge stone building. They were doing something with their costumes over there. I saw Effie undo the front of her coveralls and tape a bag of something dark to her skin, right below her armpit. Meanwhile, the men had gathered in front of the building. We followed after them and hid behind a big statue of a lion. It looked like a very important building, with wide stairs and tall doors. The men huddled on a flat spot between two flights of stairs, unzipping their backpacks and taking things out. We were so close to them, just ten steps away, but they had no idea. The place was full of people going places on their coffee breaks.

The men were arguing about something and peering over their shoulders. "Just wait," I heard Roland say. "Don't start until they're here."

Eventually, the women came out from behind the dumpsters. They looked exactly the same as before—white coveralls, pale faces—but now they had no shoes and their expressions were grim. They walked right past Rainbow and me without seeing us. They were already clowning. They signalled to the men, who started unrolling a white tarp at the bottom of the steps. It had "Stop the War" and "End the Bloodshed" written on it in huge black letters. The women took their places on top of the tarp. They stood in triangle formation, holding themselves around their waists, moaning like they had stomach aches and staring straight ahead. Some of them were crying. Meanwhile, Roland and the rest of the men walked through the crowd, handing out pamphlets, talking about how our brothers and sisters were dying on the other side of the world.

Rainbow and I climbed up onto the lion's platform to get a better view. That's when I saw the red puddles starting to appear. Blood. It was running down the women's legs and pooling at their feet. It was soaking through their coveralls in big blotches. They were moaning and wailing. They reached down and dipped their hands into the blood. They smeared it onto their faces.

People coming up the stairs below us looked at the blood, then the tarp. Their faces twisted up. They were handed a pamphlet before they scurried away, except for one woman who came up the stairs and froze, right at the top. She raised a hand to her forehead and teetered there for a second before collapsing backwards into the arms of the man behind her.

The man laid the woman down. A crowd started to form around them. People were waving their hands over the woman. "Give her some space," someone said. "Get her some water," said someone else. But the clowns kept clowning.

After a few minutes, a man came rushing out of the crowd and ran toward the female clowns, yelling, "You could've killed that woman."

Roland stepped in the man's way. He was trying to reason with him, saying that it was just theatre, that the blood was only paint and they had a right to perform here, but the man kept waving his arms around, shouting and pointing at the women. Then he threw a punch. It hit Roland right in the face and his nose started bleeding, real blood this time. The clowns stopped clowning and came to his side. Then more people came to the man's side and, within seconds, it was a full-on brawl. People were yelling, throwing fists and briefcases. Hats were coming off and rolling away down the stairs.

"C'mon," Rainbow said, jumping down and rushing forward with her fists out.

I meant to jump down and follow her. I wanted to. I should have, but I couldn't. More and more people were coming up the stairs and joining in the fight. The clowns were outnumbered. I saw Rainbow disappear into the middle of the crowd, swinging and kicking.

The female clowns were trying to roll up the tarp. Their blood spilled out onto the pavement in thick, red pools. Roland and the men started to retreat. They were backing away with their arms up, saying, "Peace." They were just about to turn and leave when I heard a shrill whistle behind me. A line of men with helmets and clubs came running along the sidewalk, toward the commotion. It was the Fuzz. There were ten of them at least, then twelve, then fifteen. They came up the stairs and ran at the clowns. They were blowing their whistles, hitting with their clubs.

I saw Rainbow fall to the ground and then I lost sight of her.

The other clowns were falling, too, curling up into balls and holding their heads. There was blood everywhere, but I couldn't tell if it was real blood or clown blood.

People were running in all directions. Police were blowing their whistles and trying to herd people back down the steps, toward the sidewalk.

I saw Roland. He had his hands up. He was talking to one cop when another hit him in the back of the legs. He fell. Another cop got on top of him. He pressed his knee into Roland's back but held his head up by the hair. Then a third cop swung his leg back and kicked Roland in the side of the head. I heard a dull pop, like a watermelon being cracked over a fire hydrant.

I screamed. The cop who had been kneeling on Roland looked up and saw me. He reached for his baton and started moving toward me.

I jumped down and ran a wide arc around the crowd. I ran up the stairs of the big stone building and in through the tall doors. It was so dark in there I couldn't see at first. I couldn't tell what kind of a building it was. It was cool and quiet and echoey like a train station but with high ceilings like a church. People were moving every which way but mostly up, in streams. They were whispering and murmuring like someone very important was napping in the next room.

I slipped into one of these streams of people and looked back toward the doors. The cop was standing in the entranceway, looking for me, left and right.

I ran up one flight of stairs and then another, weaving in and out of the crowd, until I found myself in a tall hallway with a painting of a naked angel on the ceiling.

People were floating past, smiling at me for no good reason. I followed a nice-looking woman through a set of heavy wooden doors and into the most beautiful room I'd ever seen. It had a high ceiling with paintings of pink clouds on it. It looked so real, like the actual sky at sunrise, that I wondered if I wasn't actually out there getting my head kicked in with the rest of the clowns, and this was heaven or the place just before it, a kind of waiting room where Jesus would finally get a good look and make up his mind about me.

I wasn't ready.

I moved toward a big wooden desk on my right. I wanted to lean against it, just for a second, to catch my breath. The clowns and Rainbow were gone, maybe dead. I was gone, maybe dead.

I got to the desk just as my knees gave out. That's when I heard her.

"Hell-*oh*," someone whispered. She stepped out from behind the desk and came through a little door toward me. I remember thinking she didn't look much like an angel in her fuzzy brown sweater and green skirt. She did smell like hand lotion though, and she had red, heart-shaped lips and a beautiful barrette that twinkled in the light. She had a nametag that said Joan. Did they wear nametags in heaven? Probably.

"Is this it?" I asked, meaning heaven, hell, the waiting room, whatever.

"This is it!" she whispered, helping me up. "You made it, Sweetheart!" She led me over to a chair, told me to sit and breathe and then twirled away.

Before I knew it she was back with a little paper cup of water. She handed me a candy wrapped in wax paper. I unwrapped it and put it in my mouth but, as soon as I tasted it, I knew I hadn't died with the rest of the clowns after all. It was black licorice. So this wasn't heaven. A tear ran down my cheek, then another and then I couldn't stop myself. I was shaking and sobbing and coming apart.

"Oh dear," she said, stepping away again. She came back with a box of tissues and handed me one after another until a little pile had built up on the table in front of me. "Here, have another candy," she said, sliding one toward me.

I ate it even though it was licorice too and she sat next to me, rubbing my back and telling me to breathe.

"Drink your water," she said when I had calmed down a little.

Then, when I had finished that, she said, "What's your name, Hon'?"

I stammered for a moment before arriving at who I wanted to be. "Jennifer," I said.

She rested her hand on top of mine. "And where is your mother, Jennifer?"

I said I didn't know.

"Okay," she said. "So who did you come here with today?"

My head was spinning. Everyone I'd come there with was gone: Rainbow, Roland, Tex, Effie. I started crying again, I couldn't help it.

She handed me another tissue and while I used it, I noticed she was looking at me very closely, checking out my fingernails, my hair, my clothes.

I remembered what King had said about the Fuzz, how they were always too friendly and asked too many questions. And I remembered how he'd said they could look like anyone.

So I blew my nose and gulped everything down. I sat up tall and said, "I came by myself, but my aunt is coming later."

She tilted her head. "Your aunt?"

I said some things then, I don't remember what, about how I lived with my aunt and uncle in a big house. I might've given them names. I might've said I had my own bedroom and how we all rode horses and took vacations together. It's never good to say too much when you're lying, I knew that, but I was nervous and she was watching me very closely as if she was trying to memorize my face.

When I was done, she seemed satisfied. She pulled out a pencil and a little piece of paper and said, "Well, how about we find you a nice book to read in the meantime?"

I looked around and noticed for the first time that the room was full of books. It's why everyone was here. I needed to blend in, so I nodded yes.

"Excellent," she said. "What are some of your favourites?"

My mouth hung open.

She laughed and patted my hand. "Don't worry, that happens all the time in here." Then she lifted her pencil again, "Can you at least tell me what subjects you're interested in, Jennifer?"

"Horses," I said.

"Okay," she said, but like it was really good news, like "Oh-*kay*!" She spun around and led me over to a long wooden shelf that ran down the middle of the room. She walked down the shelf, clicking her fingernails over the small drawers and explaining that the first thing we did when we wanted a book about horses was to look in the card catalogue. She kept doing that, explaining her every move and saying "we."

"Here we are!" she said when she'd finally opened the right drawer and found the right card. And I knew then, by her pure excitement, that she wasn't the Fuzz after all, but just a regular person who loved books a little too much.

I could've left then. I didn't have to keep up the charade, but the truth is it was a relief being Jennifer.

Joan wrote a bunch of numbers down on a card and then handed it to me. These numbers told us where the book was, she explained. Then she led me away, out the big doors and down a hallway, and the whole time she kept explaining how the library was organized.

I was trying to listen to her, but I kept thinking about Rainbow and Roland and the rest of them.

I tried to focus on her brown shoes clicking over the floor and how different she was from all the adults I knew, like she was from an entirely different planet where everyone tiptoed and whispered and explained things to each other all the time, but I kept hearing the sound of Roland's head getting kicked.

I squeezed the cut on my arm and the pain brought me back to the present.

She led me down some stairs and into another room full of books. We moved down the narrow aisles until, eventually, we arrived at a huge shelf of horse books.

I stood before it, looking up, but I was suddenly too tired to read the words on the spines.

"Can you pick one?" I asked.

"Absolutely!" she said, as if she'd been hoping I would say that. She disappeared around the corner for a moment and when she came back, she had a beautiful book in her hands. It was covered in green leather and had the words "Black Beauty" written on the front.

"Have you read it before?" she asked.

I cracked it open. It smelled like pencil shavings and old dinner. It was the smell of a quieter, better life, of homework and homemade casseroles. I shook my head no.

"Well, I think you're really going to love it!" she said, beaming.

"What do I do with it?"

She pinched her lips. "That's up to you. You could take it home with you. Do you have a library card?"

I shook my head, no.

"Does your aunt?"

I shook my head again.

"I see," she said, but she was squinting at me like, actually, she was having trouble seeing. "Well, you're welcome to sit at a table and read it here until your aunt arrives. Would you like that?"

I nodded, not because I wanted to read the book but because she wanted me to and, for some reason, I wanted to please her. It felt like my life depended on it.

She showed me to a table. There was another girl sitting across from me, reading a different book about horses. I smiled at her. She smiled back.

I sat and pretended to read while Joan pretended to organize some books nearby. She was watching me, I could feel it. The book was about a horse who had a wonderful life with his mother. I squeezed my arm and turned the page. The horses were happy and everything was good, but you could tell it wouldn't last. Joan was humming under her breath nearby, a song I'd never heard before. I kept squeezing my arm and pretending to read and then at some point I really was reading. The horse got moved to a new farm, away from his mother. The horse was getting "broken in" which was painful but, in the end, good for him. When I looked up, the light had shifted in the room. Joan was gone. So was the girl who had been sitting across from me.

It was a miracle. For a moment I had forgotten who I was. I had forgotten about Rainbow and Roland and the rest of them too. I shoved the book into the back of my pants. I was just going to borrow it until I got to the end of the story, I told myself. Then I'd bring it back and nobody would ever know the difference. I snuck away, down the stairs and out the door where men with hoses were already washing away the day's blood.

CHAPTER 25

AFTER

SUMMER IS UPON US. IN THE GREENHOUSE, THE MOST IMPOSSIBLE THING IS
happening: all those little yellow flowers have small, green tomatoes
forming at their centres.

Time is running out for us at Harrow House. We have to decide who
we want to become, and quickly.

Bertha arranges a tour for all of us at the local community college.

We visit the culinary school. Leonard's eyes get large, then larger,
as we walk through the commercial kitchen with its industrial-sized
pots and pans.

We visit the pottery studio, where Patrick gets to try a spinning
wheel for the first time. He giggles as his hands fall through clay again
and again.

We visit the drama department, where we come across a group of
people in tights, rehearsing something in the hallway. One of them says,
"Go to thine bosom: Knock there, and ask your heart what it doth know."

Bertha nudges Heather. "See? You could do that!" but she snorts and
makes a face like, *no effing way*.

We wander down the long, brown hallways together while Bertha goes
on and on about the merits of higher education—that it is an excellent

platform to build our lives upon, that we don't have to know exactly what we want to do yet, that it's okay to just pick a direction and begin, even if we change directions later.

At one point, I see a Jennifer walking down the hallway, her books clutched to her chest, her ponytail swinging left-right. I wait until everyone is peering in at a classroom and then I split off from the group. I follow her down one brown hallway and then another. When she disappears behind a heavy door, I go in after her and, right away, as soon as I smell the smell of old dinner and pencil shavings, I feel a sudden whoosh of hope.

It's a beautiful library, with high, vaulted ceilings and one whole wall made of windows.

People are reading in upholstered chairs all around the room. They're gathered in quiet clusters at worktables. Two librarians are murmuring to each other at the checkout desk and another one is rolling a cart full of books through the aisles.

"Tell me about a good time from your childhood," Bertha has been saying a lot lately. "A time when you *did* receive the proper lovecareandattention you so deserved!"

Mostly I've refused.

But I suppose there was one place where I did feel something like lovecareandattention. I suppose Joan gave that to me for a little while, before I ruined it.

I see Jennifer, standing before a bulletin board to my right. I walk over and stand next to her. She's reading all the posters and signs, twisting the end of her ponytail up in her fingers. Her hair smells like apples. I twist my own hair and pretend to read the signs too. *So this is what it feels like to be a Jennifer-at-college.*

She reaches up to rip a tag off one of the signs.

I do the same.

She looks at me. "What?"

I shrug. "What?"

She twirls away and passes through the turnstile.

I look down at the slip of paper in my hand. It's an ad for the librarian training program they offer here at the college. Looking at it, I feel a light, floaty feeling in my centre, like maybe Bertha's right and there can still be magic in the world.

Before we leave the college that day, Bertha gets us all the information we need to be able to submit our applications. Then she hounds us for weeks, reminding us that we have to be enrolled in time for our parole reviews, warning us that if we don't choose a program soon, someone will choose for us. Mr. Twohig helps us all fill in our applications. Annie helps us put together our personal essays. Bertha puts them all in separate envelopes and stamps them and tells us where the nearest mailbox is. It's the easiest task ever. We don't even have to think. All we have to do is walk two blocks and drop our envelopes into a slot. But on the way to the mailbox, Heather says something about how college is a total waste of life. Then she looks me right in both eyes and says exactly what Margaret once said—that we're both destined for better things which, of course, I take as some sort of sign.

I never have been much for reading signs.

We wait for our letters.

Leonard's comes first. He has been accepted into culinary school.

Patrick's arrives next. He will be starting a general arts diploma, learning everything from photography to glass-blowing.

Bertha checks the mailbox every day, but nothing comes for Heather or me because, of course, we never sent our applications. Heather, because she's going to California to catch up with Jerry, and me because I'm under her influence.

"Are you sure you sent your application?" Bertha asks me.

I nod. *Liar.*

She leans forward and frowns at me. "I'm concerned about you, Hon'. I think it may be too much for you to be sharing a room with Heather right now."

But it's already too late. I can't tell the difference between her stuff and my stuff anymore.

And then one day, just like Bertha said, time is up.

Rhonda shows up again to speak to me and Heather about enrolling in school. Heather goes first to have "a chat" about what her interests are.

By the time it's my turn, Rhonda's smile has worn off.

She asks about my interests.

I tell her I like taking care of tomato plants. I like coming up with similes and metaphors and learning to master what Francine calls "the chatter of my mind."

"Well, let's not aim *too* high," she says, scribbling something in her notes.

She gives me what she calls an "aptitude test."

Then, at the end of all that, Heather and I are both called back into the room, sat down and told we'll be enrolled at The Institute of Xcellence, a local hairdressing school. It's a night school, Rhonda explains, so we can still waitress or whatever during the day. She says we'll learn how to do manicures and updos and we'll never be out of work a day in our lives.

"Xcellent!" Heather says with pretend delight.

So it's settled. We're to become hairdressers.

This is what happens when you've screwed up as badly as us. You don't get to become. You're told who to be.

CHAPTER 26

BEFORE

I DIDN'T HAVE ANY MONEY, SO I DECIDED TO WALK HOME FROM THE LIBRARY. I walked through a neighbourhood full of bright, flashing lights, where men followed me down the sidewalk asking if I was looking for my daddy, a neighbourhood where laundry hung from the fire escapes and cooking smells filled the air, a neighbourhood that looked like a ghost town with the windows all papered over. I saw a bridge in the distance, like a doorway in the sky. Then I was upon it, with the wind aching in my ears and the cars whooshing past. I walked and walked until, finally, I came to a place I recognized, with no street signs and bars on all the windows.

It was evening by the time I got home. The house was empty. Everyone was in the yard out back. They were all in motion, moving things out of the shed. O was standing at the centre, calling out orders. I saw Effie among them. She had gotten away somehow. She was still wearing her blood-stained coveralls.

I walked right up to O and tugged on her sleeve. "They got Rainbow," I said.

She spun around, startled. "Who?"

"The Fuzz," I said. "We were watching the clowns and they got her."

She stared at the air between us for a moment, and I wondered if she'd heard me. Then she sat down, right in the middle of all that commotion, and put her head in her hands.

So she *did* care about Rainbow.

Behind her, people were rolling big barrels out of the shed and toward the bus, where it was parked in the alley.

"Was she hurt?" she asked.

I thought of everything Rainbow had been through and decided to say yes.

She closed her eyes for a moment.

The back doors to the bus were propped open. They were using two boards to make a ramp up into it.

O was staring at me, angry now. "What were you doing there?"

I shrugged.

"You were supposed to be handing out pamphlets around here. So what were you doing at the library?"

They were tipping the barrels over and rolling them up the ramp, over the bed—my bed.

O was looking at me, waiting for an answer.

I puffed my chest out. "Just walking by."

"Just walking by? In midtown *Manhattan*?"

She started to say something then—that we shouldn't have been there, that it wasn't safe—but I didn't stay to listen. I walked away, all the way up to the empty bedroom. I closed the door behind me and sat on the bed. The room was so empty I could hardly stand it. I closed my eyes and tried to feel what Rainbow and Roland were feeling, but I couldn't. I couldn't even imagine where they were now, or what would happen to them next. Would they be sent to jail? Would they find King in there and help him get out?

I reached into my pocket for the shard of glass. I was about to run it over my skin when I remembered *Black Beauty*.

I pulled it from my waistband, opened it and buried my nose in it, smelling its smells, imagining all the big, quiet homes it had been in. Then I turned to the next chapter and started reading, hoping to disappear again, like I had at the library.

I woke to Dee standing over me, holding the book in her hands, saying, "What's this?"

I stood and tried to snatch it back from her, but she lifted it up over her head.

"New York Public Library," she said, reading the words off the inside cover. "Tell me, Elizabeth, how in the world did you get yourself a library book?"

"I took it," I said.

"You *took* it? From the New York Public *Library?*" She clicked her tongue, still holding the book above her head.

I nodded.

"And what if someone saw you take it? You think we need that kind of attention around here right now?"

I shook my head. If I just agreed with her, maybe she'd give it back.

She lowered it and held it in the air between us, tapping her fingers on the cover. "I don't know if you know this, but the shit has hit the fan. We don't have time for books right now." She reached back and dropped it into the canvas bag hanging off her shoulder. Then she held another bag out to me. "You're going to show me how to do pamphlets today." She flashed a crooked smile. "And maybe if you're good, you'll get your book back."

While we walked toward a busier part of town, Dee told me O had said I was being defiant.

"What's defiant?" I asked.

"It means you've been bad," she said, "and you're on a very short leash."

We walked in silence after that, but I swear I could feel the weight of that leash pulling at my neck.

When we got to our first busy intersection, she said she wanted me to show her all my tricks, and no more funny business. So I showed her how to wait by the mailbox until a crowd had built up. I told her how

King used to do it, asking questions and holding the pamphlets out like a hand of cards. I told her my way was different, that it was best to find her own way. I explained about not staying in one place for too long, about always watching for the Fuzz, about cut and run. Then we separated and worked the intersection a few times.

Her way was even louder than King's. She stood in one spot, waving the pamphlets in the air and shouting at people until they took one.

We did one corner and then another and another and then she seemed to tire. She said she needed a minute, but I should keep going. I worked my way to the other side of the intersection and looked back at her. I saw her lean against the mailbox, smoking a cigarette, watching me.

The corner was crowded. The air was so damp it was like walking into the room after someone's had a shower, but my book was still in her bag. I could see its pointy corners sticking out. If I was good, I'd get it back.

I worked the intersection a few times. Sweat was pouring down my back and pooling behind my knees. I was standing on the opposite corner, waiting for the light to change when I saw Dee stub her cigarette. I saw her reach into her bag and pull my book out. She flipped through the pages, frowning.

I stepped off the curb, right into traffic, but someone yanked me back from behind.

It was one of those hairy Krishnas, not the same one as before, but one just like him. He had the same diaper, the same impossible hair.

"Close call," he said, crouching down to get a good look at me. His breath hung around us like an onion cloud. "Tell me," he said, "are you loved properly?"

I didn't know what to say to that.

On the other side of the intersection, I saw Dee snap the book shut. Then she turned and slipped it into the mailbox behind her. I heard it land with a thud at the bottom.

Something thudded in me. I needed that book. I needed to know how the story ended. Did the horse and its mother ever find their way back to each other?

I wobbled on my feet and the Krishna reached a hand out to steady me.

I saw Dee take out another cigarette.

A man came up and offered her a light.

She offered him a pamphlet.

He said something funny.

She threw her head back and laughed.

He was the Fuzz. Anyone could see that from a mile away. He was too clean, too friendly.

The traffic changed. I could've crossed over if I wanted. I could've shouted cut and run and saved her. But I didn't.

She'd said if I was good, I would get the book back. I had been good. I was always good. I was what everyone wanted me to be, always, but it was never enough. Not enough for Margaret and not enough for her.

The Krishna was blinking at me, still waiting for his answer.

Beyond him, I saw the man with the lighter pull out a pair of handcuffs. I saw him put them on Dee. Then he led her away, toward a black car. He put her in and shut the door.

"Krishna is the answer," the man said. "His name is pure love. When we say it, we are loved properly at last."

I looked at him. He had a crust of something, mustard maybe, dried in the corner of his mouth. He had an orange diaper and weird hair, yet even he was loved properly.

I felt the truth of my situation then. I wasn't loved anymore. Not properly. Not by anyone.

Margaret was gone and didn't seem to be coming back.

Rainbow and King were gone.

Roland was gone.

I was all by myself. And for the first time ever, instead of feeling sad about that, I sensed opportunity.

I unhooked the canvas bag from my shoulder and let it drop to my feet. Then I turned and walked away from the corner without looking back.

I took a train to Manhattan. I circled the library for a long time before finally working up the courage to go in and tell Joan the truth about the book. I would say I had taken it because I needed to know the ending, I decided, but that I had meant to bring it back. I would say it had been stolen, that I was sorry and would do anything to make it up to her. I'd wash dishes or re-shelve books for a whole year if she wanted.

"Actually, that's a very good idea," Joan said when I told her.

I was standing before her desk in the library with my head bowed.

"Well, not for a whole *year* obviously," she said, "but how about you come every day after school for a little while and help me organize things."

"I don't go to school," I said.

Her face twitched. "Does your mother know that?"

I scrunched my mouth up like King. "I don't have a mom." I knew now why he'd said that. It was easier than the truth.

"Oh," she said, only that, although I could tell she wanted to say more. Her eyes softened. "Well then, how about you just come when you can."

"Like a job?"

"Sure, okay," she said, sitting a little taller, looking pleased with herself. "Like a job." I looked over each shoulder, to make sure nobody I knew was watching. "Can I start right now?"

Before I could start, she led me through the door by her desk and down a little hallway to a bathroom. She handed me a bar of soap and told me to wash up because it was important to have clean hands when we touched the books.

We. I felt a little tingle on my scalp when she said that.

She winked and said I could take as long as I wanted, that nobody would bother me. She even gave me a fluffy towel to dry with.

When I came out of the bathroom a little while later, she looked me over and said, "Well *that* must feel better." Then she led me to a small kitchen area. There was a coffee machine, a fridge, a table and chairs. On the table there was a plate with half a sandwich, four apple slices, one and a half sugar cookies on it—exactly half of her lunch. There was a glass of milk with an ice cube in it and next to that, another copy of *Black Beauty*.

"So you can find out how the story ends!" she said. Then she squeezed me twice on the shoulder and turned back to her desk.

The sandwich was tuna with tomato and lettuce and some kind of strange, sweet pickle mixed in. I ate and flipped through the pages of the book and maybe it was those pickles or the smell of soap on my hands or the sound of Joan whispering to someone at the counter, but I felt that feeling again, the one I had felt in Jennifer's room, that my heart was a balloon.

After my sandwich, we got down to business. Joan gave me an empty cart and showed me how to wheel it around the library, picking up books from the bins at the end of each aisle. She showed me how to read the numbers on the spines of the books and match them to the numbers at the ends of each aisle and then quizzed me about where I thought each book might belong. Then, when my head was spinning, she finally said, "that's probably enough of that for one day," and she set me free to collect the books from the rest of the room.

By the time I returned to her desk, my cart was full but the library was empty.

Joan stood. She said she was heading home now and offered to walk me out.

"Where is it you live again?" she asked once we were outside.

"Over there." I waved a hand in the general direction.

"I see," she said. "Well, thank you for doing a great job today." She handed me a dollar.

I held it awkwardly in my hand. "But I'm supposed to be paying *you* back."

"I've changed my mind about that," she said, smiling but looking at me very carefully again—my shoes, my clothes, my hair. "If you ever need anything, Jennifer, anything at all, please don't be shy to ask."

I felt suddenly dizzy, like when you're standing on the edge of a roof, thinking about tipping off. I wanted to tell her that what I needed, more than anything, was to find my mother, but it was too late. I'd already lied about that. I thought about asking if I could come home with her for just one night, but I couldn't do that either. I was on too short of a leash.

"Okay, I will, thanks, bye," I said instead, shoving my hands in my pockets and walking away.

I walked home again.

On the Manhattan side of the bridge I was thinking about my new job and the dollar in my pocket and all the ways I might spend it. I was walking a little taller than usual, smelling my own soap smells and trying to swing my hair like a Jennifer.

On the Queens side of the bridge, I was thinking about how much trouble I'd be in for Dee's arrest. I was lining up my excuses in my head: that Dee had broken a promise to me, that she'd lied, that she was barely even working herself.

For the first time in such a long time, I wasn't thinking about Margaret at all. I was less than a block away from the house, rehearsing what I would say to O, when I heard a *pssst* coming from inside a bush.

My first thought was that it was Rainbow or King, but when I stepped closer, I saw it was her. It was Margaret, crouched there in the dirt.

My insides leapt.

I must've squealed because she shushed me. She peered out at the street, left and right, and then pulled me into the bush with her.

"MeMe, I need a favour," she said without any surprise at all, as if we'd just seen each other that morning.

"Yes!" I said, not even knowing what the favour was. It didn't matter. Whatever it was, I'd do it.

"Good," she said, taking me by the hand and leading me away. We walked fast, down one alley and then another. There were so many things I wanted to ask her, like where she'd been and where we were going, but she was talking the whole time, saying something about the government and the moon and a great gathering.

I was trying to listen, trying to follow what she was saying, but it didn't make sense. I kept watching her face. It had changed so much. Her mouth was twisted up and she was speaking out the side of it. Her eyes were different, too, dark and opaque like two painted-over windows. She was dressed strangely, wearing a long coat over a dress over pants, and she looked smaller than I remembered her, as if she'd shrunk in our time apart. She still had that thin, blue line running down her forehead, the small X between her eyes, but now there was a thick vein running down the centre of her forehead too, and it seemed to be throbbing. She looked like a worn-out copy of herself, like her own ghost. I wanted to hug her, but something told me not to.

She said something about payphones, how they were all a part of it. And there really did seem to be something about the payphones. Every time we passed one, it started ringing, as if someone, or the city itself, was trying to call us.

She said something about red shoes and, like magic, there were red shoes everywhere. A pair of red runners tied together and looped over the power lines above us. A block later, a single red cowboy boot lying shredded in the middle of an alley. Then, for several blocks in a row, men, women, kids, all wearing red shoes and smiling and winking at us.

We darted across four lanes of traffic. It was there, out in the middle of the road, with people laying on their horns and shouting at us, that she said about the men in brown hats. "Can't you see them?" she asked. "They're everywhere, MeMe. *Everywhere!*"

I did see one then. He was leaning out of a window up high, smoking a cigarette and smiling down at us. Then I saw another. He was sitting on a park bench across the street, pretending to drink out of a brown paper bag but watching us. Had they always been there and I just hadn't noticed, or were they only there now because I was with her? We kept moving. On a busy corner, in a part of town where the hennies were strutting past and the men were lurching at us asking "Whachyouneed?" I decided to tell her about the Pepsi Sweepstakes. I only needed two more letters, I said, and we would win a trip to Niagara Falls. I told her about the airplane, the hotel room, the all-you-can-eat buffet. I told her this was our chance to go back to the beginning and start again.

She stopped in the middle of the sidewalk. "Which letters?"

"V," I said. "And C."

All the colour went out of her face. She pointed and, there, on the brick wall directly behind me, were the letters "VC" with an X drawn through them in paint so fresh it was still glistening.

She took me by the hand, pulling me down an alley, over one fence and through a hole in another. Then, finally, in a half-empty parking lot, we slipped behind a row of dumpsters to catch our breath. It was a dark, narrow space like a tunnel, with a brick wall at the back and boards blocking the light from above. As soon as we were inside, she pulled a cardboard box over the opening. She was peering through some holes in the box. That's when I noticed more cardboard beneath my feet. There was an overturned bucket, a small tin-can stove, a pot full of water, a blanket. Someone lived here.

She pointed behind me. "Hand me that pen."

I turned and, there, on the overturned bucket was a pen: her pen, on her bucket. And that's when I understood that she lived here, that she had been living here, so close to me for who-knew-how-long. My heart, that old yo-yo, was free-falling through empty space now. I couldn't tell up from down anymore.

I handed Margaret the pen and she scribbled something on the inside of the door. In the murky light I could see the entire box was covered in writing, not letters but those symbols I'd seen her write on the road atlas so long ago.

She turned back to me, put a hand on each of my shoulders and said, "I need pamphlets." Her breath wafted into my face. It smelled like sour milk.

She was shaking me back and forth. Her fingers were digging into me. "I need to find my way back into the house, MeMe. I need to do something big and this is the only way. Do you understand?"

250

I nodded.

"As many as you can get, okay? Lots and lots." She was almost crying.

"Okay," I said. "I'll get lots."

"Good." She let go of me finally. "That's my girl. Stash them somewhere safe."

She stopped and tilted her head as if someone was whispering instructions to her. Then she grabbed my sleeve, lifted it and twisted my arm until she could see my scars, all the neat little lines I'd cut into my skin. She ran her fingers over them gently, saying—almost singing—"*Oh*-oh-oh."

She pulled me into a hug and rocked me back and forth, stroking my hair softly, like I was fragile, breakable. I could hear her heart beating in her chest. I could smell her sour-milk smells, but I didn't mind. I could have stayed that way forever. I would have, but we heard a clanging from the parking lot outside, like someone was hitting a pot with a spoon. It was close, getting closer.

She held one finger to her lips and moved to the entrance to peer out.

I should have done what I was told and shut up and stayed put, but instead, I crept up behind her and asked, "What is that?"

Her arm shot straight out behind her. She accidentally knocked me against the wall so hard my head hit the bricks. My tongue crunched against my teeth. I howled.

She grabbed me and held her hand over my mouth saying, "shhhht."

I should have listened to her. I should've stopped howling, but I didn't or couldn't.

Her hand clamped down, hot and damp over my face. It smelled like garbage, cigarettes, pennies and, beneath all that, like home. It was so tight over my face I couldn't breathe, not through my nose or my mouth. The edges of things were vibrating, everything pulsing to the rhythm of her heartbeat or mine, I couldn't tell. Then the world went dark.

I don't know how long I was out, only that I woke up later, alone, propped up against the wall in a brick doorway. Margaret was gone, no trace of her.

You might think this would have been some sort of breaking point, that at this point I would have had enough of her, but you'd be wrong. Ours was not that kind of love.

I stood and dusted myself off and made my way back to the house. I knew what I had to do. I had to steal as many pamphlets as I could and stash them in the library for whenever I saw her next. She needed me now and only I could help her.

CHAPTER 27

AFTER

VANCOUVER IS PRETENDING TO BE CALIFORNIA, WITH HER WHITE-SAND beaches, her endless sun and thirty-degree days.

Miracles are happening in the greenhouse too. The tomatoes are getting bigger and redder by the day.

The plumbing crisis is over and I'm allowed to move back into my own room. It's a relief to be away from Heather, but sometimes, lying in bed at night, I can still feel what she feels through the walls. I know she's plotting her escape.

Bertha is outraged about Rhonda and The Institute of Xcellence.

"It's like she didn't even *try* to get to know you girls," she says at the breakfast table, over French toast with mixed-berry coulis. "I mean, hairdressing is a noble profession. I'm just not sure it's right for either of you."

She says she's spoken to some people and it's possible for us to have a late enrollment, to start at the Institute in September and then switch to another college in January.

"I don't know," Heather says with a shrug. "I like hair."

"And you, Elizabeth?" Bertha asks. "Is that what you want?"

I look at Heather, who is wink-winking at me.

I shrug. "I like hair too."

"Well, okay then," Bertha says with a sigh. "I can accept that, but I can't say I'm pleased about it."

When I see Mr. Twohig, he takes a gentler approach. "We can be many things in a lifetime," he says. Then he gives me a gift—a book called *Letters to a Young Poet*—and says something about how maybe we are who we are *despite* our choices, not because of them.

Annie chooses to look on the bright side too. "Kerouac worked at the post office!" she says. She gives me a leather-bound journal. "For dreaming ..." she has written on the inside cover. Tucked inside is another poster for the Write What You Know contest.

On Saturdays, Patrick, Leonard, Heather and I go to the farmer's market and stand, all in a line, at our stall in our tracksuits and turtlenecks, looking like poster children for mental illness, like *We are mental! We are proud!* And we *are* strangely proud of our tomatoes. We sell the plants for two dollars each and even Heather gets involved, giving advice about which tomatoes will ripen first, which will be sweetest, which will be best in a sauce.

Back home, Leonard and I take the once-sickly plants and "harden them off," which means getting them used to life outside the greenhouse a little at a time. Then, when they're ready, we plant them in the yard in hooped cages, like little halfway houses.

Leonard has his hearing and then Patrick. They're both released from parole.

Bertha makes us cupcakes, which are really just banana muffins with icing on top, and we celebrate that they are no longer halfway people, but whole. In September Patrick is going to move into student housing because he's still nervous about toasters, but Leonard will try living on his own. Bertha says that each of them are a Harrow House success story.

She reminds me and Heather that we need to start thinking about where we'd like to live too. The Institute of Xcellence doesn't offer student housing, but she says she knows a great foster mom who would take us in. We both roll our eyes at the word "mom," without meaning to.

One Monday in July, Heather and I are invited for a tour of our new school. It takes two busses to get there. The Institute of Xcellence is in a grey, squat building in a strip mall alongside the highway. On one side there's a pub called Mick Donaldo's and, on the other, a store that sells nunchucks and swords.

We meet Chan, who owns the place. He introduces us to some of the other students: a Christine, a Kimmy, a Cindy, a Carmel. They have bright lipstick, bouncy perms, shirts with shoulder pads.

I catch them looking at Heather's fake tattoos, at my turtleneck.

Heather plays nice and pretends to be interested while Chan shows us around, but as soon as we're back on the bus she says, "No *way* am I going to that shithole school. *Or* living with a foster mom."

"S-hole," I correct. And I add, "But we have to."

She looks at me and, with one trembling finger raised between us, says, "I don't have to do anything and neither do you."

She says her and Tad are leaving tonight, that I can come too, that I'd better if I don't want to end up doing perms in a strip mall.

Then she gets quiet. She looks out the window and, for the first time, I see that her burn scars travel up the side of her neck too. There's even one behind her ear. What I want, more than anything, is to place my finger on those thick whorls of skin and un-whorl the past. I want to say, "Let's just stay, and go to the Institute and get off parole and be good girls for once." But I know that will never work for Heather. She'll never get a perm or play by anyone else's rules.

"I saw them once, you know?" I say.

She's still looking out the window. "Who?"

"The Dead. At Woodstock."

She whips her head around. "Get the fuck out."

"Well, I *heard* them," I say. "I couldn't really see them. Couldn't see anything because I was locked in the trunk of a car." I bring my hand to my mouth. It's the first time I've said it out loud to anyone. If only Bertha were here to see me coming to terms with my past. Well, part of my past. I don't dare say the other thing: that I was once told and, more importantly, actually believed, that Jerry Garcia was my dad. I don't want her to know how gullible I am.

Then it's my turn to get quiet and stare out the window while she looks at me like she wishes she could undo all the damage. Those words—*locked in the trunk of a car*—occupy the air between us. She doesn't say anything or ask any questions though. I like that about Heather. She knows exactly when to leave a thing alone.

"Come with me," she says once we step off our first bus, downtown. "I want to show you something."

"But we'll be late for dinner," I say.

She rolls her eyes, then spins and walks away, down Granville. I chase after her.

Everywhere we go, boys turn their heads. Their eyes travel her whole body, stopping on her ass. They whistle. She twirls and gives them the finger.

She leads me to a store with loud music playing, something loose and bluesy that I can't quite place. It's hard to tell what kind of store it is. There are used boots and suitcases and army jackets everywhere. The air is thick with incense. At the front, a skinny guy with a mohawk is sitting behind the counter, painting his nails black.

Heather nods and leads me past him, to the back of the store, where, stacked against the floor-to-ceiling mirrors, there are crates of records. We each crouch over one, flipping.

"Did you know The Dead all drop acid and trip out together on stage?" she says, flipping her hair and looking at herself in the mirror.

"That's why sometimes they'll play a song that's, like, twenty minutes long. They're just tripping."

I'm flipping through the records in my crate. I see Jefferson Airplane, Janis, Canned Heat, but I'm not paying attention. I'm feeling 80% dizzy and 20% anxious. It's the incense and the strange, familiar music and something else, call it premonition.

The song changes. Heather stands and tilts her head, listening. "Wanna know why Jerry owes me the money?"

She doesn't wait for my answer.

"Listen." She points up at the ceiling. "Hear that? That's 'St. Stephen.' It's like their biggest song ever and guess what? I wrote it! But Jerry took it from me, right out of my frickin' head!" She's jabbing her finger at her forehead now, as if pointing to the very place from which he took the song.

I would like to respond, but the room is spinning and there's a voice in my ear telling me to look up.

I do look up and, in the mirror's reflection, I see the TV behind the front counter. The news is on. A woman is talking. Her red hair fills the screen.

"And that's not the only song he took," Heather says. She's being loud now, waving her arms around. "The way I see it, I've made him a *ton* of money. Money he owes me."

It looks like it could be Margaret on the TV. I stand and, forgetting where I am, step forward, headfirst into the mirror.

"What the hell," Heather laughs.

I turn and walk toward the counter, rubbing my head.

It *is* Margaret, I'm sure of it now. A banner across the top of the screen says "Golden Gate Blockade." Another banner under her head says "Hare Krishnas Against Nukes."

So she *did* become a Krishna. And then the joke arrives, a decade too late: a Hare Krishna, not a hairy one.

The camera is zoomed in so tight her afro fills the screen. It looks as if there are small animals wriggling around in there, though it's just some people standing on the road behind her. I know this, but the average viewer won't. The camera is way too close to her head, closer than one would ever go to a normal person. *This crazy Krishna has animals in her hair*, the news people seem to be suggesting.

"What is that?" I ask the man with the mohawk.

He shrugs. "Some weirdos blocking a bridge."

Heather comes up beside me. "What's going on?"

"Turn off the music," I say. "Turn it up."

The guy looks at me funny.

Heather slams her fist on the counter. "You heard her. Turn it the fuck up."

He turns it up and then I hear her for the first time in years.

She's talking about the nukes.

She's talking about Russia and Reagan and all this macho business, all this weapon mongering, and when will it all end?

She's rambling and waving her arms around, saying love is the answer, Krishna is the answer.

I'm waiting for her to say something that makes sense, something like *Here I am, MeMe. Come and get me.*

But she doesn't. As usual, she's got other things on her mind. Nukes this time.

"We're all sitting on a timebomb," she says. "If we're not careful, it'll blow."

The picture cuts away.

A woman with a tidy blond triangle of hair comes on screen. "These commuters are *outraged*," she says. Behind her, commuters jostle and raise their fists in the air.

"Is that your mom?" Heather asks because she knows, from Group. She giggles. "Your mom is a Krishna?"

The camera cuts back to a shot of the blockade. Margaret is there, in the middle of the Golden Gate Bridge, waving a rainbow flag. She's surrounded by a crowd of people. They're holding hands and singing in their matching orange robes. She looks healthier than when I last saw her and happier, like she's loved properly at last.

Margaret tips her face up to the California sun.

"Hare, Hare, Hare," she says.

"Krishna, Krishna, Krishna," her friends answer.

She smiles and, for the first time in 3,805 days, I see her broken teeth.

I feel myself floating up, out of my body and into the darkness of her mouth.

I teeter and then fall. The world goes dark. I have been swallowed, once again.

CHAPTER 28
BEFORE

AFTER MY VISIT WITH MARGARET, I WAS LEADING A TRIPLE LIFE.

In the morning I was Elizabeth.

I woke and put on my good-girl clothes. Then I went downstairs and filled my bag with pamphlets. I sat through the breakfast meeting, all O and Samuel's talk about how capitalism was a bust and that time was nearly up, that this was our last chance to show people another way.

I always went out and worked a few corners in case anyone from the house was watching. Eventually, though, I slipped into the crowd and walked away.

I was MeMe then. I walked down every alley looking for Margaret, calling her name. I whispered *pssst* into every bush. I peeked behind every dumpster, but I couldn't find her anywhere.

Eventually, when it got too hot, I made my way toward the library. I always stopped at a few stores on the way, looking for Pepsi letters. I found the C for Vacation, but no matter how hard I looked, I couldn't find the V.

Before going to Joan's desk, I stopped on the second floor. I had found a place there, behind the books on British History, where I could stash my pamphlets.

By the time I got to the third floor, I was Jennifer.

"How *aaa*re you?" Joan would say when she saw me.

She always had little gifts for me: a toothbrush and toothpaste, a comb, a new T-shirt, nice-smelling soap. Every day she had a different kind of sandwich for me, too: ham and cheese, turkey with cheese, something called a "granny sandwich" with apples and nuts and honey. She never made the same sandwich twice. She encouraged me to read *Black Beauty* while I ate my lunch. Then, after I'd read a few pages, she always wanted to talk about it.

"What do you think?" she'd say, her eyebrows arching up.

"I'm worried for him," I'd say, or, "I wish he could just run away."

She'd always stop what she was doing then and turn to face me. "Oh?" she'd say, like I was the first person in the world to ever think such a fascinating thought. Then she'd say, "Worried how?" or, "Where do you think he should run to?"

I'd usually say something stupid then: that he should go back to the place he was born or try to find his mother.

She'd always come back with something smart and thoughtful. "Do you think, perhaps, the writer *wanted* you to feel worried for the horse?" she'd say. Or, "Do you think wanting to run away is a universal feeling?" She always had a way of making me think about the person who wrote the book and what they'd intended rather than just the story itself.

Once in a while, during our conversations, she would ask me about something other than the book, like what my aunt and uncle did for work or if I had any cousins.

At first I didn't mind. I said their names were Roland and Lulu, that she sewed dresses and he had a spaghetti restaurant. I said she had been a famous singer once and he held the record for the world's biggest meatball. I said I had seven cousins and I named them all. But then one time she asked, "What are your cousins' names again?" and I couldn't remember what I'd said before, so I had to tell another lie about how they all had nicknames. And pretty soon it was like that, lies to cover my lies.

Eventually she'd give me an empty cart though, and after that I was free. I'd wander through the aisles, collecting discarded books. I loved the calm quiet of the library rooms. I loved seeing what kinds of books people read, like how most girls my age wanted to read about horses and most boys wanted to read about dinosaurs but, every once in a while, there was a girl who wanted to read about a dinosaur or a boy who wanted to read about a horse. I loved finding books in the wrong spots and putting them in their proper places. I loved this world where everything had its place, where people could borrow a book one day and know that, two weeks from now, they would be able to bring it back without any rips or stains or missing pages.

At the end of the day, I'd stop by Joan's desk and she'd walk me out. Sometimes we'd stand on the steps outside, talking about *Black Beauty* some more before she reached into her wallet to give me a dollar or two. "You earned it fair and square," she'd say, pushing the money into my palm. Then, before we parted ways, she'd always say the same thing: "If you ever need anything, Jennifer, please don't be shy to ask."

After I left the library, I was MeMe again. I wandered through the city, looking for Margaret. I was in her world then. Everywhere I looked, I saw people with red shoes. The people who wore them seemed to be smiling at me strangely, making symbols with their hands as if they were trying to tell me something. I saw the men in brown hats too. They wove through the crowd on the sidewalk, following me. I had to zigzag down alleys and hide in doorways to get away from them.

It was usually dark by the time I got home. I'd sneak past the living room and up to my room where I'd hide the money and my Pepsi bottlecaps in a hole I'd carved in the mattress. Then I'd lie down, thinking of all the ways me and Margaret might spend the money one day.

It's hard to say how much time passed like this.

I remember I had over twenty dollars stashed in the mattress and so many pamphlets hidden behind British History, I had to start putting them in other places too: behind the law journals and the books about Antarctica. I finished *Black Beauty*, so Joan gave me a new book to read: *The Call of the Wild*. She gave me my own library cart too, with my name written on it and a nametag that said "Jennifer: Young Library Volunteer."

I remember everyone at the house started talking about the coming draft. Soon people wouldn't have any choice, Samuel said—they'd be sent away to feed the war machine whether they wanted to fight or not. This was capitalism's inevitable end point, he said. It was starting to devour us now. We had to fight back.

"Be ready, people," O kept saying. "Something's about to go down."

The next time I saw Margaret was outside the library. I had just walked away from Joan and was headed home when she intercepted me on the sidewalk. She was wearing a long leather jacket that was way too big for her. Her hands were buried in her pockets and she was jingling something around in there.

"Do you have the pamphlets?" she asked.

I glanced back at the library to check if Joan was watching, but thankfully she'd already left.

"Yes," I said.

"Good." She held her hands out. "Give 'em."

"I mean, no," I said. "I mean they're hidden. I can't get them until tomorrow."

"Why?" she looked up at the library. "Are they in there?"

Something lurched inside me.

"No," I said, "somewhere else." It was the third lie I'd ever told her. It felt so much worse than lying to Joan.

I tried to take her hand to lead her away, but she wouldn't let me. She was staring up at the library, scratching her head.

I said I had money, that I could take her for a hotdog.

She turned back to me then, finally. "How much?"

I said two dollars. Something made me leave out the rest of the money I had back at the house.

"I'm gonna need more than that," she said, laughing, and that's when I saw her two front teeth were broken at sharp angles. There was a dark triangle in the middle of her smile now. Looking through it, into her ruined mouth, made my knees so weak I almost fell over.

"How much do you need?" I asked.

She said lots.

I said I knew a way, that it would involve spilt milk and fake blood.

"Atta girl," she said.

So that day I was the klutz, crying into my puddle of spilt milk, and she stood by the cash register, waiting for just the right moment to reach in and take what she needed.

I never did ask what the money was for.

Eventually something did go down, just like O had predicted. There was a big commotion in a neighbourhood across the bridge. A bunch of men had trapped the Fuzz inside a building over there. Then more Fuzz had shown up. Then the whole city erupted. For five days and five nights everyone was out in the streets, throwing stones and tipping cars and lighting them on fire. Everyone at the house was talking about the right to love who you want and wear what you want, and every night they went out with baseball bats to defend those rights. When I went out onto the roof at night, I could hear sirens and glass shattering in the distance. I saw Cronkite, looking very serious and very sad on a TV across the alley.

After that, things really started to heat up around the house. Every day more people arrived from Detroit and Chicago. Every day there were more arrests. O said we were at war now, that it was time to take things to the next level.

One night I came home and, as soon as I walked in the front door, I saw Dee standing in the hallway with a group of people.

She spun around to look at me. "Well, look who it is. Elizabeth the escape artist."

She grabbed me by the arm and pulled me over to the group. They were all dressed in black, talking urgently about a job they had to do, a job I was now a part of. "You'd better not bail on me this time," Dee said. She handed me a backpack full of empty bottles, then led me out the front door and once again I felt the weight of my invisible short leash.

We walked down a busy street with our backpacks clanking until we came to a parking lot with a flashing neon sign saying *Girls! Girls! Girls!* Dee and the others crouched down in the red glow to discuss strategy for a moment. Then we all split off into pairs.

Dee took me by the hand and led me between the cars. "Keep talking to me," she said, "and act casual." After that she kept asking stupid, casual questions, like, "How's school?" and, "What should we do for your birthday this year?" while she peered into the windshield of every truck around us.

As soon as she said the word "birthday," I realized—with a swift kick to the chest—that mine had already passed. I was nine now and I hadn't even noticed. Neither had Margaret. At the thought of that I had to stop and bend over to catch my breath. No matter how up or down she was, Margaret had never forgotten my birthday.

When Dee had finally confirmed that all the trucks around us were empty, she unzipped her backpack, pulled out a long plastic tube and an empty wine bottle. She handed the bottle to me and told me to get ready.

"For what?" I asked, but she didn't say.

She unscrewed the gas cap on a truck and listened as she lowered the tube down into the tank. Then she knelt down, put her mouth over the end of it and sucked until, eventually, gas came pouring out.

I held the bottle under the stream while she stepped around to the front of the truck. I heard her retching up there. She rejoined me just before the bottle was full. She corked it, pulled the tube out of the tank, replaced the gas cap and wrapped the tube back up. Then she swapped the full bottle with an empty one from my backpack. She brought her finger to her lips—*shhhh*—and we moved on to the next truck.

We did seven more trucks before we met up with the others. Then we walked back to the house together, everyone sombre and silent, trudging under the weight of our bags and whatever it was we were doing.

That night Dee followed me all the way upstairs to the bedroom.

"Don't you have any blankets?" she said, looking around. "Or pillows?"

I shook my head, no. I didn't want to share King's blankets with her, even if it meant I was cold too.

"Jesus fuck, it's worse than prison," she said.

"Were you in prison?" I asked. "Did you see Rainbow and King in there?"

She snorted. "You really don't know how things work do you?" She took her pants off, rolled them up as a pillow and lay down, saying we had a big day tomorrow.

I lay on the edge of the bed, as far from her as I could get, waiting for her to fall asleep. Then, as soon as she did, I snuck out to the roof.

I could hear people working in the yard below me. They were moving on and off the bus, loading it or unloading it, I couldn't tell. They were doing something with the gasoline we had collected too. I could smell it wafting up toward me, but I wasn't interested in any of that. Instead, I lay back against the chimney and tried to remember every detail of each of my birthdays with Margaret: the one where she'd let me invite a bunch of friends over and made us a money cake with the dimes baked right into it. One girl had accidentally swallowed a dime, but I still got invited to everyone's birthdays for a long time afterwards.

Or the one where she'd woken me up in the middle of the night, carried me out of the house in my pyjamas and put me into a truck I'd never seen before, so we could go see a miracle. She never did say whose truck it was, and we never did find the miracle, but we did get to drive around all night looking at the stars while she talked about all the different paths I might take in life, how I could become a dancer or an actress or anything I put my mind to because, she said, I was one-in-a-million.

Or the one where we'd hitchhiked to a fair a few counties over and she'd flirted with the man operating the Ferris wheel, telling him he looked just like Paul Newman until he let us on for free. I remember sitting on that Ferris wheel with her, how every time we went up and got a glimpse of Lake Huron and, farther away, America, her mood lifted. Her eyes filled with light while she talked about life on the other side of the water—how in America a fair like this would have a real roller coaster and decent music, how Americans were rebels, that they knew how to party and when to fight. Then, on the way down, as we turned slowly back toward the Ontario mud, her mood changed again. She grew quiet, her face criss-crossed with complicated shadows. That was the first time I understood that we had to get away from Ontario, that her life depended on it. I wished I could go back to that moment and warn us both.

In the morning Dee kicked me awake, saying "Up and at 'em." She said Samuel wanted us all to work in pairs from now on, that if I ditched her this time, there'd be hell to pay.

We filled our bags and left the house. She was in a terrible mood. As soon as we got to our first corner, she reached over, plucked my eye patch off my head and stuffed it in her pocket. Everything turned jittery and blue. She said she'd seen me work and she'd had enough of the timid routine. She said she wanted me to be more aggressive, like her. "In case you've forgotten, we're trying to wake people up, Elizabeth," she said.

I was like her, as much as I could be. "Tired of the grind?" I yelled on corners, waving the pamphlets in people's faces. "Want to experience true freedom?"

But it didn't work. People stuffed their hands in their pockets and made wide circles around me.

Luckily, by the time we got to one of the rougher neighbourhoods, Dee had lost her focus. The hennies surrounded her, asking where she was from and if she had anything special for them. She handed over her pamphlets by the handful. They tucked them into their purses and offered to braid her hair.

I waited until Dee was busy with a woman named Candy. Then I turned and ran.

I looked for Margaret all around the library.

When my bag became too heavy, I went in, straight to the second floor, to drop off my pamphlets. Then I stopped by Joan's desk to pick up my cart.

"Where's your eye patch, Hon'?" she said when she saw me.

She made a big deal about it, asking if I could see okay, and whether I needed another one.

I said I'd lost it, and that I could see fine, but just when I said that, I noticed the air was quivering all around her.

"I think it's time I speak to your aunt and uncle, Jennifer," she said. "I'd like to invite them in for a chat. Can you give me your phone number so I can call them?"

I shook my head no. I knew what this meant. All my lies were about to catch up to me.

The air around her was moving out and out, like when a stone is dropped into a pond. She was the stone. The library was the pond.

"What do you mean, no?" she said, with her hands on her hips.

"We don't have a phone," I said. I tried to put my hands on my own hips but I missed and fell sideways into her desk.

"Honey," she said, rushing over to help me up.

She led me to the kitchen and sat me down. My cart was already there, loaded up with all the books I was to put away, and my lunch—a sandwich with the crusts cut off. She'd probably made it the night before, in her big, quiet kitchen. Me and Joan were from different universes, I remembered then. The distance between us was making me dizzy.

"Eat your sandwich," she said. She stood over me, looking at the top of my head for what felt like a long time. She seemed to be having some sort of argument with herself. "Yes, eat," she said. "Eat and we can talk about the rest later."

I opened my mouth to say thank you, but no words came out.

I picked up the sandwich because she wanted me to, but I wasn't hungry.

Luckily, a man rang the bell at her desk. She went over to speak to him.

The man wanted to see a map of New York State. Joan glanced at me before leading him out of the room.

As soon as they were gone, I snuck downstairs and out the big front doors.

When I got home later that day, Dee was waiting for me. She wasn't mad though. She had a new hairdo full of tight, swirling braids and a smile pasted onto her face like a creepy mask.

"Ready?" she said. She handed me my own backpack with my own tube and empty bottles and we went out into the city together. Before we went to look for another parking lot, we had another job to do though, she said. We had to stop and steal a bunch of bubble gum. We had to chew the gum too, one piece after another, while we walked through the city. Then, as soon as it was chewed and before the flavour was even gone, we had to take it out of our mouths, dry it off on our sleeves, and drop it into a plastic bag she kept in her pocket. She said this was for the Cause too, but I didn't believe her.

The days became a blur.

Dee liked to sleep in, so if I woke early enough, I could avoid her.

I climbed down the fire escape and scoured the city for Margaret. Sometimes I thought I saw her—a flash of red hair bobbing through the crowd. Or I'd hear someone singing in a scratchy voice by the subway entrance. Or I'd hear my name, *MeMe*, coming from around the corner.

I'd feel the old tug on my chest. I'd race forward, calling her name, but it was never her.

I must've flipped the lids off a hundred Pepsi bottles.

I must've chewed a thousand pieces of gum for Dee, in every flavour.

At some point, Joan handed me a sealed envelope and made me promise I'd give it to my aunt and uncle. Then, every time I saw her after that, she asked if they'd read it and when they were coming in.

I said they were very busy, but my aunt couldn't wait to meet her and my uncle was making her a special meatball.

"*Really*, Jennifer?" she said, looking at me suspiciously—squint eyes, heart mouth.

"Really!" I said. "They'll be here soon." But when I said it, I felt the difference between who I was and who I was pretending to be. I felt like I was a bridge stretched between two different worlds, just barely hanging on with fingers and toes.

The next time I saw Margaret was inside the library.

I was shelving dinosaur books when I smelled something strange, like cabbage rolls. Then I heard a *pssst* from the other side of the shelf.

I peered through the books and there she was.

"Do you have the pamphlets?" she said. "Are they here?" She was looking up and down the aisles, watching for people.

"Yes," I said.

"Well, go get them." She walked away, farther down the aisle. She was wearing two different shoes and a strange, ugly dress that looked like a tablecloth with holes cut in it for her head and arms. She was clowning though, trying to act like a norm. She had a piece of paper in her hand and was pretending to look for a book.

I walked to British History. I put a bunch of pamphlets onto my cart, sandwiched between horse and dinosaur books. Then I went back through the aisles, looking for her. I don't remember feeling my body.

She was waiting for me in the bird books. I wheeled my cart up to her.

"Good," she said, grabbing a pamphlet, "this is brilliant, MeMe. Now we can reach a whole new audience."

I didn't know what she was talking about until she pulled down a book about ostriches. She opened it and placed the pamphlet inside its pages. Then she closed the book, placed it back on the shelf and smiled down at me.

I stared into the jagged hole in her teeth and the ground did a thing at my feet, like when you step on the wrong elevator and, for the first moment, you can't tell if it's going up or down. Then she said, "hop to it," so I did.

We worked together, me on one side of the shelf, her on the other, taking each book down, placing a pamphlet inside, closing it, reshelving it. While we worked, she talked about radio waves and how the government had been using parts of her body to broadcast messages to the world. She talked about how, when the rockets landed on the moon, people like us would lose our freedom. She said it would be total surveillance and that it was important to reach people any way we could, that putting the pamphlets into books was brilliant, because now we could warn the smart people. She said to make sure I told O and the rest of them what we were doing so she'd get invited back into the house.

At some point Joan came looking for me. She peeked her head around the end of the aisle and asked, "Everything okay, Jennifer?"

"Fine!" I said. I could feel Margaret staring at me through the bookshelf, wondering who this woman was. I was praying she wouldn't say anything about the government or its rockets. More than anything, I wanted my two worlds to stay separate.

"I just accidentally put some books in the wrong place," I stammered. "So now I'm putting them back."

"Okay, Honey," Joan said, tilting her head at me.

I heard Margaret snort on her side of the aisle.

"Okay then," I said. "I won't be much longer."

"Great!" Joan said.

"Great!" I said.

Then, finally, she turned away and I heard her brown shoes clicking all the way back down the hall.

I was so embarrassed, I had to hang on to the shelf and close my eyes. I was waiting for Margaret to say something, to ask how I knew the librarian and why she'd called me Jennifer, or even worse, why she'd called me Honey. My ears were burning. I bowed my head and waited but she didn't say a word and, when I opened my eyes a minute later, she was gone, leaving only her cabbage smells behind.

CHAPTER 29

AFTER

"OH. MY. GOD," HEATHER SAYS WHILE WE WALK TO THE NEAREST PAYPHONE. "This is *totally* a sign. I mean, what are the chances, seriously? We just *happen* to see Margaret on TV, *in* California, on the same day we *happen* to be going there? It's a frickin' miracle. Do you think we can stay with her for a while? Just until we're on our feet? Probably, right? I mean, she *is* still your mom."

I shrug and nod, but I'm not really listening to her. The whole time there's a voice hissing in my ear, asking me, *But what do you want?*

We stop in front of a 7-Eleven, so she can call Tad. They have a low, muttered conversation. From where I'm sitting on the curb, it doesn't sound like it's going well. I hear her say something about money, something about his carburetor, something like, what does he mean *more time?*

Good, I think, *maybe we can just go home now.*

But she's determined. She makes another phone call. I can't hear that one at all. It's in a much quieter voice.

When she returns to me, she says Tad can't come, but his cousin Dan has agreed to drop us off in Oregon.

"For what?" I ask. "A hand job?"

She looks at me, looks away.

"*Two* hand jobs?"

She shrugs. Then she flops down next to me and gets quiet—too quiet, for too long. She's bouncing a knee and biting the skin around her fingernails, peeling it off and spitting the pieces in a wide circle all around her.

I feel what she feels: that her life is closing in on her, that she has to get to California tonight, no matter what. And I know that she'll do anything with just about anyone to get there.

I look at that burn scar behind her ear and realize I will do anything, too, to make things right, for her and for me.

"How much do you think you need to get there on your own?" I ask. "To California? Without Dan?"

"Why, you gonna get it for me?"

I shrug. "Maybe."

"I don't know, like two hundred," she says, laughing.

"And that'll be enough for you to get to Jerry and ask for your money?"

She nods.

"Okay," I say. "I know a way."

I give her a dollar. I tell her to go into the 7-Eleven and buy me a package of red Kool-Aid. Then, while we walk to another store a few blocks away, I pull my eye patch out of my pocket. I put it on and explain how it will work: that I'll be the klutz and she'll get what she needs out of the till.

After it's done, we walk to the bus station and buy her a ticket on the overnight bus to California.

I almost buy one for myself, too, but there's that voice in my ear again, the one I used to think of as Michael but that Bertha now insists is my "higher self." It is loud and clear and close and consistent, like a radio tuned right.

Stop being what everyone else wants you to be, it says.

"You're not coming?" she asks.

"No," I say. Only that. I hear Bertha in my mind: *No is a full sentence. It requires no further explanation.*

"Really?" She's begging almost, not with her words but with her eyes.

I plant my feet and puff out my chest like Bertha has taught us to do. "I'm sure," I say, and it's not until I say it that I really feel it.

I'm sure that I don't want to live my life on the run or join any families or chase any rock stars anymore. I've done enough of that.

I'm sure that what I want is to just stay put for once and try to be ordinary, or ordinary*ish.* I want to be a Jennifer, the kind of person who can take out a library book any time because I know that, two weeks from now, I will be the same person, living the same life, and I can return the book exactly as I found it. Better yet, I want to *be* a librarian, to live the rest of my life in quiet, vaulted rooms, helping people and putting everything back where it belongs.

"You're a good girl, deep down," Heather says, and it's clear from her face she doesn't mean this as a compliment.

And she's right. I've always done exactly what I'm told. That has always been my downfall.

I walk her out to her bus and we say goodbye in front of the vending machines.

I give her the rest of the money and make her promise that she'll stay on the bus all the way to California, that she won't hitch or give any hand jobs, that she'll find the Family and let them take care of her.

I make her promise, too, that if she does run into Margaret in California or wherever, she won't say anything about me. It's enough to know she's out there somewhere, alive, I tell her. I don't actually want to see her again.

She crosses her heart and hopes to die and then climbs on board. She finds her seat, waves goodbye out the window and, as soon as the bus engine starts, I get an old MeMe feeling. I feel the *pffft,* the going up, and then I have a vision of her living in the desert somewhere, working in a small shop with the man she loves, tattooing the Virgin Mary and hearts shot through with arrows onto the arms of cowboys and drug dealers. And even though I've been wrong in the past, I know this time, the way I sometimes just know a thing, that I'm right, that she will be okay, even happy, and by the time the bus has pulled away, I feel lighter, as if I have finally set something down, something immensely heavy that I've been carrying for years.

CHAPTER 30

BEFORE

IT WOULD BE SO MUCH EASIER TO SAY I CAN'T REMEMBER WHAT HAPPENED next or in what order, but I do.

I remember working through the M's and N's and O's, adding a pamphlet to each book. I remember struggling to hide what I was doing from Joan, falling farther and farther behind on my other work.

Soon enough, Joan stopped asking about the letter for my aunt and uncle and started asking if there was anything I wanted to talk about. And she started looking at me like the nuns used to back in Ontario, like I had a horrible secret I was just dying to tell.

I shook my head no. "I'm just tired," I said.

And I was. I was more tired than I'd ever been.

I worked through the P's and Q's and R's and then, one day, Joan asked if I'd be interested in meeting a friend of hers, a very nice lady who could chat with me about how things were going at home.

I said no thank you.

"I understand," she said, and her mouth was smiling but her eyes were not.

In the afternoons, I staggered away from the library with my head full of static.

Walking home, sometimes I'd hear a *pssst* from the bushes and then Margaret would pull me in. She always looked different. One day she was dressed like a henny, the next like a norm, the next like a hobo. She always wanted something different from me too: one day money, the next a bunch of stuff from the hardware store. And I always did my best to provide.

Then, one time, she said she needed the keys to the bus.

"Why?" I asked.

"So we can go home," she said. Or did I imagine that part? Some things remain unclear.

But she did say that O had the keys, to check her pockets, her purse, the place she slept.

That night I had to go out siphoning with Dee and the others.

I sucked on the tube. The foul liquid spilled into my mouth.

I retched. I capped the bottle. I trudged home.

Later, when I was lying on the roof, I heard Samuel giving a demonstration to Dee and the others in front of the garage below. I peeked over the edge and watched him pick up a bottle and stuff something into it. I heard a rattle, like nails hitting glass, then watched as he poured gasoline into the bottle. Finally, he sealed the whole thing with a big wad of bubble gum, the gum Dee and I had helped chew. Then he held it up and called it a bomb.

"Now you," he said, and everyone stood and moved through the same steps while he supervised.

I lay back flat against the roof and closed my eyes. I tried to sleep, but I could hear them down there, talking while they worked. They said they were going to hit the New York Stock Exchange and a bunch of banks too. They were going to tear down capitalism right where it lived, they said, on the night of the moon landing, while everyone else was distracted.

"We should hit Cronkite's house," someone said. A few of them laughed but then they discussed it in earnest. Someone knew where he lived: on East Eighty-Fourth across from the park, and then they talked about different ideas to get past the doorman.

I looked across the alley. Cronkite was on a TV over there. He was busy talking about the day's news. Then he stopped, lowered his chin, looked right at me and said, plain as day, "Do something."

But there was nothing I could do. Not yet. So instead I closed my eyes tight and tried to think about all the macaroni salad I would eat when I finally got to Niagara Falls.

The next morning, I woke with the pigeons and crept downstairs. I hesitated at the entrance to the gold shag stairs, remembering Roland's warning, that people who went down there didn't always come back, but that hardly seemed relevant anymore. I didn't care if I disappeared. I descended on tiptoe, two steps at a time.

Downstairs, people were lying all over the floor, sleeping in heaps with their bare bums showing. O was snoring on her back with her mouth wide open. Her purse was by her feet. I searched it: no keys. I patted the one dress pocket I could reach: nothing. Then I saw the glint of a chain around her neck. It disappeared down the front of her dress. I stood over her, carefully tugging on the chain. She moaned and licked her lips. I saw it then—two keys and a silver feather squished between her breasts. I pinched my fingers around the chain and started to lift. The keys pulled away from her skin. They were dangling in the air. I had started to lift the chain up and over her head. I was just centimetres away from having the keys in my hands and everything, *everything*, ending up so differently when her eyes popped open. "What the fuck?" she said. She swiped at my hand, clutched the keys to her chest, rolled over and fell back asleep.

I left the house that morning, taking my money, my bottlecaps and as many pamphlets as I could carry: two bags, one over each shoulder.

I looked everywhere for Margaret. I had to tell her I couldn't get the keys, that I'd tried, but O had caught me. I had to say that I couldn't go back to the house anymore, that it was her and me now, but I couldn't find her anywhere.

At the library, I ran into Joan on the stairs before I'd made it to the second floor.

"Are you okay?" she asked when she saw me. She stepped toward me.

"I'm fine," I said, stepping back. "Everything's fine."

She didn't look like she believed me. She handed me a tissue and pointed at my face.

I wiped. Some kind of black grime was coming off on the tissue. Roof tar, maybe.

She sniffed the air.

I sniffed too. I smelled like a hot road.

I tried to push the bags of pamphlets behind my body so she wouldn't see, but it was too late.

She squinted at me. "Do you have a paper route, Jennifer?"

"It's just pamphlets," I said.

She was still staring at me, waiting for an explanation.

"I hand them out for my uncle," I lied.

Her eyebrows knotted together. "May I see one?"

I shook my head no.

"He doesn't like me to give them away," I said. "Only to paying customers."

"I understand," she said again, but this time I was sure she didn't. Her mouth wasn't a heart anymore. It was a small, angry button.

I snuck away from the library that day without saying goodbye. I stayed out as late as I could that night. I looked everywhere for Margaret, or for a suitable place to sleep, but in the end I had nowhere else to go. I returned to the house, snuck up the fire escape and slept on the roof.

At the morning meeting I kept waiting for O to say something about how I'd tried to steal the keys, how I was selfish and working against the

Cause, but she never did. Instead, she was busy talking about the rocket to the moon and assigning everyone new tasks.

"This is the final countdown, people," she said. She pinched her fingers in the air and asked if we could feel things narrowing down, coming to a point. I saw the chain glint around her neck. I heard the keys rattle inside her dress and wondered if that's how it would sound at the end: a final jangle and then nothingness.

She put Dee and her friends on distribution and forgot all about me.

I continued with my work.

I remember working through the S's and T's and U's.

Joan never mentioned the pamphlets again, but she did start making hot lunches. She gave me a new eye patch, too, a simple black one with the name Jennifer stitched onto the band. She ran her fingers through my hair and even offered to cut it for me.

She was closing in on something, I could feel it, but by then everything was closing in.

I remember everyone, everywhere talking about the rocket and the men who were headed to the moon.

At the library, Joan set up a special display of books about our solar system. I remember standing before it one day, straightening the books with her. She had made special cookies. She offered me one, a gingerbread man with a whole bunch of crunchy, white icing to make him look like an astronaut. She watched me very carefully as I bit off his hands and feet.

Then, as soon as I had bit off his head, she announced that today we were having lasagna for lunch. She said she'd invited her friend Carol to come by and share it with us, but not to worry, that Carol was very friendly.

"Are you hungry?" she asked.

I nodded yes, but really I was thinking about her friendly friend Carol and how she had to be the Fuzz.

Joan gave me another cookie and then got called away by a woman looking for books about birdwatching.

I stood by her desk, feeling the stretch of living in two different worlds. I was trying to decide which world I would rather live in: the one where it was exciting that a rocket was going to the moon, or the one where it was terrifying.

But there was no choice, really. I knew which world I belonged to. I opened Joan's desk drawer. I grabbed her red wallet from her brown purse. I took all the money from it—twenty dollars—and tucked it into my pants pocket. Then I went downstairs to get as many pamphlets as I could possibly carry from behind British History.

And the thing is, I didn't even feel bad. By then I had already moved out of myself. I felt bad the way an empty house feels bad.

I spent days looking for Margaret behind every dumpster and inside every bush.

She was nowhere to be found and the streets were strange.

The men in brown hats were everywhere now, shaking their heads at me, like they knew what I'd done.

Wherever I went, payphones were ringing and ringing.

The Fuzz was out on every corner, too, looking mean in their moustaches.

I came home as late as I could every night. I sat on the roof, drawing a piece of glass over my arm, calling to Margaret the only way I knew how, calling to Michael, calling to anyone who might hear.

I don't know how much time passed before Rainbow reappeared. It might've been days or weeks. I just remember I came downstairs one morning and she was there, tucked up next to O at the meeting with her eyes closed, nodding *yes, yes, yes* to everything O was saying.

After the meeting, I walked straight over to her. I tried to hug her, but she shrugged me off.

"Where have you been?" I asked.

She stuck her nose in the air. "Never mind."

She was mad at me, that was clear, but I wasn't sure why. Because I'd let her get arrested? Because I hadn't followed her into the fight?

She looked different: older and more serious. She was dressed in a normal T-shirt and jeans and had a short, tidy haircut that curved perfectly around her ears. She stood before me with her arms folded over her chest. "O says I'm the boss of you now," she said.

"Fine," I agreed. If she needed to be the boss of me, if that's what it would take for her to forgive me, I was willing.

"C'mon then," she said, and she led me to the yard out back where Dee and her people were loading those bottles of gasoline onto the bus. She picked up a perfume bottle off one of the tables and shoved it at me. It was filled with blue liquid.

"It's Denial," she said, looking proud, "our new mode of delivery."

That day, while Dee and Samuel and a bunch of the others drove away on the bus to distribute their bombs throughout the city, the rest of us had to go out onto the streets with our bottles of blue perfume.

Rainbow and I were instructed to stand in front of department stores, holding the doors open, asking men and women if they'd like to try a new fragrance called "Denial" in high, bird-like voices.

We did what we were told. We sprayed the blue liquid onto people's skin and, for once, they smiled back at us. They said thank you and walked away, sniffing their wrists.

Then, after we'd been chased away from our last department store, we stood on a busy corner, twirling there in the middle of everyone, spraying jackets, purses, pants, hands, watches.

"Bugger off," people said when they saw us.

"You'll thank us later!" Rainbow shouted after them.

"Why will they thank us?" I asked.

"Because we're giving them one last chance," she explained.

"One last chance at what?"

"To wake up," she said, "before it all ends."

I spun in a circle, looking at everyone around me. They were all so busy meeting friends and hailing cabs and walking dogs and shopping. They were buying bread and wine and flowers and man-on-the-moon souvenirs. One man was hopping around on a corner, playing a flute. I tried to imagine everything—all of that happy busy-ness—coming to an end, but I couldn't.

"What will the end look like?" I asked.

"Like boom," she said, matter-of-factly and, once again, I felt her belief wash over me.

We kept working. By early afternoon, I was drowning. Standing on a crowded corner, with the sidewalk breathing beneath me, I was getting a MeMe feeling again, except about everyone who passed by, all at once. I could feel everyone's hunger, desire, hope, sadness, love, anger, loneliness, fear, longing. The tv in my mind came on. Scenes from people's lives flashed on the screen—there and then gone, one after another. I could sense everyone's million rushing, domino thoughts and it felt like I was being crushed under the weight of it all. It felt like I could barely breathe.

Rainbow was at my side, stamping around, babbling in rhymes and playing her invisible trombone. Then I got a MeMe feeling about her too, or I thought I did. I saw a shimmer all around her and, in that shimmer, I saw her life play out: how she would move on from this time eventually, scarred and overly serious maybe, pretending sometimes at a simpler past, but able to pass as normal, managing a steady job, something ordinary, at a bank or a bakery maybe, until she met a man, had a child, moved to a smaller town to live in a house near the water. She looked so beautiful in that moment, still fragile and hopeful underneath her hard shell. Then she marched over to me and shoved a Styrofoam cup into my hands. "You collect the money," she ordered and, once again, I thought I heard the word *stupid* at the end of her sentence.

The tv in my mind turned off. I moved through the crowd, rattling my cup at people.

After we started with Denial, Rainbow was my constant companion, stuck to me like glue. In the morning she shook me awake, saying, "C'*mon,*" like I was already late for something. Then she was by my side all day long, telling me what to do and how to do it, telling me when I could take a break and for how long. We sprayed people, elevator buttons, subway doors and seats, door handles, park benches and railings too. We stood on corners shouting about the end of capitalism, the end of shopping, the end of everything until the sidewalk was bounding like a trampoline and the air was jittering all around us. It did feel a little like the end then. The corners were so hot and crowded it was like being boiled alive in a great big human soup. The city was grinding and clanging. It felt like I *was* inside the belly of the beast now, like I had been swallowed whole.

I couldn't go back to the library even if I'd wanted to.

I couldn't get to Margaret, even if I'd known where she was.

There was no escape, which is not an excuse.

I remember entering a store one day and seeing a crowd of people standing before the counter, watching the TV with their mouths hanging open. Someone was counting down, "5–4–3–2–1–0." There was an explosion.

Rainbow and I ducked behind a shelf.

"This is it," she whispered. Then, while she made a wide loop around the edge of the store, stuffing her pockets with all the things we might need for the end—peanuts, batteries, pepperoni, matches, gum—I peeked at the TV. I saw a rocket rising out of the smoke. I remember everyone smiling and patting each other on the back and Cronkite's voice saying, "Oh boy, oh boy, the roof is shaking." I remember wondering if he meant that in a good way or a bad way and sensing, once more, for the last time, that there were two possibilities: one world where the rocket was good and beautiful, a sign of progress, and one where it was the beginning of the end. Then Rainbow was back by my side. The two worlds collapsed into one. It was time to cut and run.

Time went funny after that.

The days blurred together. Rainbow became relentless. She was always lecturing me about how important it was to spray as many people as we could, as fast as we could, so we could wake people up. She was always congratulating herself about how brilliant she was for getting Jennifer's mom's perfume bottle when she did, even though we both knew she hadn't planned it. She was always correcting my technique. "Get closer when you spray, Eliza*beth*," she bossed, "and make sure you say it's called Denial." And there was always that word— *stupid*—implied at the ends of her sentences.

Was I annoyed by her? Of course. I hated the way she stood on her tippy-toes when she gave me an order, the way her hands curled into fists any time I asked her a question, the way she always stood too close, with her breath wafting around me in a sour Kool-Aid cloud when she talked, the way she was always pretending to know things about the rocket that she really didn't, like how many men were on it and how they all slept—ten, she said, and they hung from the roof like bats. I wanted her to go away, but only in the way I would want a mosquito to go away, not with any special kind of hatred. You have to understand, I didn't have a single second to think my own thoughts when she was around. The only time she left me alone was at night when she went off to sleep somewhere else—in the basement with O I assumed.

I remember one day, at the morning meeting, O announced that this was it, our last day to disrupt things. She raised her hands and exploded them in the air and everyone around the circle applauded.

Everywhere we went that day, the city was strangely quiet. People were having hushed conversations and looking up at the sky as if they expected something to fall from it.

The Pepsi Sweepstakes were suddenly over, all the cardboard displays taken away.

The men in brown hats were gone.

The hennies weren't out.

The payphones had stopped ringing.

286

Even the dogs had suddenly vanished from the alleys.

Rainbow was chattering in my ear all day long.

"When the rocket lands, everyone will be looking up, and that's when we'll get 'em," she said.

And, "We've got to tear things down, so we can build them back up."

And, "Everyone's gonna get what they deserve."

I remember Uncle Cronkite, flashing on every TV, in every window throughout the entire city. Everywhere we went, he was looking at me like, *Do something.*

I remember falling asleep alone on the roof that night, looking up at the moon, wishing it would wink out.

I woke early the next morning knowing this was it: the day of the moon landing, the day Samuel and O and the rest of them were going to burn the city down.

On a TV across the alley there was a cartoon image of an insect-like ship landing on the moon, a simulation of what would happen later that night. Then the image cut to Cronkite in his blue tie and I remembered they were going to get him too. He raised his eyebrows and looked right at me like, *Save me.* Then the image cut away to a commercial for Redbird Strike Anywhere matches, which, of course, I took as a sign.

Did I see Michael standing there at the top of the fire escape, in his blue jeans and striped shirt, waving me forward, his eyes flashing every colour at once? It's hard to say. There is the moment and then there is the story of the moment. Over time one replaces the other.

I remember I crept down the fire escape into the yard. There were crates stacked everywhere with those bottles full of gasoline, Samuel and O's bombs. The bus door was standing open. I climbed on. Inside, the place was a mess. The mattress had been removed. The cupboards were bare, some of the doors torn right off their hinges. I saw my old mushroom soup can, now empty. I saw the glass bowl I'd used for my first MeMe reading lying broken in the sink. There were food wrappers and crumpled garbage all over the floor. I hated O and everyone for what they'd done to the bus, my home. I hated them for ruining it, for ruining everything, but mostly I hated them for what they were about to do. I remember hearing Cronkite in my mind: *Do something, do something, do something.*

So I found some matches in one of the drawers: Redbird Strike Anywhere.

I found my old magic book, *Fun Tricks for Good Christian Children.*

I opened the book.

I laid it flat on the kitchen table.

I folded up the corners of the pages, fanned them out and slowly, carefully lit them on fire. Then I left the bus, taking the broom with me. I closed the door behind me, locking it from the outside the way Lucky used to, by wedging the broom into the handle next to the door and then tucking it behind the side-view mirrors.

Why did I lock the bus? Was it merely habit? I can't say and besides, you will make up your own mind about that.

After I locked the door, I walked across the street and hid behind a car. I peeked over its hood, waiting, watching. I remember the curtains caught fire first and the way the flames crept along the walls toward the front of the bus.

I remember how I looked away, just for a second and, when I looked back, that's when I saw it: two hands, pressed up against the front windows. Someone was in there, wanting out. It was her, Rainbow, there was no mistaking it. I remember the last look on her face—mouth open, eyebrows up, like "Oh!" before the flames climbed her body, wrapping her up and up as she twirled the way she did on every street corner as long as I'd known her—marching, playing her imaginary trombone, her head tipped back as if she was sipping the air, as if she couldn't, wouldn't ever, get enough of it.

I stood there, stupid, stuck to one spot like a melted candle.

I remember thinking I'd always known it would end this way for me and Rainbow, that from the moment I'd first met her, I had known

I was responsible for her in some way, and that I would fail her in that responsibility, the way I always failed everyone.

I shouldn't say any of that.

I should say that, as soon as I could, I came out from behind the car and started to run for the doors, that I would have saved her, or at least tried, but that someone, Margaret, caught me around the waist and held me back, that I was, of course, powerless against her. She clapped her hands over my ears. She pulled me to the ground. Then she lay her body flat over mine just in time for the boom.

You are wondering, did I know that Rainbow was sleeping on the bus? How could I not have seen her or sensed her or smelled her there? Didn't I know how much gasoline was in the area? Wasn't I partially responsible for that?

Bertha would want me to leave Cronkite out of it, to say Margaret told me to do it, that it was her who gave me the matches and the idea, that I was suffering from folie à deux, that I was not myself, that my mind had been swallowed completely by hers.

She would want me to remind you that, had I not lit the bus on fire, worse crimes would have happened all over New York City later that day, that, given two poor choices, I, a mere child, made the better of the two: one girl to save a whole city, not to mention Walter Cronkite.

But the truth is I acted alone. It was my choice to light the book on fire, my choice to lock the bus doors.

The truth is I wanted the end to hurry up and come already. I wanted the jangle, the boom, the silence.

CHAPTER 31

AFTER

BY THE TIME I GET BACK TO HARROW HOUSE, THE BEEF STROGANOFF IS ALREADY on the table and everyone is waiting for me. I sit down next to Bertha, so it's harder for her to look me directly in the eyes.

She asks where Heather is.

I say she got off downtown (not a lie, technically), that she had to do something (also not a lie) and that she said she'd be back later (a lie, but for good reason).

Bertha nods but looks at me suspiciously. Patrick and Leonard do too.

"And how did you like the Institute?" she asks, twirling noodles onto her fork.

I shrug. "It was okay."

"Just okay?"

"Just okay," I say, and then I shove a big wad of food into my mouth before she can ask me anything else.

We all make small talk about the tomatoes and Patrick and Leonard's new living arrangements throughout the meal, but I can feel Bertha looking at me. I see her glancing at her watch.

I'll do anything to buy Heather time so, once the meal is over, I ask Bertha if we can talk. I reach into my pocket and pull out the little tab of paper I picked up at the college library, the one about the librarian training program. I give it to her.

"What's this?" she asks.

"It's what I want to do," I say. "Instead of hairdressing school. If it's not too late."

She looks at me with what can only be described as two bright lights in her eyes. "Oh Honey," she says, taking my hand in hers, "I think that's a wonderful, *wonderful* idea."

"And one more thing," I say. "Do you think, if I wrote a letter to the parole board, I could postpone my hearing?"

She comes around the table and sits next to me. "Postpone it? Why?"

"I just feel like I need a bit more time here," I say. Then, because she does love a metaphor: "It's like I'm one of those sick tomato plants me and Leonard took care of, like I'm not quite ready to live outside the greenhouse yet."

"Yes," she says as if she herself has been thinking it all along, as if it's obvious I don't have as many flowers as the others. "Okay, Hon'. Why don't you leave that with me? I'll see what I can do about it."

She goes to her office to make some calls.

I look at the kitchen clock. Any minute now Heather will be across the border. She'll be on her way to California to find Jerry and start her brand-new life.

I'm feeling pretty good about myself. I have run a successful decoy *and* made a decision about my future. But more importantly, I've helped a friend.

Then, since I'm on a roll, I go up to my room. At my desk, I pull out my red binder. I turn to the title page and because I am, deep down, a good girl, I cross out the F-word and replace it with "Effing." I sit at the typewriter then and get to work on something for Annie: my entry for the Write What You Know Contest.

CHAPTER 32

BEFORE

WE RAN FOR BLOCKS, STICKING TO THE SHADOWS, DARTING ACROSS LANES OF traffic when the coast was clear. We zig-zagged down alleys and over rooftops. We hopped fences. When there was a taxi or a car, we flattened ourselves against the wall, barely breathing until it had passed.

"Did I kill her?" I asked.

"No," Margaret said, pulling me along, faster and faster.

We ran through a good part of town. The lights were just coming on in the windows of the tall buildings above us. There was the rattle of pans, the smell of coffee in the air. The city was waking up around us, everyone starting another ordinary day.

"But I saw her," I said. "I saw her hands."

"That was just smoke," Margaret said. "A trick of the eye."

We ran through a part of the city I'd never seen before, where the windows were all boarded up and the sidewalks were full of broken glass. Here, there were cars without windows or doors parked on the sides of the street. There were men sleeping face-down on the sidewalks. They had winter jackets but no shoes, pants but no shirts. One man, who had fallen out of his wheelchair, had no legs.

"But what if it was her?" I asked.

"It wasn't," she said.

"But what if it was?"

"Shhhh," she said, pulling me into a doorway and crouching over me while a man passed by, shouting and shaking his fist at the sky.

Eventually, we came to a long bridge, the same one I'd crossed with the clowns so long ago. We had to get on a bus to cross it. Margaret tied a scarf over her hair and made me remove my eye patch. We hung our heads and sat near the back, not saying a word. When we were halfway across, I turned to look back at Manhattan, to see if it was floating in the air again. It wasn't, but above the city there was a thin crescent moon, and on that moon, soon, there would be a man.

On the other side of the bridge, we got off the bus as soon as we could. We tried to stay out of sight, running through tunnels and culverts, water splashing up to our knees. There were people living below the highways, a whole secret city. They were sleeping in the cool shade of their cardboard homes while the traffic buzzed above them. "Keep moving, they comin' for you," a woman with no teeth warned as we ran past.

In the afternoon, we came out on a long, treeless street, the same one I'd come in on. We kept moving down that street until the city was far behind us. It was just motels and car lots and bowling alleys now. We were walking through the tall grass alongside the highway. It was full of hamburger wrappers and straws. It was too loud to talk, almost too loud to think. Big trucks roared past, honking their horns and flinging sharp gravel at us.

When it was finally dark and we couldn't walk anymore, we found a bush behind a gas station. We fished a couple of old pizza boxes out of a dumpster to use as a bed. We only had Margaret's leather jacket as a blanket, but I didn't care.

"Did I kill her?" I asked.

"No," she said.

"But I saw her. I saw her hands and her—"

She leaned forward and touched her forehead to mine—Feel What I Feel. "It wasn't you who lit that fire, Elizabeth," she said. "It was Michael. I saw him do it. I was right there, and I saw with my own eyes. It was him, not you."

I felt something shift inside me, an unbearable heaviness lightening, and then I could sense him all around me: a dark fluttering in my peripheral vision, a hissing in my ears.

She pulled me down onto the cardboard next to her. She wrapped both arms tightly around me, kissed me on the back of my head and said "him, not you" over and over until, finally, it felt true and I slept.

Margaret and I walked for days, through heat and rain, and Michael walked with us. Mostly he was up ahead, shimmering in the heat waves coming off the road, waving us forward. But sometimes he was just over my shoulder, following me like a shadow, his voice hissing in my ear, saying, *Me, not you. Me, not you.* Sometimes he seemed to be everywhere at once, his face flashing in the windows of every passing car, his voice in the wind.

"Did you hear that?" I'd ask, but I never had to.

She'd already be smiling at me and nodding.

We changed our names every day. We were Brenda and Sammy, Susie and Ruth, Barbara and Jackie.

When we needed something, we sold pamphlets on corners for twenty-five cents apiece. Or we stopped at a gas station. I bled and cried. She got the goods.

Eventually, we moved away from the highway and started walking through fields and forests.

I never did ask where we were going because I thought I knew. I thought Michael was leading us home, to Ontario, to start again.

At night, we cut through people's backyards, pulling up potatoes and carrots from their gardens, picking plums and sour apples off their trees.

Once, we came across a clothesline full of clothes in exactly our sizes. We walked up and down the line, picking what we wanted. I got a pair of jeans and a T-shirt. She got a long, flowy farmer's dress. I showed her Rainbow's trick and we left our dirty clothes clipped to the line. She loved that and laughed about it for hours.

Once, on a rainy night, we crawled into an empty chicken coop in someone's backyard. We could see the blue light of a TV flashing in the windows of the house in the distance. She touched my nose and the channel changed. She touched it again. The channel changed again.

"Did the man ever land on the moon?" I asked.

"No, MeMe," she said. "You stopped him. You and Michael saved us all."

I didn't believe her, but I did think of Uncle Cronkite and how I'd probably saved him. I wondered if he'd ever know what I'd done for him.

"Let's play," she said, lifting her hands up, placing them on an imaginary pane of glass between us. I lifted mine and placed them on my side of the glass. She swept her hands up, down, across and I copied until we were perfect mirror images of each other, until you couldn't tell who was leading and who was following anymore.

You are wondering, wasn't I afraid? Didn't I feel guilty?

But the truth is, I wasn't. I didn't.

Margaret and I were together, more together than we'd ever been. It was Feel What I Feel all day long. We were hungry at the same time, thirsty at the same time, tired at the same time. At night, lying beside her, she tossed and turned and I could hear the voices bickering in her head, like a faraway radio. We were as close as we would ever be. If I could have, I would have kept on this way forever. I would have walked all the way to Canada with her, all the way to the North Pole.

But soon she started talking about a man named Jerry. She said there was a Great Gathering up ahead and that's where we were going.

She said she was working on a song, that she would deliver it to Jerry, and his Family would take care of us.

"But aren't we going home to Ontario?" I asked.

"We're going to our new home," she said, "with Jerry."

She never came right out and said it, that Jerry was my dad, the rock star from so long ago who had nearly taken her away, but she didn't have to. Some things don't need to be said.

She started working on her song more and more often. "What rhymes with shoe?" she'd say while we walked, and, "What rhymes with beginning?" She was always humming under her breath, working out the melody.

Sometimes, late at night, she had to go away from me to work on her song in private. "You two take care of each other," she'd always say just before leaving.

Once, I followed after her. I hid behind a tree and watched. I saw her cook something up in a piece of shiny foil. I saw her put it into her arm with a needle and then lie back, writhing and jolting, as if she was a puppet and someone was plucking at her strings.

Rainbow came rushing to my mind on those nights when I was alone, waiting for Margaret to come back to me. I pictured her hands on the glass, her face as the flames climbed her. I thought of the life I had imagined for her—her house near the water, her husband and child—and it seemed impossible that it wouldn't come true. I tried and tried to picture Michael standing on the bus next to me, lighting fire to the book, but I couldn't.

"Did you do it?" I would ask, but I never got an answer. He was gone on these nights. I couldn't feel him or hear him. I was all alone, more alone than I'd ever been.

We kept walking until our shoes wore out. We tossed them in a field and continued barefoot. We could hear music in the distance now. She said it was the Great Gathering, that it had started without us. Helicopters were criss-crossing above. We had to keep moving, she said, if we wanted to get there in time to meet Jerry.

I wanted to keep going, of course, but I couldn't. The bottoms of my feet were hard and black. My toes had swelled up like hotdogs and something had ahold of my throat. I was so tired even my hair hurt, even my teeth, and everything had turned inside out: hot became cold, cold became hot.

I remember at one point, she left me to sleep under a bush while she went to get me some apple juice. "Stay here," she said. "I'll be right back."

And she did come back a few hours later with a bottle of cold apple juice. She cradled my head while I drank. She stroked my hair and said "atta girl" just like a good mother would.

Eventually, one morning we came to a hill overlooking a valley. We looked down and saw it then: the Great Gathering. There were cars lined up along the road, an endless stream of glass and chrome stretching off into the distance. People were spilling out all along the sides of the road. There must have been thousands of people down there.

"This is it," she said, and she was as happy as I'd ever seen her.

I couldn't speak. My throat had closed like a fist.

She pointed to the stage way off in the distance and said, "Jerry will be there."

She ditched her leather jacket and gave me the last remaining pamphlets to hold. I didn't have any pockets, so I tucked them into the back of my pants. Then she crouched down so I could climb onto her back and we went down the hill to join everyone.

Moving through that crowd was like walking through a never-ending campsite. Everywhere, people had set up tents and barbecues and lawn chairs and campfires in little circles. We walked past one circle after another, each circle like a village, like a family. Everyone, everywhere was just like us. They had long, tangled hair, guitars, bongo drums, strange hats, rumpled clothes, no shoes, dirty feet.

The drizzle gathered in Margaret's hair like a crown of jewels.

Everyone was happy to see her. They smiled and called her sister and asked us to join them. They patted her on the shoulders and high-fived her.

She said she wanted to see Jerry. They smiled and pointed the way.

Someone gave her a peach, which she gave to me. I devoured it, licking the juice out of the palm of my hand.

Someone handed her a big green jug of wine. She tipped it back and guzzled.

Someone handed her a joint. She inhaled slowly and managed not to cough.

I couldn't see her face, but I knew what she was thinking: we'd finally arrived in the real America, the one we'd been promised.

We kept moving.

We must've walked for hours and the whole time Michael was up ahead, leading the way.

The sun came out.

Eventually it was so hot and Margaret's back was so drenched in sweat, she had to set me down.

We walked hand-in-hand for a while.

We passed a bunch of people with different-sized drums and pots and pans sitting in a circle, and even more people in the middle, bouncing around like popcorn in a bowl.

We passed a man pulling a wagon full of oranges. He was wearing underwear, a shiny cape, a cowboy hat. Every once in a while, he would stop and juggle a handful of those oranges, adding one more and one more until, eventually, they scattered and everyone dove after them.

When he saw the pamphlets tucked into the back of my pants, he held his hand out, asking, "Is that Cosmic Blue?" I handed him a pamphlet then watched as he ripped out the middle of the blue sun, scrunched it up into a ball and swallowed it whole.

We kept walking along the road.

It grew dark.

I remember seeing the lights from the stage in the distance. I remember hearing the music start: a sound like dropped cutlery, then a single guitar note ringing out, then another and another, each one sliding up like a question mark.

The crowd roared.

"We're almost there," Margaret said, tugging on my hand.

I tried to keep up with her, but my legs gave out.

I remember her carrying me for as long as she could but, eventually, stumbling under my weight.

"I've got to get to him, MeMe," she said. "I have to deliver my song to Jerry." She was trembling with the importance of it. We both were.

Jerry: my father.

"I wish there was a place to put you," I remember her saying and then, like magic, there was a car standing before us in the road. It was just like Rocky's car, a Cadillac Coupe DeVille—sky blue, with red seats. It stood with its doors wide open like some sort of miracle from the past. There was even a bed laid out inside the trunk with pillows and a homemade quilt. I remember it looked so inviting, like a quiet bedroom in the middle of all that chaos.

I can't remember whose idea it was—hers or mine— but I remember that the trunk was exactly big enough for me to stretch out in.

I remember her touching my forehead, saying "you need apple juice" and "I'll be right back." And it was like she'd read my mind.

I remember, just before she left, she touched me right above my scar and said, "You two take care of each other." Then she was gone.

I would like to say my story ends here.

I would like to say that she came back for me, breathless and apologetic. I would like to say that she gave me apple juice and sat by my side while I drank it, telling me about all the things she'd seen and about my father, Jerry, who couldn't wait to meet me.

I would like to say that I mattered and never stopped mattering.

CHAPTER 33

AFTER

I HAVE A RECURRING DREAM.

Me and Margaret are walking through a dark forest together. I feel lost, but she seems to know the way. "C'mon," she says, and I follow her down narrower and narrower paths. She stands just up ahead of me, one hand rummaging in her pockets, the other waving me forward. She's leading me down, away from the light and noise of the city. I reach for her, to grab her hand, her elbow, a fistful of her jacket, but she's always just out of reach. She's pointing to something up ahead. *Can you see that?* she says, and I do see something then, like lights in the distance. *Can you hear that?* she asks, and then I can hear something like music.

Eventually, we come to a rock wall in the forest. There is a narrow crack in the wall. It's too narrow for a person, I'm sure of it, but she puts her arms up and somehow manages to squeeze her body in. She shimmies along for a while and then the crack opens up. She's on the other side, calling back to me. "It's beautiful over here, MeMe," she says. I try to go after her. I squeeze my body into the crack, but I can't move. I'm too big or the crack is too small. I'm stuck. I can't move forward and I can't move back. I can only hear her voice calling and calling to me.

CHAPTER 34

BEFORE

I WOKE MUCH LATER IN A CLOSE, DAMP DARKNESS WITH NO MEMORY OF where I was or how I'd got there. I was lying in a pool of my own sweat. In the distance I could hear a band warming up. Someone was noodling on the guitar.

I tried to sit up but bonked my head and fell back down. I remembered then about the trunk, about climbing in. I didn't remember anyone closing it.

I pushed up against the lid with my arms, but the trunk wouldn't open. I turned over and tried with my back. The metal crumpled but wouldn't budge.

I could hear people passing by outside. They were so close. I could've called to them if I'd had a voice.

A second guitar let out some cool, clear notes. There was the crash of cymbals. The bass burbled. The microphones squealed. Then it all pulled together into a loose, bluesy song.

The crowd roared. The sound travelled through my body and found my spine, which was no longer my spine but a series of boxes all stacked on top of each other. The roar travelled up, unlocking each box, opening each one, and what rushed out was colour—pink and green and gold.

It was pitch black in the trunk, but the air had gone to shapes. It was full of circles within circles, triangles within triangles, squares within squares. It was a light show, a dance. It was like watching music. I couldn't tell if my eyes were open or closed anymore. It didn't matter.

The song changed and then changed again.

The music became so loose it barely hung together. It was barely music at all. It was a song like thought and then, in another moment, there was no me, no more thought and no one to think it. I was gone.

I was colour and shapes now. I was the roar of the crowd.

Time must have passed.

I remember Janis Joplin.

I remember Jefferson Airplane.

I remember the sunlight coming into the trunk, little pinpricks of light cutting through the dark.

The air thickened like soup. The trunk got so hot I had to make sure my skin wasn't touching the metal anywhere.

I was panting, gasping for air. *Like Rainbow, who I killed*, I remember thinking.

The truth filled the trunk. I knew then what I had done.

The dance was over. There were no more shapes anymore, no more colour.

There was only the truth, bursting open, over and over, inside my mind, like dropped fruit, and behind all that the question: *Who shut the trunk on me?*

I remember my last coherent thought, *I'm dying*, and then there was a swish and a fizzle and I went right up and out of myself. I was out in the cool air now. I was a kite on a long, long string, floating up toward the bright white sun. I was almost gone.

That's when I felt something take hold of the skin of my arm, up by my armpit, where all my secret cuts sat in neat and tidy rows. I came slamming back down into my body. There was a figure there in the dark next to me. A shadow my size and shape exactly: Michael.

He leaned in close, so close I could feel his eyelids brushing against my cheek. He took hold of my hand and placed it onto something round and hot at my side, an old beer bottle.

Drink, he said, so I tipped the bottle to my mouth. There were a few warm sips at the bottom of the bottle.

Bang, he said, so I did. I waited for a break between songs and banged the bottle against the sides of the trunk.

When I floated up and out of myself, he twisted my arm, making all my cuts sing, bringing me back down.

Count with me, he said.

And, *Wiggle your toes.*

And, *Tell me a story.*

He wanted to know about our beginnings, about Kraft Park and Margaret before Rocky. He wanted to know the words to "Boots of Spanish Leather" and "Like a Rolling Stone." He tried to keep me talking, to keep me anchored to my body for as long as he could.

According to the police reports, it was two strangers who found me. They each said they had seen a curly-haired boy, that he had taken them by the hand and led them to the trunk, that he had pointed. They each described him differently. Blue jeans, brown shirt, one person said. Brown pants, blue shirt, said the other. But this they can agree on: he was there and then gone.

They pried open the trunk. They lifted me out and carried me to a nearby house where a woman named Nan took my temperature and then ran a cold bath. "What's this?" she said when she pulled the pamphlets away from my body and saw that I was stained blue—"blue as a blueberry" the report has her saying—from butt to shoulder. She couldn't have known that I had the drugs from all those pamphlets— enough LSD to start a revolution—in my system, but she knew something was wrong.

I remember her cradling me, giving me spoonfuls of apple juice, pinching my fingers and toes, saying, "Stay with me now." I remember thinking it was Margaret and then opening my eyes and realizing it was not and knowing then, the way I sometimes just know a thing, that it was her who had shut the trunk on me.

They say the word "heartbreak" is a cliché, that instead the heart might stretch or soar or squeeze or swoop, but that's not how it felt in the moment. In the moment it felt exactly like it was breaking.

I wanted to stay there with Nan in her lemon-yellow kitchen, but I couldn't.

My mind was unspooling. I was up in the air again, looking down at the whole scene below me, the Great Gathering, thousands of people dancing and writhing and hugging and kissing in the mud below, falling in love and out of love, losing each other, finding each other.

I saw the stage like a tall ship in the distance, its sails flapping.

And there, in a clearing to the left of the stage, I saw Margaret. She was twirling in the middle of a circle of people, wearing someone else's dress. There was a man dancing with her. The people around them were clapping and chanting, egging them on. She went faster and faster like a spinning top. Her dress ballooned out around her and, from above, she looked like the most impossible thing, like an orange flower blooming in all that mud. I could feel what she felt for the last time. I could feel that she was happy and in love again and finally free. And I could feel that she had forgotten all about me. She tipped her face up to the sky. Her eyes were fluttering. Her mouth stretched into a strange smile and then she said something I couldn't quite hear across the distance, something that sounded like *hairy, hairy, hairy* or maybe, *sorry, sorry, sorry.*

I couldn't be sure. It didn't matter because, by then, the string was broken.

I was no longer tethered, not to her, not to anyone.

I was soaring up now, way above the crowd. I could see the stage and beyond that the green fields, and beyond that the river of parked cars reaching out toward the highway that stretched north to Canada in one direction, south to New York City in the other. I could see it all, the two points of my life and the distance between them. How far I had travelled. How little I had travelled.

I went up and up. I was small, getting smaller, smaller than a postage stamp, smaller than a flea.

I went up and up and I never did come down again.

CHAPTER 35

AFTER

"NEVER?" BERTHA ASKS. "ARE YOU SURE ABOUT THAT?"

She rolls the dice, hits the second-biggest ladder, moves to the top of the board.

"Okay, fine," I say. "Not for years. Eight at Mid-Hudson, two at Willingdon."

I roll, land on a snake, slide down, practically to the bottom of the board.

"A long, lonely decade," she says with a wink and a smile. "And yet here you are."

"Here I am," I say.

We're in her office, eating crackers with cheese and pickles, listening to Joni Mitchell and talking, but not about anything in particular. It's fall now. Vancouver is back to her usual moody self. Outside, the clouds sit low and dark over the city like a mushroom cap.

Bertha has worked her magic. She's rescheduled my parole hearing. I've been given six more months to "get my footing." She likes to joke that I'm the only person she's ever met who wanted *more* time in a halfway house.

I have three new roommates now: Emi, Josiah and Wayne. Together we have art therapy, group therapy, tutoring, paper routes. We talk about our triggers and practise saying no. We bring in all the green tomatoes and then rip the old plants out of the ground and throw them on top of the compost.

Bertha got me re-diagnosed too. I'm officially no longer schizophrenic. Now I'm just an ordinary person who was once too much under the influence of someone I loved, which, as Bertha likes to remind me, is not so uncommon.

Bertha also got me into the librarian training program, as a late enrollment. I start in January. Until then I'm volunteering with a librarian named Vicky at the college, learning how to check books in and sort them and then deliver them back to the shelves where they belong.

I like Vicky. She's big on systems, especially the Dewey decimal one. But she's open-minded too. She isn't bothered, for example, when I get a feeling about a person who's standing, looking lost as they spin through the racks of crime paperbacks in front of the checkout counter, or when I go over and talk to them for a while, steering them away from crime and toward, say, Steinbeck. She says this is also part of being a librarian: knowing how to read people, knowing, too, when a particular book might save a person's life. She says I'm a natural at this, that it will make me an exceptional librarian, but she says I need to hone this skill too, which is why she's been teaching me how to use the Rider Tarot Deck in our downtime, so that I can control what she calls "my hunches about people."

It's possible Bertha and Vicky are having secret meetings about me, but I don't mind.

It's Bertha's turn. She hits a snake, slides down. She sees me glance up at the bare spot on the wall, where the needlepoint used to be, the one that asked if it was possible to overcome the past.

"Why'd you take that down?" I ask.

"I think we've outgrown its sentiment, don't you?" she says, placing the dice back on the board with a click.

She winks at me, to let me know I've fallen right into her trap, then starts talking about how overcoming the past isn't possible, that our only job in life is to *become* or, better yet, to learn how to just *be*. She looks at me then, when she's done, and asks what I think about that. This is her latest doctor trick. She makes a little speech about something and then invites me to do the same.

I'd like to respond, to say something profound or at least true, but I'm distracted.

Out the window I see that same homeless man, the Canadian Huck Finn. He's rattling a shopping cart full of empty bottles down the sidewalk. I see his curly hair, his blue jeans and striped shirt. Something kicks in my chest.

He stops in front of the house and smiles up at the sky, palms out. It starts to rain then, one of those sudden Vancouver rains, like someone, somewhere has turned on a tap. He lets out a whoop.

I stand and move toward the window. It's as if I'm being pulled on a string.

He sees me and waves a hand, beckoning.

Michael, I think. And for a moment I feel my past, the whole Big Sad Story tugging at me. My scar aches. I feel that old feeling, that he died so I could live and that I can still make it right, that I must, that it is my duty. I imagine the two of us hitchhiking to California together, walking down the sides of highways on our way to find Margaret, thumbs out all day, sleeping wherever we fall at night, like a couple of lunatics. And it is tempting, of course.

But this man isn't Michael and I'm not a lunatic anymore, so before too long, I snap out of it.

I wave goodbye.

The man waves too and continues on with his shopping cart.

I come back to the table, where it's still my turn and Bertha is waiting for me, watching. I sit. I smile to let her know I'm okay. And I am. Somehow I'm 100% okay, so I wiggle my toes for luck and reach for the dice again.

Acknowledgements

WRITING THIS BOOK IS ONE OF THE MOST CHALLENGING JOURNEYS I HAVE EVER taken. I would like to thank the following people for taking me seriously and believing that what I was doing would one day amount to something even when I wasn't so sure myself:

Alexander, first and foremost, for supporting me every day, in every way. Living with a writer isn't easy. Thank you for not allowing me to give up (except when I needed to for a few days) and for watching the Woodstock movie with me so many times and for tolerating my singing and for making me spaghetti.

Helen, Art and Dylan, but I can't say for what because it is too big. My aunts and uncles too, for cheering me on.

Kaia, for living in the trenches with me for so long and then still coming to check on me after you had moved on to better things. I'm pretty sure that is the definition of true friendship.

Nicala, for the laughs, for always being interested in my work and giving me the book (you know the one) that helped me most.

Dennis, for always being willing to talk about big ideas and for being such an inspiration by showing us all how to self-rescue.

Nadine, for the camaraderie and being willing to read early drafts.

Georg Nicklas and family, for enabling a fresh start.

Wendy, for being a confidante and helping me find my teaching voice at VISA.

Val, for the swims and the talks.

Sylvia, for the many books of inspiration.

Jackie Agostinis, for the spectacular photos and mimosas in the woodshed.

The rest of my neighbours: Gus, John and Sandra, Frants and Jean, for teaching me how to live in the forest, on an island, in the sea.

My many students at the Vancouver Island School of Art who continually inspired me and reminded me why we all do this: because it's fun!

The wise and generous teachers who have helped me along the way: Catherine Bush, Annabel Lyon, and Yasuko Thanh. A huge thank you to Caroline Adderson for dishing out a much-needed dose of tough love while also holding a deep belief in my abilities when it was most crucial. Another huge thank you to Lisa Cron for giving me the tools I needed.

My UBC peeps, for the help, the laughs, the tenacity.

Chris Labonte, for being the first person to believe in this book.

Hilary McMahon, for being the second person to believe in this book. For reading, guiding me, being charming and hilarious, and most especially for being so patient!

Peter Norman, the best editor in the world, for helping me whip this thing into shape.

Caroline Skelton, for your grace during the endless fine-tuning.

Anna Comfort O'Keeffe and the whole team at Douglas & McIntyre, for believing in me.

I must also thank Christina Chan, Adam Cappuccino, and Dr. John Wong: the medicine-people who have kept me somewhat sane these years.

I owe a debt of gratitude to the kids of the James Bay Housing Co-operative for bringing me up scrappy and teaching me how to get both into and out of trouble. And to the adults of the same place, for knowing when to look the other way.

A heartfelt thank you to Hedgebrook for taking me in, giving me sanctuary and showing me the true meaning of hospitality, an experience that has forever changed me.

And huge thanks to the Banff Centre for the Arts for letting me in not once but twice to write and eat chocolate mousse at the top of the world. These are the types of experiences that keep us writers going.

Lastly, I would like to thank the BC Arts Council and the Canada Council for the Arts for their generous support. I am so grateful to live in a country that values and supports the arts.

About the Author

BUFFY CRAM is a writer of fiction and non-fiction, an entrepreneur and an amateur farmer. Reviewing her book of stories, *Radio Belly* (2012), the *Globe and Mail* pronounced her "a whip-smart storyteller who aims to shake up our reading expectations in ways that delight." She has been a fiction finalist for the Western Magazine Awards, has been nominated for a Pushcart Prize and has won a National Magazine Award. She holds an MFA in Creative Writing from UBC and lives on Salt Spring Island, BC.